I0682575

Until You Love Me

Tricia Linden

Kingsburg Press
San Francisco, California

Kingsburg Press
P.O. Box 475146
San Francisco, California, 94147
www.KingsburgPress.com

Editor: Deborah Fallon
Cover Design: MM Covers @ SelfPubBookCovers.com

ISBN- 13:978-1-946177-09-4
ISBN- 10: 1-946177-09-1
eBook ISBN: 978-1-946177-10-0

Other Books of Timeless Romance by Tricia Linden

The MacNicol Clan Through Time

A Time To Begin – Book 1

A Time To Return – Book 2

A Time To Belong – Book 3

A Time To Forgive – Book 4

.

.

.

Dreaming In Moonlight

.

.

.

Jules Vanderzeit novels

set in the Gilded Age of New York

Until We Meet Again

Until Their Hearts Desire

.

Dedication
To Dad
Thanks

CHAPTER 1

On a dark country road in upstate New York – Present Day

Becky Sue Dobson had been down this road several times before, but now it was dark and the tears filling her eyes made it hard to see. At least that's what she told herself a second before her car swerved over the edge of the mountain road, caught air, and went plunging toward the valley below. There was a screaming moment of *"Oh Shit!"* accompanied by a moment of soul-searing regret, followed closely by a jolt of severe pain. And then nothing. Only inky, black, darkness.

Sometime later, her eyes fluttered open and she found herself lying crumpled in a ball on the ground next to her wrecked car. Looking up, she saw a man dressed formally in a black suit and tie standing before her. Obviously, a man of wealth and taste, there was no denying his mesmerizingly attractive appeal. He looked Egyptian, like that old-time Hollywood actor, Omar Sharif, with his smooth brown skin, pale-grey almond-shaped eyes, and velvety curly hair.

"Trying to take the drastic way out?" he asked, his voice menacingly calm.

Becky Sue scrambled to her feet, amazed she could move at all. She knew exactly what he meant. "I didn't mean to . . ."

He viewed her with an unwavering glare. "You knew exactly what you were doing."

1

"My life sucks. Besides, why do you care?" Why should she want go on living after the way Ralph had treated her? His latest beating had been so brutal, it had caused her to miscarry. If only she had left him, like she knew she should, she wouldn't have lost her tiny unborn baby.

"Why on earth would you want to end your life when you can simply start a new one? If you end your life—this special blessing you've been given—you'll lose everything and gain nothing. Bad behavior is not rewarded," the man warned her.

"Life sucks?" Becky Sue repeated, sobbing.

"Do you think you're the only one to get rejected by a lover?" He sadly shook his head. "Rejection, loss, abandonment, it's all part of life. When will you ever learn? However, I'm feeling rather generous. There's something you can do for me, and in return, I'll help you mend your mistake and this mess you've made." He gestured with his walking stick toward the mangled wreck that had once been her car.

"Yeah, right, like you can fix my life."

"No, only you can do that. But I can show you the way."

"Oh really, why should I trust you?"

He gave her an appraising look, as if considering whether or not she was worthy. "I have an assignment for you, if you're willing to work for me. All you have to do is agree to live another life. If not, you'll have hell to pay."

Oh shit! That didn't sound good.

"Hell or time. Which do you choose?"

If she had to choose, she'd pick *time*, whatever that meant.

"That's what I thought you'd say."

Wait a minute! She hadn't actually said anything, had she? Could he read her mind?

"Complete your assignment successfully and you can move on with your life. We'll pretend this little *incident*," he pointed again to the wreckage of her car, "never happened. Fail, and you'll be facing that time in hell you're so dreadfully afraid of."

She'd made so many mistakes, surely she deserved some time in hell, but still, if there were a way to avoid all that extra pain, she'd be a fool not to try.

The man pulled a card from the inside pocket of his coat and handed it to her. "Allow me to introduce myself. I'm Jules Vanderzeit, the Maestro."

The name meant nothing to her, but at least he hadn't said he was Lucifer, or Beelzebub, or any of the other names she associated with the devil.

"I orchestrate time for the sake of learning. Words don't teach. Experience is the teacher."

What? Was he a teacher? Was she was going to be his student?

He then plucked a set of papers seemingly from out of thin air and handed it to her. It looked like a contract of some sort, tightly typed and filled with legalese.

"Sign this and you can be on your way to your first assignment."

She looked up from trying to read the document, which might as well have been written in Greek for all the sense it made to her. "And if I don't?" she asked, trying to sound bolder than she felt.

Mr. Vanderzeit pointed to the wreckage of her car. "You're stuck with the consequences of *that* mistake."

Ugh. That couldn't be good.

As if wielding a wand, he held out a beautifully gilded fountain pen. "Sign the contract, or face the consequences of your actions. It's your choice."

Becky accepted the pen. When she had finished signing her name, a sharp point on the gilded pen pricked her finger and a spot of blood dropped onto the page. "Oww! That hurt." She brought the offend digit to her lips, sucking away the pain.

"Blood never lies. Now take my hand and we can begin your assignment. You'll need some training; a week should do. After that, you'll be on your own, more or less."

She touched his hand, and in a flash, she was standing at the edge of a cliff overlooking the rugged sea below, feeling as if she were about to lose her balance. Taking a quick step back, a feeling of déjà vu washed over her. Was it just her imagination, or had she been here before?

~*~

Saturday, November 11, 1893 – New York City

Rebecca flinched as her father abruptly entered the room, marching heavily across the polished hardwood floor of the parlor while the crystal chandelier tinkling softly above. Her involuntary response was one she had tried repeatedly to overcome but never truly mastered. Stanton Wheland had the power to intimidate her, though she liked to think she had learned not to show it.

"What do you think you're doing here?" her father barked in lieu of a greeting.

"I've come home," Rebecca said with a lift of her chin. "I plan to stay."

"Like hell you will," Stanton ground out. "You're his problem now. Go home to your husband."

"But I want to come home." She had lived here most of her life, of course it was still her home.

"This is no longer your home. Go back where you belong." The look in his eyes told Rebecca he rather enjoyed delivering this hurtful piece of news.

Staring at the man she both loathed and feared, Rebecca stood her ground, determined to show no weakness. After enduring four months—more than one-hundred and twenty lonely days—in a dreadfully bad marriage to a man she did not love and who didn't love her, all she wanted was to return to the home. The home she had once shared with her loving mother and brother. The thought of spending another day with James Jaffray, the man her father had chosen for her to marry, was enough to turn her stomach. Merely being in the same house as him filled her with despair.

Though her father had the power to intimidate nearly everyone he met, Rebecca hoped she was strong enough to defy him. She needed this reprieve.

"James doesn't love me. And I don't love him. Our marriage is a sham."

"What does that matter? Marriage ain't about love, little girl, it's about obligations and commitments. You have a commitment to fulfill and Jaffray has an obligation. You're his problem now. Go home."

Rebecca might have been raised by an unloving father, but she was used to getting her way. Not because she was kind and sweet—as her father had taught her, that was for weaklings. It was her mother who taught her how to use her femininity and guile as tools to get what she wanted, and she had learned from the best.

"And if I refuse?" she asked, stiffening her spine.

"Doesn't matter. I don't care where you go, but you can't stay here." Not bothering to use the bell cord, her father shouted out to the hallway, "O'Conner, get in here."

A moment later, a short, stocky Irish man scurried into the room.

"Put Mrs. Jaffray's trunks back on her carriage and take her back to her husband's house," Stanton ordered.

"Yes sir, Mister Wheland." The groomsman jumped to comply with his master's commands. Everyone jumped when Stanton Wheland barked.

Rebecca glared at her father. She felt like crying and stomping her feet, demanding she be allowed to stay, but she would do none of that. Such a show of emotion in front of her father would only serve to prove she was weak. She would not admit defeat. Nor would she return to her husband's house. James had never struck her—in fact he hadn't touched her since the week of their wedding—it was his lack of attention that had sent her running.

They rarely dined together and he hardly, if ever, showed her any true affection. Sure, he may have tried at the beginning, especially when he wanted her in bed, but less than two weeks after consummating their marriage he had stopped visiting her bedroom altogether. At first, she'd been grateful for his lack of interest. The mere thought of physical intimacy made her sick to her stomach. By the time she began to regret the loss of his affection, it seemed too late to make amends, and she felt too rejected to try.

While her father was also unloving and unkind, at least she had learned to tolerate his presence when he was around, which wasn't often. Usually, he was off conducting business, overseeing his vast financial holdings, or simply too busy to care. Her father was not only rich, he was handsome, and when it suited him, he could even be charming. Usually to others, of course—rarely to her. Unfortunately, he was also utterly without humor. For all his God-given advantages, it seemed her father viewed life as a competition, a harsh game where the score was measured by the riches one collected.

Besides, it was different for fathers. Husbands were expected to show their wives some measure of affection. At least that was what she had wanted to believe. Just as she believed her father had loved her mother, before she died.

5

Rebecca had been one month shy of her thirteenth birthday when her mother died from a lingering fever, and with her passing, it seemed all the love, joy, and laughter Rebecca had ever known was slowly drained away, leaving her with only her older brother Randolph on whom she could rely.

The holidays were fast approaching and she refused to spend them living with James Jaffray, a virtual stranger who wanted nothing to do with her. There had to be another way, somewhere else she could go. If only she had a maiden aunt or a kind old grandmother who could take her in, but no, there wasn't another welcoming family member in all of New York. If Randolph were here, she wouldn't be having this problem. He would give her shelter, but he was away in London on business. So, it was either her father or her husband, and neither of them wanted her.

Faced with such a daunting dilemma, she suddenly had a brilliant new idea.

Frustrated but not defeated, Rebecca turned and marched out of the room with her head held high, not bothering to look back or say good-bye. After leaving the parlor, she scurried up to her room to retrieve a key she had once hidden there, before making her way out to the porte cochère where her traveling carriage stood. When O'Conner was done loading her belongings, she took satisfaction in giving him new instructions. Her father did not control her anymore, and she would not be shipped off like cargo.

"Rather than taking me home, to Mr. Jaffray's house, I need you to take me to the train station," she said, infusing her voice with sweetness. Before he could object (not that it was any of his business), she added, "I need to visit our cottage on Long Island."

"But Ma'am, it's closed up for the season. Only the caretakers are there. Mr. Wheland's not been there for a good long while. You'd be all alone."

"You needn't worry about me. I'm quite capable of taking care of myself," she said, still smiling.

"But Ma'am, your father ordered me to take you to your husband's house."

"Yes, yes, I know, and I can assure you, I will go there later." *When I'm good and ready.* "Now, please, if you don't mind, I need you to take me to the train station." Rebecca tried to maintain an aura of sweetness but the man was getting on her nerves. It wasn't his place to question her instructions. Why must she put up with such insolence?

"Well, if you insist, Ma'am."

"Yes, O'Conner, I insist. I shouldn't want to report any unnecessary rudeness to my father."

"Yes, Ma'am," he said with a bobbing nod. It was an empty threat, but it was enough to get him moving.

Without waiting for his assistance, Rebecca climbed into the carriage and settled into the front facing seat.

O'Conner rushed to take his place beside the driver, and Rebecca listened to ensure he passed along her request as instructed. With a lurch, the carriage headed off down the street, and Rebecca sat back to relax and make her plans, determined to find a way to avoid both her husband and her father.

~*~

From the train station in Hampton Bay, Rebecca hired a hack to take her to her father's summer house on the shore. It had been a long and exhausting day, and the sky was nearly dark when she finally arrived. As the hansom cab pulled into the long drive, Rebecca was disheartened to see the house looking darker and more foreboding than she had remembered. Unlike the last time, when she had been here in summer, most of the trees had shed their foliage. Their naked branches surrounding the house only added to the feeling of cold abandonment. Instead of welcoming her as it always had before, the distant crashing of waves upon the shore and the scent of salt in the heavy, damp air only added to the home's feeling of isolation. No one was there—the windows were dark, and the place appeared cold. It made her wish she had wired ahead to the caretaker to let him know of her arrival and have the house prepared.

Rebecca reached into her handbag and pulled out the key she had taken from her father's house. Until today, it had been nothing more than a childish souvenir, a reminder of a youthful prank she had played on one of her many nurse maids. In all the upheaval with her father, it was a blessing she had even thought of it. She had never used a house key before; she had never needed one. Doors were always held open for her. She had never been to Raven's Point in winter—no one ever went there in winter—but with this key to the servant's entrance, she'd have access to shelter and a place to call her own.

She planned to stay no more than a few days, a week at the most, only until her brother returned from London. Randolph would know what to do.

7

If she went missing for too long, either her father or James would discover her whereabouts and send someone to fetch her back home. But she was done with them. Being owned and ordered about by men who cared nothing about her was not her idea of a satisfying life, certainly not the life she wanted for herself.

As they pulled into the drive, Rebecca leaned out the window and shouted up to the driver, "Take me around back to the servant's entrance and unload my cases there."

"The servant's entrance?" the driver shouted back over the wind.

"Yes, the back door to the kitchen. I have the key," Rebecca shouted back, relieving a smidgen of the anxiety she was feeling.

As soon as she gained entrance to the house, she had the man unload her traveling bags from the carriage and take them to her room upstairs. She was cold, tired, and soon she would be hungry, but her first concern was for heat. Staying a few steps behind, she followed the hired driver up the back stairs to her room. She was unfamiliar with this part of the house, and although the newly installed electric lights were working, the stark shadows made her uneasy.

When they reached her room, Rebecca waited in the hallway while he set down her luggage. "While you're in there, can you please light the fire?" she asked as she peeked in from the doorway. "I'll pay you extra."

"Yes, Ma'am. As ye wish."

She waited in the hall until he was done with his task, uncomfortable being alone with a stranger in the empty house. The sooner she could get some warmth in this place, the better she would feel. Chilled, she rubbed her hands up and down her arms.

Once the fire was burning in the grate, the driver returned to the hall. "Will ye be needing anything else, Ma'am?" he asked.

Grateful he was respectfully keeping his distance, Rebecca attempted an air of confidence. "Do you know how to get the boiler started?"

"No, Ma'am. I'm a hack driver, not a mechanic."

Her shoulders sagged. Darn. It was doubtful he was even willing to try. That task would have to wait for the caretaker to arrive, but at least she had a fire in her room.

"Are you sure you want to stay here by yourself?" he asked, looking concerned.

While he seemed kind enough, it occurred to her this man knew she was alone. That could be a problem. "My brother is coming to meet me, I'm sure he'll be here soon. And there's a caretaker living on the property," she said with a lift of her chin. The part about her brother, of course, was a lie, but Rebecca didn't care. This man did not need to know her business or think she was easy prey. "When you leave, please use the servant's road. You've been most helpful, but I need you to stop at the caretaker's cottage and send him here to the main house. Tell him I need his assistance."

"As you say, Ma'am."

Rebecca retrieved a few coins from her handbag to pay him, including the extra for lighting her fire. The driver kindly tipped his hat and returned to his hack, then drove off into the night.

When thirty minutes had gone by and there was no sign of the caretaker, Rebecca wondered if the hack driver had even followed her instructions and told him to come. Cold and frustrated by what she deemed an unacceptable delay, she hiked down the back road used by the servants and delivery trucks to find the small building where the caretakers lived. After knocking several times without an answer, she peered in through the kitchen window. Pressing her face to the glass, she could see a newspaper and pipe lying on the table and dishes drying on the sideboard. While it was obvious people were living there, it seemed no one was home. Apparently, the caretaker and his wife were out for the night. Drat, could she not depend on anyone to help her. It seemed she truly was all alone.

Frightened and colder than before, Rebecca returned to the main house. Surveying her surroundings, she wondered how she was going to survive through the cold November night without more heat. If only she had thought to make her escape in July or August, none of this would be a problem.

Her marriage to James Jaffray had taken place on July seventh, and she had known from the start it was a big mistake. She had confided her misery to her older brother, Randolph, but under pressure from their father, he had convinced her to at least give it a try. Now, four months later, all she wanted was out. James would probably say she hadn't tried hard enough, but how could she love or even respect a man who ignored her day after day. It was hard to believe she had once found James Jaffray

9

handsome and charming, and even desirable. That was before she had been forced to marry him.

As Rebecca shivered in her bedroom, wondering what she could do to make it warmer, she began to realize how poorly she had thought this through. This house was designed to stay cool in the summer, not warm in the winter. Even the pale pink floral paper on the walls and sheer lace curtains at the window were a reminder of warmer days.

Unfortunately, her brother Randolph was in London on family business. If he were still in town, Rebecca was sure he would come to her aid. But he was gone, and until he returned, she was on her own.

So here she was, approaching the dead of winter, alone in her father's summer cottage, planning how she would leave her husband. Of course, this was no mere beachside dwelling. Her father had wanted to make a dramatic statement with the size and location of his house when he set it high upon a cliff overlooking the roaring Atlantic Ocean. But who was she to complain, especially since she was using the large, empty mansion to give her shelter.

Though her father insisted on keeping the house her mother had loved, he rarely stayed here after her death. Every prominent family she knew had a summer home somewhere outside of Manhattan, and it seemed her father would be no different. Surely, the only reason he kept this ocean-side house was to impress their neighbors. Nothing was too grand for Stanton Wheland.

There was a fire in the grate, the lamps were lit, and Rebecca was still wearing her coat. She had done all she could to warm her bedroom but it was still too cold to make it through the night. While it wasn't cold enough to cause her any serious harm, she much preferred the comfort of a warm, cozy bed. Much as she dreaded it, Rebecca considered the idea that she may need to venture outside in search of fuel. There was probably a woodshed somewhere on the property, but she had no idea where it was. Like the boiler, that would need to wait until the caretaker returned.

But she was perfectly capable of gathering wood for herself. Perhaps she could find some fallen branches and maybe a log or two. Surely, she could manage such a simple task. Rebecca may have been raised as a pampered heiress, but she was finished being dependent on other people. It was time for her to take charge of her life.

Grabbing a lantern from her room, she headed down the back stairs and out into the large lawn separating the house from the ocean cliffs. It was nearly dark and the light from the lantern gave her comfort.

Holding the lantern high, Rebecca stumbled over stones and tree roots blocking her path as she searched for the fallen branches in the shrubs and trees surrounding the estate. She had already made good progress, and her arms were nearly full when she spied nice sized branch that would surely burn until morning. Stooping to retrieve it, she felt rather pleased with her efforts. No one would ever expect to see Rebecca Wheland doing something so mundane as gathering wood. As she stood with the log nestled in her arms, a low hanging branch smacked the backside of her head, causing her to lose her footing. Dropping her load and the lantern, her arms flailed as she fell forward and rolled several feet down the slopping hillside.

Feeling scared, but grateful she had managed to survive unscathed, she stood and brushed herself off. As she looked about for the lantern she had dropped, she realized she was standing precariously close to the edge of a cliff overlooking the rugged sea. *Dear God, that had been close.* Her heart pounded in rhythm with the crashing waves below. She was about to take a step away when the muddy ground beneath her gave way and she felt herself slipping, about to plunge over the cliff. Suddenly, in the blink of an eye, everything she had thought important, including her grand plan of running away, no longer mattered.

~*~

Seven Days Later, Saturday, November 18, 1893 – New York City

"I can do this," Becca reminded herself as she stepped into the entrance hall of the mansion on Fifth Avenue, and made her way to the drawing room. Her heart pounded with a mixture of cautious curiosity and fear as she prepared to greet her husband. How would he react to her homecoming? His wife had gone missing seven days ago and she didn't have a good explanation for where she'd been. Certainly not a believable one she could share. Her eyes roamed about the room with its high ceilings, crown molding, polished marble and elegant decor, taking it all in. This was her husband's mansion, the place she now called home, and she needed a moment to absorb it all. This wasn't going to be easy, but there was no going back.

11

She barely had time to remove her coat and gloves before James stalked into the room and lashed out with unchecked animosity. "It's about time you decided to come home. Where the hell have you been, Rebecca?"

Becca paused a moment to take in the sight of her husband. Even in his shirt sleeves and waist coat, James Jaffray appeared polished and sophisticated, a man born to money. He stood a few inches taller than her with short, thick, wavy, dark brown hair, a strong angular jaw, pronounced cheekbones and an aristocratic nose. While he wasn't overtly handsome, his features were certainly attractive enough to catch a woman's eye. Or maybe it was his imposing personality; it seemed to fill the room. Not surprisingly, his silver blue eyes bore down on her with anger and suspicion. She had known this was coming, and still, this moment of reckoning was harder than she had expected.

It would be nice if she had a better story to tell. Repeatedly she had thought about what she was going to say, and yet now that she was confronted with the man to whom she was married, those blasted well-rehearsed lines failed her, fleeing from her mind like a skittish hummingbird unable to still its wings long enough to settle upon a perch.

Taking a deep breath, Becca addressed her husband. "I went to my father's house, as I'm sure you know, but now I've come home. Isn't that what you want?" She hoped she sounded more confident than she felt.

He eyed her with disdain. "I want to know where you've been. You may have gone to your father's house, but you also left there the very same day. You've been gone for seven days, *Rebecca*, so let me ask you again, where the hell have you been?"

She really did not like the way he said *Rebecca*, as if it were a curse word or something nasty in his mouth. Setting that aside, she cleared her throat and said, "I . . . I thought you knew. Didn't O'Conner tell you? I went to my father's cottage on Long Island."

"You expect me to believe you've been at Raven's Point this whole time? Alone?"

"Yes," she nodded, feeling a quiver of dread move through her. "But I can assure you, it wasn't very pleasant." Thoughts of Rebecca's accident flashed through her mind, which was bad enough, but facing James, an enraged man who was mad as hell at his wife, made it even worse. Nothing she could do would make this a pleasant homecoming.

"What the hell were you doing there? Isn't it closed for the winter?."

"Yes, so it is, but I needed a place to think, and it helped to be alone." How inane. Give her a minute and she would start stuttering.

"To think?" Suspicion darkened his eyes.

"Yes, to think."

"About what?"

"Everything, I suppose. Anything I wanted."

"Tell me, Rebecca, what the hell do you want?" Mr. James Jaffray looked to be about at the end of his rope.

Becca hemmed and hawed and blinked a few times. "Do you really want to know?"

"Yes, I really want to know."

Pausing to consider all she had been through, Becca wondered if she should answer him truthfully.

~~~

James clenched his teeth, too frustrated to speak. He really shouldn't give a damn. His wife had run off, surely to be with another man, and he really shouldn't care. But he did.

Lately, it seemed as if she could barely stand to be in the same room with him, but like it or not she was his wife, and by God, she was going to behave as such. He wouldn't have it spread all over town that less than six months into their marriage, his wife was having an affair. Thankfully, so far they had managed to keep it out of the papers, and hopefully it would stay that way. The few callers to the house had been told Mrs. Jaffray wasn't receiving. When his sister asked how his new wife was faring, James had simply mentioned she wasn't feeling well and let it go at that. In truth, he had no idea how she was feeling; she hadn't been home for him to know. It didn't matter that it had taken him two days to realize she was gone.

"James, I'm not sure now is the right time to talk about this. I'm tired, and cold, and hungry. As I'm sure you can appreciate, a vacant cottage on Long Island in winter is not very pleasant. And, yes" –she held up a hand as if to stop his rant before he had a chance to respond– "I know it was my choice to go there. Right now, all I want is to take a hot bath, have a bite to eat, and retire to my room. Can we discuss this in the morning?"

Rebecca stood there looking at him with a blank expression, as if it were of little concern that she had gone missing for seven days. How could she be so indifferent?

Not that he should be surprised. This was so like her to sidestep the issue. As usual, she was refusing to talk to him, her special brand of punishment, but tonight he was going to get some answers.

It wasn't normal for a newly married woman to go off on her own without a word to either her husband or her father. No one had known where she was until Wheland's groomsman, O'Conner, came to him and privately admitted he had taken her to the train station though he had been ordered to bring her here. Rebecca had told O'Conner she planned to take a train to Long Island, alone. Who the hell went to a beach house in November? Without servants? The place would be cold and empty. He didn't believe for a minute she had actually gone there alone. Angry as he had been, he hadn't been foolish enough to go racing after her. He had no desire to find her in the arms of another man.

James wanted to lash out at her, but held his temper in check. Gentlemen did not rant or rave. As calmly as he could manage, he said, "You need to tell me one thing before you leave this room. Are you having an affair?"

Rebecca looked shocked. "Oh my God, James, no. How could you ask such a question?" She actually shuddered, as if the idea were repulsive.

He took some satisfaction in knowing he had at least stirred an emotion out of the woman. "I don't think it's unreasonable, given the circumstances. It's not as if you love me. Face it, Rebecca, neither one of us wanted this marriage, but by God, you are not going to make a fool out of me by having an affair only weeks out of our marriage bed."

"Months, James. By my count, we've been married over four months."

"You know what I mean." Much more of this and they would be shouting at each other, as usual.

"Calm yourself, that's not what happened. I simply needed to get away. Some time alone, by myself. Forgive me if I didn't seek your permission, but I've come back. Isn't that enough? What good will it do to discuss this now? You're right, we have a loveless marriage, arranged to clear your gambling debts."

"My investment losses," he corrected her.

He didn't gamble, he invested, and unfortunately, he had invested poorly. After inheriting the family business, he had become an innovator in building stock railroad cars. No one built better or more efficient railcars and replacement parts than Jaffray Manufacturing; he had cornered the market. But the stock market panic earlier this year had hit the railroads hard, and cost him more than he could afford, and he had needed a significant loan to cover his losses. Stanton Wheland had agreed to cover his debt interest free if James agreed to marry his daughter. What could he do? Without the loan he would have lost everything, possibly even this house. His back was up against a wall and Stanton's offer was too good to refuse. So what if he had to agree to marry a woman he hardly knew? At least he would remain afloat at a time when banks were failing left and right, and the idea of a business loan for half a million dollars was little more than a daydream.

"You got what you wanted, money to keep your company afloat, but what did I get? Oh wait, I know, the benefit of your precious name and this beautiful box to call home. Who could ask for anything more?"

She spoke with such unemotional calm, it was almost as if she were delivering some well-rehearsed lines. What she said wasn't nearly as important as how she said it. She was hiding something, he was sure.

Rebecca turned from him and pushed the servant's bell. Within minutes their butler entered the room.

"May I be of service?" Jenkins asked.

"Yes, I'd like my maid sent to my room to prepare my bath. I shall be up shortly," Rebecca told him.

"Yes, Madam." The butler nodded. "Will there be anything else?" Jenkins asked, directing his question at James.

"No, thank you. That will be all," James confirmed. When Jenkins had exited the room, he said to Rebecca, "This isn't over."

She looked at him almost kindly. "Can we please discuss this in the morning. If I stay to argue with you, my bath will get cold."

He drew a deep breath, resisting the urge to shake her. "Have it your way." Stepping over to the sideboard, he poured himself a drink. He needed one, badly.

"Will I see you at breakfast?" She seemed hesitant, as if his answer were important.

"If you're still here," he replied sarcastically. Taking a drink of his brandy, he savored the burn as it went down. "I certainly won't be going into the office on a Sunday."

She smiled, almost sweetly. It made him wonder what she was thinking. "Rest well, James. I look forward to seeing you in the morning."

~~~

Becca stepped out into the foyer on her way to the grand central staircase and paused to listen. From the front drawing room, she heard the gentle clinking of glass upon a table, an indication James was settling in with his drink. Good for him. He needed to relax.

Slowly, with a weary step, she climbed the stairs to the private rooms on the third floor. That hadn't gone well, not nearly as well as she had hoped. Though she had tried to remain calm, she had allowed his anger and raw emotions to draw her into an argument. Anger begets anger; like begets like, so it was written. It was up to her if there were any hope of changing the mood in this house. As she well knew, a person could not live with such anger and not be affected.

Upon reaching the third-floor landing, she heard water being run in the bathroom down the hall to her left and headed toward the sound, anxious to slip away to the sanctuary of her private chambers. Hopefully, this short reprieve would give her an opportunity to gather her wits and rally her composure. She would need them both when she faced her husband in the bright light of day.

CHAPTER 2

Sunday morning, November 19, 1893

James sat at the breakfast table wondering if Rebecca would actually make an effort to join him or if she planned to avoid him as usual. As a betting man, he'd put his money on the latter. He'd been through hell for the last week, wavering between grave concern that his wife was missing (and possibly dead) and utter rage that she was probably having an affair.

When he went to Stanton Wheland for the loan he needed, he'd never expected to be saddled with a shrew of a wife. His brief acquaintance with Rebecca Wheland had led him to believe she was quiet, unassuming, and most importantly, attracted to him. How could he have been so wrong? Prior to their marriage, he had mistaken her silence for docile acceptance, when in reality, she wanted nothing to do with him. He eventually realized she had gone along with the wedding as a way to escape her father. It seemed she had jumped from the fire into the frying pan, believing life with the devil she didn't know was better than the devil she did.

He could relate. Much the same had been his motivation for going to Stanton Wheland instead of Jules Vanderzeit. Earlier that year, when the stock market panicked and railroad stocks fell, there had been few options open to James when he went looking for the short-term loan he needed. Wheland had let it be known he had the necessary resources available, but his bail-out came at a price. Hard and repulsive, Wheland was a stocky man of average height with a full head of thick white hair and sharp, cold eyes that peered out at the world from a face burrowed with bitterness and the excesses of success. The telltale hints of his Scottish brogue had a way of making his voice seem harsh and unfriendly even when he was attempting to be sociable. For Wheland, making money was the purpose of his life.

As loathsome as Wheland was, James had believed him better than Vanderzeit, the only other person who had offered to provide the money he needed to get through this rough patch. He had worked for Vanderzeit, a man known as the Maestro, in the past, and he wanted to keep it that way—in the past. Not surprisingly, Jules had come to visit James after he learned of his significant losses in the stock market and had offered to give him the money he needed if James was willing to sign another contract pledging six more years of his life to the Maestro.

That wasn't going to happen. Not in this lifetime. Not if he could avoid it.

James had already suffered through seven years of servitude to Jules—it felt more like seventy—as the man sent him flip-flopping through time on errands to retrieve musical artifacts at his beck and call. James had been to ancient China, medieval Spain, and once even to a city in the future Republic of Europe. All too often, it seemed he got the hottest, or coldest, or dirtiest assignments this side of hell, a real slice of life.

However, he could no longer afford to go flipping through time at the whim of Jules Vanderzeit. When his father died shortly after his contract with Jules expired, James had become president of the family business. Jaffay Manufacturing made railcars and replacement parts for the transportation industry. It was simply a matter of bad timing that he had invested so deeply to enlarge his factories in upstate New York shortly before the market fell in May. While still asset rich, the crash had left him scrambling for ready cash to pay his bills, including the basic requirements needed to sustain his lifestyle and keep the factory operating.

Stanton Wheland's offer to James had seemed like a very sweet deal indeed, certainly the lesser of the two evils. He'd been perfectly willing to take Wheland's proposal of an interest-free loan along with a healthy young heiress as his wife. He saw no downside. The problem, as James discovered afterwards, was that although Rebecca was physically healthy, she was not sound of mind. She held a grudge against everything and everyone. Unfortunately, there was no going back. He would never default on a debt, or cause his family to suffer the scandal of divorce. Much as it irked him, Rebecca Wheland was his wife and his responsibility, now and in the future.

The latest issue to plague him had been her week-long disappearance. When he first realized she was missing, he had no intention of letting her absence become known to her father or anyone else until he knew for certain if Rebecca was dead or alive. Thank goodness O'Conner had confessed to taking her to the train station or he may have needed to contact the authorities. According to the groomsman, Rebecca had told him she was going out to Long Island to stay at Raven's Point, her father's summer cottage. She claimed she had gone there alone, which sounded too suspicious to be true, but at least he had confirmed where she had gone.

He thought he had done a fairly good job of holding his anger in check when she finally returned home. The temptation to blow up at her had been enormous, but she had come home willingly, without anyone knowing of her seven days' absence. He wanted to keep it that way. It was better to eat a bit of crow than have their dirty laundry displayed for all of Manhattan to see.

When Rebecca walked into the breakfast room as if nothing were amiss, James felt a mixture of shock and unabashed interest. What on earth would this woman do next?

~~~

Following the scent of bacon and coffee, Becca made her way to the dining room and took her place at the table. A footman stepped forward to serve her breakfast. While he poured her tea, she rested her hands peacefully in her lap and casually observed the man sitting across from her. James Jaffray. Her husband. He might seem like a stranger, but there was no denying he was a handsome man, which certainly created more problems than it solved. Questions swam upstream through her mind. Who was this man, deep down inside? What made him tick? What would it take to soften their divide? Surely, he wasn't always mean and angry. Admittedly, Rebecca had a lot to do with his hostile reaction, taking off as she had, but still, she was his wife.

Becca wondered if it were possible to soften his demeanor or if he was the type of person who got angry for the sake of getting angry. If that were the case, there was very little she could do to make her life better except endure. From personal experience, she knew angry people weren't willing to change their ways, nor would they listen to reason. They didn't even respond to love, not that such a course was practical at the moment.

She supposed she should say something. The mood in the room was colder than ice in winter. If she didn't do something to break the chill, she risked catching a cold, or the flu, or pneumonia. A smile lifted her lips as her mind bounced illogically through these worst-case scenarios and she silently laughed at her foolishness. This might not be easy, but at least she could try to have some fun. Perhaps humor, subtle but consistent, was the way through this quagmire.

"Did you sleep well last night, my dear?" she asked with a pleasantly sweet smile. She even batted her lashes a few times for good measure.

James barely glanced at her before returning his focus to the food on his plate. If he had noticed her flirtatious gestures, he gave no indication. "Fine, thank you. And you? How did it feel to be back in your own bed?"

Oohh, ouch. So he still wanted to throw verbal darts. She needed a way to deflect them.

"As comfortable and *lonely* as ever," she said. Oops, that may have been a bit too forward, and too revealing. She needed to keep that in check. Interestingly, it seemed to get his attention. He finally looked up.

"Are you missing the warmth of your lover?"

"Mmm, yes, the warmth of a lover on these cold winter eves would be ever so nice. Do you know where I can find one?" It was best not to smile too broadly as she said that.

"Probably back on Long Island, or wherever it was you left yours."

Ouch again. "James, James, James," she said with a shake of her head. "We went over this last night. I don't have a lover. I merely needed time to think. Is that really too much to ask. I believe my time alone has been good for me."

"I hope you don't plan to do that often."

"No, not at all. In fact, I was thinking it may be helpful if we tried to start fresh."

His eyes narrowed as if he disapproved, or maybe he simply didn't trust what she was saying.

"I'd like us to start over, give us a chance to become better acquainted, maybe even friends. We are married. It might be helpful," she offered with a small measure of hope.

"It would be more helpful if you didn't take off for days at a time." He set down his coffee cup with a noticeable clink.

Heaven forbid, were they back to that again? "Really, James, you need to let that go. Can we just move past my little holiday away and carry on?" she snapped, firmly setting down her delicate teacup.

Judging by his evil glint in his eyes and the devilish smile curving his lips, he seemed to enjoy her distress. "Your little *holiday*? Is that what you're calling it?"

Darn, she had allowed him to ruffle her feathers. She needed to do better. Smoothing a hand down the front of her skirt, she said in a softer tone, "Call it what you want. I'm sorry if I disappointed you." That hadn't been easy to say but she carried on. "It felt as though I'd been cooped up in this house for months while every day you go off to your office and your friends at the club."

"Is it my fault you lack for friends?"

Another ping, she should have been prepared. Nevertheless, it gave her the opening she needed. "No, but with your help, I believe that can be changed. In fact, I'd like to become more involved with the Women's Assistance League and perhaps other charities. It will give me something to do and a way to be more involved in society."

"Society has not exactly opened its doors to the Whelands. What makes you think it will start now?"

"Because of you, my dear, and your well-respected family name. While my father may have burned plenty of bridges with his nasty business transactions, you and your family are still viewed as upstanding citizens of New York society. Nobody knows of the deal you made to make me your wife." Actually, a few did, but there was no need to go into that now. "I believe we can put this to good use. For starters, I would like very much for us to secure an invitation to the annual Women's Assistance League Holiday Charity Ball on December eighth."

"I should think the invitations have gone out by now." He seemed ready to discount her suggestion and went back to eating his eggs and bacon.

21

He was probably right, but when she checked through the cards and letters piled up on her writing desk, an invitation to the ball was not among them. That was such a disappointment. It would have been so much easier if it had. "You may be right; however, it isn't unusual for invitations to be handed out right up to the day of the event, especially if the organizers believe we are interested in making a substantial donation to their cause."

He eyed her with blatant disbelief. "What would lead them to believe such a thing? It's taking all I have to keep up appearances. I don't have excess money to give away at charity balls." He set down his knife and fork. It seemed she had his attention now.

"You know, and I know, but societies' matrons don't necessarily know the details of our financial situation. I understand there will be an auction of some outstanding paintings at the event. If we let the right people think we're interested in bidding on one of the pieces, I'm sure we could garner an invitation."

He stared at her in stony silence. Darn, he wasn't going to make this easy.

Short of begging, she needed to sweeten her plea. "Please, James. Is it really asking so much for you to get us an invitation to a holiday ball? Think how happy you'll make me. It will give me something to look forward to."

"You expect us both to attend?"

"Would it be so painful to be seen out in public with me? You're worried I've taken a lover. Certainly, any gossip or concerns in that area would be put to rest if we present ourselves as a happily married couple, and happily married couples have a tendency to attend social functions together."

"This sounds like an excuse to purchase another fancy ball gown."

Becca sighed. "I'm sure I already have something in my wardrobe appropriate for the occasion." One only needed to peek into her closet to see it was bursting with gowns to choose from. She had no doubt she could find something appropriate to wear.

"That's a new one. When did you become thrifty?"

"Since I have a ball I want to attend, and I need your help. My goodness, James. You claim you want a happy marriage, the least you could do is support me in this effort." Considering his lack of enthusiasm, maybe he didn't really want a happy marriage, only the image of one. It caused her to ask, "You do want a happy marriage, don't you?" When he stared at her for an inordinately long time, she added, "Or at least the pretense of one."

"I'll see what I can do, but I'll make no promises."

"Perfect. That's all I ask. It might also be helpful if I send out my calling card to some of my old friends." And perhaps a few of his, if she could find out who they were.

"I didn't think the Whelands had any friends."

She batted her lashes again. "In society, the term 'friend' is relative."

~~~

James studied Rebecca as she sat across from him, looking uncommonly relaxed, and sipping her tea with a half-smile curving her lips. He found he was intrigued by their little exchange. Their conversation this morning was more than they had spoken to each other in weeks. Maybe her time away really had done her some good. Not that he condoned her actions.

He hadn't noticed it last night, but today she seemed thinner than he remembered, as if she had lost weight in the seven days she was gone. No doubt the lack of servants to wait on her hand and foot, night and day, had taken its toll. But that wasn't all. Her hair, he noticed, was gathered loosely atop her head in a flattering style instead of the severely unattractive tight bun she usually favored. Interestingly, the deeply embedded frown lines that usually framed her mouth seemed to have vanished completely. When she looked up at him and smiled, sweet little laugh lines danced around her eyes. He had always thought of Rebecca Wheland as little more than plain, but today, if his eyes didn't deceive him, she was really quite pretty.

Such a notable change in her appearance made him wonder. Was she doing this all for him? Or was there someone else? He couldn't shake the belief that a woman didn't disappear for seven days unless another man was involved. She claimed she wasn't having an affair, but the change in her mood and appearance, though subtle, indicated she had something up her sleeve.

Maybe her time away truly had done her some good. It certainly appeared that way. Perhaps he should simply be grateful and make the most of it. She had suggested they attempt to make a fresh start, but he wondered if such a thing were possible. A woman as mean and ornery as

Rebecca Wheland didn't seem likely to change overnight. And becoming friends with her was even harder to imagine, especially considering they hadn't had sex since the first week of their marriage, which was fine with him. Bedding Rebecca was akin to fucking a corpse. For the most part, she had simply lain there, stiff and cold, without an ounce of affection or enjoyment. Rebecca, as he knew her, didn't have a passionate or gracious bone in her body. Thankfully, since they maintained separate bedrooms and she had locked him out of hers, he rarely saw her. Now it seemed he couldn't stop looking at her.

James watched as Rebecca delicately cut off a piece of bacon and lifted her fork. Full, pink lips parted to receive the morsel. But that wasn't all he noticed. "Have you always eaten with your left hand?" he asked.

Rebecca glanced down at the silverware held in her hands. "I'm nearly ambidextrous. I can feed myself equally well with either hand." She laid down the fork and knife and picked them up with the opposite hands, then proceeded to repeat the process. "I can work a needle with either hand, but I must confess to choosing my left over my right when it comes to writing or crochet. I injured my right hand once in a riding accident and my bones tend to ache when it's cold. I've learned to adjust." After switching the utensils once again, she asked, "Are you saying you've never noticed this before?"

"Why would I?" They rarely dined together. He usually left for his office while she slept late and remained ensconced in her private chambers. For the past few months, he had taken most of his evening meals at his club downtown and arranged to arrive home late enough to ensure with a fairly high degree of predictability that Rebecca would be back in her bedroom, retired for the night. He had no idea what she did to keep herself busy during the day, nor did he care. The less they saw of each other, the less they argued. It didn't make for a happy marriage, but at least they maintained a quiet home. This morning at breakfast was the longest and most pleasant conversation they'd had since . . . ever.

"Maybe that's our problem. A man should take notice of his wife." Rebecca set down her knife and fork and gave him an incredulous look, which he supposed he deserved. "It seems there's much we don't know about each other. Perhaps, if we're willing to set aside our past, we may even find some common ground where we can make peace."

When he gave her a skeptical look, she continued, "You needn't worry. I don't expect you to fall head over heels in love with me, but think about it, James. We've committed to spending the rest of our lives together. Wouldn't it be so much better if we were able to get along? That's why I bolted and hid away at my father's cottage. The idea of living the rest of my life in misery, alone in this home, was more than I could bear. Having time alone, *really alone*, made me think I haven't given this . . . this . . ."

"Marriage," he supplied.

"Yes, this marriage enough of a chance. I was going to say relationship, but that seems a bit presumptuous."

That almost brought a smile to his lips. Almost, but not quite. "You don't think, as a married couple, we have a relationship."

"Up until now, I'm sure you would agree, it hasn't been very good."

She'd get no argument there. "What are you suggesting?"

"Well, for starters, what do you have planned for today? Perhaps we could spend the day together."

James grinned boldly at her suggestion. "Have you forgotten while you were away? It's the last day of the New York Horse Show at Madison Square Garden, and I, for one, plan to attend. I've had a box there all week, which you would know if you were here."

Rebecca perked up noticeably. "Am I allowed to go with you?"

This was something new. Rebecca had not shown an interest in horses before now. "Only if you want to. After your little disappearing act, I'm surprised you'd want to spend the day with me."

"Quite the opposite. I think it's most important to be seen together." She glanced up at the large wall clock hanging above the side table. "Do we have time to attend church service?"

He nearly laughed. "When was the last time you were in a church?"

Her eyes darkened momentarily before she waved off his offensive quip with a forced smile. "I've been known to attend from time to time. Afterwards, we can attend the horse show together. Perhaps, if you behave yourself, I'll let you hold my hand to keep me warm. With our gloves on, of course." Her forced smile transformed into one that appeared more genuine.

Was his wife flirting with him?

Looking almost giddy with excitement, Rebecca continued, "I believe there's an eleven o'clock service at Grace Episcopal Church. I'm sure I can change into something appropriate and be ready in time."

He couldn't deny there were benefits to appearing at church services and the horse show with Rebecca, and while he wasn't yet sure if this was how he wanted to spend his day, it seemed Rebecca was determined.

She said to the footman standing nearby, "Please send my maid to my room so she may help me change."

Not so fast. He wasn't ready to concede to her wishes. "Are you referring to Katie?" he asked, feeling mildly annoyed.

"Excuse me?"

"Our servants, they have names. Your maid has a name. Why don't you use it?"

Rebecca seemed less than happy to be reprimanded. "Since I only have one maid in this house, one personal chamber maid that is, I am sure this footman knows who I meant."

"The footman's name is Wallis."

"Oh my goodness, I am sure *Wallis* knew who I meant."

"If you took more of an interest in running this house, you would know their names." James didn't know why he insisted on focusing on this issue, but for some reason he couldn't let it go, as if her lack of care for their servants was somehow linked to him.

Rebecca stared at him steely eyed. Apparently, he had ruffled her feathers, again. He almost felt relieved, as if his footing was back on solid ground. He could handle angry, unhappy Rebecca. Kind, flirtatious Rebecca had thrown him off guard.

"Shall I start today, on the Sabbath?" she questioned. "Perhaps we should line them up in the foyer for another formal introduction since I obviously didn't benefit from the first. Next, I can sit with our cook and draw up menus for the week to promote my authority over running this house."

James bit back a curse. "My house." He stopped short of saying *our* home. He doubted she shared that sentiment. He understood from O'Conner that she had gone to her father's house intent on staying there, but Stanton had refused her. What a sad experience that must be, to be denied lodging in one's own family home.

26

She seemed to detect his unspoken reference to home. Her eyes turned sad. She braced her hands against the edge of the table and bowed her head with her eyes closed. What emotion might she be feeling? Sadness, regret, anger—or worse, rejection? When she looked up her expression showed renewed determination.

"I am going to attend services at Grace Episcopal Church. You are welcome to accompany me or attend the horse show alone, as you intended. I leave it up to you." She stood with a measure of grace and dignity and exited the room.

James felt a degree of respect for her that he had never felt before.

Becca went to her room to dress for church. The November day was cold and she chose a warm, dark green velvet dress for the outing. With Katie's assistance she changed her clothes and then sat at her dressing table while her maid arranged her hair.

"Do you want it pulled back in your usual style, Ma'am?" Katie asked as their eyes met in the mirror.

"No, something softer, I think, to flatter the shape of my face."

"Yes, Ma'am. I know just the thing. Something I saw in the Ladies' Home monthly."

"I'm sure it will be fine. I trust your judgment."

As Katie combed out her hair, Becca asked, "Do you like working here?" She watched in the mirror to catch the maid's reaction. Katie's hands stilled for a brief moment before she continued dressing Becca's hair.

"I like it here well enough, Ma'am," she said keeping her eyes focused on Becca's head. "I ain't one to complain." There was a fearful look in her eyes. Becca wasn't surprised. From what she knew, servants tended to be fearful of losing their position.

"You're not complaining, I'm asking. Do you get on well with the other servants?"

"Well enough, Ma'am," Katie replied with a nonchalant shrug.

Apparently, her maid was wary of saying too much and breaching the code of silence shared by the downstairs staff. "I must confess, Katie, though I'm sure you know, I've not made the appropriate effort to engage the staff. I hope to set that right." When Katie's eyes widened in surprise, she added, "My adjustment to my husband's house has not gone well. My

27

time away has shown me it's time for a change. I plan to meet with Cook tomorrow to go over the menus for the week."

In for a penny, in for a pound. If she was going to commit to this transition, she needed to be bold. She also needed to consult with James to know if he planned to be home for any of his meals. Would he be willing to dine with her or was this a doomed, useless effort? Oh well, one must try, she told herself.

"I'm not asking you to gossip, you understand, or reveal precious secrets, but can you tell me one helpful hint about Mrs. . . . ." Becca paused, because of course she didn't know the cook's name.

"Granger."

"Yes, of course. Thank you, Katie."

Katie gazed off with a thoughtful look. "Mrs. Granger always says she doesn't like to waste food or Master Jaffray's money. She doesn't shop for more than we can use, and leftovers are always put to good use. There's no waste in this house."

"Thank you. That's very helpful to know." Judging from this morning's breakfast, she was sure Mrs. Granger was a qualified cook. "I wonder what dishes are her specialties."

"Roasted beef stew with potatoes and carrots."

That didn't seem like anything special. Becca gave Katie a questioning look.

"Mr. Jaffray is a meat and potatoes kind of man. He doesn't ask for anything fancy."

Becca wondered if he would be willing to change, to try new things. It seemed doubtful, given what little she knew of him. Her suggestion that they spend the day together had not been well received. He hadn't agreed and then went on to pick a fight, a classic way of avoiding her offer. He had made her so upset she had wanted to withdraw her request that they attend church services together, but she resisted. She left it up to him and fully expected him to decline. She had little reason to believe he wanted to be seen in public with her, and Grace Episcopal Church was considered the center of fashionable Manhattan.

He was most likely preparing to leave for his club to avoid her company as soon as possible. Nevertheless, she would carry on with her plans. It would still be beneficial to be seen at church services. Most of New York's society matrons attended service and her presence there would boost her chances to secure an invitation to the holiday ball. Of course, not just any ball. It had to be the Women's Assistance League Holiday Charity Ball on December eighth.

That ball was her one chance of purchasing the painting she so badly needed, the Magic Flute by V.W. Stevenson. When that was done, all this nonsense would be over.

~*~

James paced the length of the foyer as he waited for his wife to come down. In his wildest imaginings, he wouldn't have expected to be attending Sunday services, and most certainly not with his anti-social wife. He couldn't remember the last time he had stepped inside a church for anything other than a wedding or a funeral, and he didn't do christenings. Even more unexpectedly, it looked as though Rebecca also planned to accompany him to the horse show at Madison Square Garden.

He glanced again at the stairs. She wasn't yet there and he was tempted to go about his merry way as he'd originally planned. As he paced down the hall, he debated with himself on the soundness of such an idea. Should he give in to Rebecca's request or carry on with his day? She had said she wanted to start anew. It was an encouraging start, but he wondered if he should acquiesce so easily to her demands. Was this a show of weakness on his part? Then again, she hadn't really made a demand, only a request, and a nicely put one at that. If he wasn't mistaken, she had actually flirted with him.

Too bad he had to go and spoil it all by pointing out her lack of care for their servants, or rather, his servants. With the exception of Katie, her personal maid, James or his mother had hired everyone on his staff. After his father died, he had sold off the old family brownstone near Washington Square and built this new house on Fifth Avenue close to Central Park. With significant support from his mother and sister, they had furnished and staffed this house and made it their home. Prior to that, for the seven years it had taken to work off his contract with Jules, he had been gone more often than he'd been home. Always another business trip, as he called them.

He was home now, hopefully to stay. His contract with Vanderzeit was over but the memory never left him. When he had fallen through the ice with his youngest brother Martin and made a deal with the Maestro to save their lives, James had no way of anticipating the consequences. But

29

all that was behind him now. No more Maestro, no more contract, no more time travel.

Earlier in the year, his sister Charlene had married Steven Shepard and moved to a home of her own with her husband, but she still lived in Manhattan. Currently, Eleanor, his mother, was in Savannah, staying with Martin to avoid the cold winter weather of New York. She had left the first week of November, shortly before Rebecca disappeared, and was thankfully unaware of what had happened.

He couldn't really fault Rebecca for not knowing the names of his staff. Even after his marriage, his mother had continued to run their home. Rebecca had seemed to accept the arrangement, which led him to believe she simply didn't care, or maybe she saw no reason to upset the status quo. He wondered if his mother's departure had figured into Rebecca's decision to run off as she did. Perhaps the idea of running his house in his mother's absence was too daunting for her. Or perhaps he was simply giving her the benefit of the doubt since she had flirted with him at breakfast.

Turning to retrace his steps, he took another look at the central staircase. No Rebecca. He still had time to change his mind, put on his hat and coat, walk out the front door to his carriage, and instruct Mr. Bates, his driver, to take him to his club where he would hide out until the horse show began. Did it matter that Rebecca would be disappointed and justifiably upset?

Yes, it did.

Their marriage had gotten off to a bad start—a horrendously bad start—but maybe, if they were both willing to try, they could make this work. Wouldn't that be a kick in the backside to old Wheland, to one day discover his castoff daughter was happily married.

It would also be a blessing for him. No man in his right mind wanted to spend years of his life in an unhappy marriage if there was something he could do to avoid that, especially if that something was within reason.

Footsteps sounded on the stair. James looked up to see Rebecca and for a moment, his breath stopped. Was this beautiful, stunning woman really his wife? How had that happened? He couldn't remember her ever looking this good, even on the day he married her. She wore a sweeping cloak richly brocaded in russets and greens over a hunter green velvet dress. The wide hood of the cloak was drawn up to frame her face and a single ringlet of chestnut hair hung down her slender swan-like neck. She caught his eye and gave him a shy, sweet, feminine sort of smile that shifted her appearance from plain to pretty, and even alluring. The overall effect was dazzling.

He blinked and gave himself a slight shake. He mustn't allow himself to become distracted by a pretty face, although if one must be distracted, this was certainly a face to do the job. Her efforts deserved an acknowledgment.

"You look lovely," he greeted her.

"Thank you, James. You look quite dashing as well. Shall I take this to mean you're going to accompany me to church?"

"It will be my pleasure." He wondered where that sentiment had come from, but when her face lit up with a bright smile, he didn't care. He would be honored to go anywhere with her by his side. He offered her his arm. "Mr. Bates has already brought the carriage to the front."

"Splendid. I shall have to thank Mr. Bates for braving the cold to wait for us."

"We should go. We don't want to miss the opening hymn," James said although he wasn't even sure if services were started with an opening hymn.

"Agreed. A late arrival would be awkward." She took his offered arm and he led her to the carriage.

As they rode the short distance to Grace Church, James couldn't help but sneak glances at Rebecca. Was this pleasant, smiling beauty sitting by his side really his wife? It almost seemed too good to be true, as if some fairy godmother had come and switched his old, mean Rebecca with a fairy princess and he was living in a fairy tale. He wondered what had happened to her while she was gone to elicit such a change. Could it truly be as simple as she said, that she needed time away from him to think? Something had provoked this change, and given enough time, he fully expected to discover what that something was.

"It's awfully cold. Do you think it's going to snow?" Rebecca asked, turning to look at him. Her checks glowed red from the cold and the green specks in her hazel eyes seemed brighter than he had ever noticed before. The fresh scent of her lavender soap filled the air of the enclosed carriage.

"Not yet. It's still too dry. Perhaps by Thanksgiving," he offered as his perfunctory weather forecast.

"Ohhh, snow at the holiday. That will be pretty." Her face lit with the idea.

"Not in New York, at least not for long."

Her smile flattened. "You're right, the soot and mud will all too quickly take its toll, but maybe for a day or two all will be crisp and white."

He was talking about the weather with his wife, not arguing. It seemed so strange and yet so natural.

She turned slightly toward him in her seat. "I have a confession to make."

His stomach clenched. Was she going to confess to having a lover on their way to church? If she thought her timing would absolve her of her sins she was grossly mistaken.

"I'm a bit nervous," she said. "I haven't been to church for ages. I'm sure it's been a year or more."

James let out a sigh of relief. "I can't remember the last time I attended Sunday services. I'm sure I was still in knickers."

Rebecca laughed. He liked the sound. "I remember my father taking me when I was young and holding my hand. He made me feel safe."

"Your father held your hand?" That didn't sound like Stanton.

"He must have at least once. I guess, when something special happens to you as a child you remember it above all others. I suppose if it wasn't special, I wouldn't have been so impressed." With a downfallen look, she stared pensively out the window.

As he watched her, it occurred to him that Rebecca had purposefully hidden her beauty under a façade of anger and resentment. The father who may have once loved his little girl had all but abandoned her after his wife died. Rebecca hadn't wanted to be sold off as chattel by her father and she had done everything in her power to thwart his wishes.

James reached for her hand. He wanted her to feel safe and special again. "If lightning strikes or we're laughed out of the chapel, at least we're in this together."

The way her smile lit up her face, one might have thought he had just pledged his undying love, which was far from true. At least she was smiling again, and for some reason, that made him feel good.

When they arrived at Grace Cathedral, the usher took them to seats midway up the nave on the far-left aisle. James surmised the location was due to them being unknown visitors and yet obviously of some financial standing based on their appearance alone. He took a cursory look around and gave passing nods to the men he recognized. Near the front, he noticed Pierpont Morgan and his wife, Frances.

They took their seats only a few minutes before the service started and already James was fighting the urge to fidget, an old habit from childhood. He glanced over at Rebecca. Unlike him, she seemed peaceful and serene. Her eyes slowly scanned the church as if drinking in the sight of the stained-glass windows and tall stately columns.

She caught his eye and leaned in close to whisper, "Churches are so peaceful, don't you agree? It's as if all the prayers said here have infused this space with a sense of awe-inspiring calm."

"I suppose so," he agreed, although until that moment such a thought never would have occurred to him.

She reached for the missal stored in the pew in front of them and as the service began she joined the congregation in song. She had an accomplished voice, pure and melodic, the type of voice a mother would use to sing her child to sleep.

Not that he expected them to have children any time soon. Their few attempts at lovemaking had been such dismal disappointments he was in no rush to repeat the experience. Rebecca had responded with all the emotion and pleasure of a dead fish. Understandably, she had been an inexperienced virgin, and he had expected her to be somewhat stiff and frightened at the initial event. Still, despite all his efforts to be a considerate lover, each attempt had produced the same dismal results, until she effectively snuffed out any desire he might have to try again.

As he listened to her voice joyously raised in song, James couldn't help but think there were depths to her passion she'd withheld from him. The thought inspired both disappointment and hope. He supposed he couldn't blame her for withholding her affection. She had been forced to marry a man she didn't love and hardly knew. Resentment had been the easy, and perhaps, only logical response.

But now, as he caught a glimpse of the warmth and joy she was capable of displaying, it gave him hope. Hope that given enough time, he and Rebecca could find common ground on which to stand. The thought of making love to a warm and receptive wife was somewhat arousing and he was grateful for the cover his winter overcoat provided. Surely such thoughts were inappropriate in a house of God! James made a concerted effort to focus on the service. Coincidentally, the sermon was on the temptation of Eve to Adam. It was a fitting reminder that the temptation of women was often the downfall of men.

~*~

When the service ended, they stepped out to the curb to await their carriage. A number of his friends and business associates came by to express their regards. Most of these men and their wives had been sitting near the front of the church in their established pews, indicating they were long-standing members of the congregation. Morgan seemed particularly pleased to note his attendance. Rebecca had been right—as a foray into society as a married couple, this was a sound idea.

"Jaffray, good to see you. I didn't know you attended Grace Church. In fact, I didn't know you attended church at all," Morgan said as he drew near. J.P. Morgan, known as Pierpont to his friends, was a large man with massive shoulders, piercing eyes and the unfortunate facial disfiguration of a large, discolored, purple nose, made worse by the early winter chill.

James had known the man for quite some time, and while they did business together, they rarely if ever discussed their personal lives. James preferred to keep it that way, especially since marrying Rebecca, but now he had very little choice if he didn't want to appear rude.

"I don't usually, but perhaps it's time I did. Allow me to introduce you to my wife, Rebecca. Rebecca, this is Mr. Pierpont Morgan and his wife, Frances. I'll be working with Pierpont later this week."

"It's a pleasure meeting you," Pierpont said, reaching out to shake Rebecca's hand. Morgan was known to intimidate people upon their first meeting, as if daring them to acquiesce to the force of his character rather than shrink from the ugliness of his nose. James wondered how Rebecca would react.

"J.P. Morgan?" Rebecca asked, sounding impressed as she shook his hand and looked him square in the eyes. Apparently, Morgan's physical appearance didn't intimidate her.

"Why, yes. Has James mentioned me?" Pierpont glanced quickly at James before he turned his attention back to Rebecca. He seemed intrigued by her question, as was James since he didn't make it a habit to discuss his business associates with anyone.

"You're working on restructuring the railroads, aren't you?" Rebecca asked.

James received another questioning look from Morgan. "I didn't think that was common knowledge," Pierpont said with a menacing glare.

Rebecca shrugged it off. "My father must have told me."

"Her father is Stanton Wheland," James explained.

"You're Stanton's daughter!" Morgan looked momentarily unsettled before his expression turned amiable. "You certainly have changed since the last time I saw you. Marriage must agree with you."

"I believe it has its advantages," Rebecca offered. "Mrs. Morgan, since our husbands will be working together, would it be acceptable for me to call upon you?"

James froze, wondering what the hell Rebecca was thinking. Mrs. Morgan held the socially superior position to Rebecca, even if Wheland was her father. As such, she should not ask to call upon Frances, she should wait patiently for Mrs. Morgan to call upon her, if that were to happen.

Frances and Pierpont exchanged a brief knowing glance and he gave her a nod. "Since you asked, I'm at home on Wednesdays," Frances said.

James breathed a little more freely.

"Lovely, I shall hope to see you then," Rebecca said, smiling kindly.

"Our carriage has arrived. Allow me to assist you, my dear." Pierpont lent a hand to his wife. "It was a pleasure meeting you, Mrs. Jaffray."

"The pleasure was mine. Thank you, Mr. Morgan, Mrs. Morgan. May you enjoy the rest of your day," Rebecca replied, maintaining her smile.

James waited until they were alone in their carriage before he asked, "How well do you remember meeting Morgan at your father's?" He wondered what business the two men might have exchanged.

"It's hard to say. So many men passed through our front parlor to do business with Father. They all seemed the same to me. I don't know how I was able to recall hearing about his involvement in the railroad. Are you sure you didn't mention it to me?"

"Quite sure. Our work is still preliminary. Very few know." When would he have? He and Rebecca rarely spoke more than a few words to each other. Today was already surely a record.

"I didn't know your work together was confidential, but now that I do, you can be assured I will treat the information with greater care."

35

Since they had plenty of time before the last event of the horse show was scheduled to begin, James instructed Mr. Bates to continue north on Fifth Avenue to Central Park. As they rolled down the street ensconced in their carriage, a snug little world seemed to envelop them. The hustle and bustle of Manhattan faded into the background, leaving a comfortable silence. While James relaxed lazily against the heavily padded cushions of the coach, Rebecca leaned forward slightly to peer out the window. She seemed absorbed by the sights along the street as if she were a newly arrived visitor to the city instead of a longtime resident. Rather than feeling ignored, James was intrigued as to why she should display such a newfound interest in the city.

"You seem inordinately enchanted with the passing scenery," James commented.

Rebecca turned her gaze from the window as he had hoped. "I'm sorry, I didn't mean to ignore you, it's just that I've allowed my curiosity to run wild. Have you ever considered what goes on behind the façades of those brownstones and newly built mansions? What might it be like for the people living in these homes? Block after block of the same dull brownstones, interrupted now and again by some new modern mansion that takes up a whole block. I wonder how long it will be before more and more of these row houses are demolished to make way for the nouveaux riche flooding into New York."

"Surely you're not against the nouveaux riche." While the Jaffray family had a long and well-established history in New York, Wheland, with his millions, was easily considered one of the newly rich.

"Not at all. They are inevitable, and a boon to the economy," Rebecca said.

James studied his wife. "When did you become interested in real estate?"

Rebecca chuckled lightheartedly. "I am my father's daughter. His attention to the market must have rubbed off on me. I can't help but think that holding land in New York must be a profitable venture."

"Land investments are almost always profitable. It's obtaining the ready funds for such ventures that is usually the hindrance."

"And yet each of these families has found the necessary resources to make their home here. But, please, you must excuse me. I have a tendency to let my imagination run rampant. I should be focusing my attention on

36

you. I appreciate you taking this time to be with me. Oh, look, we're about to enter Central Park. I wonder if we'll see anyone we know."

It was a common enough activity, even in November, for couples and families to take a Sunday ride through the park. The leisurely drive was a convenient opportunity to see one's neighbors and to be seen in return. It wasn't unusual to see two or more carriages pulled off to one side of the roadway as the occupants took time to exchange greetings and a bit of gossip.

Rebecca once again leaned forward to gaze out the window as a woman pushing a baby carriage strolled by. With a jerk, she settled back against the seat cushions. "I suppose I shouldn't do that."

James gave her a questioning look.

"I mean, it's probably not nice to stare out the window. But really, do you think it's safe to have a baby out in the dead of winter?"

Her concern seemed somewhat out of place. "It's hardly the dead of winter, but I'm sure the child is bundled up warmly."

"Well, I would never, if I didn't have to. Babies can be so fragile." Her eyes glazed over as she focused on the opposite wall of their carriage.

It occurred to James he knew very little about Rebecca. Did she want children? Most women did, but perhaps she didn't, considering their dismal failure in the bedroom. Like so many other things, they had not yet discussed the subject.

The few times they met before their hastily rushed wedding had been in the presence of her father, and Stanton had done most of the talking. If he wasn't discussing business, he was busy planning the wedding ceremony, guest list and reception. Rebecca had been given little say in the matter and at the time James hadn't really cared. He'd been too focused on the goal of securing the interest-free loan to keep his business running smoothly.

Prior to the market crash he had always had more than enough ready cash to meet his needs, but when his margin was called on the railroad stocks he owned, it had wiped out every liquid cent he had. A depression in the market was not a good time to sell anything and expect a good return, so he had gone looking for a loan to hold him over until he could negotiate new contracts for his railcars and equipment. At first, he had acted as if the drain on his resources was not an issue, believing the longstanding benefit of his good family name would see him through. It

37

didn't take long for him to realize everyone was drained and the railroads were holding back on new purchases. There were very few places he could go to get the funds he needed.

Desperate times called for desperate measures, but the thick of a panic was not a good time to make life-altering decisions. Much of his incentive for dealing with Wheland had been his desire to shield his mother and the rest of his family from knowing how desperate their finances had become.

Now, with the benefit of hindsight, he saw how deeply his single-mindedness had affected Rebecca. No matter what came before in their marriage, if she sincerely wanted to start anew, he owed her that favor. Unexpectedly, he was consumed with a feeling of . . . optimism. It took him a moment to identify the feeling, it had been too long lacking in his life, but suddenly the idea of improved relations with his wife was decidedly appealing.

Could he truly look upon Rebecca as a desirable mate? The idea had significant merit. They both had been given a raw deal, but rather than allow it to devastate their lives, maybe they could turn it to their favor.

James turned his attention back to his silent wife. "Are you all right? Aren't you enjoying yourself?" he asked, as he reached for her hand.

As if startled awake, she turned to face him, flashing a magnificent smile. "Yes, thank you. It's wonderful to see all the handsomely dressed carriages and wonder who is inside. I was thinking ours is one of the nicer ones. Surely, we've drawn an eye or two, wouldn't you think?"

It pleased him to hear her compliment his carriage. "I can point out a few that I know if you like."

"Could you really? That would be grand."

Her enthusiasm was like that of a child released in a sweet shop. "That carriage there in front of us is the Morgan's. They must have come here directly from church services like us."

"Yes, I remember seeing their carriage. It's about the only one I know."

"There, just past the curve, is William Vanderbilt's rig. I wonder if George is in town. Since he finished building his home in Ashland he's rarely here."

"Yes, I know of the place, he calls it the Biltmore. Do you know the Vanderbilts well?"

"My mother is friends with Alva. A more pugnacious and determined woman I have never met. It's rumored she has turned to England to find a titled husband for Consuelo." James immediately regretted the underlying meaning of his words and looked to Rebecca for her reaction.

She sadly shook her head. "When it comes to arranged marriages, I know I am not alone. Can you imagine for a moment, knowing your only worth in this world is to serve as marriageable chattel for your father? Although in Consuelo's case, I believe it's worse since it's her mother doing the bidding."

"Were you close to your mother before she died?" So many questions he had never asked.

"I'm grateful I had a parent who loved me." Sadness shifted through her eyes.

Feeling he had stepped on forbidden ground, James quickly changed the subject. "That carriage over there belongs to Robert Goelet. You were talking earlier about New York real estate. His family owns property up and down Fifth Avenue."

"Really! What do you know of him?"

James listed some of Goelet's better known holdings, and Rebecca responded with a startling show of interest. Clearly, he had underestimated her intelligence.

"You surprise me. Not many woman care to discuss real estate," James said.

"I'm sure I'm not very different from most women. I'm more interested in what goes on inside these homes than their worth. I've always had an interest in art, design and architecture."

They were near the cross-through street of Central Park where most of the carriages would turn around and head back. "Would you like to make another pass through the park?" James asked.

She nodded with a shy smile. "If we have time. I should think we need to get home so I can change for the horse show."

"I think we can manage," James assured her.

~*~

It hadn't taken long for James to change for the horse show, but he should have known better if he thought Rebecca wouldn't keep him waiting. It seemed to take forever for a woman to complete a simple

39

change of garments. He picked up his hat and was ready to walk out the door without her when Rebecca finally came waltzing down the stairs.

"Please forgive me, James, I didn't intend to make you wait. It took me longer than I expected to choose what to wear," she said as she neared the bottom of the stairs. "Do you think I look all right?"

She looked better than all right, she looked amazing. It seemed she was determined to dazzle him and everyone else at the horse show with her gown and pearls. She would fit right in with the rest of the ladies who filled the box seats at the arena and wandered about the promenade in the garden displaying their furs and jewels. Unexpected as it was, he easily saw the benefit of having Rebecca at his side.

"I think you'll do in a pinch," he said, holding back his praise.

"Thank goodness, I wouldn't want to be an embarrassment to you."

"I wouldn't worry too much about that." James was encouraged by her earnest effort to please him. It gave him hope for their future together.

Jenkins helped her put on her fur coat and a moment later they were on their way, giving James a moment to relax as they rolled down the streets toward Madison Square Garden.

The horse show attracted the elite of New York society, who came to view the equine parade from the comfort of their private boxes decorated in the black and yellow colors of the Horse Show Association. Throughout the week, prize horses had been paraded through the arena and thousands of dollars had been exchanged as studs and mares were bought and sold by men seeking to enhance the stock of their stables. For Rebecca, it seemed the real show was the crowd filling the place. The New York Horse Show was considered the opening event of the winter season, and for the women, it was viewed as another excuse to display their fashions; an opportunity to see and be seen.

If she hadn't been with him, he would have spent the day in the company of the other lone men who drank, smoked, and discussed the favorable and unfavorable attributes of both the horses and women on display. But Rebecca was with him—she stayed close by his side as they viewed the proceedings together—and as such, he acted accordingly.

Thankfully, nothing unpleasant occurred during the course of the event. No disagreements, no show of temper, no pouting from Rebecca when he stepped away to speak with one friend or another. And yet, James couldn't shake a feeling that Rebecca was only with him for show, much like the horseflesh being paraded around the arena. Often pensive, as if she were unsure how to conduct herself in his presence, she seemed too quiet, too compliant. It harkened back to the days before they were married and she had done her best to impress him with her quiet grace, and not let her true feelings show.

As they rode home through the darkened streets, Rebecca said sweetly, "I'd like to thank you for spending the day with me. I know you had other plans."

"You needn't thank me, I had a perfectly acceptable day." A man should want to spend time with his wife, and a wife shouldn't have to thank her husband for spending a Sunday afternoon with her. But Rebecca and James weren't a normal couple. They were strangers trapped in a marriage not to their liking.

"Do you have anything exciting planned for this coming week?" Rebecca asked.

"Can't say that I do," James answered tersely, suddenly anxious for the day to be over.

"Aren't you meeting with Mr. Morgan to discuss the railroads?"

"Preliminary meeting only. Nothing too exciting." His meetings with Pierpont were extremely confidential, not something he wanted to discuss with anyone, especially Wheland's daughter. If news leaked out on his negotiations, he risked losing a very lucrative contract for his company.

"Oh, I see," she nodded. "I look forward to calling on Mrs. Morgan. She said she was receiving on Wednesday."

"That should be nice for you." He was certain Morgan wouldn't be sharing the subject of their meetings with his wife, and even if he did, he doubted Frances would share such information with Rebecca. Women simply did not discuss business at social calls.

"I've let Mrs. Granger know I want to meet with her tomorrow to discuss our menus for the week. Is there anything you would like me to include, any dishes you favor?" Rebecca seemed determined to strike up a conversation, but menus and social visits hardly held any interest for him.

"Mrs. Granger has been our cook for a few years now. I'm sure she knows my preferences."

She finally seemed to understand he was no longer in the mood for meaningless conversation and they spent the rest of the ride home in uncomfortable silence.

It was quite late by the time they returned home. Rebecca claimed she was pleasantly tired and begged his leave to retire to her room. It shouldn't surprise him that she was so quick to quit his company. Apparently, she had gotten what she wanted and was anxious to return to the solitude of her rooms. James was happy to oblige, as he, too, wanted some time alone. It had been a most unusual day. Going from having a barely tolerable marriage to having a compliant wife who wanted to please him was more taxing than he would have thought. He needed a relaxing drink, a nice port perhaps.

Yesterday he had been out of his mind with worry about the whereabouts of his wife and her possible scandalous activity, and today he had spent several unexpectedly pleasant hours in her company. The sheer contrast was jarring, and he wasn't sure what to make of it. He certainly wasn't ready to believe Rebecca had completely changed her feelings for him simply because they had spent one companionable day together. Considering what he had been through in the last twenty-four hours, he deserved a drink. Maybe he would make it a brandy.

~*~

Becca went to her room, grateful for the opportunity to rest and shed her role of dutiful, loving wife for a while. She wanted to relax and write in her journal before she retired for the night. The day with James had gone well—in many ways, better than she had expected. He had been nice. There may have been a few times when he had let his past resentment show, but for the most part, James had been nice, even respectful. What a blessing. Respect was such a vital element in any relationship and his behavior was encouraging. If she had any hope of making it successfully through the next few weeks, she needed to continue to foster his respect and good will.

When they arrived home, she and James had each retired to their separate bedrooms for the night. She had no reason to expect anything different. Earlier in the day it had seemed he was warming to her efforts, but a chilling frost had set in on the ride home and she didn't know why. It was only day one of this effort, she reminded herself. She couldn't expect them to become best of friends overnight just because they had spent a few pleasant hours together. Still, she hoped he would warm up enough to support her desire to attend the Women's Assistance League holiday ball. If she failed to secure the highly coveted invitation, she might as well call it quits. She could think of no other way to obtain the painting she needed from the Delafield family since it was already announced they were donating it to WAL for the charity auction. It was equally doubtful someone would bid thousands of dollars on the piece only to turn it over to her, and the painting was expected to fetch a high price.

Come Monday, James would return to his routine of heading off to his office and days full of business meetings, while Becca would step into the role of managing their household affairs. First on her agenda was to meet with Mrs. Granger, their cook, to discuss the menus. It was important she fully embrace the role of mistress of the manor if she was going to make this work. Regardless of whatever stupid, ridiculous, petty mistakes Rebecca may have made in the past, she needed to move forward with a fresh start. Becca couldn't change what had happened in the past, but she could certainly do her best to ensure a successful future.

After Katie assisted her in preparing for bed, Becca wrapped herself in a warm flannel nightgown and climbed into bed with her journal in hand. Delicate shadows from the lamplight danced across the polished wood floors. It seemed only fitting that her room should face west, while James' private rooms faced east. He preferred to rise with the sun and be off on his way. He was an important man with important business to conduct.

CHAPTER 3

By the time Becca went down to breakfast the following morning, James had already left for his office downtown. After their ride home together, she wasn't surprised he was avoiding her. It seemed James was determined to maintain his distance, as before. Becca, however, was equally determined to change all that. The sins of the past could not be allowed to continue.

After a light breakfast of tea, toast and eggs, Becca let Mrs. Granger know she wished to meet with her in the library at the top of the hour to discuss the menus for the week. While waiting for the cook to join her, Becca surveyed the library shelves filled with books James had collected. His interests varied from history and ancient literature to law and modern classics. Business journals were stacked on one of the tables in the room.

A smaller section was devoted to books on such diverse subjects as etiquette, transformational spirituality, and domestic economics along with novels by such popular authors as Jane Austin, Charles Dickens and Mark Twain. This little corner, with its Louis XVI desk, was undoubtedly the space used by Eleanor Jaffray, her mother-in-law. Becca picked up the book *Little Women* by Louisa May Alcott, took a seat at the desk, and began to read while she waited.

At ten o'clock sharp, Mrs. Granger walked into the library carrying a notebook and a recipe box. Tall, stout, and heavyset, the woman looked as if she greatly enjoyed her cooking. Becca guessed her to be in her fifties if not older. The hair peaking from beneath her lace cap was dull, dishwater grey and her dark brown eyes were nearly black.

Becca set aside her book and asked Mrs. Granger to take a seat across from her. "First off, Mrs. Granger, I want you to know I have no intention of interfering with the way you run your kitchen. Everything I've seen tells me you're a highly qualified cook," Becca began, hoping to make a good first impression.

Mrs. Granger gave a nod of understanding.

"Now then, obviously breakfast is fine as it is. The eggs, toast and breakfast meats certainly suffice, however I wonder if you plan to serve ham anytime soon." She had only been in the house for a couple of days. It was possible Mrs. Granger had served ham every day for a week and she wouldn't know.

Mrs. Granger eyed her suspiciously. "Mr. Jaffray has never asked for ham to be served in the morning."

Fair enough, Becca understood the reason for the cook's reaction. "We won't know if he likes it until we try. I've had it at my father's house and would like to have it served here occasionally, if it can be made available." She gave the cook a terse smile and waited for her to respond.

"I have a ready source, if that's what you mean. I trust our regular butcher can supply us with a bit of ham from time to time if I ask."

"Good. How about we try it one day this week and see how Mr. Jaffray reacts. If he indicates it is not to his liking for any reason, we can leave it off the menu as before. Is that agreeable with you, Mrs. Granger?"

The woman seemed to sit a little straighter in her chair. "Your suggestion has merit. We can give it a try."

"Very well. When do you think we can expect it?"

"I place my orders with the butcher on Tuesdays and Fridays, when he comes to deliver. If I order a ham tomorrow, it can be here on Friday, unless you be needing a rush."

"No, no rush is necessary. I think Saturday will be a good day to add it to our meal."

Mrs. Granger wrote this down in her notebook. It seemed they were making progress. Becca felt confident enough to continue.

"I also wanted to ask about orange juice. When can that be served?"

"Orange juice?" Mrs. Granger asked skeptically.

"Yes, orange juice at breakfast. We don't need much, only a glass or two will do."

"It's winter, Ma'am. We can't get fresh oranges in winter."

"Umm, yes, right, I suppose I was getting ahead of myself." She should have known; fruits and vegetables wouldn't be available unless they were in season. It was plain the cook wasn't interested in being supportive without a good reason.

"Mrs. Granger, I must confess, I am going to need your help. I've never been the mistress of a manor before. My mother died when I was quite young, so she never taught me. My father had a head housekeeper who took care of all the domestic details of running our home. I never had to concern myself, but I would like to try. I'd like someday for us to entertain here and know I've done things right. Can you help me with this?

Mrs. Granger's look remained stern, but Becca believed she saw some softening around her eyes. "Perhaps you should ask Mrs. Hewes to join us."

Becca had learned that Mrs. Hewes was the name of their housekeeper. "If you think so, then by all means."

Mrs. Granger nodded and went to the bell rope near the door. A moment later she instructed Wallis to ask Mrs. Hewes to join them. When the cook returned to her seat, Becca wondered what she should do to fill the time as they waited for Mrs. Hewes. She felt highly uncomfortable trying to fill a role for which she had very little training. A more experienced woman would know exactly how to handle this situation.

"I see you've brought your recipe box. Should we look over some options for this week?" Becca asked.

"We can. Or I can just show you what I've already planned for the week."

Mrs. Granger seemed to take some bit of enjoyment at making Becca look foolish. A jolt of "stupid" punched her in the gut. Of course, their cook hadn't waited for Becca to confer her blessing before she planned for the week. Foodstuffs had to be ordered ahead of time.

"Yes, please," Becca said through a strained smile. "I'm sure you've already given this some thought."

Mrs. Granger shook her head and sighed. "Same as I do every week, along with Mrs. Hewes and Mrs. Jaffray, when she's here."

If Becca didn't assert her authority now, she might as well call it quits and slink back to her bedroom to suffer through endless hours of boredom. She squared her shoulders and said, "I'm sure you're used to working with my mother-in-law, but she has gone to Savannah to be with her youngest son. I am now the mistress of the house."

Mrs. Granger's brows rose sharply on her forehead, but she kept her thoughts to herself, as well she should.

"Now then, I'd like to see what you have planned for this week." Becca didn't expect to make any changes, unless it was necessary. There were certain foods she could not eat and she needed to know if any them were scheduled to be served.

Mrs. Granger pulled a sheet of paper from her notebook and handed it to Becca. It listed the meals scheduled for the week. A second sheet included ingredients on hand and those that needed to be ordered. She scanned through each item and to her relief found nothing she needed to change. She was still looking over the menu when Mrs. Hewes arrived.

Mrs. Granger turned to her co-worker and said, "It seems *Mrs. Jaffray* is in need of our services." The cook's tone put Becca ill at ease, as if she were being mocked, and she didn't like it.

Rebecca's attitude in the past probably justified this reaction, but still, no servant should treat her employer with such disrespect, especially not after Becca had confided in her.

Mrs. Hewes was a matronly woman of average height. Her dull brown hair was streaked with grey, and her pale blue eyes seemed sad and tired. She took a seat next to Mrs. Granger as directed, her weary eyes darting questioningly between Becca and Mrs. Granger, taking in the situation.

"What can I do for you, Ma'am?" Mrs. Hewes directed her question to Becca.

"Understandably, while Mrs. Jaffray, my mother-in-law, was in residence, I respected her position as mistress of this house. Now that she's gone to Savannah to visit her son, I intend to assume my rightful duties as my husband's wife." Becca was done playing nice, especially with Mrs. Granger who had shown her very little respect.

Mrs. Hewes nodded with a look of affirmation, but Mrs. Granger continued to scowl.

"To begin, I expect to see the menu plan for each week, which I will approve or adjust as needed." This would give Becca control over what was served and avoid the possibility of ingesting foods she was allergic to. "Mrs. Granger and Mrs. Hewes, I expect you to continue to work together to create these menus as I will rely on your knowledge of the fresh produce and meats available at market. Please take note, Mrs. Granger, I do not care for eggplant and I cannot eat tomatoes."

She paused, expecting the cook to make a note in her book, but she didn't.

"Aren't you going to write that down?" Becca asked.

Mrs. Granger gave her a condescending smile. "I think I can remember that."

"I would feel better if you wrote it down."

Mrs. Granger narrowed her eyes, looking quite miffed, but jotted down a note in her book.

It was obvious Rebecca and the cook had not gotten off to a good start, and she was not going to placate the woman in hopes of making it better. Mrs. Granger would have to work with her or risk being replaced. "I also want to see the accounts for the kitchen expenses."

At this Mrs. Hewes and Mrs. Granger exchanged a nervous glance. Something was amiss.

"Is there a problem with that?" Becca asked.

"Umm, no Ma'am, it's just that Mrs. Jaffray never paid it no mind," Mrs. Hewes said.

Becca wasn't surprised. The older woman had lived a life of unrestricted financial freedom, but Becca knew very well that James was stretched thin until he secured new contracts for his railcars. "Things are different now and I prefer to receive a full accounting of all expenses. The one thing I did learn in my father's house was how to balance a ledger. To give me some background on the household's spending, I want you to bring me the ledger for this year. When I have time, I will look it over."

Mrs. Granger seemed a little dumbstruck while Mrs. Hewes simply looked nervous. Becca wondered if Mrs. Hewes was a willing co-conspirator in Mrs. Granger's fight against her or if something else was going on.

"You want to see the accounting records for the full year?" Mrs. Hewes asked, looking concerned.

"Yes," Becca confirmed.

"You weren't even here for half of it," Mrs. Granger mumbled brusquely.

"I fail to see how that affects my request." Becca replied.

"I merely wonder if you're taking on more work than necessary," Mrs. Hewes offered.

"Thank you for your concern, but allow me to worry about that. I expect to have the ledger on my desk by the end of the day."

"Which desk is that?" Mrs. Granger asked, sounding impertinent.

Becca knew her writing desk in the bedroom apartment would not suffice for the task she had in mind, which meant she needed to commandeer her mother-in-law's desk here in the library to use as her own. "While Mrs. Jaffray is away, I'll use this space as my office. I'm sure she won't mind." Hopefully, neither James nor Mrs. Jaffray would disapprove. Becca waited for the two women to respond in some manner, but they both merely sat across from her in blank, unblinking silence.

"Well then, if there is nothing more to discuss, you are dismissed to return to your duties. Thank you for your time."

"You're welcome," Mrs. Hewes said.

The two women rose in unison and headed for the door. Mrs. Granger left without saying another word.

Becca sat back in her chair and let out a sigh. She had her work cut out for her.

~*~

Though Becca was anxious to improve her standing with her upper crust neighbors, she had no social calls to make today, no invitations to tea or lunch. Instead, for a bit of solace, she took some time to inspect her wardrobe. If a woman wanted to make a good impression on society she needed to dress the part, and Becca always had a fondness for fine and pretty things. Much as she preferred, Rebecca's closets and dressing room were neatly organized by style and purpose, ball gowns in their own special section, evening wear in another, and closest to her boudoir were all her day dresses for various functions such as tea, shopping, museum visits and social calls.

It was comforting to see the array of morning dresses, afternoon dresses, tea gowns, and large picture hats embellished with flowers and plumes of ostrich feathers neatly displayed and awaiting her use. Sadly,

49

she noted, the fine silk lingerie with matching robes from Paris were still tied together with colored ribbons as when they first arrived and were unpacked from their shipping trunks.

The most important closet through which she wandered was used to store her ball gowns. Lined with cedar and perfumed with aromatic sachets, the room held dozens of exquisite gowns carefully arranged on polished shelves and shrouded in a protective muslin bag. Every gown was stuffed with tissue to retain its shape, clipped with a number, and listed in a ledger accompanied with sketches of the gown, notes on when it was purchased, and the date and occasion when it had been worn. These outfits, with their layers of extravagant silks, satins, brocades, taffetas, tulle, velvets, and lace were all designed not only to reinforce a woman's wealth but also to dazzle. Many of the gowns, especially the most recent additions, had not yet been worn, giving Becca the thrill of anticipation for wearing something new when she attended the WAL charity ball.

Morning gave way to afternoon, and after taking a break for tea, Becca was too distracted to think about the daunting task of reviewing accounting and expenses. Nonetheless, she stopped by the library and was pleased to see that the ledger had been left on her desk. There was some satisfaction in knowing Mrs. Granger had done as she requested. Without bothering to give it more than a passing glance, she stashed it away in a drawer before returning to her bedroom to change for dinner. The ledger could easily be put off for another day.

For dinner she chose a pale pink silk evening gown that flattered her figure. She hoped James would appreciate her effort. She also hoped he would come home to join her for dinner. She knew he tended to stay downtown and take dinner at his club, but she hoped that would not be the case tonight.

Shortly after six thirty, when Katie informed her that Mr. Jaffray had indeed returned home, Becca felt both relieved and excited.

Promptly at seven o'clock, she descended the stairs and proceeded to the front parlor, but James wasn't there. Disappointed, she took a seat on the settee nearest the hearth and waited. A few minutes later, he entered the room and after a dutiful greeting, sat on one of the wingback chairs across from her. Becca felt an urge to stand and twirl for him, she felt so pretty in her silk evening dress with her hair stylishly arranged, but she resisted.

~~~

James had thought long and hard about coming home after work, and in the end, he decided if he really wanted to give Rebecca a fair chance, he needed to go home. His behavior during their return from the horse show the night before had been less than kind. His only excuse, and it wasn't a good one, was that he was unaccustomed to being around this new, nicer version of Rebecca. He still had doubts regarding her motives.

From what he had pieced together, Rebecca had left his house on Saturday and had taken some clothes with her to her father's house. O'Conner confirmed she had left there around two o'clock in the afternoon. Instead of coming home to his house as Wheland requested, O'Conner told him that Rebecca had insisted on being taken to the train station so she could visit her father's summer cottage on Long Island. Apparently, Stanton and his daughter had fought and Rebecca had been noticeably upset when she left.

James had been away that weekend on business, so it wasn't until late Monday evening that he realized his wife was missing. Interestingly, except for her personal maid, none of his servants seemed overly concerned that Rebecca hadn't been home.

Convinced that Rebecca had run off to be with a lover, James had refused to go chasing after her. Let her dig her own grave. When she came home a week later, she swore she had not had an affair. That alone was hard enough to believe, but then she had insisted she wanted to start anew, which was almost as suspicious as the idea that she had been alone while she was gone.

The only reason to believe she might have been telling the truth about needing time alone to think was the noticeable change in her attitude. Before her absence, they had barely exchanged pleasantries. Now, not only was she kind and pleasant, he actually found her attractive, something that had not happened before. While this new aspect of his wife thrilled him, there was a part of him that still didn't trust her and wondered if he ever could.

"James, my dear, I'm so happy you could make it home for dinner," Rebecca greeted him. "I know you're busy with Mr. Morgan this week working on that railroad business. It must be so tedious. Would you like a drink before we're called to sit for dinner?"

51

"Brandy—no, make it a sherry," he told her. She got right up and began pouring his drink, not bothering to call for a servant.

"How was your day?" she asked as she handed him his drink. "Did you and Mr. Morgan make good progress?" Not only was she pretty and attentive, she was also interested in his work. When did that start?

"This business of restructuring the railroads is quite a chore. It's going to take some time, but I'm sure you don't want to hear about that."

"Only if you want to talk about it. Perhaps you'd rather leave the office behind. Did you happen to have a chance to mention the Women's Assistance League holiday ball?" she asked, reminding him of her sudden interest in social events.

"I must confess, the subject completely slipped my mind. Never even thought about it." He wondered if that would incur her wrath. Even if he had thought about it he would never discuss such a thing with J.P. Morgan.

"I understand. You have much more important things to deal with." She sat slightly forward with her hands clasped demurely on her lap.

"How about you? Did anything interesting happen here at home?" The question was rather pedantic but he wasn't used to engaging in small talk with his wife.

"Nothing out of the ordinary. I met with Mrs. Hewes and Mrs. Granger to discuss our weekly menus and household expenses. I understand your mother handled all that when she was here, but since she's away visiting your brother, I thought now would be a good time for me to take over those duties."

"That seems reasonable," he agreed. He hadn't really given it much thought, but it occurred to him that while his mother was at home, she had managed all the household tasks. As his wife, it was only fitting Rebecca should want to take on that role.

"I've asked to look over the household accounting. I'm sure everything is in order, but it's something I did for my father."

James gave a thoughtful nod. "That's probably a good idea." Especially now that funds were tighter than they used to be. "I don't believe Mother ever took much of an interest. It'll be reassuring to have someone take a closer look."

Rebecca smiled brightly, apparently pleased by his approval. "I completely agree. I hope to have time later this week to look over the ledger. I'm using your mother's desk in the library. I hope that's all right."

James nodded absentmindedly and rose from his chair. A few measured steps took him to the window, where he swirled the drink in his hand and looked across the well-kept grounds below. He had the strangest urge to join Rebecca on the settee, to sit at her side—something he had not done before. Not even when they were courting, if what they did before they were married could be called such.

The past be damned. If he had any hopes of making his marriage work, he needed to give Rebecca the fresh start she had requested and toss aside his disrespectful behavior toward her. James set his glass on a side table and strode back to the settee. As he took a seat at her side—close enough to enjoy the subtle scent of her perfume—Rebecca's expression registered a moment of shock and then quickly transformed into one of delight. Pleasing her pleased him.

Her expression softened as she reached out and grasped his hand. Small as it was, her gesture reminded him what little effort he had made to show Rebecca any true affection, much less appreciation. In many ways, he had resented her as much as he resented her father, if not more so. To him, she had become a living embodiment and daily reminder of his desperate financial straits. He'd felt shackled by her mere presence, especially since he hoped his financial stress would be short term while he knew his marriage was not.

Her gracious reaction confirmed he needed to show her more consideration. He had consistently withheld all affection and appreciation, and yet she still reached out to him. He needed to change how he treated her, and by God, he would. He wondered how one went about wooing one's own wife. Should he look upon her as he would any desirable unmarried woman? Or should he act under the assumption that she was already his for the taking?

As he took a deeper look at Rebecca, he realized she was truly an alluring woman. She was fair of face, well-bred with graceful manners, and as he was beginning to learn, capable of sincere affection.

Was it possible to find true love and affection in his marriage?

His thoughts stumbled to an abrupt halt.

He was getting ahead of himself if he thought it was likely he would suddenly fall in love with Rebecca Wheland. Mutual appreciation with some affection was already more than he had ever allowed himself to consider. He need not jump to lofty ideals of love. Nevertheless, James flipped his hand over to return her squeeze and let the clasp linger.

"You're looking lovely tonight," James said with complete honesty.

Her eyes glowed. "Thank you, James," she said with a coy smile. Lowering her voice, she added, "You're looking quite handsome, yourself."

Of course, he had only dressed for dinner as usual, but more importantly, he realized she was flirting with him. His wife was actually flirting with him, plying him with ego-stroking compliments. The realization sent a small measure of joy melting through his body. Looking at her with fresh eyes, he suddenly thought about kissing her temple, just at the place where her lovely chestnut brown hair swept up from her forehead. He leaned forward, felt her breath brushing the skin of his neck, and was just about to touch his lips to her skin when Jenkins came to the door to announce that dinner was ready to be served. Damnable bad timing on the butler's part.

In sharp contrast to the moment of intimacy they shared in the parlor, dinner was quiet and subdued. Any further ideas of flirting with his wife were diminished under the watchful eyes of his servants. He was not comfortable putting his affections on display, especially not in front of them.

"I read in the Times that the Sunday afternoon musical reception hosted by Mr. and Mrs. Martin was poorly attended," Rebecca said, relaying a bit of gossip from the society section of the newspaper, the only part women tended to read. "The paper suggested it was due to the poor selection of talent, but it also mentioned Mrs. Martin's less than favorable relations with Alva Vanderbilt. Do you suppose that's true?"

"I expect so. Society's matrons tend to move in packs and follow the herd," he said as he sliced off a bite of roast beef.

"But I understand Mrs. Vanderbilt isn't even in town. She's gone to London with her daughter," Rebecca said, reaching for her wine glass.

"Alva would never let a little thing like the Atlantic Ocean keep her from being informed on the activities of her friends, especially the ones who feel it's necessary to stay in her good graces." James took a drink of wine and waved off Jenkins from pouring more into the half empty glass. He'd had enough for the night and they were nearly finished with their meal.

"I suppose you're right. With the holiday season upon us, I expect we shall receive any number of invitations to parties. At least, I hope so."

"Yes, I expect so." In previous years, as a bachelor, he had left it up to his mother and sister to inform him when his presence was required as their escort at one event or another. Most likely, that task should now be placed upon Rebecca.

"I look forward to attending our next party on your arm," she said with a sly grin. "We may be married, but I expect there are more than a few women who will miss the benefit of your charm and good looks on the dance floor."

"Am I no longer allowed to dance?" James asked with a lift of his brow.

"Only with your wife and perhaps other women who are older and married," she teased.

"Would you be jealous if I danced with an unmarried woman?" he asked.

"No, not jealous. Jealousy indicates a lack of trust and security. I prefer not to harbor such emotions. I believe I can trust you, James. I can only hope you think the same of me."

Not yet, he thought, *but maybe someday.*

Rebecca seemed to sense his hesitation. "I'm not a fool, James. I know I'm not your first choice for a wife, but that doesn't mean we can't make the best of this."

Begrudgingly, he silently acknowledged she was right on both counts.

"You're a handsome man. I'm proud to have you as my husband. If I haven't shown sufficient appreciation in the past, I wish to make amends. It's not my desire to make you unhappy, not anymore."

Her honesty surprised him. In return, he would do the same. "Pardon me if I find it hard to believe a tiger would change her stripes overnight."

"Even a caged tiger eventually learns not to bite the hand that feeds her. With proper petting, you may even make her purr, if you can get close enough. What cat doesn't like to be petted until she purrs?"

Suddenly, the idea of making Rebecca purr held great appeal. Was she truly ready to resume bedroom relations, this time with feelings of passion? The idea of starting over and being able to create a truly loving marriage was sounding better by the minute. Sparks of warmth and hope welled up in his chest. "What do you have in mind?" he asked before finishing the rest of his wine.

~~~

Speaking of tigers, James had the look of one ready to pounce on its prey and Becca realized she may have just pinned herself into a corner. She wasn't ready to start sleeping with James and didn't know when, or if, she ever would. She was still carrying the wounds and scars from her last attempt at romance. Neither her heart nor her body was ready to make such a leap. It was one thing to strive for a respectful relationship, but becoming lovers was more than she was ready for—at least not now, not yet, and maybe not ever. If she threw water on the fire she saw burning in his eyes, she risked losing all she had accomplished, but she wasn't about to sell her body to make this work.

"I believe we're making great progress. We're doing something we've not really done before, which is talking, and being nice to each other."

From the look of disappointment on his face, she could see the fire was dying. She needed to do something to keep the embers burning while keeping the flame under control.

"Surely you would agree a lack of mutual respect has contributed to our marital discord," she added.

"As well as other issues we share," he scoffed.

She didn't want to delve too deeply into what the other issues might be, although she had a fairly good idea what he meant. She tried to focus on something positive. "I know we're husband and wife, but I don't believe we've made much of an effort to be friends. I would like to start by being your friend. And hopefully you want to be mine."

"Friends?" The look on his face was incredulous. "You want us to be *friends*?"

"Well, yes. I think it's a good place to start." Darn, she had used the F word. She knew better than to tell a man she only wanted to be his friend—men rarely received that well—but she didn't know what else to say. Surely, he didn't think . . .

"Being friends is all well and good, but don't you think husbands and wives should be lovers?"

Apparently, he did. It was time to back pedal. "In the best of circumstances, I would agree, but obviously we haven't started with the best of circumstances."

"No, we haven't." Was that a flash of hurt she saw in his eyes?

"I still think it would be best if we forgo bedroom visits until we have progressed further along in this process of restarting our marriage."

His face grew dark and shadowed. "Ours is a marriage of convenience, nothing more. Certainly not *friendship*. I desperately needed a loan and your father conveniently found a way to marry off his daughter."

"Please, James. Let's not do this. Does it really matter how we got here? It's not as if we can change all that."

"You're right. We can't change the past, but I damn sure intend to learn from my mistakes. One of which was thinking you'd change. Keep your door locked, Rebecca. You can be sure I have no intentions of breaching your defenses."

He tossed his napkin on the table then stalked out of the room.

Feeling totally deflated, Becca watched him walk away. She hung her head in her hands and sighed. Everything had been going so well. If only their sexual relations—or lack thereof—hadn't raised its ugly head. It was her fault for flirting with him as she had done, but that was hard to avoid, especially with a man as virile and masculine as James. She should have known, for a man such as him, everything revolved around sex, money, or power.

Becca thought she had been alone in the large dining room, but when she looked up, she saw Jenkins standing near the servant's entrance, his eyes focused off into space. She wondered how much he had seen or overheard. Not that it mattered, since the servants probably knew all of their dark and dirty secrets.

Suddenly too tired to care, Becca retired to her room, with the door unlocked, and summoned Katie to assist her as she changed into her night clothes. Her maid obviously sensed her dejected mood, but respectfully said nothing, for which Becca was grateful. Thankfully, if nothing else, this partnership was progressing smoothly. She appreciated her maid's loyalty.

57

Sitting alone in her big, lonely bed, Becca picked up the book she'd been reading and tried to settle in for the night. She stared at the open page of *Little Women*, but the words remained a blur. Her mind was elsewhere.

For a while, it had seemed she was making significant progress in repairing her relationship with James, but the thought of engaging in sexual activities—even ones with the potential to be quite satisfying—at this stage of the game was more than she could handle. Yes, she found him attractive, handsome, and interesting—she wasn't blind—but she wasn't about to create false feelings she didn't have to satisfy his sexual needs. There was no reason to believe James loved her, and though she found him attractive and cared for him in a friendly sort of way, she didn't love him either. Couples who really loved and cared for each other would show each other mutual respect. Surely, that wasn't too much to ask.

It wasn't so much that she didn't want him in her bed—if she thought about it long and hard enough the idea held some appeal—but she also wasn't ready to let down her defenses and open herself up to such a relationship. She had been down that road before and still vividly recalled the lingering pain.

It felt as though she had taken one step forward and two steps back, placing her further behind than before this whole thing started. But she was used to that, it was the story of her life.

With a sigh, Becca set aside her book and rolled over, then fluffed the pillow under her head, hoping to find some rest. Though she felt lonely, she was grateful for this warm, soft bed in this big, safe house. Out there, in the world outside, people were cold, hurt, hungry and dying. New York held more than its fair share of the desperately poor. Bad things happened, she knew, because some of them had once happened to her, but here in this time and place, she was safe. How lucky she was for these blessings.

If she were unmarried, she might be considered a spinster, but she didn't see herself that way. Why should she? At twenty-five she could easily pass for younger, perhaps twenty or twenty-two. Being small boned helped. People saw small and thought it meant young, even fragile. She understood young and fragile, she had once been both of those things, but not any longer. After all she had been through, she had learned how to develop a hard-outer shell to protect what was left of her tender heart.

58

Being young didn't mean being naïve. Naïve had come and gone some time ago. A woman didn't suffer through an abusive relationship and remain naïve.

~*~

James retired to his room and slammed the door. Damn that had hurt. Rebecca had played him for a fool with her talk of petting and purring, stringing him along with no intentions of making good on her flirtations. Was her improved disposition another façade? Why would she run hot one moment, only to turn cold the next? His only relief was that no one had been there to see her tease and reject him, no one other than Jenkins. Thankfully, he trusted his butler to keep such unseemly happenings to himself. The rest of the staff might gossip—he was sure they did—but he trusted Jenkins with his deepest, darkest secrets. Never had the man let him down.

Sadly, for a few fleeting moments, he had actually allowed himself to think Rebecca truly cared, that she held some affection for him. What a mistake. She didn't want to be his wife, not in the true sense of the word. Rebecca only wanted to be his *friend*. A friend who lived in his house, and yet stayed in her own room. Granted, it was probably her way of trying to make peace in their relationship, but no man wanted to be stuck in a loveless marriage, or saddled forever after with a woman who only wanted to be his *friend*. A marriage bed was not a place for *friendship*. A marriage bed should be a place for *passion*.

Sure, he'd made plenty of mistakes, but he wasn't an old dog. He could, and would, learn new tricks. Rebecca's request to forgo bedroom visits until they were better acquainted was quite a bold declaration, but James suddenly saw the challenge it presented. Perhaps it was time to seduce his wife. What could be better than driving Rebecca to beg for his attentions? Perhaps he would even go so far as to refuse her, at least once, to let her know how it felt. The satisfaction in giving her such a taste of her medicine may very well be worth the effort.

Of course, he risked creating a bigger rift in their marriage than already existed—or potentially falling in love with a woman who only wanted to play games—but what did he have to lose? He was already barred from her bed, and up until lately, they'd rarely even exchanged kind words. How much worse could it get? He'd simply guard his heart, not let

59

himself be swayed by her tenderness or flirtations. Perhaps it was time for him to be the one in charge of their little game.

CHAPTER 4

James snugged his coat tighter as the early morning train rolled out of the station and headed toward Long Island. There was a noticeable chill in the air, and the gloom of cloudy winter skies complemented his dark mood. After his clash with Rebecca the night before, he decided to take the day to check out her story. His gut instincts told him something was wrong and until he could find out what it was, he could give it no rest. Since Pierpont was busy meeting with the boards of two of the largest railroad companies, and his presence wasn't needed, James decided he needed to take a trip out to Wheland's cottage and have a look around, though he had no idea what he might find.

Last May, when the stock market panicked and the railroad stocks fell, James hadn't been looking to get married, and if he were, the last woman he would have considered was Stanton Wheland's daughter. But he soon discovered a man didn't always get to pick and choose his fate the way he might have planned it. Much the way Jules Vanderzeit had stepped in when James and his brother had fallen through the ice, Wheland had been there as a safety net to prevent James from losing his business. Neither had been a good choice, but each had served their purpose, and for that, in many ways he was better off.

He could understand why Wheland had wanted Rebecca out of his house. His daughter was edging toward twenty-two and the specter of spinsterhood was gaining ground. Both Vanderzeit and Wheland had stepped forward in his hour of need with deals to offer. Of the two, he had believed Wheland's to be the lesser of the two evils. Yes, it meant he was married to a woman he hardly knew, but Vanzerzeit's offer had him jumping through time for another six years, and he had already had his fill of that crap.

He had recently turned thirty, well into the time when a man should settle down with a wife, but he had been too busy working for the Maestro, building his railcar business, and making investments in the stock market. His sister, Charlene, was already married, so when Wheland offered his daughter in exchange for the loan, James had figured there was room in his house for another woman. He had imagined Rebecca would busy herself with her social pursuits, much as Charlene had done, and stay out of his way. And for a while, she had.

For months, they had lived separate lives under the same roof. Then, without a word of notice, she had disappeared for a week and when she returned, she claimed she had gone away to think about their sham of a marriage. She claimed she had gone to her father's summer cottage, alone, in the brink of winter. Only a fool would accept an excuse such as that, and he had no intention of being made a fool. He hadn't believed her and now he was on his way to Long Island to check out her story for himself.

A few hours later, the train pulled into the station at Hampton Bay. James made his way over to the ticket agent and waited until the man was free. He had brought along a picture of Rebecca taken at the time of their wedding. Even then, her dour expression had shown her discontent at being married to him.

When the couple in front of him was done with their business, he stepped up to the window and handed the clerk the photograph. "Do you happen to remember if this woman passed through here a week or so ago?"

The station agent took a good hard look at the photograph before he spoke. "Is there a reason why you're asking? I don't like to get involved in no trouble."

"There's no trouble. She's my wife and I'm trying to track down where she was last week."

The clerk took a moment to study his face and must have judged James to be honestly concerned. It seemed he was willing to help. "From what I can remember, if I'm thinking of the right woman, she arrived here late Saturday evening week before last and left last Saturday. I recall when she arrived because she asked about hiring a cab to take her out to her family home. Said something about arriving earlier than was expected and no one was here to meet her. I flagged down Johnny Tate to take her there. Then she came back the following Saturday and bought a ticket back to Manhattan. A right pretty little thing, real kind and all. I was happy to lend a hand."

Rebecca was kind? "Was she alone each time?"

"Why, yes. That's why she needed to hire a hack, although I don't think Johnny brought her back. Must have been someone else."

That was an interesting bit of information, and very helpful. If the hired cab didn't bring her back, he wondered who did. It might have been a caretaker at the cottage, or it could have been someone else. "Do you know where I can find Mr. Tate?"

"He'll be round front if he didn't get a passenger from this train. Otherwise, he'll be back around to meet the next one. He's about the only driver out there, it's slow this time of year, but he makes do by sticking with it."

"Thank you, you've been very helpful."

James went out to the front of the station platform, but the street was empty. The driver must have picked up a passenger. He went back inside where it was warm, pacing back and forth in front of the station's windows as he waited. This was burning up time, but since there wasn't another cab around he had no other choice. Thirty minutes later, the hansom came into sight.

James stepped out to hail him as he drew near. "Are you Johnny Tate?"

"Yes, sir, that's me. Do ye need to hire a cab?"

"First I need to ask if you remember giving this woman a ride Saturday before last." James showed him the picture of Rebecca.

"Sure I do," the drive said, adjusting his scarf around his neck and blowing on his gloved hands as he rubbed them together. "I was a might concerned about her, being alone and all like she was. I took her out to Raven's Point, out on the bluffs overlooking the bay. It's one of the bigger places out here but it don't get many visitors."

Raven's Point was the name of Wheland's summer cottage. James knew he had the right driver. "Did you also bring her back here last Saturday?"

"No, sir, I didn't. She must have gotten her brother to bring her. She had said he was coming out here to join her but I never picked up another passenger to go out that way."

James got an uneasy feeling in his gut. Rebecca had lied to both the ticket agent and driver about meeting Randolph. Her brother was away in London. Someone else must have been with her at the cottage. It seemed Rebecca hadn't been alone as she claimed. He needed to go to Wheland's estate to find out who else had been there. "I need you to take me to Raven's Point."

"Yes, sir, hop in."

No one was at the main house when they arrived so Mr. Tate directed him around to the caretaker's cottage on the servant's road. The driver informed him the caretaker hadn't been around when Rebecca arrived, so he had obliged her by lighting a fire in her room. "She had asked me to send up the caretaker on my way out, but he wasn't there and I needed to get on my way. There was one more train coming through that night and I wanted to catch it, but there weren't no passengers for me to pick up."

"You left Rebecca Wheland here alone without any servants to tend to her?" James asked, both angry and amazed.

"Well, now, she never did introduce herself to me, but like I said, she told me her brother was on his way so I didn't figure she was in need of my assistance. It seemed a might strange for her to be visiting a summer home in winter, but you rich folks seem to do as ye please, and as long as it's a paying fare, I don't ask many questions."

"I need to take a look around. Are you able to stay awhile to give me a ride back to the train station?" James asked.

"Yes, sir, but I'll need to charge you for both ways, you understand."

"Certainly, that's not a problem."

James had just stepped down from the cab when an elderly man came out from the caretaker's cottage. "Is there something I can help you with?" he asked.

"Yes, please. I'm James Jaffray, the owner's son-in-law. I understand my wife, Rebecca Wheland Jaffray, was here last week."

The old man nodded. "Yep, she was. My wife and I took care of her while she was here."

"I'd like to talk to you about her stay. Do you mind if I come in?" It was cold outside and James figured this could take a while.

"Certainly, sir." Turning to the driver, the caretaker said, "You might want to take the horse to the carriage house out back and get yourself out of the cold." He pointed down the road behind him as he spoke.

"Mighty fine of you to suggest." Mr. Tate tipped his hat and drove off toward the carriage house.

James followed the caretaker through the door and removed his hat and coat once inside the warm and cozy cottage. Scents of baked bread and pipe tobacco lingered in the air. The front sitting room, like the rest of the house, appeared clean, tidy and well lived in. Much of the furniture was thickly padded and upholstered in brightly patterned fabrics, and the wool rugs covering the floor were well worn. Knitted throws were draped on the backs of the chairs. It seemed the caretaker's wife had a lot of time on her hands.

"Name's Krammer, this is my wife Mary. What can we do for you?" the caretaker said as they took their seats.

"What can you tell me about my wife's stay at Raven's Point? Was she alone, or did someone come here to join her?"

"Other than Mary and me, she was alone the whole time, near as I can tell. She had to spend the first night alone, the poor little lady, but she seemed to manage well enough. You see, it was Saturday evening and we had gone to the village to meet some folks from our church. We had no word anyone was coming to the house, so we didn't know she was here until the next morning when she came knocking on our door. She'd spent the whole night bundled up in her room, the only room with a fire. I went straight away to the big house and got the boiler going. It took the whole day to take the chill off the place. I worried a bit about the extra fuel being used, but she assured me Mr. Wheland wouldn't complain."

"Do you have any idea what she did the whole time she was here?" James asked.

Mrs. Krammer spoke up then, squeezing her husband's arm in comfort and support. James felt a pang of jealousy at the easy companionship of this happily married couple. "We did spend more time up at the big house, fixing her meals and such, but we didn't see much of her. She kinda kept to herself, real quiet like. She read a lot, and took lots of walks down to the beach. Sometimes I saw her standing on the cliffs, looking out at the ocean. She seemed kinda melancholy if you ask me."

James could easily believe Rebecca had been unhappy, staying here alone in the big house with winter closing in, but he had a harder time accepting she had been alone the whole time. "Did you ever see her with anyone else?"

Mr. Krammer shook his head. "No, sir, never. Not a once. What I noticed most was how quiet she was, like my Misses says. I told myself to pay it no mind, but she hardly said a word other than please and thank you when we brought her the meals. She weren't no trouble at all, only wanted to be sure we kept her room well heated. Said she hated the cold. Can't say I blame her, but we've gotten used to it, staying here year-round like we do."

"And yet, you say she went for a walk every day?"

"Yes, sir, right about noon, when the sun was out and it was the warmest. I'd often see her take the path to the shore. She always had a book with her. I guess she went out there to read, but she always left alone and always come back alone. There's no other way to access that stretch of the shoreline other than from this property. If you don't mind me saying, she looked a might sad, and lonely, and maybe afraid, like something had her worried. But at the end of the week, she said her time here was done and she needed to get back home. She thanked us kindly for our service though we hadn't done all that much except keep the fire in her room burning day and night. I took her back to the train station and I expect she went back to New York," Mr. Krammer informed him.

"Is she all right?" Mrs. Krammer asked, wringing her hands together. "We didn't do wrong not to alert her father, did we?"

"Mrs. Jaffray is fine, you needn't worry, you did no wrong," James assured them. "In fact, I'd like to thank you for doing such a good job taking care of my wife. If there are any extra expenses because of her stay, you can send them to me." He drew his card out of his coat pocket and handed it to them. "If you can think of anything else, I would appreciate it if you would let me know."

Mr. Krammer scratched his chin, looking thoughtful. "Nothing comes to mind. The only other unusual piece of news I can think of was that mention of an unidentified woman washed up on the shore a few days ago,

66

but that had nothing to do with your wife. It was speculated the poor unfortunate soul had jumped to her death. The police came by and talked to us, asked us if anyone had gone missing, but I knew Miss Wheland had gone back to Manhattan. I'd taken her to the train station myself."

Not wishing to spend any more time pointlessly gossiping about local events, James made his goodbyes and called for the cabbie to take him back to the train station. Everything Rebecca had told him was confirmed. She had come to her father's summer cottage alone, she had stayed here alone, and she had left alone. Perhaps she really had come here to think, as she had said.

~*~

Becca settled in the library to begin her review of the household ledgers. Not exactly exciting entertainment, but at least it gave her something to do. Once again, James had left the house before she had risen from her bed. Obviously, he was still trying to avoid her. She wasn't surprised. After what had happened the night before, she hadn't expected he would want to see her, and she hadn't exactly risen early to be by his side. There was no reason to start the morning on a dark note.

Earlier, alone at breakfast, she had read the morning society pages looking for any mention of the upcoming Women's Assistance League holiday charity ball. Her methodical scan of the paper revealed nothing new. No one had said this was going to be easy, but she really needed an invitation to that ball. Hopefully, she would have an opportunity to ask Mrs. Morgan about the event when she called on her tomorrow, but until then, she would have to bide her time.

Not really looking forward to her task, she opened the accounts ledger, thinking she would start with the entries for January of that year. Within minutes, Jenkins came to inform her she had a visitor.

"Mrs. Shepard is here to see you," Jenkins said as he entered the room.

Grateful for the interruption, Becca looked up from the ledger. "Mrs. Shepard?"

"Mrs. Charlene Shepard, your sister-in-law," Jenkins said with a slight lift of his brow. "She's waiting in the front parlor."

"Yes, of course, James' sister. I simply hadn't expected her." It seemed awfully early for a caller, even one who was family, but Becca happily closed the ledger and set it back in the desk drawer. "Please arrange to have tea brought in," she added before heading out to the parlor.

"Charlene, what an unexpected pleasure," Becca greeted her guest as she entered the room.

"Rebecca, I'm so glad to see you're receiving. James told me you weren't feeling well." Charlene Jaffray Shepard was near Becca's age with clear blue eyes, petite facial features and an hourglass figure. Her dark brown hair was piled high atop her head in a puffy pompadour style and topped with a wide brimmed hat. Sitting perched near the edge of her chair, she looked rather uncomfortable, as though she might jump up to leave at any minute.

"I hadn't expected you so soon after my recovery." That must have been how James explained her absence: a bout of illness. It worked for her. "How is everything with you?" Becca took a seat on the matching floral print upholstered chair next to her guest. Unlike Charlene, she sat all the way back and let the chair support her. Just looking at Charlene's stiff posture made Becca's backbone ache.

With an earnest look of concern, Charlene reached out her gloved hand to cover Becca's as it rested on the arm of her chair. "I saw Fanny Morgan and she told me you and James were at church on Sunday. How did you ever manage to get him to church?"

"I simply asked." She gave her sister-in-law's hand a slight squeeze before she withdrew her hand and set it on her lap.

"Oh, please, it couldn't have been as easy as that. Mother has been after him for years to save his soul."

"Perhaps he did it as a kindness in honor of my recovery."

"You can't be serious!"

Before Charlene could say more, the footman entered the parlor carrying the tea tray Becca had requested from Mr. Jenkins. With a nod from her, he set the tray on the side table next to Becca.

"Will there be anything else, Madam?"

"I think this will do. Thank you, Wallis," Becca said with a polite smile, making a point of using the servant's name.

Wallis nodded respectfully then exited the room.

Becca looked at Charlene. "Would you care for tea?"

"Yes, thank you. How thoughtful of you. Hot tea on a cold November day is always welcomed."

As she poured them each a cup of tea, Becca asked, "Have you heard from your mother since she left for Savannah?"

"She's only been gone a couple of weeks and already she's written half a dozen letters. Mother believes in keeping up with her correspondence, as I'm sure you know."

Actually, she didn't, but Becca nodded in agreement. If James had received letters from his mother, he hadn't shared them with her. Why would he? They barely spoke as it was, and none of it was the usual, polite, small talk typically exchanged by married couples to keep each other informed.

"The weather is pleasing, and she's happy to be gone from New York, now that winter's setting in," Charlene continued on. "She misses us dreadfully, but loves spending time with Martin. I think she's hoping he'll find a wife soon. She doesn't like to see him alone, especially during the holidays."

"Which is all the more reason for her to be with him at this time of year." For Martin's sake, Becca hoped he would be allowed to pick a wife of his choosing, and not be forced into a marriage of convenience. James probably believed he had been forced to sell his soul to the devil when he agreed to marry Stanton Wheland's daughter, even though he did it so his family would never experience a drop in their social status. Charlene would no doubt be appalled if she knew the whole sordid story, which Becca believed she did not.

"Does Mother know of your recent . . . illness?" Charlene asked, sounding a bit too concerned.

"I'm a bit behind in my correspondence, as I'm sure you can understand. I planned to write to her later today. In fact, I was in at my desk in the library when you called." Maybe she would have eventually gotten around to writing her mother-in-law a letter, if she had thought of it; however, most likely she wouldn't have if Charlene hadn't mentioned it.

"I'm sorry to have disturbed you. Perhaps I shouldn't keep you. Since you were ill for nearly a week, and not receiving, I couldn't wait any longer to see for myself that all is well."

"Think nothing of it, Charlene. I welcome the company. It's a pleasure to see you."

Charlene's repeated mention of her illness made Becca wonder if she knew more than she was saying. Becca believed it was best if she avoided discussing her week-long *illness* until she could speak with James and find out exactly what he had said.

"Good. I had hoped you were up to receiving visitors, since you plan to call on Fanny Morgan." Charlene blew gently on her tea before taking a sip.

"Do you know Mrs. Morgan well?" Becca tasted her tea. It was delightful but not all that hot.

Charlene set down her cup and looked at her queerly. "Well, of course, dear sister. She was the one who sponsored my acceptance into the Women's Assistance League. Don't you remember? I know it happened before you and James were married, but surely you haven't forgotten my celebratory dinner." She paused and raised her gloved fingers to her lips. "Oh, no, that's right, as I recall, you didn't attend."

"I must have been too busy with the preparations for my wedding," Becca said with a false smile. That was most likely a lie. She wondered if she had even been invited to Charlene's celebratory dinner.

"Fanny told me you asked if you could call," Charlene said, referring back to Mrs. Morgan. "I must say, that seems a bit forward of you."

It seemed nothing got past Charlene. Becca couldn't help but wonder what Frances Morgan had said about her. Had she been cast in a negative light? At this point, she had no reason to believe polite society thought highly of Stanton Wheland's daughter. Most likely, Charlene considered Mrs. Morgan her social superior, implying Becca should have waited until Mrs. Morgan called upon her, but she didn't have time for society to come knocking on her door. Becca needed to take matters into her own hands.

"Yes, well, Mr. Morgan and James are . . . are business associates. It seems only fitting I should make the effort to know Mrs. Morgan. Since you're a fairly new member, are you planning to attend the Women's Assistance League holiday ball this year?" Becca asked, moving on to more important matters.

"Why, of course. Steven and I wouldn't miss it for the world. It's the event of the season. And such a worthy charity. This year the money will go to providing additional shelter for the outside poor and orphans."

"I agree, it's a very worthy cause." Becca nearly huffed. She wondered how much of the money raised would actually go to the *outside poor*, the term polite society used to refer to the homeless people living on the streets of New York. While the filthy slum tenements operated by rich landlords weren't much better, at least those people had a roof over their heads even if the lodgings were crowded and completely inadequate. She shuddered to think about it.

Setting aside her feelings on that particular issue, she focused on a more important task. "I expected James and I would have received our invitation by now. The ball is less than a month away. Although I might have overlooked it, having been ill and all." Perhaps she could convince Charlene to obtain the coveted invitation for her.

"But my dear sister, you're not a member of WAL."

Or perhaps not.

"The holiday ball is not exclusive to only members. It is a charity event after all." This much she knew was true. "Both you and Mrs. Jaffray are members. It seems only fitting James and I should attend since his mother won't be able to."

Charlene looked unconvinced. "I suppose I could talk to Fanny for you, but I understand you're going to visit her tomorrow. Perhaps you should mention it then."

"Perhaps I should." Great. This must be Charlene's way of telling her she wouldn't help.

Becca rubbed her temple, suddenly annoyed. Why couldn't anything be easy? Why couldn't the right and perfect solutions just fall into her lap? Why did everything always have to be so darn hard? She shook off her dismay and focused back on Charlene. It wouldn't do to have her sister-in-law see how important this was to her, or how strongly she wanted that sacred invitation. People tended to take advantage of you if you appeared weak or needy. She would simply have to ask Mrs. Morgan, as Charlene suggested. That had been her idea anyway when she asked to pay her a visit. She might as well stick to her original plan and leave Charlene out of it.

"What else do you have planned for today?" Becca asked, only to be polite, not because she cared.

"I have a number of other calls to make, but of course it goes without saying, you were first on my list." Charlene smiled sweetly, and Becca had to give her credit, her expression of concern seemed almost sincere. Perhaps her sister-in-law really did care, although it was hard to believe that any of the Jaffrays cared much for Rebecca Wheland.

71

"I appreciate your concern, dear sister, but now that you've seen for yourself how well I'm doing, I shouldn't want to keep you from your appointed rounds."

Charlene looked dismayed, as if she wasn't used to be dismissed. Schooling her face back into one of sweetness, she said, "I understand. You're probably anxious to get back to your correspondence."

Oh yes, the task of writing to her mother-in-law. Maybe she would mention in the letter how much she would like to attend the WAL charity ball. Maybe Mrs. Jaffray could pull a few strings from down south in Georgia.

"Yes, my letter to your mother. And I have some household accounting I was going to look over."

"You do the household accounting?" Charlene sounded surprised.

"Yes, I plan to review the household ledgers. Don't you?"

"No. Mother never thought it important. I leave that all to Steven."

Becca had no intention of pushing that task onto her husband. James had enough to handle, she didn't need to add to his burden. Besides, she wanted to make herself useful. Sitting around all day with nothing to do other than social calls, or reading a good book, would soon grow dull. She was listless enough as it was. She need not add idleness to her day.

"I learned accounting from my father. It's a small thing I do to help James. He's already so busy at the office."

"Yes, so I've heard. I get the impression he's rarely home."

Where the hell had that come from? Becca hated the way siblings knew so much about each other's lives. "It's been a busy time for him," she fibbed, not wanting to admit James often stayed away to avoid her.

"That reminds me. Next week is Thanksgiving. I know we've always celebrated the holiday here in this house, but now that I'm married and have a home of my own, I was thinking I should host the dinner, especially since Mother has already left for Savannah and won't be here. I swear, the older she gets the more she hates the cold."

Becca wondered if she should fight her sister-in-law for the right to hold the celebration. After all, James was the elder sibling, and they were also newly married, the duty should fall to them. "I would need to speak to James. I'm sure you understand why the dinner should be held here."

"Yes, James is my elder brother, but Steven wants to include his family. If we host the dinner, we can all be together at our house. We've finished remodeling the downstairs rooms and I would love to show off the new décor.

It was tempting to contest Charlene on this, but maybe, if she indicated she was willing to play nice, her sister-in-law would be more willing to help her get an invitation to the WAL charity ball. "I promise, I'll talk to James, and certainly put in a good word for your suggestion. I'm sure you know how important it is for him to spend the holiday with his family."

"Wonderful. I'll tell Steven." Charlene smiled brightly, as if all her worries were solved.

"I imagine he'd also welcome the opportunity to attend the charity ball with you and Steven, if given the chance." Becca paused, waiting for her sister-in-law to respond.

Charlene's smile faded. "Rebecca, you know it's not up to me."

"No, of course I understand. You're still a new member." Becca smiled politely, though she wasn't convinced Charlene was without connections. "But still, isn't there anyone you can talk to?"

"Well, you know, it's possible I could speak to Fanny. She is quite close to Mrs. Markens, the head of the invitation committee. It's possible she has some say in the matter." Becca got the impression Charlene was hedging her bets to avoid losing the opportunity to host Thanksgiving.

"That's all I ask, Charlene. As sisters, I believe we must help each other whenever we can. Family is so important, don't you agree? I'm sure Steven would agree, especially knowing how much he wants to spend Thanksgiving with his parents. And James would be devastated if we couldn't all be together. I'll be sure to speak to him about your request."

"Please do. James can be unreasonable when it comes to breaking with tradition. I would hate to disappoint him."

"I understand completely. I'll let you know how it goes when we've had a chance to talk." Becca wondered when that would be, considering their recent spat.

Charlene set down her teacup then smoothed out her skirts. "Just look at the time. I've been here much longer than I expected. I may have to miss visiting with Miss Sanders today."

"Don't let me keep you any longer. You've been such a dear to make time for me in your busy day. Perhaps I should come by later in the week and let you know what James has to say about Thanksgiving."

"Please do, as soon as possible. There are so many preparations I need to make, such as choosing the flowers and the food. My chef, Monsieur Lamont, will be so upset if I wait until the last minute to confirm. You know how temperamental French chefs can be."

If they were anything like ornery Mrs. Granger, Becca could relate. She stood along with Charlene and saw her to the door. "I expect you shall hear from me by the end of the week. Will that be soon enough?"

"Thursday, at the latest, if you don't mind, would work best for me."

To Becca, it sounded as if Charlene was already planning to host Thanksgiving dinner; the only remaining question was whether or not she and James would attend.

Once Charlene was off on her way, Becca returned to the library to resume her review of the accounting ledgers, or more correctly, to begin. So far, she hadn't managed to get past the first page.

The ledger began with the first week of the year and continued on to this past week. She began by flipping through the pages to review each week, looking for grocery purchases that seemed unusual or excessive. At first glance, it appeared the household expenses varied little from week to week. Thankfully, she found whenever Mrs. Granger had ordered more meat and produce than usual she added a note of explanation. Her notations included such items as: E.J. – dinner party for 6, C.J. – engagement party for 27, or E.J. – WAL luncheon for 12. Seldom did she see J.J. listed as the reason for additional expenses.

The various listings for Mrs. Jaffray's parties reminded Becca she had told Charlene she would write her mother-in-law a letter. She set aside the ledgers and began the daunting task of corresponding with James's mother. What should she say? If Eleanor had written to James, he hadn't shared it with her. She decided to keep the tone of the letter polite, cordial, and somewhat impersonal.

Dear Mrs. Eleanor Jaffray,

I hope this letter finds you well as you are enjoying your stay in Savannah with Martin. I regret my delay in writing as I should; however, as you may have heard, I have not been feeling myself lately.

Please be assured, all is well here. I have recovered nicely from my recent illness, and although James is quite busy, he is also well. Hopefully, he will take some time to relax a little during the holidays.

Charlene came by today to visit and we discussed the upcoming Women's Assistance League holiday charity ball. I think it would be lovely if James and I could attend with Charlene and Steven, however I am unable to locate our invitation. Since you are such an involved member of the League, it seems only proper that James and I should attend in your stead.

Also, James and I saw Mr. and Mrs. Morgan while attending services at Grace Church. In keeping with our long family association with the Morgans, I plan to call on Frances later this week. I shall send her your regards.

Please send our love on to Martin.

Sincerely,

Mrs. Rebecca Jaffray

It wasn't much, but hopefully it would do the trick. She rather liked the part about seeing the Morgans while at church with James and hoped it would be a feather in her cap in regards to inspiring Eleanor Jaffray to support her desire to attend the charity ball.

~*~

Not surprisingly, James didn't come home until late that evening. Becca had been waiting in the downstairs drawing room, reading *Little Women*, listening for him to come in the front door. When he did, he bypassed the room where she was sitting and headed straight for the stairs. She acted as if she didn't mind. James would come and go as he pleased. She doubted there was much she could do to change that, but now that he was home, she needed a few minutes of his precious time.

Setting aside her book, she got up and followed him as he went to the parlor on the second floor. By the time she entered the room he was already pouring himself a drink.

"Charlene came by to see me today," Becca said as she leaned against the door jam, hesitant to enter.

Pausing with his glass in mid-air, James responded with a look wonder. "Did she now? How interesting."

"Yes, I thought so too. She said you told her I was ill last week and she wanted to assure herself of my full recovery. Frances Morgan informed her she had seen us at church on Sunday. Since I didn't know I had been sick, I didn't know what to say. Maybe you should enlighten me on exactly how you explained my absence."

James's expression remained neutral but Becca sensed his discomfort, as if she had inadvertently hit upon a nerve. He took a swallow of his drink—brandy from the looks of it—before he responded. "I didn't say anything about your *absence*. When she asked about you, I simply told Charlene you were unwell and weren't receiving. She knows better than to ask me for details, which is probably why she came to check for herself."

It was comforting to know James didn't share his secrets with his sister, most likely because it spared Rebecca the embarrassment of having to explain her actions to anyone other than James.

She could just imagine the conversation her unexpected absence would inspire with Charlene:

"I heard you went to your father's summer house on Long Island. Whatever were you thinking? No one goes to Long Island in November."

"I went there to think, and to be alone."

"To think! To think about what?"

"Saving my marriage, if you really must know."

"Really! Your marriage needs saving after only four months?"

"My marriage needed saving since the day we were wed."

But that didn't happen, or anything like it, since James had kept her secret to himself, for which she was indeed grateful.

Becca smiled appreciatively at her husband. "Thank you for your discretion. I appreciate your concern for our privacy."

James gave her a disparaging look. "I suspected you had run off to have an affair. Not exactly news I wanted spread all over town. The fewer who know of your poor behavior, the better."

Becca stood a little straighter. "I've already told you, I wasn't having an affair. I was alone. I wish you would believe me." She turned from the doorway, ready to leave. It was useless trying to talk to James. He had made his opinions about her perfectly clear.

"Actually, I do believe you."

She stopped and turned back to face him.

"I've done some checking. Everything I've heard supports your story."

While it was a little discomforting to hear he had checked out her story, she wasn't entirely shocked by his actions. As her husband, it was his right and responsibility to know the whereabouts of his wife. Whether he trusted her or not was not the issue.

James raised his glass toward her. "Why don't you stay? Have a seat, relax, have a drink with me."

She narrowed her gaze. This was a surprise. It made her wonder what he had in mind. Curious, she stepped away from the door, and took a seat in one of the upholstered chairs fronting the fireplace.

"What will you have?" he asked.

"Umm, what do you suggest?"

"Nearly anything you might want," James said with a lift of his brow. He went to stand in front of his liquor cabinet. "Whisky, brandy, port, or would you prefer a little sherry?"

"Sherry sounds nice." Becca noticed she was sitting perched on the edge of the chair with her back straight and stiff, much as Charlene had done when she came to visit. Not wishing to appear nervous, she made an effort to relax and scooted back on the chair.

"I have a Manzanilla I think you may like." He held the bottle up to the light. "It's often underappreciated, but I find truly good sherry is a neglected treasure of the wine family."

Becca watched as James poured the fine aged wine into a tulip-shaped glass, then gently swirl the golden libation while his hand caressed the expensive crystal.

"This seems so unusual," Becca said as she accepted her drink from James. "I rarely drink." Their hands briefly touched and she felt his warmth, rather surprising considering he had only recently come in from the cold.

He smiled and looked directly at her. "Perhaps you should have a drink more often. It helps to lighten the mood." He took the chair across from her and raised his glass. "Shall we toast?"

"To what?" she asked, blinking.

"To restarting our marriage. Isn't that what you called it?"

Was he making fun of her? It was hard to tell for certain, but she joined him in the toast. "To our marriage." She took a hesitant taste of the fine liquor. So smooth, it went down easy, and she took another swallow. The sherry's warming effects quickly spread through her body. This could be dangerous if she wasn't careful.

"What else did you and my sister discuss today?"

Becca thought back to her visit with Charlene. "She asked if she could host Thanksgiving dinner this year. She said it's because she's a newlywed with a new house and wants to entertain Steven's family and ours. How do you feel about that?"

"Fine, let her."

"But you're the eldest of the family. Shouldn't the holiday celebration be held here?"

"Mother has always been the one to host Thanksgiving. Since she's not in town, I'm fine with the task falling to Charlene." He shrugged and Becca couldn't help but notice his broad shoulders. Strong and muscular, they seemed well suited to carrying the weight of his family's burdens. "Who would we invite besides Charlene and Steven?"

Yes, who would they invite? Certainly not her family. It was obvious Stanton Wheland wasn't welcomed here. And she didn't know if her brother Randolph would be home for the holiday.

"It's best if Charlene is allowed to host Thanksgiving." From the tone of his voice, Becca knew this subject was closed. Time to move on to less volatile topics.

She looked down at her glass, seeking inspiration, and took another sip. "Charlene also mentioned your mother, and reminded me I needed to write her a letter, which I've already done. I hope you don't mind. You've not mentioned if she's written, but I expect she has."

"A few times, I believe. Nothing out of the ordinary. Only to say she's arrived safe and sound. I wouldn't think she expects me to respond. I rarely write."

Her first thought was to be appalled that he hadn't told her, but she quickly set that aside. She and James simply didn't communicate as well as a married couple should. "As your wife, that's a task I should perform." Becca took another sip of her sherry. James was right, this was an underappreciated treasure.

"As my wife, there are a number of tasks you should perform. But I expect you really don't want to have that conversation." His smile was both smug and alluring, leaving her with little doubt as to what he meant.

She hadn't expected lust to come up so quickly, but for some reason, her nether region was sitting up and taking notice. Darn unreliable hormones. "I'm not sure I know what you mean." Yes, she did. So why was she playing dumb?

"Would you like me to explain? Or is a demonstration in order?" He drank the rest of his brandy and set aside his glass.

Oh, yes, a demonstration would be quite nice right about now. But, no, she really shouldn't. She didn't want to lead him on, or give him any ideas, although she was pretty sure he had enough ideas of his own. She blinked hard and took another sip of her sherry.

"A demonstration?" she squeaked, her voice sounding much higher than usual. She noticed now how close they were sitting, and how his eyes locked onto hers. She was taken in by the extraordinarily long lashes framing his silver blue eyes. The combination was so startling, Becca could scarcely resist staring.

Leaning forward, he cupped her chin in his hands. "I know it's been a while, but I'm sure you remember. Although I wouldn't blame you if you forgot. Our first attempts were rather forgettable."

Our first attempts? Was he referring to their wedding night? If that was the case, there was nothing to compare. For her, this was all very new, and strangely exciting. "Perhaps I need some reminding." Oh, my goodness, she was flirting with him again. It was as if she couldn't stop herself. Becca swallowed the last bit of her sherry.

James took the empty glass from her hand and set it on the side table next to his. "Maybe this will help." Sliding his hand to the back of her neck, he leaned in and pressed his lips to hers. His kiss was soft and seductive.

Instinctively, she opened her lips to receive him, and heard him groan. Dang, but he was good at this, his lips soft and inviting. He smelled of spice and musk, and tasted like the brandy he had been drinking. All very manly, and all very appealing. Why on earth had Rebecca rejected him? At this moment, for the life of her, she didn't know. Nor did she want to.

It took several seconds for her to remember that theirs was a marriage of convenience, not of love, and certainly not passion. Why her insides should be doing flip-floppy little summersaults was beyond her.

Shivers of sensation skidded across her skin as he ran his hand down her arm, and played his thumb across the back of her fingers. Tugging at her hand in a silent, gentle command, he pulled her to stand and wrapped her in his arms. Feeling soft and mushy, she melted against him. Her legs felt wobbly, but he held her upright, firmly encased in his arms.

His kiss was one of passion and promises, and yet Becca was torn in every way possible. She wanted his kisses but feared she should push him away. As a woman, it was up to her to put a stop to this before it went too far. She did the only sensible thing she could. She wrapped her arms around him and returned his affection, her body humming with desire. He was handsome, and sexy, and masculine and he smelled so darn good. This wasn't right, but it felt too good to stop.

Unexpectedly, James pulled back and set her on her feet. He looked deep into her eyes as if to assure himself of the passion he had stirred. "It's time to go to bed, Rebecca."

To whose bed? Did he expect to join her in her bedroom, or did he prefer she go to his? At this moment, he could take her anywhere he wanted to go. She looked up at him in silent wonder, waiting, anticipating.

He took another step away and softly said. "Go to bed, Rebecca."

"With you?" Good God, she hoped so.

A look of guilt, or was it remorse, passed through his eyes. "No. Alone. No bedroom visits until we have progressed further along in restarting our marriage. I believe those were your very words."

She felt the room tilt as the moment suddenly took a turn for the worse. Wait! Was he sending her off to her room, alone?

She wanted to slap his face, she felt so insulted. And embarrassed. And turned on. "You . . . you . . . you mean you seduced me under false pretense?"

"Our whole marriage is a false pretense. Good night, my *friend*." He turned on his heel and left the room.

Becca slumped in her chair, too stunned to remain standing. That dirty, rat bastard. He had given her a dose of her own medicine and the taste was bitter indeed.

But he was right, their marriage was a false and sad pretense. Everything about her was false.

~*~

James forced himself to leave the parlor and head up the stairs to his room, alone. He had come very close to taking Rebecca to bed, and was fairly certain she wouldn't have resisted. But he stuck to his plan. He had wanted to give her a taste of her medicine, seduce her and leave her wanting more. And the scheme had worked, better than he had planned, but not at all what he had expected.

When he first plotted this idea, he had been sure she was going to reject him, throw up some roadblock against his affection, but she hadn't.

Instead, she had yielded to his kiss, returning it with a passion he wouldn't have guessed existed in her cold, hard heart.

For a moment, he almost turned around and went back to her. But then what? Should he ask for her forgiveness; admitting he had deliberately seduced her only to leave her wanting? Not likely.

While there was no denying, for the first time in months, he wanted to bed his wife, if he did so now, it would only prove she had power over him. And that wasn't what he wanted.

He also had a strong feeling that no matter what he did, the damage was already done. Having already executed the deplorable deed, he couldn't expect to so easily secure her trust. It was doubtful she would welcome his affections after he left her like that. Besides, if she gave in now, there was a very good chance she would regret it in the morning. While he may have uncovered previously unknown passions in Rebecca, he had no reason to believe she loved him anymore today than she had on the day they married.

Until he won her love, until he knew for certain she was truly ready to be his wife, heart and soul, he would leave things as they were. Let her come to him. He had already done his best to show her he cared.

CHAPTER 5

Becca forced herself to climb the front stairs of J.P. Morgan's house and ring the bell. Much like the man, his brownstone mansion was large and imposing. Thankfully, his wife, Frances Louise, seemed less intimidating. Inside, the home was warm and inviting, even if it had the feel of being an art gallery. As she followed the butler into the house, Becca took in the vast number of paintings lining every wall. Pierpont Morgan was known as an insatiable art collector and it showed in his home. The collection was equally impressive as the home itself.

Just knowing that Mrs. Morgan had agreed to let her call gave Becca a glimmer of hope that her visit would be successful. Her mother-in-law Eleanor Jaffray and Charlene were friends with Mrs. Morgan; she hoped that would weigh in her favor. The butler took her to a smaller side parlor decorated in hues of rose and pink, most likely the ladies' sitting room of the house. Frances Morgan was there waiting for her, dressed in a modest but exquisite dress of sage green silk. Her thick, dark brown hair was done up in a smart French chignon that flattered her petite features. Much as Charlene had done, Mrs. Morgan sat perched on the edge of her chair, but unlike Charlene, Frances Morgan looked perfectly at ease. She dominated the room with a queenly air that left Becca second-guessing her request to visit.

Becca greeted her host as she was ushered to take a seat across from her. "Mrs. Morgan, thank you so much for accepting my call."

Mrs. Morgan nodded politely, without smiling. "It's my pleasure. As you know, my husband is well acquainted with your father."

The last thing Becca wanted to discuss was Stanton Wheland. "I understand you're also friends with my mother-in-law, Eleanor Jaffray," she said, thankful for this connection. "She sends her regards."

"Yes. Dear Eleanor. I understand from Charlene she has gone to winter in Savannah with her younger son. Charlene visited me earlier this week."

"Yes, so I was told. Charlene came by to see me only yesterday. We had a very pleasant visit."

"She does tend to stay busy." Mrs. Morgan's comment didn't exactly sound like a compliment.

"Yes, well, my sister-in-law is happiest when she's surrounded by family and friends."

"Aren't we all?" Mrs. Morgan agreed.

"I expect with the holidays fast approaching there will be several opportunities to visit with family. It's a busy time of year. Have you any special plans?" Becca wondered how long she should continue with this small talk before she got to the real reason for her visit. She didn't want to appear too pushy, but common etiquette demanded she keep this first visit short, no longer than fifteen minutes at most.

"Pierpont and I plan to take the children to London shortly after Thanksgiving to be with his parents."

Interestingly, Becca noticed that Mrs. Morgan seemed to keep her answers short and asked no questions of her. She forged on as if that wasn't a concern. "How splendid for you. Does this mean you won't be here for the Women's Assistance League charity ball in December?"

"I rarely attend. I prefer to support the league in a more private manner."

In other words, she gave money. That was probably much less messy than having to rub shoulders with any of Manhattan's less desirable nouveaux riche who might be in attendance. Or perhaps, since this was a year of great recession, the Morgans didn't want to appear too showy. J.P. Morgan already had a reputation for being too rich and powerful for many New Yorkers.

"I am hoping to attend, since both Eleanor and Charlene are members, but I must have missed receiving my invitation. I hesitate to be a bother, but I was wondering if you are able to assist me in this regard?"

Mrs. Morgan gave her a doubtful look, as if Becca had said something wrong. "It pains me to say this, but I don't see how I can. Stanton Wheland has made it clear he does not agree with my husband regarding his railroad holdings. And Pierpont has made it clear to me I am to do nothing to benefit Mr. Wheland."

Or his daughter. Mrs. Morgan hadn't said those words, but her meaning was clear. "Surely you don't believe the sins of my father should be passed onto me. I've done nothing to deserve such censure."

"If Pierpont is against providing assistance to Mr. Wheland, as his wife, I must extend his wishes to include his daughter."

"But you were so kind when I met you at church on Sunday." At least it seemed that way at the time. "If you don't approve of my father, why did you agree to my call?

Mrs. Morgan looked mildly astonished. "Would you have rather I refused you in public? You should be grateful I chose to make this a private affair."

Becca drew back in horror. "But your friendship with Charlene and Eleanor Jaffray—?"

"Shall endure regardless of Mr. Jaffray's association with the Whelands. This may not be what you want to hear, but there is nothing I can do."

She was being set down. The only upside to this excruciating experience was that the set-down had not happened in public, which it easily could have been, if Mrs. Morgan had so intended. She was at least grateful for that small consideration.

Becca sat in silence, not knowing what to do or how to react. Should she just get up and leave? Should she fight back? What good would that do besides making her appear petty and unkind, like Stanton Wheland, proving she truly was her father's daughter? She stared at Mrs. Morgan in wonder.

"It seems there is nothing else to be said," Mrs. Morgan said, interrupting her thoughts. "Good day to you, Mrs. Jaffray."

After fumbling through a hasty goodbye, Becca rushed out the front door of the Morgan mansion and scurried into her waiting carriage. Her heart thumped wildly in her chest, so great was her embarrassment.

She barely had a moment to settle in when she saw she was not alone. Sitting across from her was Jules Vanderzeit, the Maestro. Impeccably dressed as always, including the top hat upon his head, his hands rested peacefully atop a walking stick. Seeing him unexpectedly like this, she was immediately taken back to that rainy night when her life was not only turned upside down, it was forever changed. In an instant, she vividly recalled her former life, when she'd been Becky Sue Dobson, driving down a lonely country road in the twenty-first century.

"What a pleasure to see you, Becky Sue," Jules said, referring to her by a name she no longer used.

Becca blinked in astonishment. Dang, this man had the most annoying timing. "It's Becca now, thank you very much, and I can't say the same about you."

"Now, now, now, let's not be rude," Jules objected, wagging a finger in her face. "I'm only here to check on your progress. Have you secured an invitation to the ball, Cinderella? Or maybe I should call you Sleeping Beauty. Will you be able to get that painting for me as we agreed?"

He was referring to the painting of the Magic Flute by V.W. Stevenson. The one she was supposed to buy at the auction during the WAL charity ball. And, no, she wasn't any closer to securing an invitation, but she didn't want to admit that to him.

"I was just visiting with Mrs. Morgan, as I'm sure you know since you're sitting in my carriage outside her home."

"Did your visit go as well as you had hoped?" His condescending smirk told her he knew perfectly well it had not.

She huffed and looked out the window.

"Just as I thought." Jules used his walking stick to rap once on the roof of the carriage and it surged forward as the driver started them on their way. "There have been some new developments. The body of a young woman has washed up on Long Island."

Stunned, Becca's hand rose to cover her mouth. "Do they know who it is? Have they run her prints?" It was less than a week since she took this assignment; surely, she still had more time.

"Run her prints? Please, this isn't the twenty-first century. The body was badly decomposed. Apparently, she was torn up on the rocks by the tide and her face was somewhat smashed, making it extremely difficult to identify the body. Her clothes were barely clinging to her body."

"But you think it was Rebecca Wheland?"

"I know it was her. That's neither here nor there. As far as anyone knows, Rebecca Wheland Jaffray is alive and well and has just paid a visit to Mrs. J.P. Morgan. Your secret is safe."

Becca relaxed against the carriage seat. "But oh my goodness, I hate to think of that poor woman's accident. How she died, it was so sad." She hadn't been there to witness the unfortunate accident, but Jules had told her what had happened.

"You needn't worry, I went to the authorities and claimed her as Becky Sue Dobson. She was given a proper burial."

"Why on earth would you do something like that?" She never knew what to expect next from the Maestro.

"It's what I do, I tie up loose ends. That's not the issue. What's at stake here is whether or not you're able to get an invitation to the Women's Assistance League holiday charity ball."

It didn't help to show fear in front of Jules. Though in many ways he had treated her kindly, she knew he was ruthless. With a lift of her chin, she said, "I'm working on it. I have great faith in my success. It turns out both Eleanor and Charlene Jaffray are members of WAL"

"Yes, I know, I always know these things, but I fail to see how this will help you."

"With their connections, I should have no problem getting an invitation to the ball."

"But you haven't yet, have you?"

"No, I haven't," she confessed. She might as well be truthful. Jules would know if she was lying. Jules always knew. "There's still time. I am certain I will."

"I certainly hope so for your benefit. I would hate for you to fail and face the consequences. You may think your life was hell before, you should see what Fate can throw at you when you fail in your assignments. Your experience with Ralph will look like a walk in the park."

Jules was referring to the pitiful excuse for a man that she had called her boyfriend. A man who had argued with her, and screamed at her, and

86

accused her of the most hateful things, only to apologize and ask for her forgiveness, claiming he would never do it again. But he did. Over and over again, she had let him belittle her, and each time she had taken him back. Until that day when his brutal beating caused her to lose her unborn baby, and turned her whole body black and blue. She had been so devastated, she had nearly killed herself, thinking it was all her fault. It wasn't until after Jules came to her rescue that she had realized it wasn't her fault that Ralph got mad. It was his own damn doing. Now, in exchange for her attempt at suicide, she was doing penance working for Jules Vanderzeit, a man known as the Maestro.

For a second chance at life, she would do anything. Even pretend to be Rebecca, a woman who had unexpectedly died in a senseless accident.

Though she had only seen a black and white image of Rebecca Wheland, it was startling how much alike they looked. When Jules had shown her the ancient photograph, Becky Sue was almost convinced she was looking at a picture of herself in period clothing. It was obvious she was the right person for the task Jules assigned her, and Becky Sue had agreed to present herself as Rebecca Wheland Jaffray. As part of her assignment, she needed to buy the painting of the Magic Flute by V.W. Stevenson when it went up for auction at the annual Women's Assistance League holiday charity ball. This was her penance for foolishly running off the road, an accident that could have caused her death.

So, as Jules requested, and as her contract with him stipulated, she had travelled back in time to the 1890's, taken in the identify of Mrs. Rebecca Jaffray, and had started calling herself Becca, not Becky Sue. Oh, and she had also agreed to live with a man she didn't know, and was pretending to be his wife. Could life get any stranger? She didn't think so.

"Nothing could be worse than almost being beaten to death by someone I thought I loved." *And who I thought loved me.* "You have no idea."

The smirk faded from Jules's face and his expression softened as his eyes became misty. "Unfortunately, my dear, yes I do. I've seen so much more than you could ever imagine. *You* have no idea. And yet, everyone believes theirs is the only story that matters."

"It's the only one that matters to me." Too emotional to hold his gaze, she turned to look out the window once again.

"Except now you have a new life to live, a new story to tell. For your sake, I hope you do it well. I would hate to have you fail and need to start all over again. Such delays are never welcomed, but are often necessary."

Her temples began to throb; she reached up to rub them. "You speak in such riddles. I never know what you mean."

"I expect you will someday, when the time is right. But for now, let us focus on your assignment. Have you any thoughts on how you will be allowed to attend the ball, now that Mrs. Morgan has turned you down?"

Becca hemmed and hawed for a moment, wondering what she could say. "Not really, but I think Charlene may still be able to help. I know you warned me that Rebecca was not well-liked, but I didn't realize how few friends she has."

"Yes, yes, I know. The sins of the father being forced upon the daughter and all that rot. Bad luck, such as it is, poor girl. No wonder she wanted to run away. But running away only got her smacked in the head and dumped in the ocean."

"Jules! How can you be so cruel?"

"Remember, I've seen it all before. Nothing new here." He patted his mouth as he yawned. "Back to your story, your new story. You have an opportunity to set things right, or at least change them for the better. Doesn't that sound appealing?"

"Well, yes." Actually, she was starting to enjoy the prospect of making Rebecca a more likeable person, especially with James, her husband of convenience. It wasn't going to be easy. First impressions were hard to overcome, and almost everyone, including James, already had a negative impression of Rebecca. "Although sometimes, I must admit, I question why I even bother," she said almost as an afterthought.

"It takes your mind off what you are actually doing."

"And what might that be?" She thought she was doing penance for running off the road and nearly getting herself killed.

"Have you ever noticed how life is less about what happens to you and more about how you react?"

Becca looked at Jules as if he were speaking Greek. "Are you saying I shouldn't have reacted to Ralph's beating with grief and guilt?" *And wanted to die?*

"I'm not saying your reaction is right or wrong, but let me remind you, Rebecca is dead because of her foolish choices, and how she reacted to what happened to her. And you, my dear, are here to take her place. With a job to do."

A startling thought suddenly occurred to Becca. "Am I changing history?"

"Whose history? The past is not stagnant as you've been lead to believe. We do not change history so much as act within it. There is more to heaven and earth than you have yet to imagine."

"Sometimes you make no sense." Nothing in her world seemed to make sense any longer. Wasn't it exactly her job to change the past, and hopefully learn from it along the way? It seemed to her the Maestro's whole goal was to change the past, to touch unraveling threads and compose a whole new fabric, connecting each thread with the other until the landscape of the tapestry was completely changed. The arrogance of one man to think he had the right to change the fabric of time was beyond her understanding. "Maestro," indeed.

But like it or not, Becca did as she was told, to the best of her abilities. The sins of her past were unforgivable, but she was willing to serve her penance. Needed to make amends. It did no good to dwell on the past, or pine for a future of what might have been. She needed to stay focused on the current time and move forward from here, taking each new moment as it came and staying attentive to all opportunities to make things right.

"Because I have more experience than you, I'm able to see the big picture," Jules said with an air of confidence.

Right, the big picture. "If I'm able to obtain this one special painting for you, I'll complete my contract, correct? Then I can be on my merry way. Isn't that what you told me?"

"Something like that," Jules nodded.

As Becca looked out the window of the carriage she noticed they were no longer headed toward home, the home she now shared with James. "Where are you taking me?"

"Isn't it obvious. We're taking a ride through Central Park."

"What if someone sees my carriage out here and it gets back to James? He may get suspicious again. He already thinks Rebecca was having an affair. Personally, I think she wanted to divorce him."

"Very hard to do in this day and age. She would almost need to prove *he* was having an affair, or actually have one herself. But I believe you

89

may be correct, all the clues indicate she wanted to leave her husband. Instead, she died." Jules gave a sad shake of his head. "Such a rash and permanent solution to a temporary situation."

"She didn't view her marriage as temporary. Like you said, these people don't believe in divorce." Jules had given her a handful of books to read while she was at Raven's Point as part of her training. One was a historical overview of this time period, another was on manners and etiquette, but the ones she had enjoyed most were the memoirs of Consuelo Vanderbilt and Mrs. Harry Lehr. Of course, none of these books had been written yet, but they would be someday.

"Being married wasn't her problem. Her problem was choosing to be unhappy." Jules rapped his walking stick on the floor of the carriage as if to emphasize his point. "It would serve you well to take note of that."

"Well, I don't want to divorce James. I just wish he would treat me nicer."

"Understandable. By the way, what excuse did you give for your absence?"

Becca looked back out the window and gazed off into the distance. "As if you don't know . . . I told him I needed time to think, and I wanted us to be friends, maybe give our marriage a second chance." Her excuse sounded weak even to her, but it seemed not many people liked poor Rebecca, including James, and she wanted to change that. She turned back to face Jules. "I told him I hoped we could restart our marriage."

Jules seemed amused. He raised a brow. "Have you slept with him?"

"Good heavens, no! I just needed an excuse for acting differently around him than before. I'm hoping he'll help me get an invitation to that stupid ball you want me to attend."

Jules wagged a finger at her. "Tsk, tsk, tsk, Rebecca. You needn't act all uppity. This is serious business."

"Don't you think I understand?"

"Sometimes I wonder if you truly do. You agreed to take on this assignment as your penance so you can move forward. Onward and upward, as they say. You need to see it through to the end, and let's hope you're successful, for your sake. While I admit I want that painting, if you don't get it for me, I can assure you, someone else will. I always get what I want."

Becca huffed. "Give me some time. I'll get that darn painting for you. I haven't run out of options yet. If only Stanton Wheland wasn't such a jackass to everyone, maybe this wouldn't be so hard. I guess I have my father to thank for all this."

"That's very good."

"What? That my father is hated by everyone in Manhattan?"

"No, that you called Stanton your father. It's very important for you to think of yourself as Rebecca, because for now, you are."

"You don't need to worry. I'm doing a very good job of being Rebecca. A new and improved version perhaps, but to everyone I meet, I'm very much Rebecca."

"Still, I recommend you avoid Stanton Wheland. I doubt you can fool him."

"Don't be so sure. I don't think he knows his daughter very well." *And he sure as hell doesn't know what I'm capable of.*

They had reached the midway point of Central Park, and she noticed that the driver turned the carriage into the lane that crossed through the park. It was a bright, sunny day, and even in winter, the park was lovely. She would have felt content to drive along its curving lanes for hours, but she also needed to be mindful of the time. James would question her if she were late.

"What about Randolph? Have you heard from him?" Jules asked, taking her mind off the passing scenery.

"You mean Rebecca's . . . umm, my older brother? No, I haven't. Isn't he away on business? London or something like that?" Jules had told her so much before he sent her out on this assignment, it was hard to keep it all straight. She'd been so nervous when she first arrived at James's house, she had forgotten the names of many of her servants, even though Jules had gone over the list with her at least twice. It wasn't easy to step into someone else's shoes and not make mistakes. It was one of the reasons she kept a journal.

"Yes, London. He's working on a bank investment with his uncle, but he's expected home for Christmas, perhaps sooner if his plans change. I'm keeping an eye on the situation."

Not surprisingly, Jules seemed to have his *eye* on everything. It was rather unnerving. But if her brother were going to be here for Thanksgiving, she wondered if she could get him invited to join them at

91

Charlene's. She didn't really care where Stanton Wheland celebrated the holiday dinner.

"How will I know if things change?"

"Don't worry. Randolph will contact you. You and your brother are fairly close. You both share a dislike for your father."

"Don't you mean hatred?"

"Too strong of a word. I prefer dislike."

Becca rolled her eyes.

He continued, "You should not hate anyone, it will do you no good, but you need not like everyone either."

That was good to know.

"Well, here we are." Jules rapped on the roof of the carriage with his walking stick and the carriage came to a stop outside the Dakota, a luxury apartment building located at Seventy-second Street and Central Park West, a sparsely developed area remote from the core of the city's center. "I must leave you now. I have another client to see."

"Oh, my, I've always wanted to see the inside of the Dakota. May I come with you?"

Jules gave her a stern look of disapproval. "You most certainly may not. I do not allow my clients to mingle, and you cannot be seen at the Dakota.

She pouted at the refusal. "Why not?"

"Because you don't have business here. I'm sorry, but I must send you on your way. I'll be in touch when needed."

"I'm sure you will."

Jules tipped his hat to her then exited the carriage. "Take her home, Mr. Bates." The carriage surged forward and she was once again on her way home, no closer to obtaining an invitation to the ball than when the day had started.

~*~

James had known Charlene would come to call sooner or later. It wasn't like his sister to mind her own business. Not when she could keep herself busy minding his and everyone else's. She had seen him walking down Fifth Avenue and had insisted on giving him a ride home in her carriage so they could visit. He knew better than to argue, and he couldn't exactly deny his sister access to his home. Not too long ago, before she married Steven Shepard, she had lived here, too.

Upon their arrival, James asked Mr. Jenkins to bring tea to the front parlor for Charlene. He then went to the liquor cabinet to pour a glass of sherry for himself. It was too early for brandy, but he reserved the right to switch to the stronger dram if needed.

His sister was still removing her gloves when she asked, "Did you know Rebecca wants to attend the WAL holiday ball this year?"

"Which holiday ball?" he asked, looking up from his drink. He wondered if he had heard her correctly. Did she just refer to a "wall" ball?

"The annual holiday charity ball put on by the Women's Assistance League, W.A.L., surely you are familiar with it."

It took him a second before her words sunk in. "Oh, yes, I believe Rebecca may have mentioned it to me." He hadn't really paid her much mind because he really didn't care whether or not they attended. A holiday charity ball certainly wasn't important to him.

"I wish she hadn't come to me for help, I hate to turn anyone down," Charlene said, making the pouty face he knew so well. When Charlene went into a pout, it meant she wanted to get her way. And interestingly enough, she usually did. His sister could charm nearly anyone around her if she put her mind to it. Except him. After all these years, he had grown immune to her methods.

"I thought you came to visit her," James said, scrutinizing his sister.

"You know what I mean. I may have been visiting her, but she presented me with her request." She waved off his judgmental glare as if it were of no concern.

James declined to point out that if Charlene hadn't come to visit, Rebecca wouldn't have been able to ask for her help. It wouldn't do any good if he did. He took a swallow of his sherry. It was good, very good, but perhaps the brandy would have been a better choice.

"If only Rebecca was a member of the Women's Assistance League, none of this would be an issue. Everyone who is a member of WAL is invited to the charity ball," Charlene was saying.

"Isn't it a little too late for that? I thought the ball was next month." Why was he letting his sister pull him into her problems?

Charlene gave him an exasperated look just before she acknowledged the tea tray brought in by Jenkins with a gleaming smile. "Thank you, Jenkins. You may set it there," she said, indicating the side table.

Their butler set the tray next to Charlene. "It's nice to see you, Miss Charlene." Even though she was married, Mr. Jenkins had always called her Miss Charlene and James suspected he always would. "Will there be anything else?"

"This will do quite nicely. Thank you kindly, Jenkins." Charlene waited for the servant to exit the room, and then, without missing a beat, she turned her attention back to James. "I'm thinking ahead, James. I'm thinking of next year. Of course, she would need a sponsor, and since we're not allowed to sponsor other family members, it would need to be someone besides Mother or me. I know she has not made a good impression on society, but isn't there anyone you know whose wife might be interested in sponsoring her, as a favor to you. You know everyone in New York."

James might not know everyone, but he knew the men who ran New York. Some of them were accepted into the upper echelon of society, and some of them weren't. When it came to business, having the right resources at the right time was far more important than screening their social credentials.

Still, that didn't change how he felt on the subject. "I really do not care if Rebecca is able to attend that damn ball. Why should it matter to me?"

"Because she's your wife. Because if your wife is to be accepted into polite society, she needs to make the proper connections. You're married now. You have a responsibility to your wife to ensure her place in society." She poured herself a cup of tea and as a matter of etiquette offered to pour one for James. He declined her offer with a wave of his fingers.

He supposed she was right. Men tended to care more about getting business done while their wives cared far more about their acceptance into society. Often, for women, it was the only thing they cared about.

"If she wants an invitation to that ball, she can get it on her own. She doesn't need my help," James said.

Charlene looked appalled. "Why would you fight her over such a little thing as an invitation to a ball?"

Because it was the only thing he knew she wanted. But he felt no need to share that bit of insight with his sister. "I have other issues to occupy my time. I don't have time to worry about invitations to holiday balls."

"Well you should. You've been married for over four months. You need to ensure your proper place in society or you'll be left without access to the best families and their homes."

Much as he hated to admit it, she was right. Fighting Rebecca on this would only come back to bite him. "I'll think about it."

"Fine. That's all I ask. A man of your resources should have no problems securing an invitation to a ball." Charlene looked pleased, as if it were already a done deal.

James saw no reason to burst her bubble.

"Now as for Thanksgiving, did Rebecca tell you, I'd like to hold the dinner at my house?" Charlene took a sip of tea and smiled sweetly. The same smile she used whenever she wanted something to go her way.

"Yes, she mentioned it. Although I'm sure you know, she thinks we should hold the dinner here." He preferred to have Charlene do the honors, but it was best to let his sister believe there was a chance he didn't. That way it would seem he was doing her a favor.

"James, I need to host Thanksgiving. This is my first year in my new home."

"This is also Rebecca's first year in her new home. Shouldn't I take that into consideration?"

For a brief moment, Charlene's eyes narrowed as she bit down on her lips. She looked ready to burst, but she quickly reined in her emotions, returning to her manipulatively sweet smile. He had to give her credit; she was good at masking her emotions. "James, I've already assured Steven we would host. His parents are coming. Surely, you don't expect them to come here."

"Calm down, Charlene." *For heaven's sake, this really wasn't worth a fight.* "I'll tell Rebecca I've decided to let you host the dinner. I thought about having it here, but apparently it means more to you." Perfect. Now his dear sister would feel indebted to him, a helpful situation if he found he needed a favor.

"Thank you, big brother. This is one less thing for me to worry about. You can't image how busy I am. I have a lady's tea on Saturday, and don't forget the opening night of the opera on Monday. We'll all be there."

"If you're that busy, are you sure you want to do Thanksgiving?"

95

"Don't be silly. It's nothing I can't handle." Charlene gathered up her gloves. "Before you can change your mind, I really must be going. Steven will be home soon and I like to be there when he arrives."

His sister stood and James did likewise.

"Good day, dear brother. I shall see you next week for Thanksgiving, if not before." With a flourish of swishing skirts and a kiss to his cheek, Charlene made her departure.

James sat down and took another drink of his sherry, grateful for a moment alone to relax.

A moment later, Rebecca walked in the front door. It seemed the fun times never stopped around here. Good Lord, couldn't a man get some time alone to enjoy his drink? Then again, considering the way he had treated her last night, maybe now was a good time to make amends.

"Was that Charlene I saw driving away?" Rebecca asked as she stepped into the parlor.

"Yes, you just missed her." James looked longingly at his drink, but set it aside after taking one last sip.

"Did she come to see me?" Rebecca asked, looking hopeful.

"No, not really."

Her shoulders slumped noticeably. "Then why was she here?"

"She came to confirm that she would be having Thanksgiving dinner at her house."

"Oh." Rebecca looked crestfallen. "I had planned to visit her tomorrow to give her your approval. I guess she couldn't wait." Her cheeks were rosy from being outside and her hazel green eyes had a doe-like innocence. The effect was decidedly appealing.

"Apparently not. That's Charlene for you. So where were you today?" James was grateful he had stuck to the sherry; he needed to keep his wits about him. Rebecca looked vulnerable and tempting, not a good combination.

Rebecca removed her hat before answering. "I went to see Mrs. Morgan, don't you remember, we discussed it last Sunday at church."

Oh, yes, now he remembered. He hoped her meeting went well.

"Afterwards, I had Mr. Bates drive me through Central Park. Such a lovely day for a ride through the park, I wish you could have been there."

"That sounds pleasant. Did you ask Mrs. Morgan about the ball?" Since Charlene had mentioned it, he thought he should ask. Let her know he cared.

Rebecca tilted her head as if thinking carefully before she answered. "It did come up, but she informed me she wouldn't be attending. Apparently, the Morgans are expected to be away from the city. I believe they're spending the holidays with Mr. Morgan's family in London."

"Yes, I recall Pierpont mentioning his upcoming trip." James reached for his glass and took another sip. It looked as though they were going to be here for a while.

"Oh!" She took a deep breath, looking slightly pained. "I wish you would have shared that bit of news with me."

"Why should I? I didn't think it was important."

She flipped her hand through the air with a sigh. "You're right. It's not. I was just thinking it might have saved me a trip."

"Didn't you enjoy your visit with Mrs. Morgan?" Pierpont was an important business associate of his and Fanny Morgan was one of the most gracious women he knew.

Rebecca fidgeted with ribbons on her hat, looking decidedly uncomfortable. "Umm, my visit with Mrs. Morgan was quite enlightening."

"But it went well, right?" He was beginning to worry. If Rebecca had done or said anything to offend Francis Morgan he needed to know. Maybe Charlene was right. He needed to pay more attention to Rebecca's social standing.

~~~

Becca paused, her hat in her hand, wondering how much she should confide to James. Her visit with Mrs. Morgan had not gone well at all, not for her. It had been enlightening, as she had said, but she wouldn't call it successful.

Not unless one considered being dismissed in private instead of public a success. Learning how deeply Rebecca was disliked—or to be more precise, how strongly Stanton Wheland was hated, especially by J.P. Morgan—was an unexpected revelation. Apparently, she was already deemed guilty by association. She really couldn't blame Mrs. Morgan. Rebecca had done nothing to distance herself from her father or change society's impression of her. Well, maybe she blamed Mrs. Morgan a little.

97

The woman could have shown her some compassion Nevertheless, Frances was married to J.P. Morgan, a man known throughout history for his business acumen, not for his humanitarian aid.

"As well as one could expect, all things considered. Surely you can understand, it was only my first visit, so I didn't stay long." Eager to move away from the subject of her visit with Mrs. Morgan, she added, "I see you're having a drink. Do you mind if I join you?"

"Please do." James stood and went to the sideboard holding decanters of liquor and glasses.

Becca set her hat and gloves on a nearby table. It was rather gratifying to know if she left them there, Katie or one of the other servants would ensure they were returned to her room. Ah, the luxuries of being married to a rich man. Except even being married to a rich man was no guarantee she'd be able to complete her assignment and satisfy the Maestro.

"What are you having?" she asked, eyeing his half empty glass.

"Sherry. Would you like the same?"

"Yes, please." Becca stepped further into the room and took a seat near the fire. Ahh, the delights of a wood-burning fire on a cold winter's eve. How romantic, if you were lucky enough to be with someone you loved. If not, it was merely a source of heat. She briefly held her hands toward the blaze, grateful for its warmth.

James poured her a drink and added more to his. Perhaps it was good he had gotten a head start. Last night, after only one glass, she had nearly thrown herself into his bed. Sadly, she might very well have ended up there if he hadn't stopped her from making a complete fool of herself. She supposed she should be grateful for small favors. It would hurt far worse if he had turned her away after they made love. It was much easier to face him this way.

"You're home rather early. It's not even dinner time yet," she said, accepting her drink from James. She took a sip, relishing the warming sensation it sent coursing through her body.

James took a seat across from her next to the hearth. Apparently, he wasn't averse to being in her company; she took this as a good sign. Hopefully last night's little display of rejection had only been in retribution for her suggestion they should keep their marriage out of the bedroom, at least for the time being. For a man such as James, her declaration could be considered quite a put-down.

"One of the benefits of spending several long days at the office. Once in a while I get a reprieve."

"And I get the benefit of your company." Without waiting for his response, she raised her glass in a salute then took another sip. Dang, this stuff was good. She could get used to this, sipping sherry near an open fire with a handsome man, who was her husband, no less.

"Do you enjoy the benefit of my company?" James asked.

"Yes, James, I do. I enjoy it very much. Besides, it's frowned upon to drink alone." She took another sip of her sherry.

"Is that what we are now? Drinking buddies?" he asked with a raised brow.

"No, of course not. We're husband and wife." Darn. That answer was probably going to get her into trouble, or at the very least open a smelly can of worms.

"A married couple who are *friends*, am I not right?" he asked, looking rather pensive.

"I would like to be your friend, James, if that isn't too much to ask." *And hopefully, maybe someday, something more.* That was a surprising thought.

"Is that all you want?" he asked, his voice seductively low.

Dang, he was asking an awful lot of questions. Was he trying to test her or simply push her buttons? Either way, it was working. She was getting close to throwing a real nice hissy fit. Her disappointing visit with Mrs. Morgan, and then the ride with Jules had upset her more than she liked. And to top it all off, she'd come home and found out that Charlene had asked James about Thanksgiving even though they had agreed she would take care that.

"What do you want from me, James? Should I throw myself at your feet and beg forgiveness, or seduce you into making passionate love to me?" she asked in a bit of a huff.

That seemed to shut him up. For a brief second, he looked stunned. But just as quickly, he recovered. "Perhaps a little of both."

Dang, he seemed awfully pleased with her suggestion. "Well, if I need to beg your forgiveness, then you also should beg for mine."

"Excuse me! Do you really believe I should beg for your forgiveness? My sins are no worse than yours. I've tried to be a considerate husband."

"Oh, really, James. A considerate husband? Does a considerate husband ignore his wife day after day? Or seduce her only to reject her? Is that your ideal of a considerate husband? You know, I could be a pretty darn good wife, if you would only let me. But no, you have to treat me as if I have some horrible social disease."

"You're the one who locked me out of your bedroom."

"I'm the one who asked you to give our marriage a fresh start, so we could be friends before we became lovers. But for some reason, that suggestion is distasteful to you. As if the idea of being my *friend* is too much to ask, but sleeping with me would be just fine."

"Only if that's what you want. Look, I'm sorry—."

Becca rolled her eyes. "Yes, I know. We're too proper, and uppity, and rich for something so basic as friendship between husband and wife." She really didn't know what had set her off on this tangent, but now that she was here, she found she rather liked it. It felt good to get this off her chest.

James studied her as if she had sprouted horns, or was speaking a foreign language. Which in many ways, she was. Sadly, she was too angry and frustrated to care.

"Husbands and wives should be lovers, as well as friends." James was starting to raise his voice.

"Well, we're neither."

"When would we have had the chance?"

"Never. We never had a chance. We were doomed from the start." Suddenly the wind blew out of her and she felt deflated. "You needed a loan, and my father needed a man to pawn off his daughter to get me out of his house. Lucky you, you hit the jackpot. Money to pay off your debts and an heiress as a wife. I don't blame you for what happened. Not anymore. If anything, I blame my father, but he's not here and what's done, is done. I'm tired of looking back. I'd like to look forward. But not if it means we sit here and fight every night." She finished off her drink in one gulp then set down the empty glass. "I'm going to my room to change for dinner."

Why should she even bother to dress and sit for dinner with a man who didn't care for her? The effort seemed useless.

"Never mind. On second thought, I'll have Katie bring a tray to my room so you don't have to be bothered by me."

She stood to walk away, but he called after her.

"Rebecca, wait."

"Not tonight, James. I'm simply too tired to fight anymore." With tears burning her eyes, she turned and continued on to her room.

She felt horrible about taking her frustrations out on James, but nothing had gone well today. First there was her disappointing visit with Mrs. Morgan, and then seeing Jules, who reminded her she still needed to fulfill her contract with him. If that wasn't enough, when she came home, she was told Charlene had gone behind her back to speak to James about Thanksgiving. And now, to top it all off, though he'd done nothing to deserve it, she had managed to pick a nasty quarrel with James. It was as if she had just kicked her dog simply because he was there.

It seemed the only thing left to do was go to bed and hope tomorrow would be a better day.

~~~

James sat for a moment in stunned silence. Sadly, but not surprisingly, it seemed the old, angry, resentful Rebecca was back. Something had obviously set her off, and he had a feeling it was more than just him. He was tempted to go after her and try to talk some sense into her, but was fairly certain such an effort would only provoke more anger. Neither of them needed more of that.

He thought back over their conversation; it had started off well enough but had quickly turned sour. It seemed she was still feeling upset over the trick he had pulled on her the night before. He had intentionally aroused her passions with the intent of refusing her. That couldn't have felt good. He had only thought to give her a taste of her own medicine, but the results were far from what he intended.

When she had suggested they give their marriage another chance, he had assumed that included bedroom visits, but apparently, she had not. With all her talk of friendship, she had made it abundantly clear she had no interest in allowing him into her bed. He had taken her refusal as a challenge, and then he had taken it too far. The set-down he gave her must have hurt.

They had gone this long without marital relations, he supposed a while longer shouldn't be an issue. After all, neither of them was going

101

anywhere, at least he hoped Rebecca didn't plan to pull another disappearing act.

He sincerely wanted her to be happy. A successfully married couple should be considerate of one another. He yearned for that, and yet few men admitted to having such a loving relationship with their wife. Although to be honest, men rarely spoke of such things. As long as their wives maintained a proper home and hosted all the right people at all the right events, and participated in all the right social groups, everything was fine.

He wondered if part of her anger was because he had refused to help her get invited to that damn charity ball. His lack of concern in that regard certainly didn't seem to help her mood, but might there be something else? Was she upset because Charlene had upstaged her by asking to host Thanksgiving?

Then it dawned on him. She was not well respected. Not by him, not by her father, not by his sister, and not by society at large. She was struggling under the weight of Wheland's legacy. Was it any wonder she felt so angry and rejected? Thinking about it this way, he supposed she had a right to be upset. No wonder she was trying so hard to be his friend, she had so few. He felt a suddenly pang of regret over the way he had treated her.

As he thought back over the past few days since her return, he realized Rebecca was sincerely attempting to improve their relationship and he had done little to support her. He needed to give her credit for her efforts. While it was unlikely he was suddenly going to fall head over heels in love with his wife, he had to admit, their relationship could stand some improvement.

Rebecca wanted respect, but he had withheld his respect because her father had forced him to marry her. Not her fault. Society at large also withheld its respect because she was Wheland's daughter. Again, not her fault. However, if she thought running away from her problems deserved respect, she was wrong. If she thought simply announcing she wanted to make their marriage better earned her respect, she was still wrong, but at least she was on the right track.

When Rebecca demonstrated to him by her actions, and not just words, that she truly supported him as his wife, maybe then she would earn his respect. He wasn't going to hold his breath waiting for that to happen, but a part of him acknowledged he hoped she would prove herself worthy and prove him wrong.

CHAPTER 6

Thursday, November 23, 1893

It wasn't easy to bounce back from the disappointment of the previous day, but Becca decided to make the effort. She truly regretted the way she had lashed out at James—not that he didn't deserve her ire, but anger never solved anything. If anything, she had probably only made matters worse. Once again, one step forward, two steps back. Could she never get ahead?

It seemed he liked to push her buttons. Maybe it would be easier to just sleep with him, as he wanted, and get it over with. But no, she had no intention of basing their relationship on mere physical pleasure. Besides, what real pleasure was there in having sex with a man she didn't really love? For men, it didn't seem to make a difference, sex was sex, but for a woman, sex was an intimate act of love. Maybe she was being a hopeless romantic with her head in the clouds, but it didn't matter, she wasn't going to settle.

She might be living someone else's life, but by God, she was going to do it her way or not at all. And her way included loving a man before she shared her body with him. Okay, maybe she didn't need to *love* him, but she certainly needed to believe they cared for each other, which as of yet, did not seem to be the case.

So much of her past was foreign to her, but then again, so was her future. The only real moment she could hang on to was the present, and do her best to keep moving forward from here. It was time to rise and shine and face the day.

After taking breakfast in her room, Becca called Katie in to help her dress for the day.

"I was thinking I would wear the burgundy wool skirt and shirtwaist. I don't expect to be going anywhere," Becca said as she stood in front of her walk-in closet. The day was chilly and she rather liked the idea of curling up in the library to finish reading *Little Women*.

"Ma'am, did you not tell Mrs. Shepard you would visit her today?" Katie reminded her.

"Oh, yes, that's right. Thank you for reminding me."

Her plan to pay a call to Charlene had completely slipped her mind, or maybe she simply had thought it was no longer necessary, since Charlene had taken it upon herself to go directly to James to get his approval for her to host Thanksgiving dinner.

Still, it was probably best to make the effort to visit Charlene. At this point, she had more than enough enemies; what she needed were more friends.

"What do you suggest? Should I go with the dark blue day dress, or the black and grey stripe?"

"Those both seem rather conservative for your sister-in-law. I would suggest a pop of color, perhaps the plum-colored silk, or this russet gown with the stamped velvet trim," Katie said, pulling out the dress for her to see.

"Let's go with the russet gown."

"Very good choice, Madam," Katie said with a smile. "It highlights the color of your eyes."

It was good to know, if nothing else, she had a trustworthy servant looking out for her best interests. Katie couldn't exactly be considered a friend since Becca was her employer, but still, she appreciated the loyal bond they shared. Not every servant in this house was as considerate to her.

Friends. It seemed like such a simple request, and yet, making friends didn't come easy. What could she do to make up for Rebecca's past? She couldn't force people to like her, not even if they were family. She supposed the only thing she could do was try to be kind and hope that was enough to overcome whatever self-destructive mistakes Rebecca had made in the past. Besides, who was she to judge? She was far from perfect. She had certainly made enough of her own mistakes. Hopefully, it was not too late to change.

~*~

Becca was grateful she had agreed with Katie's suggestion and worn the russet gown. It felt expensive and fashionable. While she had thought her home with James was rather new and impressive, Charlene's house was one of tasteful tradition. Based on the size of the brownstone and its location near Washington Square, it was obvious Steven Shepard was from one of the old, well-established and wealthier families of Manhattan.

After being greeted at the front door by the butler, Becca was shown to the front parlor to wait for Charlene. Jewel-colored drapes, velvet-covered chairs and thick wool rugs filled the front parlor, making it feel like a rich, exotic Turkish bazaar. A few minutes later, her sister-in-law entered the room with a swish of silk skirts accompanied by a wafting floral scent. She made quite a grand entrance as she came to take a seat beside Becca.

"Rebecca, how nice of you to call. I'm sure James told you I stopped by yesterday."

"I think he mentioned it." Only because she had seen Charlene leaving the house.

"You must forgive me, but I simply could not wait another day to make my final plans. I had to place my order for the flowers and table decorations, and this is such a busy time of the year for my florist, I couldn't take the chance he would be out of supplies. But you needn't worry, he promised he could fill my order without any problems. Thankfully, the Shepards have always been his loyal customers. The house will be filled with mums, daisies, lilies and of course, roses. I love roses. It will be stunning, just you wait and see. I can hardly wait myself. I'm so excited to be hosting my first Thanksgiving dinner. Mr. Lamont has assured me he purchased one of the largest turkeys this side of the Hudson River. Nothing is too good for my family."

As Becca listened to Charlene ramble on and on about her big party, she began to share in her sister-in-law's happiness. Obviously, hosting the holiday dinner meant much more to Charlene than it ever could to Becca or James. Seeing Charlene's delight soon made Becca forget her problems, she was so drawn in by her sister-in-law's good cheer. Charlene might not be able to get the invitation to the ball she needed, but she shined as a devoted member of her family.

"Speaking of family," Becca said when Charlene paused to take a breath, "I may not have mentioned this before, but there's a possibility my brother, Randolph, may be in town for Thanksgiving. If he is, I hope you don't mind if he joins us. I don't know what plans my father has, but I would so much prefer to have Randolph dine with us."

Charlene looked happy enough to pop. "It would be our pleasure. The more, the merrier. There will be plenty to eat. I already told you about the turkey, didn't I?"

"Yes, and your flowers, it all sounds delightful. And only a week away. I'm sure you have so much more to do before then."

"You cannot imagine. I don't know how Mother did it all year after year. We need to have every piece of silver polished and ready for inspection by Wednesday. Do you think Randolph will want to bring a guest? I worry about uneven numbers at the table."

"I really couldn't say. He hasn't returned home yet."

Charlene tapped a finger to her chin. "I wonder if there is anyone appropriate I can ask at the last minute, although I don't see how. By this time, everyone has already made their holiday plans."

"I really wouldn't worry. He may not return until the first part of December. He's in London working on a banking investment."

"When will you know? Thanksgiving is only a week away. Surely, if he were coming home, he would have sent word by now." Charlene was beginning to look a little worried.

Becca didn't know what to say. It was very possible Randolph had been in contact with their father, but since she was avoiding Stanton Wheland, she had no way of knowing for sure. "You may be right, it may be only wishful thinking. I just wanted to be sure, if he is in town, he would be welcomed to join us."

"Why, of course, of course. Uneven numbers at the table is of no concern when family is involved. I don't know Randolph well, but he seems to be a fine gentleman. Are you two close?"

Becca hesitated to answer. What could she say? She didn't even know Randolph. "He's my only brother."

"Why of course you're close, just like James and I are. How silly of me to ask. You wouldn't want him at Thanksgiving if you weren't."

"Thank you for being so understanding. I'll let you know as soon as I hear anything, or if he returns to town." Becca bit nervously on her bottom lip. She still needed to ask about that darn ball before she left. "Charlene, I hesitate to ask, but have you given any more thought to how James and I can attend the WAL charity ball?"

"It would be so easy if you were a member, but of course that can't happen until next year. Is there a reason you're so interested in attending this year?"

"Actually, yes. I've been told the Delafields are donating a painting for the charity auction and I would very much like to bid on it."

Charlene's eyes opened wide with delight. "Oh, the Delafields are such lovely people, I'm really not surprised. Which painting is it? Do you really plan to make a donation to the foundation?"

My goodness, how did one keep up with Charlene? "Yes, the Delafields are lovely, they're donating the Magic Flute by V.W. Stevenson. And, yes, I suppose I want to make a donation, by bidding on that painting." She hoped Charlene hadn't misunderstood. This wasn't about buying her way into the ball, this was about getting that particular painting.

"That may change things. Maybe I should talk to Caroline Beaumont. She may be able to help. She's in charge of the donation committee."

"I'm not sure I understand. How do you think she might help?" The last thing Becca wanted was to get trapped into making a donation in order to attend the ball. Where would she get the extra money? As Rebecca Wheland, she had a reasonable amount of money in her account to use at the auction, but it wasn't enough to *buy* her way into the ball and bid on the painting.

"If she knows you want to purchase a painting that has already been donated for the event, I'm sure she'll help get you an invitation. I'll just need to speak with her."

Becca's hopes began to soar.

Charlene continued, "Unfortunately, that won't be until after Thanksgiving. She's gone to New Haven to be with her husband's family."

And just as quickly, her hopes dropped. This meant she would have to wait another week or more before she would know for certain if Mrs.

Beaumont could help. Becca forced herself to keep smiling and tried to look on the bright side. She may not be any closer to getting the coveted invitation, but at least hope was in sight. Until she knew otherwise, she would hold onto that glimmer of hope until it was thoroughly extinguished.

"Charlene, if you could do that for me, I would be ever so grateful. It means a lot to me to attend the ball. I'm so looking forward to getting that painting. Just imagine how splendid it would look hanging in our parlor." Becca relaxed ever so slightly. Hopefully, she was one step closer to completing her assignment. "You've just made my day."

Charlene beamed proudly. "Think nothing of it. It's what I do best, making other people happy." She took another sip of her tea before she continued. "It's hard to believe there's less than a week until Thanksgiving. How does the time get away from me? I have the lady's tea on Saturday, and the opera on Monday, it all seems too much."

Becca felt a tinge of envy. She wished she had such a busy social schedule. "If anyone can handle it, Charlene, I'm sure you can."

"Aren't you kind? You really should come to the tea on Saturday. It's nothing big, only a handful of ladies." Charlene began ticking them off on her hand. "Let me see, there will be Julia Perry, Eliza Rutherford and of course Amy Sterling and her sister Myra. She's Mrs. Archer now, you know. I was so happy for her when she met Donavan, so much better than George Barclay, God rest his soul. Emma Sands was going to come, but she sent her regrets today so I've room for one more. You will come, won't you?"

Ah, so that was it. For a brief moment, Becca had felt honored to be invited, but just as quickly, she realized she was only being invited because Miss Sands had canceled. Still, an opportunity to mingle with the ladies at tea was too appealing to refuse simply because she was a last-minute replacement.

"This is rather short notice, but yes I believe I can make it. What time will it start?"

"Two o'clock. That isn't a problem for you, is it?"

"Two o'clock will be fine." Becca made a mental note to write this all down in her journal.

"Wonderful, I'm glad that's all settled. Now all I have to think about is the opera on Monday. Everyone will be there for the grand reopening. I expect we'll see you and James. I know he rarely attends, but it is opening night for the season."

Did James have tickets to the opera? If he did, this was news to her. He hadn't mentioned any plans to attend the opera, but if there was any way she could arrange it, she wanted to go. She had never seen a New York opera before and didn't want to miss this chance. "James has been so busy lately, we've hardly had a moment to discuss it, but I see no reason why we shouldn't be there." Especially if they already had tickets, and from what Charlene said, it sounded as if they did.

"Splendid. Steven and I will make a point of coming by to visit your box during the intermission. We'll be attending with Steven's parents. Mr. and Mrs. Shepard donated heavily toward the interior reconstruction after that dreadful fire, and since this is the grand reopening I'm sure it will be quite impressive."

James had box seats! This was getting better and better by the minute. "That sounds wonderful."

"Marvelous. Of course, I expect we'll see you at the big party afterwards. I'm grateful Mrs. Shepard is hosting and not me, I really couldn't add another event to my list. You will drop by, won't you? I know Mr. and Mrs. Shepard are looking forward to seeing you and James."

"I'll talk to James, but I'm sure we will," Becca said, trying to restrain her excitement. Opera and an after-theater party, she could hardly wait.

From the anxious look on Charlene's face, Becca could tell it was time for her to leave. "My goodness, I've kept you much too long. You must have a hundred things to do besides sitting here chatting the day away. I really should be going."

"Rebecca, you're such a dear to understand. Don't forget, tea on Saturday."

Charlene gave her a quick hug before seeing her to the front door. Becca stepped cheerfully down the front stairs feeling better than she had in days. There was finally a light in the dark tunnel she'd been traveling through, and not only that, it looked as if she was going to the opera. This was a very good day indeed.

It was easy to see why Charlene was so well liked; she presented an unending persona of optimism and good will. While Becca wasn't completely enamored with her sister-in-law, there was much she could learn from her, and how to be a respected member of high society was one of them. All she needed to do was watch, listen, and learn.

~*~

When Becca returned home, she went straight to her room to change. While she waited for Katie to come and assist her, she took a moment to plop on the settee in her sitting room to relax, although since she was wearing a corset, she wasn't truly able to plop. It was more of a relaxed lean, but still, she felt relieved. She had made more progress today than ever before. Not only did she have fairly high expectations for getting an invitation to the ball, she felt she had also made significant gains in securing Charlene as a friend and confidant. She had to give her sister-in-law credit. Whatever past blunders Rebecca had committed, Charlene seemed able to look past them in the name of family. In her eyes, Charlene was a real friend.

She had only been relaxing for a moment when Katie entered the room.

"You called, Ma'am?"

"Yes, I need you to help me change into something more comfortable. Let's go with the skirt and blouse I picked out this morning."

"Certainly, Ma'am, as you wish." Katie immediately went to the walk-in closet to get the outfit.

As the maid spread out the skirt and blouse on her bed, it occurred to Becca that the servants always knew what was going on in a house. Maybe Katie knew if James planned to attend the opera. She wondered how she could bring up the subject without making it obvious she didn't know what her husband was planning.

"Katie, Charlene reminded me about opening night at the opera on Monday. Do you know if Mr. Jaffray has his tux ready?"

"Yes, Ma'am, he informed Mr. Jenkins today. It's already been cleaned and brushed."

This was wonderful news. This meant they were going to the opera. Her heart did a little skip, but she tried to remain nonchalant. "I suppose I should pick something to wear and not wait until the last minute. Will you be so good as to pull out a few of my nicer gowns so I can decide?"

111

"It would be my pleasure. I was hoping you wouldn't wait until the last minute. It makes it so much easier if any repairs are needed. Hems have a nasty way of coming undone."

That was probably because they were always being dragged along the ground. She took a seat near the window and waited while Katie went to the separate closet set aside to hold the fancy dress gowns. One by one, her maid brought out half a dozen gowns for her inspection, each more beautiful than the last. Rebecca must have loved to shop and spend money on expensive clothes. No wonder her father wanted to pass her on to a husband to take over her expenses.

Thinking about expenses reminded her of the ledgers sitting in her desk in the library. "After this, I really should spend some time in the library going over the household accounts," she said aloud.

Katie looked up from what she was doing. "I believe Mrs. Granger has taken the ledger to update it with this week's shopping list."

It was a little disconcerting to learn the cook had taken it upon herself to retrieve the ledger from her desk, but Becca said nothing about it. "Oh, yes, that's right. As I recall, she places her orders on Tuesday and Friday."

"Correct, Ma'am. I heard her say she was already behind since she had to make a temporary list for her orders on Tuesday."

"I'm sorry to hear that, but I've been too busy. It seems every time I get started, something comes up. Please ask Mrs. Granger to return the ledger when she's finished. Maybe I'll have time this weekend."

"Yes, Ma'am," Katie said as she laid another gown across the bed. "What do you think?"

This wasn't going to be easy, there were so many beautiful gowns to choose from, but she shouldn't be surprised. After all, these belonged to Rebecca Wheland; the woman had grown up rich.

In the end, she decided on a midnight blue gown with black lace and jet-black beading, and a rosette trim along the bottom edge. With Katie's assistance, she also picked out the necessary accessories and jewels to accompany the gown. Now all she needed was for James to come home and confirm they would be attending the opera together.

~*~

Becca paced aimlessly through the house, waiting for James to come home, anxious to confirm their plans to attend the opera. Each room on this level connected to the next through wide and tall pocket doors. When these doors were slid open, they created one immense space, allowing her to meander unimpeded through the front parlor and library at the front of the house to the central hall, with its access to the grand stairwell, then on to the dining room, and finally to the grand salon at the back of the house. She paused in the grand salon to admire the small garden courtyard it overlooked before retracing her steps back to the central hall to begin her round again.

As she wandered through the rooms, she noted how this design was particularly useful if the house should be put into service to host a large party, and wondered if she would ever be here to see such a day. She could almost picture the space festooned with dozens of flowers, mostly white roses, and filled with finely dressed guests happily enjoying the evening as they sipped champagne while classical music played softly in the background by hired musicians. Already, the mansion was beginning to feel more like home, a great departure from her first impression when she felt like an impostor who did not belong here.

Before taking this assignment, she had been poor Becky Sue Dobson, working as an entry level bank teller, living in a cold, small two-room flat in Brooklyn. Now she was married to a wealthy man, living in a big house in Manhattan with over a dozen rooms, servants to tend to her needs, and fine clothes to wear. Neither the old Rebecca nor Becky Sue had been happy with their lot in life, but she was Becca now and planned to do things differently. Often, it seemed as if the ones with all the riches didn't appreciate how good their life was, but she'd been poor, and being rich was so much better. Becca couldn't change the past, but she could certainly do her best to ensure a successful future.

When it came to a choice of partners, at least James had only ignored Rebecca, he hadn't abused her as Ralph had. Ralph had been jealous, disrespectful, and emotionally controlling. As Becky Sue, she had foolishly fallen for his false words of love and protection. As Becca, she was much smarter because of her past experiences.

James had been born into a glittering world of entitlement and luxury and yet he strived to achieve more. He had been willing to take on Stanton Wheland to ensure his family's place in society went unharmed by financial ruin, and from what she could see, he was a knowledgeable businessman. He wouldn't be working with the venerable J.P. Morgan if he weren't. With James, it seemed the more she knew him, the more he fascinated her.

He could be cold and nearly cruel, but he could also be kind and seductive, as she had seen the night he kissed her. That had been nice, better than nice, until he so abruptly put a stop to it. He also wasn't a pushover, nor was he unreasonably mean. Unexpected as it was, Becca realized she found him intriguing, and a bit of a challenge. It didn't hurt that she also found him attractive, handsome, and seductively appealing, but that was all beside the point.

While everything wasn't roses and songbirds, at least not yet, Becca had a hopeful feeling of optimism. If all went well, she might finally have the ways and means to make her life better. She knew who she had been, and who she didn't want to be. It was time for a kinder, more considerate Rebecca Wheland Jaffray to emerge, and Becca was just the person to be her.

Interestingly, Becca could easily relate to the poor departed soul. Her own mother had been a mean, screaming shrew, probably a lot like Stanton Wheland in many ways. Undoubtedly, there had been times when her mother had been kind, but those few memories were overshadowed by feelings of dread and fear every time she thought of Martha Dobson. She didn't miss her mother, but unfortunately, she couldn't shake the hold Martha had on her. Sadly, her father, a hardworking man who stood by his family, had let his wife have her way. Perhaps he saw it as a way of keeping the peace, but Becky Sue saw it as a weakness. She had been Papa's favorite, his sweet, little girl, and she had loved him dearly. But when she left home, Becca had promised herself she would never be like her mother, nor would she ever marry a man who couldn't stand up for himself. The man of her dreams had a backbone.

That helped to explain why she had been so enamored with a man like Ralph. From the moment she met him, he seemed like a man who took charge of any situation. However, she soon learned he was really the type of a man who liked to order her about with an appalling lack of respect.

But not anymore, and never again. Never again would she let herself be overshadowed by an overbearing and controlling man such as Ralph had been. If James proved to be such a man, she would do much as Rebecca had done, and make her escape. Although unlike Rebecca, she had no intentions of losing her life over him.

She had probably made her twentieth turn through the rooms when she heard the front door open. She rushed to the grand stairwell and listened. James was home. She was tempted to run down the stairs to greet him, but she didn't want to appear too eager. It was best to remain calm. From experience, she knew he would either ascend the stairs and make his way to his office or he would go to the front parlor on the first floor near the front of the house. She waited and listened. Sure enough, after handing off his coat and hat to Jenkins, he was coming up the stairs. Becca stepped away from the stairwell and waited.

"I thought I heard you come home," she said and he emerged on the landing. "How was your day?"

He eyed her skeptically. "Were you waiting for me?"

"I would like to speak with you. Shall we go into your office? Would you like me to pour you a drink?"

"What's this about, Rebecca?"

She went to him and linked her arm in his as they walked into the richly paneled room. "Charlene reminded me today about the grand reopening of the Metropolitan Opera House and I wanted to discuss our plans for Monday." She wanted to sound as if she fully expected them to attend together, which she very much hoped they would.

"You needn't worry. I've already informed Jenkins to have my tux made ready."

"Yes, I know. I've already picked out my gown." Turning to him, she asked again, "Did you want that drink or no?"

James declined with a shake of his head and they each took a seat on the settee near the hearth. He leaned back, looking relaxed, and rested an ankle atop his knee.

"What time to you think we should plan to leave?" she asked, trying to sound upbeat.

"The opera starts at eight-thirty. We'll need to leave by eight if we hope to arrive by the rise of the curtain. The streets around the opera house will be packed."

"I'm sure you're right. It is the grand reopening, I should like to arrive on time. I'm sure you know, Charlene also expects us to make an appearance at the Shepard's for their after-theater party."

"She has reminded me several times, but why are we discussing this now?"

"You must admit, James, we haven't had much time to discuss this before. I know we've had our differences, but you really must forgive me. I haven't been myself lately." She almost laughed at the truth of her last statement.

James sighed. "I never know what to expect from you these days. One minute you seem intent on developing some meaningful friendship, and the next you're up in arms."

"I wouldn't exactly say I was up in arms, but yes, I suppose there were a few things I needed to get off my chest. I apologize for giving you the brunt of my sour mood." He was right, her life these days was full of highs and lows, and too many dark moments of doubt.

"Do you feel better now?"

She contemplated his question. Did she feel better? "There were things that needed to be said, but no, I didn't handle it well, if that's what you mean. Please accept my apology."

"Accepted. And I apologize for falsely seducing you." There was a hint of a smile on his lips. Dang, but he had nice lips. "I suppose I can't blame you. It feels as though we've been walking on thin ice around here. I'm not sure I liked it better when you avoided me, but I certainly don't want to fight with my wife every other night."

"There's something we can agree on," she said smiling brightly. Maybe they were making progress.

"Are we to proceed as friends?" he asked, sounding somewhat hopeful.

"I would *love* for us to be friends."

James seemed amused by her comment. His brow rose ever so slightly and she detected a hint of a smile. Becca wondered if she could actually get him to laugh, and decided it would be her goal for the night. If she couldn't get him to laugh, she at least hoped for a look of honest contentment, and perhaps a smile.

"What do you suggest?" James asked.

"We could start out by being nice to each other. Tell each other how our day went. Perhaps share interesting little stories. Or make plans to attend events together."

As she studied his face, she noticed how a lock of his wavy chestnut hair curled over his ear. She suddenly felt an urge to reach out and tuck it behind his ear, or smooth back the thick wave that fell over his forehead, but she kept her hands to herself. James looked as if he had gone a few too many days from his last trim and she feared if she drew attention to his wayward locks he might be reminded to see his barber. Since she rather liked this scruffy version of her stiff, upper crust husband, she wasn't sure she wanted him to return to his strict grooming standards. Then again, she couldn't imagine James Jaffray looking anything other than handsome and uniquely attractive. How strange to think she was actually attracted to this man who had suddenly become her husband.

James shook his head and folded his arms across his chest. "Hmm, I must confess, I cannot think of one interesting story I have to tell. I went to work, saw Pierpont, Sloane, and Phelps and shared a cigar at lunch with Pierpont. I swear, he can smoke a dozen of them a day. One was enough for me."

Becca laughed lightly, hoping it didn't sound too forced. "See, that was an interesting story. I didn't know J.P. Morgan liked to smoke so many cigars."

"He's like a blasted chimney. He must keep his valet busy trying to get the smell out of his clothes."

"I wonder how Mrs. Morgan stands it. Let me state for the record, here and now, thank you, James, for not smoking, especially not in the house. Do you know what that does to the drapes? I never could stand to spend more than ten minutes in my father's office because of that smell. It never left."

His smile widened, it almost qualified as full-fledged, but not quite. She was nearly halfway to her first goal. "I've been there, I know. Does he never open the windows?"

"I couldn't say; that was one room I tried to avoid, especially if he was in it." Becca paused for a moment and shook her head. Strangely, it almost felt as though she were relaying a memory from the past, instead of only imagining Rebecca's life. Becca's connection to the ill-fated woman seemed to grow stronger each day, as if she were starting to remember things only the real Rebecca could have known. Such an idea was nonsense, and yet strangely compelling.

"I guess I've tried to avoid several things in my life, you being one of them. But not anymore. I avoided standing up to my father until it was too late. I avoided thinking about marriage and hoped the need for it would go away, but that didn't work very well, did it? Father was strongly against me being a spinster and living in his house for the rest of my life. That's why he forced me upon you." Substitute Martha Dobson for Stanton Wheland and it was all the same. Her mother's constant fighting and yelling had driven her out of the house the moment she turned eighteen. That was when she had gotten involved with Ralph, her first big mistake.

James reached out and touched her hand. "I know, Rebecca, I'm sorry."

His acknowledgment of her pain warmed her heart. "And worse of all, I avoided you when you might have been my one true friend in all of this. Oh my, I have a lot to answer for, don't I?"

"No more than I."

She smiled demurely and leaned forward, beckoning him close with her finger. He leaned forward, closing the distance between them. "Want to be co-conspirators?" she said in a hushed voice. She caught a whiff of his scent; clean, musky, and strongly masculine. She breathed deeply, as deeply as her corset would allow.

He eyed her warily. "How do you mean?"

"My father thinks he has damned us both, if you'll pardon my use of such a word."

His smile broke free. Score one point for her. "Agreed."

"I say we prove him wrong by attending the opera together appearing as if we're a happily married couple. He'll surely be there. Wouldn't it just drive him mad to know his plan to ruin our lives isn't working?"

James threw back his head and laughed. "My God, Rebecca. I like the way you think."

Final score, she had reached her goal in more ways than one.

"Do you think really think we can fool him?" he asked when he had stopped laughing.

Becca felt a wide smile breaking across her face. "I don't see why not. It shouldn't be too hard. You can stay by my side and I'll gaze up at you from time to time with loving eyes, not too much of course, we wouldn't want to overdo it."

She was good at pretending, she had done it for most of her adult life. For years she had pretended Ralph's disrespectful and controlling ways didn't matter, until she finally left him. And then, after she had driven off the road on that cold, rainy night, she had agreed to pretend to be someone else to satisfy her contract with Jules. Certainly, she could pretend to be part of a loving couple. Especially with a man she was growing fonder of each day.

"I think you may have a plan," James said with a look of approval.

"So, we have a deal?" Becca asked, thrilled to her core.

"We have a deal." James reached out and shook Becca's hand.

For the first time since she took this assignment, Becca felt a measure of hope for success. For once, it wasn't only about buying the painting Jules wanted. Thanks to her budding relationship with James, it felt as though she had something to look forward to besides worrying about the charity ball or the painting or Jules Vanderzeit. All of that was still there, but they need not be the only, all-consuming issues in her life as she had thought them to be.

As Becca slipped comfortably into bed later that night, she felt more hopeful than she had in days, and for that, she was grateful.

CHAPTER 7

The cakes and cookies were warm and tasty, the tea hot, and the gossip even hotter. Becca could hardly believe her ears to hear what these polite ladies of society deemed fit to talk about. Mostly it was about other women of their social set, what they wore, and which parties they attended. Barely a word was exchanged about current events in politics or the world at large. Money, and those who control it, was simply not discussed in polite company.

She supposed it should come as no surprise. Whenever a group of privileged, catty women gathered in one room, they were bound to let their claws out. It seemed this group of young women was not much different from their modern counterparts. Heaven bless the rich and idle housewives of New York, although to be fair, of those present, Julia Perry and Amy Sterling were not married.

"It's beyond me why these newcomers insist on pushing their way into our fashionable circle," Eliza Rutherford was saying. "We've all known each other for ages, why should they think we are in want of new friends?"

"Oh, please, dear Eliza, I can still remember when the Vanderbilts were considered undesirable outsiders, and look at them now. Everyone falls over themselves to get an invitation to one of Alva's parties," Amy Sterling rebuked. Of the ladies gathered at Charlene's Saturday afternoon tea, Becca liked Amy and her sister, Myra Archer, the best. They seemed the most practical and interesting of the group. Both sisters were tall, thin, blonde, and very pretty. The sisterly resemblance was striking, although Amy was slightly taller, and in Becca's opinion, the more interesting of the two.

"Alva is different and you know that," Mrs. Rutherford shot back. "Besides, the Vanderbilts have been in Manhattan for generations, it simply took time for them to earn their place."

"You mean *spend* enough to earn their place." Brows were raised, but Amy Sterling stood by her comment. Even Becca knew it wasn't polite to mention money.

"Still, newcomers or not, it doesn't explain why they should strive to be part of a group that is not interested in accepting them." Eliza offered her comment before taking another sip of tea, her face pinched in an expression of contempt.

"My goodness, Eliza, your family has lived in New York on the same street for decades. I'm sure you take it for granted you belong here, but regardless of what you may think, Manhattan does not stop at Washington Square. All the fashionable families are building homes north, toward Central Park," Myra said, apparently in support of her sister.

"I rather agree with Eliza," Miss Julia Perry said, speaking up. "If we do not maintain our elite status, what is to become of us? Those beyond our inner-circle must content themselves with merely the appearance of exclusivity, for they shall never truly have it."

Mrs. Eliza Rutherford nodded adamantly in agreement. She plucked a cake from her plate, brought it to her mouth, sniffed and then set the cake back down, apparently changing her mind.

Becca caught Amy rolling her eyes over her teacup, and nearly laughed.

"Our exclusivity, as you call it, is wholly self-designated, and subject to change if enough money is spent," Miss Sterling commented. "Just look at the Metropolitan Opera House as an example. Half of us here would not be attending the opening night on Monday if the old Academy of Music still existed. It was simply too small to accommodate all the truly important people."

As she listened to them go on and on about their family trees, it hadn't taken long for her to peg Mrs. Eliza Rutherford and Miss Julia

Perry as snooty supporters of the old Knickerbocker society and its founding families. From what Becca could decipher, while Mrs. Rutherford and Miss Perry fully approved of Charlene, it was a bit of a comedown for them to be attending this tea with Amy Sterling and Myra Archer even though Charlene had indicated the Sterlings were an old and respected family of New York. Judging merely by the clothes they wore, Amy and Myra were also quite wealthy.

If confession was good for the soul, Becca would have to admit, she didn't like Mrs. Rutherford all that much, but she was Charlene's friend, so Becca kept her thoughts to herself and quietly played nice. For the most part, she let them have their say as she listened, taking it all in as she nibbled on her second pecan cookie. My, but they were good! She needed to be careful or she would overeat, and that would not bode well in front of these women.

Though Mrs. Rutherford and Miss Perry hadn't said enough to confirm whether or not they approved of Rebecca Wheland Jaffray, if questioned, she would guess they did not. Undoubtedly, Stanton Wheland and his family were viewed as one of these offensive newcomers. The more Eliza and Julia disagreed with Amy and Myra, the more Becca approved of the Sterling sisters. Thankfully, it seemed Charlene did not share Julia's and Eliza's opinions, as she was notably gracious to all of her guests.

"Speaking of opening night at the opera, am I correct to think you are all planning to attend the Shepards' party afterwards?" Charlene chimed in.

Mrs. Rutherford seemed to welcome the change of conversation and finally smiled, losing her foul look of contempt. "Of course, dear. Bernard and I wouldn't think of missing it. The Shepards host such elegant parties, always dignified and proper. We've never been disappointed." She turned to smugly smile at Amy as if to make her point.

Amy seemed not to care.

"I quite agree," Miss Perry said, siding once again with her self-designated exclusive friend. "Do you recall Mrs. Babcock's party last spring? They actually had monkeys at the event, if you can believe that."

Several of the women giggled with their hands covering their mouths.

"For myself, I'm quite interested in seeing what gowns will suddenly appear from the trunks sent over from Worth," Charlene said with a delighted grin. "We were denied an opening night last year because of that nasty fire, such a disappointment. Fortunately, we can thank Mr. Carnegie for building his new music hall in time to give us a season or I hate to think what we might have done for entertainment."

"Charlene, there's no denying Charles Worth is an amazing dress designer, but this season I obtained my gowns from Madam Osborne," Amy informed her hostess. "I discovered her a few years ago. She is simply the best in all of New York. She's much more aware of our fashions here."

"I quite agree, I have visited her salon several times," Charlene countered, "but still, Amy, even you must agree, we are all anxious to see what Mr. Worth has produced."

"One can always tell a Worth gown." Mrs. Rutherford brushed a hand across her skirt. "Nearly all of my dresses and gowns come from Worth."

Could she sound any haughtier?

"When was the last time you were in Paris?" Myra asked, referring to where the famous designer lived. "Was it one or two years ago?"

Mrs. Rutherford declined to answer and turned her attention to Miss Perry. "Have you an escort for the evening?"

"I will be attending with my father and Mr. Leggott," Julia answered.

"Leonard Leggott?" Amy and Myra said in unison.

"Yes." Miss Julia Perry looked less than sure of herself. "Is there a reason you should ask?"

"Not at all," Myra said with a look of reassurance.

"Bravo for you. He's very handsome," Amy said, smiling with approval.

The sisters exchanged a knowing glance; Becca wondered what secret they shared.

"What about you?" Charlene turned her attention to Becca. "What will you be wearing on Monday?"

For a moment, Becca froze. Up until now, she had been content to sit on the sidelines, watching the women engage in their verbal sparring. Now it felt as if all eyes were on her. Thankfully, she recalled seeing the dressmaker label on the gown she had chosen to wear. "I must admit, I'll be wearing a gown from Worth."

"I'm sure it will be splendid," Amy said, coming to her defense. "However, if you ever wish to visit Madam Osborne, please let me know. I would be happy to make an introduction."

"That's very kind of you." Becca smiled kindly at her newfound friend. "I shall keep that in mind."

"Now that you're married, you must have James take you to Paris. It's such a shame you weren't able to go after your wedding." Charlene sighed heavily as if it had been the end of the world.

"It wasn't a good time for him to get away, as I'm sure you know," Becca said, defending her husband. Apparently, Charlene was not aware of James's tenuous financial status. Regardless of the lack of marital bliss shared by James and his newly married wife, she doubted James had the surplus funds needed to make a trans-Atlantic crossing, much less to take his new bride shopping for expensive gowns. Her brother must have chosen to hide his monetary losses from his family, and the subsequent loan from Wheland that had saved his business at the cost of his bachelorhood.

"You may be right, he has kept himself busy," her sister-in-law chirped happily. "But you must admit, you're both due for a visit to France."

"I'm sure James will make the proper arrangements when the time is right." While Becca would openly welcome trips to Paris or anywhere else in Europe with James, she had no reason to believe she would be around long enough to enjoy such a benefit.

"Perhaps next year, when you celebrate your first wedding anniversary," Charlene offered, sounding hopeful.

"Perhaps," Becca agreed, and let it go at that.

It was nearing four o'clock, and as if on cue, the other four ladies began to say their good byes, thanking Charlene for a lovely afternoon.

"We must do this again soon," Amy said as the women made their way to the front entrance hall. She reached out and gave an affectionate hug to Mrs. Rutherford, who was a good four inches shorter than Miss Sterling.

"It will be at my house next time," Myra chimed in as she accepted her coat from Charlene's butler.

"It will be my pleasure," Miss Perry confirmed. With a bright smile, she accepted a kiss to her cheek from Myra and gave one in return.

"I wouldn't think of missing it," Mrs. Rutherford agreed. She paused as a footman helped her on with her cloak. "Can we count on seeing you again soon, Mrs. Jaffray?"

"Oh, yes, Rebecca," Amy agreed, "you really must plan to join us. I have so enjoyed your presence."

Becca's eyes darted from one woman to the other, wondering where this display of friendship had been all afternoon. "Certainly. I shall await your invitation."

Charlene leaned close to Becca and whispered, "Can you stay a moment longer, dear sister?"

Becca nodded. "Of course, if you wish."

After the other ladies had departed, Charlene guided Becca back into the parlor. "I was right to have invited you today. Emma and I are usually united in our opinions and I am happy to see I had you on my side. I doubt I could have made it through the day if I had to face them all on my own."

Becca hadn't thought she had taken anyone's side, or even done much to provide assistance other than her silent moral support, but if Charlene believed that to be true, she had no desire to correct her perception. "Might I ask, do Amy and Myra usually get along well with Miss Perry and Mrs. Rutherford?"

"Why yes, we're all splendid friends. I understand it may not always look that way, but take no mind of their sparring. It wouldn't be any fun if they didn't test each other's nerves."

"I'm so glad you cleared that up for me," Becca said, still feeling a bit confused.

It must have shown on her face. Charlene added, "My job is to keep them civil, and your quiet presence helped me tremendously. You were right not to take up with one pair or the other. Neither would have forgiven you."

It seemed her best course of action had been to keep her thoughts to herself after all. What was that old saying? When in doubt, to avoid looking the fool, it's best to remain quiet or risk proving it's true.

She smiled brightly and gave Charlene a hug. "Thank you so much for inviting me today. I truly have enjoyed myself."

"You're quite welcome, it was my pleasure. It's what I do best, make other people happy."

Becca departed from Charlene's, feeling the day had been a greater success than she had dared to imagine.

~*~

James once again agreed to attend Sunday services at Grace Episcopal Church with Becca. When she made her request upon returning from Charlene's tea on Saturday, James had acquiesced without a word of disagreement, almost as if he had expected her to ask. Becca hoped their presence at a highly respected church community could benefit their standing in society. After the encouraging reception she had received at Charlene's tea, Becca felt it was her duty to do all she could to improve their place with Manhattan's elite, especially if she had any hope of obtaining an invitation to the ball, as she needed. Many of the most fashionable people of the city attended Grace Church and besides assisting in her assignment, such connections would surely help James deepen his business contacts with all the right people.

She also hoped this simple show of unity would help to strengthen her connection with James. Merely walking into the grand cathedral with him at her side, with its beautiful stained-glass windows and soaring vaulted ceiling, infused her with a sense of calm and a feeling of hopeful expectations. Listening to the joyful singing of the choir made it easier to believe everything was going to be all right.

Upon their arrival, Becca had purposefully chosen seats on the other side of the church from Mr. and Mrs. J.P. Morgan, but as they exited the crowded building, there was no polite way to avoid them. Becca wondered if Pierpont would stop to greet James. Most likely, Frances Morgan had already discussed Becca's recent visit with her husband, and knowing that Mr. Morgan had encouraged his wife to shun her still hurt bitterly.

Becca told herself Mrs. Morgan's set-down shouldn't sting so badly, after all it was directed at Rebecca Wheland, not her. But she felt so deeply connected to the woman she had replaced, and so filled with compassion for the way she was perceived, the slight felt personal. Knowing she wasn't the person Mr. and Mrs. Morgan believed her to be, Becca quickly decided she would be neither friendly nor cold, but merely civil. She would treat them with the same affable respect she would wish for herself.

Becca had read recently in the papers that J.P. Morgan was a staunch supporter of the Episcopal Church and contributed heavily to its building fund. Perhaps her attendance with James would weigh in her favor. She certainly hoped so, but she braced herself for the encounter, briefly squeezing James's arm before she forced herself to relax.

"Jaffray," Pierpont's voice boomed, "two Sundays in a row? Does this mean we can expect to see you here more often?"

"It's too soon to tell, but yes, it seems my wife wishes to make a habit of this church-going business." James tipped his hat to Pierpont's wife. "Good day to you, Mrs. Morgan."

"That's what our wives are for, to keep us in line." Mr. Morgan glanced with approval at his wife before he continued, greeting Becca with a simple acknowledgement. "Hello, Mrs. Jaffray." No tip of his hat.

Mrs. Morgan simply nodded, no other greeting.

Becca met their gaze squarely and greeted them cordially. "Good day, Mr. Morgan, Mrs. Morgan. What a pleasure to see you again." Her smile felt forced and her stomach muscles clenched. She hoped this encounter would not last long. Certainly not long enough for Mrs. Morgan to say something rude that might disgrace her in front of James.

"By this time next week, I expect you will be on your way to London," James said affably.

James looked at her as if expecting her to add to the conversation.

Feeling awkward, but hoping to make James happy, Becca pasted on a smile and said in her most pleasing voice, "I hope your voyage is a safe one. I understand Trans-Atlantic crossings can be rough this time of year. May you be blessed with favorable weather for your voyage." Having fulfilled the minimum requirements of politeness, she looked off into the distance, wishing they would move on.

"How kind of you," she heard Mrs. Morgan say.

Meeting her gaze, Becca gave her a polite nod. It was more than she had expected from the woman who had disapproved of her only days before.

One glance at Mr. Morgan let Becca know he was taking this all in. His look of smug satisfaction led her to believe he supported his wife in her rejection of her. When he turned to address James, his expression was all business. "I don't like to talk shop on the Sabbath, but I have some final details I'd like to discuss," Morgan said. "Can you be in my office tomorrow?"

127

"I'll be there first thing, say eight o'clock. Will that work for you?" James looked slightly bewildered, as if this summons to Morgan's office was unexpected.

"I'll see you then." Mr. Morgan tipped his hat to them both and escorted his wife down the street to where their carriage awaited them.

Relieved that the encounter had gone as well as it did, Becca headed off with James to locate their coach and driver. It could have been so much worse if Mrs. Morgan had decided to embarrass her in front of James. Instead, thankfully, she had been graciously civil.

"What was wrong with you back there?" James asked the minute they had settled into their own carriage.

So he had noticed. It was probably best if she told him about her visit with Mrs. Morgan. If she didn't he would think her unacceptably rude. "I'm sorry I didn't say anything before, but Mrs. Morgan was less than kind when I went to call. It seems Mr. Morgan is not on good terms with my father and their dislike is passed on to me." She took a deep breath before she continued. "She refused to assist me with an invitation to the charity ball because I'm Stanton's daughter." She felt childish relaying this information to her husband, but she needed to be completely honest with him. She would hate to have him learn it directly from J.P. Morgan himself.

"You can't be serious. I know Wheland is an ass, but would they really think to take it out on you?"

"Of course they would, James. I'm guilty by association. I'm only relieved to think Mr. Morgan has not held our marriage against you. I guess, thankfully, business is business, and he must respect your opinions when it comes to working with you."

"Pierpont has never hidden the fact that he dislikes your father, but I had not believed he would set down my wife." Sounded somewhat peeved, James' furrowed brow signaled his annoyance.

It warmed her heart to hear him defending her so, but she suspected there was a time not too long ago when he would have let Rebecca be socially hanged and left out to dry without coming to her aid.

"I was going to attend a horse and carriage auction with Bernard Rutherford later today, but I shall send my regrets," James said, surprising her.

"Why would you do that?"

"You seem distraught. I don't want to leave you alone."

The idea that he would give up his entertainment to comfort her filled her with joy, but his protectiveness wasn't necessary.

"I'm perfectly fine, James. I appreciate your concern, but this is nothing I haven't experienced before." Every young girl who passed through high school had experienced being shunned, made fun of, or simply left behind by the popular girls. This was very much the same, only now she was older and better equipped to handle such slights. "I shall survive."

"I don't want my wife mistreated in public." James eyed her with a look of concern she had not seen before. It was reassuring to see how far they had come in only one week.

"Mrs. Morgan wasn't mean to me. She just didn't say very much. Thankfully, her set-down wasn't done in public. If anything, I appreciate her consideration. Plenty of women would have delighted in publicly displaying their disapproval. I can at least be grateful she spared me that disgrace." It was hard for Becca to think of Mrs. Morgan as gracious, but it was more important for James to not think poorly of Morgan's wife. The last thing she needed was for him to say anything rash to his business associate.

"You speak as if you owe her a favor."

"Not at all, but I should still treat her as I wish to be treated, with politeness. Remember, the good book says to do unto others as you would *have* them do unto you, and once in a while, I try to follow the good book." Laughing, she gave him a quirky smile, hoping to lighten the mood. She had stewed on the slight from Mrs. Morgan long enough—it had contributed to her nasty quarrel with James—she would not let it poison her thoughts any longer.

Chuckling, James seemed amused by her reference to scripture. "Are you certain you won't mind my absence this afternoon?"

"While I enjoy your company immensely, I would not deny Mr. Rutherford your companionship at the horse show. I met Mrs. Rutherford at Charlene's yesterday and would like to remain in her good graces, so let's not talk of you skipping out on Mr. Rutherford. Can I look forward to you being home in time for supper?"

"You can rely on it," he replied, looking brilliantly handsome in his Sunday suit. The twinkle in his eye made her heart swell.

"Wonderful. I shall expect a full account of your day to entertain me as we dine."

He leaned close to her in the carriage and kissed her forehead. "You've changed, Rebecca. I feel as if I am just getting to know you."

"Me too," she said, referring to their efforts to become friends.

Setting his arm across her shoulders, he continued to hold her close. "I wouldn't have expected this only a couple of weeks ago."

She leaned into his warmth, savoring his show of affection. "I'm sure there was a day in the not too distant past when you didn't expect to be married, least of all to me. Fate has an interesting way of changing the way we think, wouldn't you agree?"

"I couldn't agree more." He placed two fingers under her chin and tilted it upwards so he could see her face.

She gazed into his eyes, wondering what thoughts were swirling about in his head. Had they reached a milestone and turned a corner toward a better relationship, or was this merely a show of compassion for the slight she had received from Mrs. Morgan. When he leaned in and kissed her, gently and passionately, she had reason to believe it was the former. The taste of his lips, warm and full upon hers, made her ache for more. Palming her cheek with his hand, he kissed her with such affection, she wondered if she would get her wish. But a moment later, she felt the carriage slowing and James pulled back.

"We're home," he said as a groomsman came to open their door. "I best behave myself."

She lingered a moment longer in his arms, breathing in his manly scent—spicy with a hint of musk—before she allowed him to help her down from the carriage. "Quite right. We wouldn't want to give the neighbors something to talk about."

He chuckled again. "When did you become so witty?" James escorted her to the front door and saw her safely inside before he kissed her once again. "I'll see you later for dinner," he promised softly into her ear.

Much more of this and she would be dragging him up the stairs to one of their bedrooms. While not necessarily a bad idea, she wasn't yet ready to make such a bold move. "Go. Enjoy your afternoon. I'll be fine."

"Only if you insist." He seemed reluctant to leave.

"I insist," she nodded.

With a final peck upon her cheek, he turned and bounded down the steps to the waiting carriage.

~*~

James leaned out the window watching his home fade into the distance, thinking about his wife. Two weeks ago, when she had run off and disappeared, he had been afraid she had done something stupid, something to bring shame upon him and his family. Now he felt protective of her, ready to defend her against the cruelty of others. When had that happened? This new version of Rebecca fascinated him, something he had not thought possible, and he wondered how she managed to manifest such a change. Was it truly due to her week alone at Raven's Point as she claimed? Or had something else contributed to her transformation? Whatever the reason for her change of heart, he hoped it was here to stay and not some short-term pretense to wiggle her way up the social ladder at his expense.

Somehow, she had managed to inch her way into his life and everything he had believed to be true was being tested. He could no longer look at her as someone he had married for the good of his family. Suddenly, she had become someone he liked, someone he could even admire. It was enough to turn his world upside down. Rebecca was no longer the woman he had thought her to be. This new emerging Rebecca had charm, grit, and determination, and startling as it was, he liked it.

With stunning disbelief, he realized he was starting to appreciate his wife. When had she become different from every other woman he knew? When Rebecca had returned home from her excursion—her attempt to run away—she had seemed quite changed, a much different woman than the one he had married. This new Rebecca didn't avoid him or sulk about the house in misery. She stood up to him, and like it or not, she forced him to examine what was wrong with their marriage. While he was still learning to trust this new Rebecca, it didn't take a locomotive running him over to know how right she was.

Recently, it seemed every time he thought of her, feelings of desire snaked through his body. It started in his chest and traveled south, winding its way down to his groin until his cock was standing at attention. At first, he had denied the attraction, too stunned to believe it was possible. He still found it hard to believe he was attracted to her. Who would have seen this coming?

Yet, he wasn't fully convinced this new Rebecca was everything she pretended to be. It was too soon to believe she wouldn't return to her old familiar ways of sulking and generally making his life miserable, but for the moment, he was willing to give her the benefit of the doubt. Like any truly good speculative venture, it was often best to keep a sharp eye on this asset to see if the opportunity would pay off and prove itself worthy of additional investment.

When he returned home for dinner later that day, he found the image of a devoted wife waiting for him in the upstairs parlor. He paused for a moment at the threshold, simply observing Rebecca as she gazed into the fire warming the room, her book forgotten in her lap. She presented such a delightful appearance of domestic peace and tranquility, he hated to disturb the scene lest he discover it was only a mirage. She must have felt his presence, for she turned to look at him. For a brief second, he thought he read melancholy in her eyes, but it was quickly replaced with a look of joy, as if she were truly happy to see him.

"Did you enjoy your day?" Rebecca asked. She set aside her book on a nearby table and stood to greet him.

"It was fine enough. Rutherford has a fine eye for horseflesh." He stepped forward and kissed her lips. "But I think I shall enjoy my evening even more." It was nearly startling for him to say this thought aloud. There was a time when he hadn't thought this day would come, when he'd have a loving, attentive wife to come home to. For months, it had looked as if he and Rebecca were doomed to tolerate a loveless marriage, but now, his future with her looked brighter than ever. He took a seat next to her on the settee and she turned slightly to face him.

"Did you see anything you liked?" Rebecca asked, looking genuinely interested.

"Rutherford placed a bid on a couple of horses, but I have no need to add to my stables." He also currently lacked the funds. As it was, he needed to economize wherever possible to make his payments to Wheland and not fall behind in the rest of his business. Thankfully, he was working on a deal with one of the largest railroad companies in New York State to supply them with new railcars and equipment for their lines. If the deal went through, his financial worries would become a thing of the past.

Rebecca nodded in understanding. "Still, it's always nice to window shop, even if you are not buying. Every woman knows that."

132

"You haven't bought anything new in quite some time," he said, thinking how tightly her purse strings had been tied since her marriage to him. "Does that bother you?"

"Not at all," she said, shaking her head adamantly. "I have more than I need. Don't get me wrong, I like all my pretty little things—every woman does—but I'm happy with what I have."

James cocked his head, trying to view his wife with new eyes. Was she truly happy with her life, as she said, or was this merely a ploy to make up for her unexplained absence? Based on her actions, which he believed spoke louder than words, it would appear she was genuinely happy. It was time to give her the benefit of the doubt and meet her half way.

At the end of dinner, James regretted that he needed to spend some time in his office. Pierpont had asked to meet with him tomorrow and he wanted to be prepared. He wasn't sure what Morgan wanted to discuss but he felt it was best to go over his notes from their recent meetings to be sure he wasn't hit with a surprise. He was still working on some last-minute bookkeeping when he looked up and saw Rebecca standing in the doorway.

"Is there something you need?" he asked.

"I didn't mean to bother you, James. I know you're busy. I just wanted to stop by on my way to bed." She took a step forward into his office, but then stopped, looking stiffly uncomfortable.

"You can come in, Rebecca. I don't bite."

Laughing in response, she seemed to relax. "I merely wanted to say good night." Rushing forward, she gave him a sweet kiss on his cheek.

Her simple gesture seemed awkwardly charming; a noteworthy indication he might have underestimated her discomfort in the area of sexual intimacy. No doubt, it had something to do with why she was so reluctant to allow him back in her bedroom.

Like most young women, she was undoubtedly fearful as well as inexperienced in the ways of intimate relations between husband and wife. Their earlier unsatisfactory attempts would certainly support such a theory. He hadn't exactly forced her to consummate their marriage, but he had let her know what was expected. And she had complied, if only barely.

As she was about to leave the room, he stopped her. "Rebecca, you needn't be afraid of me."

133

Turning back, the smile she gave him seemed uncertain, and at the same time, hopeful. "That's reassuring." She hesitated a moment longer, but then continued on her way.

Rebecca had asked him to give her time to adjust to their marital union, and though it was disappointing, he supposed there was no need to push. Although at times like this, when she looked so innocently enticing, he was sorely tempted. Since her time away, she seemed so changed, he wondered if perhaps there was a well of affection he not yet tapped into.

Acutely aware that if he pressed for more, she could easily revert back into her moody, unfriendly shell, he settled for her good-night kiss on the cheek, and watched her head off to bed alone. It wasn't easy, but he told himself, it was for the best, lest he be tempted to test just how far her limits of friendship would bend.

~*~

The next morning, James had just finished his breakfast and was preparing to leave for his office when Becca met him in the downstairs hallway.

"I'm sorry I missed you. I was hoping we could have breakfast together," she said, wondering if he had time to stay and have a cup of coffee with her to discuss their plans for the opera that night.

He stopped to give her a brushing kiss, which she gladly accepted. "I have to run, I have that meeting with Pierpont this morning."

"I hope your meeting with him doesn't take too long. It's the opening night at the opera, and as unfashionable as it may be, I would like to arrive before the curtain rises."

"I expect to return with plenty of time to make myself presentable. It's the women who require half a day to prepare."

"I suppose you are right. Other than my meeting this morning with Mrs. Granger to go over the menus for the week, I plan to devote my day to shameless pampering in preparation for the gala event." Delighted with the prospect of dressing up in a fancy evening gown to attend the important social event, Becca was nearly bursting with anticipation, but she held it inside, not wishing to look silly in front of James.

"Please pass along how much I enjoyed the ham at breakfast on Saturday. It was a nice departure for our usual fare."

A happy buzz zipped through her. "Ah, so you did enjoy the ham. It was my suggestion, if I'm allowed to brag."

134

"You most certainly are," James said, looking adorably handsome. "Especially when I'm pleased by the results."

Becca reached up and straightened his tie, though it really didn't need it. She merely wanted an excuse to touch him. When she was finished, she patted his broad, muscular chest. It felt warm beneath her fingers. "There now, you look perfectly presentable."

"What would I do without you?" James kissed her again before he headed out to begin his day.

If given a chance, she could easily get used to all this kissing hello and goodbye. She felt delightfully happy, as if nothing or no one could possibly intrude on such a perfect beginning to a perfect day.

So much had changed so quickly. Could a person really turn their life around in little more than a week? Surely, she was getting ahead of herself. It was much too soon to be thinking such things. Besides, while it was important for James to accept her as Rebecca, and hopefully enjoy her company, her real reason for being here was to get an invitation to the Women's Assistance League charity ball and buy that painting for Jules so she could complete her penance.

And then what? Jules had indicated she would be sent back to resume her previous life, but she was starting to wonder if that was what she really wanted. He'd told her that if she succeeded, she would be allowed to move forward. "Onward and upward," he had said, and she had assumed he meant with her life. But she no longer had any interest in returning to her old life. She rather liked being Rebecca, or more correctly, Becca. If she succeeded in getting Jules the painting, would he let her stay here with James if she asked? At this point, she wasn't sure who she really was, but she was darn sure she no longer wanted to be Becky Sue Dobson.

After she drank the last of her tea from breakfast, Becca asked Mr. Jenkins to remind Mrs. Granger of their meeting in the library at ten o'clock. She hadn't exchanged more than a dozen words with the household cook since their first meeting a week ago. Most of their communication seemed to take place through Katie or another one of the staff, which was fine with Becca since her first encounter with Mrs. Granger had not been pleasant.

Becca was reading the latest letter from her mother-in-law when she heard the library door open. Looking up, she noticed it was a few minutes past ten. Mrs. Granger joined her in the library carrying her notebook;

however, it seemed the cook had neglected to bring the household ledger with her. Katie had assured her she had passed on her request to Mrs. Granger. And Mrs. Hewes had confirmed hearing the conversation.

"Thank you for joining me. I have a busy day, so let's get right to it," Becca said as soon as Mrs. Granger had taken her seat. "To begin, let me pass along that my husband did enjoy the ham served on Saturday. I would like to be sure we include it at least once a week."

"Hmm, that was unexpected," Mrs. Granger huffed. "I haven't included it in the menus." The cook pulled a sheet of paper from her notebook with a finely printed list of menus for the week and handed it to Becca. Her expression was one of pure defiance.

Becca narrowed her eyes. "I thought it was agreed we would prepare the menus together."

"I'm sure I told you I need to have my grocery lists ready by Tuesday to place my orders with my suppliers."

"That's why we're meeting today. On Monday." There was no excuse for Mrs. Granger to ignore her instructions, but Becca decided she had other more pressing issues to address. She didn't want to turn this weekly meeting into a fight. "Since you have gone to the trouble of making *suggestions* for what is to be served, allow me to look it over." Becca wanted to make it very clear that as mistress of this house, she would have the last say on the daily meals. She scanned the list. The woman had impressive handwriting, she would give her that.

"A might late to be making changes now," Mrs. Granger mumbled.

"You're wrong, Mrs. Granger. As mistress of this house, it is never too late for me to make changes."

"Like wanting orange juice in the dead of winter?" The cook practically sneered.

Becca ignored her sarcasm. "If my husband or I want orange juice in the dead of winter, your job is to find a vendor who can supply it. Do you understand?"

"Am I to not worry about the cost?"

"You have a duty to inform me of the cost, which is why I've asked to see the household ledger. I understand you took it upon yourself to remove it from my desk."

"I needed to update it with last week's orders. You wouldn't want me to get behind in my duties, now would you, Mrs. Jaffray."

"When you were finished, you should have put it back. Is there a reason why you didn't return the ledger when you were done?" This was obviously a battle of wills and Becca had no intention of backing down.

Mrs. Granger shrugged as if it was of little concern to her. "I knew I would need to update it again tomorrow. You seemed too busy to worry about the ledger. I didn't see when you would have the time."

There was some truth in what Mrs. Granger said, but this was not about whether or not Becca had time to review the ledger, it was about an employee doing as she was told, and respecting her authority. She considered for a moment if it was worth the battle. If she pushed too hard, she risked winning the battle only to lose the war. Becca didn't know how much longer she would be in this position and the last thing she needed was to create an unnecessary uprising in the servant's hall. In two weeks, the holiday ball would be over, and win or lose, she would probably be gone, either successfully done with her penance or off to another assignment until she could get it right. Dang, she really had no desire to go through something like this again.

But that didn't mean she should allow people to push her around or let them take advantage of her while she was here. Her simple request to look over the books and stay informed on the menus had started out as a way of fitting in and to give her something to do while she pretended to be Rebecca Wheland. Now it was about her (Becca), and her desire to be respected. She would fight this battle, and win the war. She would not let Mrs. Granger intimidate her as Ralph had done. No more would she give in to the bullying of others and their disregard for her needs and desires.

"I want that ledger back in my desk by noon tomorrow. That will give you plenty of time to update it with this week's purchases. Do I make myself clear?"

"Yes, Ma'am. I understand you perfectly." The cook stared at her unblinkingly.

"Now, I want you to add ham to the breakfast on next Saturday." Becca added a note to the finely printed list before she continued.

Mrs. Granger looked as if she were about to complain, but Becca paid her no mind and continued to scan the menus.

"Mr. Jaffray and I will not be home tonight for dinner, so no changes there. As for Tuesday and Wednesday, I would like to see more seasonal vegetables added and less squash. These meals seem heavy on starch."

Wearing these tightly cinched corsets meant she needed to watch what she ate. She made another note on the menu sheet.

Mrs. Granger looked incredulous. "Are ye planning to change every meal?"

Becca looked up and smiled kindly. "Why no, Mrs. Granger, only the ones I've mentioned. Now to continue, as you know, Mr. Jaffray and I will be at Mrs. Shepard's for Thanksgiving, so you're welcome to go ahead with Friday's meals as you've suggested." She could tell her use of the word *suggested* did not sit well with Mrs. Granger. Too bad. The woman needed to learn her place in the kitchen or find somewhere else to ply her trade. If push came to shove, she wondered if Charlene could help her find another cook. Maybe a French one, like hers.

It was time to write another letter to Eleanor Jaffray. She wanted to keep the lines of communication open with her mother-in-law in case she needed to make an urgent plea. James had handed over the most recent letter received and she had begun a rather nice correspondence with the Jaffray matriarch, though Mrs. Jaffray still hadn't said a word about her request for an invitation to the WAL Ball.

When she was done making her notes, she handed the menu sheet back to Mrs. Granger. "Please make these changes and have a copy of the menus back on my desk along with the ledger."

Mrs. Granger squared her shoulders. "Will there be anything else?"

"No, I think we're done here. You may return to your duties in the kitchen."

The cook stood to leave, looking fit to be tied.

"Oh, yes, there is one more thing, Mrs. Granger."

The cook stopped and narrowed her eyes. "Yes, Mrs. Jaffray."

"Thank you for your assistance here today. Your cooperation and service are greatly appreciated." Becca smiled graciously.

The cook looked stunned, as if she didn't know whether or not to take Becca seriously.

For the moment, Becca's work here was done.

CHAPTER 8

Once her meeting with the loathsome Mrs. Granger was concluded, the rest of the day went by in a whirl of activity. This was her first time attending such an extravagant event and Becca was over the moon with excitement as she prepared for her night at the opera. With Katie's expert assistance, Becca dressed in the exquisite midnight blue evening gown with jet-black beading. As she walked and turned, the rosette trim along the bottom hem swished with a pleasing effect. Jewels had been brought from the safe for her to wear, including stunning sapphire earrings and a matching sapphire and diamond necklace. Long three-quarter length dark blue gloves covered her hands and arms. Katie styled her hair in a lovely chignon with one long elegant ringlet draped gracefully down her neck. She hoped James would be pleased.

As she descended the stairs from her bedroom to the front reception hall, she stopped halfway down with one gloved hand on the baluster. James stood at the foot of the stairs looking wickedly handsome in his tuxedo, and the look he gave her was one of dazed admiration. As his appreciative gaze swept over her, the swarm of butterflies she'd been feeling all afternoon took flight in her belly.

"Well done, Rebecca. You look lovely." The deep, gravely texture of his voice was heart-stoppingly seductive.

"Really, James? You're not just saying that, are you?"

139

"Did you not look in the mirror?"

"Thank you, James. You look rather dashing yourself." She was happy to see he hadn't made it to the barber; his slightly too long hair was brushed back and perfectly oiled. Together, she believed they made a very attractive couple. No matter what else happened, as far as she was concerned, the night was a success.

"Have you been waiting long?" Becca asked as she walked down the last few stairs into the reception hall and sashayed up to his side, linking her arm in his.

"Not long at all, but if I had, seeing you look so beautiful makes it all worthwhile."

He was going to make her blush if he kept this up.

"Shall we be off?" he asked.

"Oh, yes. I'm very excited, aren't you?"

He gazed at her with appreciative eyes. "I usually find these events to be tedious and boring, but I have a feeling tonight will be an exception."

"I swear, Mr. Jaffray, you say the most charming things." Becca stood on her tiptoes and kissed him on his cheek.

Her show of affection earned her a smile and kiss to her hand. As James brought her gloved hand to his lips, he held her gaze. The warmth of his hand heated her skin even through the thin fabric, and the spark in his eyes sent goose bumps dancing down her spine.

Jenkins stepped forward with their evening wraps, breaking the moment. He assisted first Becca with her opera cape and then James as he donned an elegant black wool coat. A moment later they were settled in their coach and on their way.

Their carriage slowly paraded up Broadway toward the imposing site of the Metropolitan Opera House and turned on Fortieth Street to reach the covered entrance that would give them access to their box seats. If Becca had expected to be impressed by the grandeur of the building, she was somewhat disappointed. Although substantial, it lacked beauty. The severe brick Italian Renaissance exterior reminded her more of a boxy office building than a grand European opera house.

Jostling through the throngs of theatergoers, Becca did her best not to gape at the finely dressed patrons. The opera scheduled for tonight was Gounod's *Faust*, and every seat and box was expected to be occupied. Staying close to James, they climbed the sweep of crimson-carpeted stairs and maneuvered through the crowd to their box on the second tier. A maid was there to assist her and James with their coats. Each box contained a small sitting room behind the loges where the women could make final adjustments to their costume, or the men could retreat to ease their boredom with a cigar or a glass of brandy.

After taking her seat, Becca slowly scanned the crowd assembling in the first and second tiers surrounding the theater known as the Golden Horseshoe. This was the section that housed the boxes owned by the rich patrons of the new opera house. The label seemed quite fitting as the money on display would make Fort Knox envious, and those who had agreed to back this venture to earn these coveted seats were deemed the lucky ones. Tradition dictated that the ladies sat at the front of the box while the men took their seats behind. Attending the opera was as much a social event as it was entertainment and everyone understood the importance of being seen looking their best. Every lady in attendance looked her best, dressed in fine, expensive gowns, and was heavily adorned in jewels. Not a hair or thread was out of place.

Becca vividly recalled the feeling of longing she had felt as she gazed at white table-cloth restaurants and luxury hotels she could never hope to afford on her salary as she walked through the financial district on her way to work as a bank teller. To now be in the company of people who viewed those types of establishments as standard fare was more than she would have allowed herself to dream.

Several of the boxes lining the Golden Horseshoe were still empty when the orchestra began the overture, indicating the opera would soon be starting. Many of the upper crust deemed it unfashionable to arrive before the middle of the first act, but Becca couldn't resist taking one last look around before the lights were dimmed. Her gaze swept around the large room, taking it all in. When she came to one of the last boxes near the stage, she froze, her gaze held in place by the man sitting there, his eyes locked on hers.

It was Stanton Wheland. She knew him from a grainy picture Jules had once shown her. The photo hadn't done him justice. Stanton appeared elegantly handsome in his formal evening attire, an older, dignified looking gentleman with thick, grey hair that touched his collar. He reminded her of the actor Sam Elliot, although, from what little Becca knew of him, he was nothing like the thoughtful, considerate men which the great actor tended to portray.

"I see Stanton is here," James said as he sat beside her.

"You noticed him too?" She turned her attention to James. The soft lighting of the theater only enhanced his pleasing features: augmenting the sharp lines of his face, deepening the color of his chestnut brown hair, and highlighting the smooth glow of his freshly shaved skin. In Becca's eyes, there wasn't another man in the building who could hold a candle to her husband.

"A hard man to miss, wouldn't you agree?" James said with a hint of mischief in his eyes.

"Yes, even if he weren't my father." A glance back across the theater showed he had noticed them as well and was studying their box.

James leaned toward her and whispered in her ear, his breath warm upon her neck. "Shall we let the show begin?" he asked placing his arm across the back of her chair.

Dear God, did he not know the effect he had on her? "Yes, let's," she answered breathlessly, turning toward him. Was this really all for show, or was there any truth to his actions? She hoped it was the latter. She and James seemed to run hot and cold, unable to find a foundation on which to stand as the sands shifted beneath their feet. Becca wondered if with time and effort, she had a chance to change all that.

"Perhaps it would help if you laughed a little, as if you're entertained by what I'm saying," James said, still speaking in a whisper, still leaning close, warming her neck with his breath.

Becca smiled broadly and laughed lightheartedly. "I can assure you, Mr. Jaffray, I am more than entertained at this moment"

"Really? Would you care to elaborate?"

And let him know how she really felt? It hardly seemed appropriate in public. She reached up and ran her gloved hand across his cheek, wishing she could do more, knowing perfectly well such public displays of affection were frowned upon. Saved by the dimming of the lights, she pulled her hand back to rest it in her lap. "Hush now, the opera is about to begin."

"As you wish, Mrs. Jaffray." He sat back in his chair and faced forward, his thigh seductively close to hers.

Still reeling from the effect of his words, Becca turned her attention back to the stage as the curtain began to rise. She hadn't heard him refer to her as anything other than Rebecca, and not always in the kindest voice. The way he called her Mrs. Jaffray just now had her insides melting with a yearning she hadn't known she possessed. What would it be like to truly be married to this man, to truly live as husband and wife, as a happily married couple, and not simply be playing a role assigned to her? More importantly, was she willing to explore the possibilities, regardless of where it may take her?

She breathed deep, pushing those thoughts from her mind. Such notions were foolish and frivolous, she admonished herself. There was no use dwelling on what would never be. That was not why she was here. Still, in the darkness of the theater, her mind effortlessly wandered to thoughts of happily ever after, regardless of how impractical they might be.

It seemed only a matter of minutes before the opera reached its first intermission. As the house lights were turned up, Becca's thoughts returned to matters of a more practical nature.

"If you will excuse me, James, I would like to visit the ladies' dressing room," Becca said, using the proper term for the ladies' restroom.

"Certainly, my dear. While you're out, I'll get us both a drink." He stood and escorted her to the back of the box.

Before she had a chance to slip away, Stanton met them at the outer door of their salon, blocking their exit.

"Rebecca, my dear, you're looking lovely. I nearly didn't recognize you," Stanton said looking less than pleased. His eyes scanned her from head to toe, as if taking an inventory of her gown and jewels and assessing their value.

"Thank you, Father," Becca replied, trying to sound unaffected by his backhanded compliment. Mr. Wheland might not think highly of his daughter, but she was determined to remain gracious as befitting her role as James's wife.

"Jaffray." Stanton gave a nod to her husband. "I'm surprised to see you here tonight, *together*."

"It's opening night. I would think it was expected," James replied, looking less than happy to see his father-in-law standing at their door.

143

"Yes, Father, as you can see, James and I are quite enjoying ourselves. Is that why you came by? To check on your darling daughter?"

Stanton glanced from Becca to James and back again, a dark glare shadowing his eyes. "It didn't seem that way a couple of weeks ago. Seemed to me, you were ready to leave him."

Becca was appalled by his rudeness to say such a thing in front of James. "No, Father, you're mistaken. I can assure you, I couldn't be happier."

"Really? I find that hard to believe," Stanton said.

"Believe it," James said, smugly. "A lot can happen in a week or two."

"I suppose you're right. It only took one day for the market to crash and wipe out several fortunes. So, Jaffray, how are you faring these days?

Becca felt her husband relax beside her, a smile returning to his face. "Quite well, actually. Many of my investments are making quite a comeback. In fact, some are performing better than I could have predicted."

"Is that so? Does this have anything to do with your meetings with Morgan?" Stanton asked, looking smug.

James seemed unfazed by Stanton's knowledge of his business activity. "Couldn't say. Privileged information, you understand. Now, if you will excuse us, my wife and I need to step away."

Stanton was still blocking the door and for a moment, it looked as if he was not going to move. His gaze turned to Becca. "I would like a few minutes to speak with my daughter, alone."

Becca felt frozen in place. The last thing she wanted was to be alone with Stanton Wheland.

As if sensing her distress, James answered for her. "Not tonight, Wheland. Rebecca is with me."

Stanton continued to stare at her, as if he wanted to say more. It made her wonder if he suspected she wasn't really his daughter. But how could he know? From all appearances, she was Rebecca Wheland, married to James Jaffray. Finally, he nodded curtly, and stepped aside. "Perhaps we can speak later at Shepard's party," he said in a demanding tone.

Drat, she had so been looking forward to going to the after-theater party. She hoped Stanton wasn't going to ruin it for her.

"We'll be there, but it would be better if we didn't see you. Once in an evening is more than enough." James pushed past Stanton as he escorted Becca out of the room and into the rush of people making their way through the hallway.

Seeing Rebecca's father up close like that had been more unsettling than Becca had expected. She had known the father-daughter relationship was contentious—Jules had warned her—but it took seeing his hatred up close, and personally feeling his wrath, for it to fully sink in. It wasn't until she was alone in the ladies' dressing room before she could settle her nerves and feel at ease once again.

When she returned to their box to take her seat, James was already there.

"Are you all right?" he asked, looking slightly anxious.

Becca tried to look brave and smiled. "Yes, thank you for asking. I must confess, that was nastier than I had expected. It makes me feel justified for staying away from him as I have."

"You never need to see him again if it upsets you."

"Do you really mean that?"

"Of course. Why should you be exposed to his wrath? He's lost that right. You're mine now. I'll take care of you."

James had just become her hero. She had to blink away the happy tears misting her eyes. "If you keep being nice to me, I may cry, and we wouldn't want him to see that. We're supposed to be happy."

"Is this happy enough for you?" He lifted her chin with his fingers and placed a chaste but lingering kiss upon her lips. If Becca could have her way, it would never stop. She melted with the passion of his kiss, pulling back only when she heard a judgmental cough coming from a neighboring box.

~*~

The Shepard's home was ablaze with lights, decked with flowers, and crowded with merry guests. Charlene stood next to her mother-in-law and greeted them when they arrived, complimenting Becca on her hair and gown. Becca returned the favor, gushing over Charlene's exquisite blush white gown and the multiple strings of pearls draping her bodice. Through it all, Becca felt pretty and charming. Best of all, she felt welcomed.

James had stayed protectively close to her side for much of the evening, averting the threat of another unpleasant confrontation. Once

Stanton had left the party, Becca started to relax and released James to mingle with his gentlemen friends while she sought out Amy Sterling and her sister Myra. The sisters introduced her to Myra's husband, Donavan Archer, and later they caught up with Julia Perry and Eliza Rutherford, who were sitting near the punch table entertaining each other by providing running commentary on everyone in attendance.

Eventually, she made her way into the ballroom, and took a seat on one of the many chairs lining the wall to watch the dancers on the floor. Not long after, she was pleasantly surprised when she felt James's hand on her shoulder. It was a comfort to know he was there. When the music changed to a waltz, he asked her to dance. He was an excellent dancer, and in his arms, she felt as if she were floating across the floor. As she whirled around the room, shapes and colors whizzed by, but all she could see was the handsome face of the man holding her in his arms. How had she gotten so lucky?

"Are you enjoying yourself, Mrs. Jaffray?" he asked as they stepped to the music.

"More than I can say, Mr. Jaffray," Becca replied.

"You look happy."

"I am. I'm happier than I've been in quite some time." She gazed into his eyes as he swept her across the floor. "Thank you, James."

"It's my pleasure."

Knowing it hadn't always been the way, she sent up a prayer of gratitude for this moment of bliss.

When the music ended, he escorted her from the floor and stayed by her side as they watched the other dancers. A waiter passed by and he plucked two glasses of champagne from the servant's tray, passing one to her. She caught a glint of mischief in his eyes.

"Thank you, James," she said again, leaning in close to be heard over the music. "You've made me feel special, as if you're glad I'm your wife." *Maybe even proud.* She took a sip of the bubbly, enjoying the taste on her tongue.

"What makes you think I'm not?" He tucked her free hand into the crock of his elbow and began strolling with her along the edge of the room, sipping from his glass as they walked.

"Let's be honest, James, I know I haven't always made you happy. But I'm working to make it better." Becca wondered if there was an empty alcove in this vast house where they could find some privacy, but she doubted it. The place seemed filled to the brim. Becca lifted her glass in greeting to Amy Sterling as she passed by.

"I've noticed. You're doing an excellent job," James said as he too silently greeted people he knew with a nod or a raise of his glass.

His acknowledgment of her made her smile even brighter. He seemed a bit hesitant, and she could tell there was something he wanted to say. She looked at him expectantly, silently encouraging him to speak.

"Please forgive me, but I must ask, why the sudden change? It's almost as if you're a whole new person."

Becca felt her smile drain from her face as her brain whirled for something to say. Trying to ignore the beads of sweat pooling down her back, she whipped out her fan and began to wave it back and forth, the room suddenly seemed stuffy.

"Don't get me wrong," he said, picking up on her anxiety, "I like the change, but you must admit, it seems rather sudden."

She took a deep breath and gathered her thoughts, recalling what Jules had told her. Rebecca chose to feel unhappy. "To be honest, I got tired of feeling sad all the time. I finally realized that blaming you was not going to make me feel better. If anything, it made me feel worse. Once I realized I'm the only one who can control how I feel, it was easy to change, although I will admit, I continue to experience moments of doubt."

He stopped walking and pulled her to the side of the room next to a large potted palm. "Doubts? About what?"

Self-exposure was such a risky thing, but she pushed on. Maybe it was the champagne she was drinking that allowed her to speak so freely. "I worry about being accepted by society, and if I'm able to make you happy." *Or if I even belong here.*

"What about you? What will make you happy?"

"For starters, an invitation to that darn WAL ball." It was the first thing that had come to her mind, but when his expression turned stern, she knew she had said the wrong thing.

"Is that all that matters to you? Making a good impression on society?"

"No, James, that's not what I meant." She could feel his guard rising, a mask of indifference slipping into place. "It's just that we're having such

147

a wonderful time here tonight, and I was thinking how nice it would be to do this again."

"So, attending parties is what's important to you."

The way he spoke, it felt as if he had put her in a no-win situation. Yes, attending the WAL ball was important to her, she needed to get that painting, but it wasn't the only thing that mattered. "Being Stanton's daughter isn't easy. I'm sure having Wheland's daughter as a wife can't be easy for you, either. I'll admit, I think it would be easier for us *both* if we didn't need to worry about our place in society, but making you happy is far more important than any of this." She waved her hand through the air, indicating the festivity taking place around them.

"Do you really think attending these social events makes me happy?" He swallowed the rest of his champagne and set his empty glass on a nearby tray.

She removed her hand from his arm, unsure if she could face his discontent. "Right now, I don't know what to think."

"It's getting late. We should leave." James had stiffened at her side, and despite the crowded room, the air around them suddenly grew cold. He must truly be angry with her to want to take her away from the party.

"Yes, James, as you wish," she said, keeping her eyes averted. The last thing she wanted was to cause a scene. And certainly not in front of the cream of New York's high society, the very people she hoped to impress and gain their acceptance.

James guided her to the reception rooms on the first floor to gather their coats and called for their carriage. Within minutes, the gaiety of the brightly lighted house filled with merrymaking guests was left behind, replaced by cold silence filling their coach. Becca sat as far from him as possible in the limited space of the coach's interior, stiffly avoiding any show of weakness, or affection. She would neither cower nor plead for understanding. Not when James showed so little respect or consideration towards her.

His words had hurt her deeply, reconfirming he didn't trust Rebecca. And by extension, he didn't trust her. For a while she had imagined herself in a fairy tale that actually had potential for a happy ending, but this wasn't a fairy tale, this was a nightmare, and the sooner she shed her childish desires to live the life of a princess, the better off she would be. Forget about love, and trust, and respect, and all the other emotions so vital for a happy marriage. This relationship had started as a sham, and it would end the same way.

She had foolishly allowed this roleplaying to get the best of her, imagining a better life for herself. She had fooled herself into thinking she could take the place of Rebecca Wheland and prove to the world she was a better person. But she wasn't. She was still only Becky Sue Dobson, working for Jules Vandezeit, a master manipulator. He wanted a painting and she wanted atonement for an error that could never be mended.

Atonement would not come from fulfilling her assignment, nor would it come from trying to make someone else happy. She had only herself to account for. Come December eighth, after the WAL ball was over, win or lose, succeed or fail, she would be leaving this life, this temporary charade, and would return to being poor little ole Becky Sue Dobson. Rebecca Wheland was dead and Becca Jaffray wasn't real. Unfortunately, none of this was real, except for the way she felt.

~~~

James tried to temper his disappointment, but failed. Rebecca liked to say she wanted to make their marriage better, but when he had asked her what she wanted, the first thing from her mouth had been that damn invitation to the WAL ball. He shouldn't have been surprised by her answer; he should have expected it.

He didn't care one bit if Rebecca went to that damned ball or not, but it seemed the more she pushed to go, the more he wanted to push back. A part of him acknowledged he was merely being contrary for argument's sake, but he also wanted to show her who was in charge. He could get an invitation to the charity ball in a heartbeat, if he so desired. He knew all the right people to ask. If nothing else, all he needed to do was send a cable to his mother and the invitation would be at their door the next day. But he didn't. He resisted. It didn't necessarily make him feel better, but it gave him a measure of control, which he liked.

James had wanted to believe Rebecca had changed, that creating a happy marriage meant more to her than securing a high place in society, but she had proved him wrong. She was too much like her father to put love and family before prestige.

Earlier in the evening, James had encountered Wheland before he left the party, and it hadn't gone well. Speaking with Wheland never went well.

"That was a nice little *show* of affection at the opera, I'm glad to see you two getting along. You and Rebecca deserved each other," Wheland had said, none too kindly. "You provide the old, respected family name Rebecca needed to take her proper place in society and she's provided you with the financial support you need to keep her fed. Together you make a mighty fine pair."

"She wants nothing to do with you," James had insisted.

"Let me remind you, Rebecca is still my daughter; that will never change. I know she wanted to leave you, and yet here you are, by her side, putting a happy face on your marriage, as if you weren't bought and paid for. I'm your father-in-law. Get used to it."

"You're a bastard, you know that."

James had wanted desperately to hit the man, but he hadn't. He had simply walked away. Wheland was a fundamentally flawed person, a greedy, grasping, competitive businessman inclined to lie and cheat to get what he wanted. Rebecca had grown up in Wheland's household and James had found it hard to believe she had managed to cut herself away from her father's cloth. Her comment about the ball had proved him right; never trust a Wheland. They always had an agenda, they always wanted something. Wheland had wanted to marry off his spinster daughter, and Rebecca wanted to stake her place in society. In both cases, James was merely a means to an end, a tool for them to manipulate as they saw fit.

Undoubtedly, this was the real reason Rebecca had been so upset when Mrs. Morgan had refused to provide her with an invitation to the ball. When Fanny didn't jump to do her bidding, Rebecca believed she had been insulted and in return had given Fanny the cold shoulder. And to think he had actually taken her side in the matter. He should have known better.

Why should he think Rebecca Wheland was any different from all the other social climbing women who used their husband's wealth to make their mark in New York?

For the past few weeks, James had been working on a very profitable deal to provide railcars for one of the largest railroads on the east coast. He was very close to signing a contract that would secure his wealth for years to come. Although he hadn't yet shared this news with Rebecca, James was sure Stanton Wheland was aware of the negotiations. It explained why Wheland wanted to speak with Rebecca alone. No doubt, he had wanted to discuss the matter with his daughter, hoping she could confirm the rumor. Stanton and Rebecca might appear estranged, but that didn't mean Wheland wouldn't use every avenue at his disposal to garner inside information.

All things considered, he had plenty of reasons to mistrust his wife. Just because she had decided to play nice for the past week didn't mean this tiger had changed her stripes.

He stared at Rebecca as she cowered in the far corner of the carriage, avoiding contact with him, as if his mere touch might tarnish her. Did she actually think he would force his affections upon her? It seemed she had no problems flirting and accepting his kisses when they were out in public and unable to do more, but as soon as her foot crossed the threshold of his house, she would be off to her own bedroom, safely locked behind her door. Looking away, he shook his head, more disgusted with his marriage than ever before.

CHAPTER 9

Tuesday, November 28, 1893

It was nearing mid-day when Becca finally roused herself from her bed. Depression had a way of surrendering itself to sleep and she had stayed in bed much longer than she intended. Not that it mattered. She had nowhere to go, no place she needed to be, and no one who cared. In the dark, dreamless hours of sleep, she could forget her problems, forget her past life and all its mistakes, forget her mission, which was doomed to fail, and even forget herself. She could even forget the way James had retreated into his shell, walking away from her the moment they returned home. But daylight always came, intruding into the darkness, and forcing her to face the day.

She had started the previous evening believing she was living a fairy tale, that she truly was the golden princess going to the fancy dress ball with her handsome Prince Charming. But their relationship was so fragile, so brittle and breakable, it had taken only one misspoken comment to send it cracking into pieces. Everything had been going so well, she and James were having a grand time, the best time ever since her arrival, and yet it only took a reminder of her blasted assignment to bring their delicate dance crashing to an end.

If only she could take back those words.

When James had asked her what would make her happy, did she tell him that *he* made her happy, or that all she wanted was to be a good and faithful wife and make him happy, or something to that effect? No! She had once again mentioned her need for an invitation to that darn WAL ball.

And how did that make her look? Like a social climbing, insensitive snob, only interested in attending more parties. She didn't see herself that way, but apparently James did. It was almost as if he was looking for a reason to not believe in her. She had imagined she could overcome his dislike of Rebecca, but he had proved her wrong. When he looked at her, he still saw Rebecca, a woman whose father had forced him into a marriage for financial gain. The guilt of that alone would be bad enough, but to know how badly Rebecca had treated her husband only added to the mountain she needed to climb.

Jules had warned her she was overly sensitive to the emotions of those around her, and it seemed he was right. He claimed this was both her greatest asset and her biggest burden. Sensitive as she was, she could easily take on the role of another once she tapped into the emotions that motivated their lives. However, she was also susceptible to being sucked into their drama, making it her own, taking on their misery, sorrow or even discontent. It was an element of her psyche she needed to protect.

Knowing how to handle her emotions towards Stanton and James was more challenging than she had anticipated. If she allowed Rebecca's preconceived emotions to take charge it would reap disaster. If she had any hope for success, she needed to control her emotions, forge her own path and keep on going. The choice was up to her, as were the consequences.

After dragging herself from bed and getting dressed for the day, Becca decided it was time to once again try to tackle the household ledger as she had been intending to do. She was not the type of person who liked to leave any task undone and it nagged at her that she had put it off. She told herself it was understandable, with all she had going on, but she still had an obligation, at least to herself, to follow up on what she had started.

After breakfast, she went directly to the library and sat at the desk she was using. Thankfully, and rather surprisingly, Mrs. Granger had returned the ledger as she had asked. Becca opened it and began to go over it again, thinking her task shouldn't take very long. From what she remembered from her initial review, everything appeared to be in order. She would take another look to assure herself that Mrs. Granger was truly being financially responsible to her employers and let it go at that. While she hadn't gotten a good first impression of the elderly cook, she hoped that wasn't an indication of how their relationship would proceed going forward, even if her days here were numbered and counting down fast. She had less than two weeks until the ball.

She went back to the beginning and went over each week's entry with a discerning eye. When she got about half way through the year, she realized something didn't seem quite right. The weekly shopping lists and amounts paid seemed reasonable, but for some reason, the total amount paid out each week seemed unreasonably high. She decided to try a different approach and dig deeper.

When Becca had reviewed the ledger before, it hadn't occurred to her to add up all the amounts spent on groceries each week. She had been more interested in checking if the amounts paid for various purchases seemed reasonable, and that they weren't being overcharged. It took some time and effort, but when she took the time to add up the sums for the grand total for each week, a startling pattern began to emerge.

At first, she had thought perhaps Mrs. Granger had made a simple error in math, but soon she realized the household expenses had been inflated by a few dollars each and every week. Sometimes it was a couple of dollars, sometimes it was as much as five. Added all together, week after week, it began to add up to a significant amount.

Becca found the wages of each servant in the kitchen staff listed in the ledger, and according to her calculations, Mrs. Granger had skimmed enough money from James to triple her income. Obviously, none of the household staff were paid very much—the poor dears, they worked so hard—but that didn't give Mrs. Granger the right to steal from her employer.

Her first inclination was to confront Mrs. Granger, she was so distressed by what she found, but she quickly realized the flaw in that idea. Challenging Mrs. Granger would only cause hate and discontent and probably denial. She needed to go to James and show him what she had found, and hope he would listen. Even though they were not on the best of terms, hopefully, if she showed she really had his best interests at heart, it would help to soften his mistrusting heart. She wondered how he would react. Would he thank her for her efforts, or would he take the side of his loyal servants and assume it truly was an accounting error on the part of their cook. At this point, it was hard to know for sure. In Becca's mind, it could go either way. Yes, she was certain of her findings, but James had made it clear more than once that he trusted his staff to have his best interests at heart.

James was also a reasonable businessman. He knew the value of a dollar and the wrongness of being swindled by his own staff. Apparently, his mother had trusted Mrs. Granger enough to accept the weekly totals submitted for the cost of their groceries and had not thought to double check the cook's math as Becca was doing. How would James react knowing she had gone behind his mother to question the completeness of her work? As far as she knew, it could go either way. It might look as if she mistrusted his mother. This could upset the smooth functioning of the staff. They would need to hire a new cook, which could take weeks, and the rest of the staff may resent her meddling in their affairs. This was not a cut and dry situation, but now that she knew, she couldn't look the other way and let Mrs. Granger think she could continue to cheat her employer.

To be sure of her findings, Becca went through her figures a second time and even went to the effort of creating a second set of books, a set that correctly added up the amounts spent each week. She hoped by doing this exercise, she would have a better argument when she presented the proof to James. It took some time and by the end of the day she was bone tired. When she looked up at the clock, she saw it was past seven o'clock. Where had the time gone?

She had waved off Katie when her maid came to ask if she wanted to change for dinner. She had been too absorbed in her work to take a break. Now it seemed she had missed the dinner hour and James was still not home. If he had planned to be home for dinner, he would have been here by now. Apparently, he was avoiding her once again.

Pausing to rub her eyes in the dimming light, Becca decided to stop for the day. She set the ledgers in the drawer of her desk and locked it, taking the key with her. The issue with Mrs. Granger would have to wait until later.

~*~

Wednesday, November 29, 1893

After spending the whole day thinking about it, Becca knew what she needed to do. James was late again coming home, but this time, Becca was willing to wait. She wanted to discuss the accounting errors, or more correctly, the theft perpetrated by their cook at her husband's expense. It burned at her insides to think one of his so-called-loyal servants had taken advantage of James in this way. Like a lioness protecting her den, she needed to pounce while their foe was within range, since Mrs. Granger was scheduled to be gone from Thanksgiving morning until late Friday afternoon. Several days ago, Mrs. Granger had asked for the time to be with her family. At the time, there had been no reason to deny the cook's request.

Becca waited for her husband in the upstairs parlor. It was warmer there and close to the library where the ledgers were locked in her drawer. She would still be able to hear when James arrived home. It was a little disheartening to think she needed to lie in wait for her husband. If she didn't, she expected he would simply head directly to his office or bedroom or some other room in the house without seeking her out. No wonder Rebecca had felt ignored in her own home.

Becca was starting to doze off, her book falling shut in her lap, when she finally heard Jenkins greeting James at the front door. How their butler always knew when someone was arriving seemed a mystery to her, but she was grateful to hear their voices from the first-floor entrance hall. Becca set down her book and dashed out to the hallway, waiting for James to climb the stairs.

As he rounded the stairs to the landing, he looked both tired and pleased, as if his day, while long and taxing, had gone well. When he saw her standing there, he greeted her with a weary smile.

"Good evening, Rebecca. Have you been waiting for me?" he said as stepped into the hallway.

"I know it's late and you're probably tired, but I was hoping we could have a few minutes to talk."

"If this is about our quarrel after the Shepards' party or that blasted WAL ball, I'd rather not." From the look on his face, she could see he was in no mood for a fight.

"Oh, no, James, not at all." She had resolved to put such subjects out of her head; it had already caused enough of a rift between them. She lowered her voice, not wanting Mr. Jenkins or any of the other servants to possibly overhear. "This is about one of our servants. I know it's my job to oversee the household, and normally I wouldn't bother you with such things, but I think you may want to know about this." Seeing the haggard look in his eyes, she began to second-guess her plan to burden him with another issue and quickly added, "But it can wait if you're too tired."

"No, I'm not too tired, but I think I'll have a drink while we talk, if you don't mind." He nodded towards the front parlor.

"That sounds like a good idea. I think I may join you."

Side by side, they entered the parlor. Though she sorely wanted to touch him, to reach out and link her hand in his, she resisted. Instead, she went directly to the sideboard holding the liquor supply.

"I think I'll have a sherry, I very much liked the last one you served me," she said, remembering the night he had seduced her and left her wanting more. "What will you have?"

"I'll take the same." He took a seat near the hearth, the same chair where she had been sitting, and eyed her book with a raised brow, *Pride and Prejudice* by Jane Austin.

Yes, it's a romance, she thought, defending her choice of reading material, *but it's also a classic*.

As she poured the drinks, James asked, "So tell me, what's this all about?"

She handed James his glass and he took a deep swallow. After settling into the chair across from him, she too sampled her drink; it was every bit as good as she remembered.

"It's about our household expenses and our cook, Mrs. Granger." She glanced down at her drink, thinking she wouldn't mind taking another sip, but decided against it. Besides not wishing to appear as a lush, she needed to keep her wits about her. "I'm sorry to report this, but I think she's been stealing from us."

James sat forward in his chair. "Stealing? Are you sure? That's a pretty strong accusation."

"Based on the ledger she's been keeping, if you've been paying the weekly amounts she has submitted for the household groceries, then yes, I think I'm correct."

"Where is this ledger? I want to take a look at it."

"It's there, in the library," she said, pointing to the connecting door. "Locked in the desk I've been using."

"Show it to me." He was on his feet and already headed for the door, leaving his drink behind.

Following close behind him, Becca quickly went to her desk and unlocked the drawer. After turning on the desk lamp, she opened the ledger and showed him her findings.

"This is the original ledger with Mrs. Granger's figures, and these loose sheets are my calculations double checking her work. As you can see, it looks as if she listed the correct amount paid for each item, at least that's what I'm guessing, but the totals she submitted each week to cover her expenses are inflated by three to five dollars each and every week. I don't think this is simply a matter of bad math. From the consistent pattern, I think she deliberately misrepresented her expenses and pocketed the extra money."

James quickly scanned through a page and flipped to the next, going through several pages. "Well I'll be damned, Mrs. Granger cooked her books."

Based on James's glib reaction, Becca wondered if she had overestimated the importance of the matter. Maybe the few dollars Mrs. Granger stole each week didn't warrant her strong reaction. A second later, she realized he was as concerned as she was.

With his head still bent over the books, he said, "She'll have to be let go. I cannot tolerate such deception. And we'll have to question the rest of the staff. I want to know if anyone else was in on this. Do you have any idea how much she took in total?"

Becca shuffled through the pages until she found the one with the grand total and showed it to him. "Here, this is the net damage, but it's only for this year. I haven't gone further back. I didn't want to alert her of what I had found by asking for the older ledgers. I wanted to speak with you first."

"This is serious." James huffed out a sound of disgust. "I wonder why my mother didn't find this?"

"I imagine she didn't bother to check the totals for each week. The amounts paid for each item seemed reasonable and consistent, so she accepted what Mrs. Granger presented her. I did that myself at first, but then I noticed one of the weeks didn't add up, so I went back and checked them all. There's no telling how long she's been doing this, but I would guess it started before this year. She probably tried it once, thinking she could claim it had simply been a math error on her part, but when it went unnoticed, she continued to inflate her figures every week. You could have paid for three cooks for what she's taken in this year alone."

James sat there shaking his head for a minute. "I can't believe she did this. Mother trusted our servants, as did I. I would never have thought this was happening if you hadn't taken the time to double check her figures. Rebecca, this is remarkable. You're remarkable."

Becca felt her insides swell with pride and appreciation. "What shall we do? Several of the staff, including Mrs. Granger, asked for time off on Thursday for the holiday. Only Mrs. Granger won't be back until late Friday afternoon, in time to make our dinner."

"That's not a problem. This can wait until after she returns. Until then, I don't want anyone else to know what you've found. On Friday morning, we will gather the staff together and speak to them each separately to hear what they have to say. Once we've conducted our investigation, we'll have a better idea if anyone else was involved. Until then, I don't want to alert the staff. Do you agree?" He spoke to her in earnest as if she were his partner, his equal.

"Completely, James. I agree one hundred percent. I'm so glad I was able to speak with you. I knew you would know what to do."

"Thank *you*, Rebecca."

"You don't need to thank me. I'm your wife. It's my duty to look out for your best interests. I'm just sorry I hadn't done this sooner." It was late, but Becca was glad she hadn't waited to tell him what she had found. James needed to be informed.

"There's no need for regrets. You've discovered the error and now we can deal with it. I hate to lose Mrs. Granger, she's a competent cook, but we're going to have to let her go. It makes me wonder if any of the other staff were involved."

"Hopefully, we'll know more after we've had a chance to question them, as you've suggested. And I agree, I think it's best if we question them one by one so they aren't able to collaborate their stories. I am a little worried about letting her go the day after Thanksgiving, it seems a little cruel."

"It was the risk she took when she started stealing. Would you rather we let her stay until after the New Year? What she did is both illegal and immoral. She should be grateful we're not having her arrested." James

159

stood and rubbed his eyes. He looked dog-tired. "Lock this all away and we'll deal with it on Friday. It can sit until then."

Becca gathered up the ledger and accounting sheets and placed them safely in her desk, then locked the drawer. As she stood, James came to her side and pulled her into his arms.

"Thank you again, Rebecca. I'm sorry I doubted you."

His show of affection and appreciation filled her with joy. Finally, she was taking steps forward instead of backwards. She also heard the weary tone in his voice and knew it was past time for him to go to bed.

"Come, James. It's late, let's go to bed." This time, Becca reached for his hand and together they climbed the stairs to their bedrooms on the third floor.

At the top of the landing, James cupped her face in his hands and kissed her goodnight. The gentle caress of his lips on hers only lasted a second, but to Becca it was a glorious moment. "Good night, darling."

For a brief moment, it seemed he might ask her to join him in his room, and Becca held her breath. "I'll see you at breakfast." He dropped his hands to his side and turned to walk alone to his bedroom.

Becca sighed, watching him walk away. Like it or not, it seemed she would spend another night sleeping alone. How much longer could this last, she wondered? Because, along with everything else, she was getting rather tired of their *friendly* arrangement.

CHAPTER 10

Thursday, November 30, 1893

In years past, Becca had always enjoyed Thanksgiving Day with a sense of profound gratitude. It was a blessing to live in a country that made giving thanks a national holiday. Truly, she had so much to be grateful for; a warm bed, lovely clothes and food on her table. Today, however, she was feeling a little less of the holiday spirit. She wasn't looking forward to confronting Mrs. Granger about her ongoing pilfering of money for the past year, though she knew it needed to be done.

At breakfast that morning, James looked as if he had not slept well. There were dark circles under his eyes and his movements seemed slow, his strength seemed sapped. Still, when they prepared to leave for Charlene's house, he was dressed handsomely in a grey wool serge suite with a dashing cutaway jacket. Just the sight of him, so finely dressed, made her heart go pitter-pat.

Upon arriving at Charlene's house, they were ushered into the large salon where Charlene's family and friends were gathered to chat before being called to dinner. Becca sat sipping a glass of wine, quietly watching the conversations taking place around her. As her sister-in-law flitted from one group of guests to the other, it was obvious she enjoyed being the hostess. Becca was happy for her.

Almost instinctively, her eyes were drawn to James. He was standing near the windows speaking with Charlene's husband Steven, and Mr. Theodor Perry, another guest at holiday dinner. His daughter, Miss Julia Perry, whom Becca had met before at Charlene's Saturday tea, sat nearby speaking with Steven's younger sister about the opening night of the opera. Emily Shepard was too young to have attended the grand event and wanted to hear all about the gowns worn by the women. Because they were sitting nearby, it would almost appear as if Becca was also engaged in their conversation, but she really wasn't listening. Her thoughts were elsewhere.

Today was Thanksgiving, and she should be thinking of all the things she had to be grateful for, but at the moment, that really wasn't working. She found it hard to settle into the spirit of the holiday, though there was much she had to be thankful for, including the latest news that James would soon be an uncle. Earlier that day, shortly after they arrived, Charlene had let it slip to Becca that she was expecting a baby. Becca was delighted for her and Charlene looked happy enough to burst. It was nice to know at least someone was having pleasurable relations in the bedroom.

Becca wondered if that day would ever happen for her and James. Not the getting pregnant part so much—the pain of losing one baby was enough, thank you very much—but the idea of having pleasurable bedroom relations with the man to whom she was married certainly seemed appealing. Much better than sleeping alone while there was a handsome, virile man right down the hall. Then again, she hadn't exactly invited James into her bedroom. Maybe she should.

When she first arrived to take on the role of Rebecca Jaffray she had thought it was best to keep her relationship with James above board and out of the bedroom. After all, she hadn't expected to stay long and saw no reason to muddy up her already damaged life with gratuitous sex. She'd been assigned to get the painting Jules wanted, assured if she succeeded, she'd be returned to her old life. But that idea no longer appealed to her. She also knew, if she failed, she would be sent somewhere else, to another place and time until she could complete her contract with the Maestro. That possibility held even less appeal.

She had grown up in the twenty-first century where everything moved at the speed of technology, and she hadn't been happy. Since spending time in the gilded age of 1893, she'd been able to experience a lifestyle

162

previously beyond her reach. If given the chance, would she return to her old life? Highly unlikely, and yet, she didn't feel as if she belonged here either. Thanks to Jules's detailed training and instructions, she had learned suitable manners to mingle with the elevated circles of New York's elite society, but she was vastly aware she had not been born to this rank. Being accepted by the upper crust of Manhattan required more than fine clothes and proper manners, it required an attitude of entitlement and self-confidence which Becca feared she lacked. She was playing the role assigned to her by Jules, doing what the Maestro wanted, because she had basically signed her life away when she signed his blasted contract.

James had once asked her what she wanted. What would make her happy? She hadn't had an answer, other than to think of that darn invitation to the WAL ball. But what if she could have anything she wanted? What would that be? At the end of the day, she supposed it was the same thing everyone wanted; to live a happy life with a man who loved her. And maybe have his child.

That last thought surprised her. She hadn't believed she had gotten past the fear of losing a baby. But what if . . .

"Rebecca, are you all right?"

Becca flinched and nearly spilled her wine. Lost in thought, she hadn't noticed that James had come to sit by her side.

"Yes, yes, perfectly fine," she answered, speaking quickly. "Just doing a little woolgathering, I suppose." She took another sip of her drink.

"You've not said much since we arrived."

"I spoke to Charlene when we first arrived, and for a while, to Miss Perry and Miss Shepard." Although when she looked to her side, she realized the two young ladies had moved away and were now talking to Mrs. Shepard. Drat, she hadn't been paying attention. Not wishing to dwell on where her thoughts had been, she added, "I think it's wonderful you agreed to let Charlene host Thanksgiving dinner. It's obvious she loves playing the hostess."

James looked over at his sister and smiled with brotherly pride. "She does look happy. She's in her element. Charlene is happiest when she's taking care of others."

"Yes, I've noticed that about her. I suppose you've heard her big news." Becca was sure the secret had made its way around the salon twice by now, Charlene had been so excited to let it slip.

"Yes, I heard."

"You're going to be an uncle, James. How do you feel about that?"

"I expected it would happen sooner or later. It seems my sister and her husband wasted very little time."

Unlike Rebecca and James, who had spent the last four months avoiding each other like opposing magnets; come too close and I'll push you away. If one of them could only reverse their polarity, wouldn't that make for a much better connection?

Becca surveyed her husband's face. He looked happy for his sister. Although, it occurred to her that James wasn't really her husband. She had never stood before God and man and vowed to be his faithful, loving wife, nor had he vowed the same to her. She wondered how he had felt going to his wedding, knowing he was marrying a woman he didn't love, much less know very well. From what Becca knew of this time, she figured it wasn't all that unusual. Marriage for the social elite was just as often a business transaction as it was a union of love.

"I've noticed you've been working late again. Is it anything important?" *Or just an excuse to avoid coming home.* But she'd leave that unsaid, like so many other things she was keeping to herself.

He averted his eyes when he spoke and she had the feeling he would rather not discuss this particular subject. "I'm always working on one business deal or another. It's what I do, Rebecca."

"I wasn't trying to pry. It was only polite conversation." She reached out her hand to touch his knee, a rather forward public gesture, even for a wife. "You know, as cold as it's been, I don't think we shall see snow for another day or two," she said, recalling a conversation they had once had in the carriage as they drove through Central Park.

James returned his gaze to her. "One can never tell with the weather. It's subject to change on a whim."

"The weather and women, aren't we both considered changeable and unpredictable?" She managed a weak smile but heard the melancholy in her voice. She wondered if it was time to let go of the shore. All her life, she'd been waiting for a life raft to come by and rescue her. Maybe it was time to start swimming with the current to see where it would take her.

~~~

James couldn't agree more. Women were extraordinarily changeable and unpredictable. Especially, Rebecca. Every time he was prepared to dislike his wife, she did something to confound him and turn his opinion of her upside down. Earlier, he had noticed her faraway look as she sat with Miss Perry and Miss Shepard, even though they were engaged in animated conversation right beside her. Actually, she had looked a bit sad. He had heard the news of his sister's condition and wondered if Rebecca had heard it too. If so, he would expect her to be happy, it seemed all women were happy when one of them was carrying, but Rebecca seemed somber. Concern for her feelings had drawn him to her side. For some reason, he didn't like seeing her sitting all alone.

Rebecca lowered her voice. "I know you've been busy. I hope I didn't unduly burden you with our conversation about Mrs. Granger."

"Not at all, why would you think such a thing?"

"We've hardly spoken to each other since the night of the opera. I don't know what to think."

"I'm sorry. I may have over-reacted," James admitted. His ire hadn't entirely been her fault. His run-in with Wheland had grinded his gears and he had taken it out on Rebecca. "I've been distracted. It's that business deal I'm working on. It's not done yet, but if this deal comes through things should be a lot better."

"Is there anything I can to do to help?"

He chuckled at her eagerness, but shook his head, no. "I can't imagine how."

"Actually, neither can I, but I want you to know I'm here if you need me."

"You've helped me enough by finding that error in the bookkeeping," he said, thinking back to the effort she had taken to expose the cook's stealing, "but let's not talk about that here." He'd been impressed with her attention to detail. She hadn't just tossed out some unfounded accusation. She had gone through each week's numbers, adding up the cost of each item listed and comparing her sums to those of Mrs. Granger. The effort must have taken hours.

"I agree." She looked down at the nearly empty wine glass in her hand. "I should talk to Charlene. She shouldn't drink while she's expecting."

"Why not?"

"Um, I heard it's not good for the baby. Something about what the mother eats and drinks affecting the baby. But really, I probably shouldn't discuss such things with you. I'll make a point of speaking with Charlene in private, if I get a chance. I'm so very happy for her."

For a moment, the look on her face made him wonder if she was envious, although he supposed all women wanted to be mothers. Marriage and babies seemed to be their lot in life, and he had no reason to think Rebecca was any different. Seeing how proud and happy Steven was, knowing his wife was carrying, made James want some of that. Hopefully, maybe someday.

A moment later, they were called into dinner and spent the rest of the evening sitting side-by-side discussing nothing more than polite dinner conversation would allow. Interestingly, when they settled into the carriage a few hours later, James noticed a change in Rebecca. There was a look of determination on her face he had not seen before. This was so like her, changeable and unpredictable.

As soon as their carriage had pulled away from Charlene's house, Rebecca turned to him and said, "Ask me again." Her expression was one of earnestness.

"Excuse me?" James was taken off guard.

"Ask me again, what will make me happy."

He didn't know what she was up to but he was willing to play along, for the moment. "All right, Rebecca, what do you want? What will make you happy?"

"For you to respect me enough to trust me. And for you to trust me enough to stop avoiding me."

"Trust you!" He hadn't seen that one coming, but certainly he trusted her, especially after her discovery of Mrs. Granger's stealing.

When Rebecca told him about the cook's larceny, he had been both surprised and grateful. He had never expected she would take such an interest in ensuring the soundness of his finances. Even now, she continued to amaze and confound him.

What confounded him most was that he cared about her enough to regret he had mistrusted her, and yet, he had felt justified because he resented her for all she represented. Every time he looked at her, he was reminded of his failed business investments and his need to go to Wheland for a loan. But what if he changed the way he viewed their situation? What if he stopped seeing his marriage to Rebecca as a failure on his part, and

166

instead saw it as a very shrewd bargain? Seeing it that way, it was safe to say he had gotten the better end of the deal.

Wheland had never appreciated his daughter and had bargained her away because he saw her as a drain on his assets. James, on the other hand, was beginning to see, she could very well be the best investment he had ever made. Marrying her had saved his railcar business. While there may have been a time when he never would have believed he could love his wife, those days were slipping farther and farther away. Lately, it seemed as though he had hitched his hopes to a mighty strong engine, and it was picking up speed as it rolled down the tracks. Rebecca was proving she could be a loving and supportive wife. It was time for him to get onboard or risk being left at the station.

"Do you remember last year when we met at Mrs. Haversham's ball?" Rebecca asked.

He had to think back, it was such a random question, but he couldn't come up with a distinct memory.

"I remember," she said, with a hint of a smile. "It's when we were introduced for the first time. I thought you rather handsome. I still do. I told Randolph about my impression of you, and I think he may have mentioned it to father. I've recently started to wonder if that's why he picked you to be my husband. In his own distorted way, perhaps Father was trying to make me happy. Don't get me wrong, I know he wanted to get rid of me; having a spinster daughter did not sit well with him. But still, maybe there was some little part of him that wanted to pick the right man for me, in his own distorted way."

Distorted was right, but it was rather gratifying to think Rebecca had always found him handsome.

"What I'm trying to say is, regardless of what has come before, I'm your wife, and you're my husband, and I will not give up on us. As long as we're together, I will not give up. It seems I've given up and given in my entire life, first to my father, and then to you. It's time for me to be my own person. To live this life I've been given and stop wishing for something else, something better to come along. Today is a day of Thanksgiving, and James, if nothing else, please know, I am thankful to have you in my life."

Wow! Where had all this come from? She hadn't exactly made a declaration of love, but this was pretty darn close. "Why the sudden change in tune?"

"It's been a long time coming, especially since my return from my . . . my time away. Up until now, I realized I've only been humming a tune, humming along, but humming is boring. You may not like it; I don't know what you like, or what you want, or much of anything, since you so rarely talk to me. But I will no longer be your silent, meek little mouse of a wife, walking on ice and hoping for a thaw. Will you join me, James? Will you support me in my desire to be a good, and faithful, and loving wife?"

He wasn't sure what to say. A good and loving wife? Did that include letting him back into her bedroom? Or was it still too soon to ask?

Almost as if she could read his mind, she said, "My bedroom door is open. It hasn't been locked since I returned. You've simply not tried. Every princess has an image of a knight in shining armor willing to break down the door of her defenses and make her swoon with desire. Hopefully, I'm a little past the swooning part, but I think you get my meaning. A woman likes to be seduced, made to feel cherished, and wanted, and needed."

"As seductions go, I would say yours is a might bold." He had to admit, his seduction of his wife, if it could be called such, left much to be desired, but he refused to believe it had all been his fault. Until recently, she had given him very little reason to believe his attentions would be welcomed, much less returned. Now, it was almost as if she had made a decision to drive the train down the track and it was full steam ahead. Just the thought of what that might mean had him growing hard inside his trousers.

"Maybe that's my problem. I've never been good with dangling the carrot. The art of seduction has eluded me. Is that a problem for you?"

The carriage had come to a stop. They were home. A moment or two more of this conversation would be nice. A long ride through town seducing his wife would be even better. Hopefully, the mood wouldn't dissipate the moment they walked into the house. "Would you care to continue this discussion in a more private room of the house?" he asked as a footman came to open the carriage door.

"I should hope so. This *discussion* has only just begun." She reached out her hand and let him assist her down from the carriage.

Inside the front door, they went through the process of handing off their coats, hats, and gloves to Jenkins before James led her up to the small sitting room located on the third floor between their two bedrooms.

"Ah, a very good selection, neutral space but not too far from the battlegrounds," Rebecca commented as he led her into the room.

James smiled at her apt description. "Is that what our bedrooms are now, battlegrounds."

"Hmm, perhaps a poor selection of terms. Hopefully, by the end of the evening we shall view them differently."

"I quite agree. Would you care for a drink?" he asked, gesturing to the servant's bell. He wouldn't mind one for himself, but that would require a delay to their discussion since liquor wasn't kept in this room, and he was rather in a hurry to hear what his wife had to say.

"None for me," she answered.

"I can do without as well. Now, what were we discussing before this little interruption?"

"I believe the topic was seduction, or lack thereof." Her eyes held mirth, as if she was enjoying their little game. "Now that I think about it, I believe it was the lack of seduction on your part that has contributed to our separate lifestyle."

He was about to rebut her statement but she continued speaking, gracefully holding up a hand to halt his words.

"Before you get too riled up, let me explain. Our marriage was arranged by my father, hence, no seduction required on your part. Our wedding night did not go well, for which we are both to blame, but again, essentially no seduction on your part. It's my observation that men like to seduce women. It's the hunter in them, and yet your hunter instincts have not been tested since we've met."

"Are you challenging me, Mrs. Jaffray?" he asked, retracting his ire as he mused over her interesting observation.

"Do you have any idea how much I love hearing you call me Mrs. Jaffray?"

His brows spiked. "Really. I had no idea."

"When you call me Rebecca, you sound as if you don't like me very much."

He recognized the truth in what she said. He resented Rebecca Wheland, and all she represented, but when he thought of her as his wife, she seemed different somehow. "Would you prefer I call you Mrs. Jaffray all the time?"

She chuckled, a mirthful sort of sound. "I don't think I would mind."

"It seems rather formal, don't you think?" He had heard other couples call each other Mr. and Mrs. and had never cared for the practice.

"Then perhaps something more friendly, something that is special between us." She paused, as if giving it some consideration, then added, "Perhaps you should call me Becca."

"Becca? Hmm, yes, I like the sound of that. It suits you."

"But only when we're alone, not in front of others," she said in a whisper, as if she were sharing a secret.

"Like now?"

"Yes, like now." She reached up and began to pull pins from her head, setting them one by one on the table next to her as she unraveled her elaborately styled hair. The simple act was both intimate and completely unexpected. She must have noticed his startled reaction and said, "Do you mind? I think this hair style has reached its expiration."

"Not at all, please continue," he said, enjoying the show. He had never seen a woman undo her hair in front of him like this and he found it more arousing than he would have imagined.

"Would you mind helping me find all the pins?" she asked, looking marvelously seductive.

"My pleasure." He went to stand behind her and she lowered her hands, letting him take over the task. Sighing, she closed her eyes as he ran his fingers through her hair. It felt unbelievably silky in his hands. He noticed a faint scent of lavender and leaned closer to breathe it in. Taking his time to find each and every pin, he delighted in the way the heavy tresses fell across the back of his hand and over his wrists. Lingering, he wound thick curls over his fingers as he searched for the last few pins. When he could find no more, he gently massaged her scalp and was rewarded with her moan of pleasure.

"Oh my goodness, James, that feels so good. I'll give you thirty or forty minutes to stop."

He chuckled at her jest and continued to massage her head, enjoying the feel of her hair in his fingers, before he spread it out across her slender, white shoulders like a veil of silk.

"I don't know why I've waited so long to do this." He bent down and pushed her hair aside to kiss her slender pale neck, noticing the pulse racing beneath her skin, before moving further along her shoulder, his hands tracing a teasing path down her arms.

"I can't say the thought hasn't crossed my mind."

He paused for a moment. "Do confess."

"You must know I find you attractive." He noticed how her breathing had increased, her breasts rising and falling mere inches from his eyes.

"As your husband, I would hope you do." He caressed his way back up her shoulders and neck, softly rubbing his nose across her warm skin, and inhaled her subtle scent. She arched her neck, moaning out a little purr. Yes, he would make his kitten purr.

"But we didn't get off to a good start, and I didn't know how to change that." Her voice sounded breathless and airy.

His hands settled on her shoulders. "How could you? I wanted to be the one doing the choosing. I wanted to be in control." For too long, it had felt as if her father had robbed him of his rightful control, but now Becca was giving it back.

She gazed up over her shoulder at him through lidded lashes. "Now that you're in control, what do you suggest?"

"I'd like to ravish you," he said, somewhat surprised by his own boldness. He nipped her earlobe and whispered at her ear, "With your permission, of course." Although at this point, he knew she would not refuse him. It was obvious, she wanted this as much as he did.

Her smile was wicked, and enticing. "Permission granted."

When he took the seat beside her on the settee, he made sure they were touching from thigh to knee and he wasted no time in turning, cupping her face, and lowering his lips to hers. He'd meant to take it slowly, but the moment he felt her melt into his embrace, he realized it was going to be harder to control his desires than he had anticipated. The recent weeks of being in her company and pretending he wasn't attracted to her had created a powerful train of desire. Now it rushed through him, staggering in its strength.

He rested his forehead to hers and whispered against her lips, "Good lord, woman, how I want you." How did this happen? How had she managed to break through his defenses?

171

He blazed a trail of kisses down her neck and along her shoulder, peeved by the hindrance of her tightly formed bodice. His fingers struggled to undo the top buttons of her gown, determined to release her from her virtuous shroud. She made no attempt to stop him.

He worked his way through the buttons of her bodice only to reach the top of her corset. Damn, more barriers to be breached. "Why must women lock themselves up in such . . . such . . ."

"Ridiculous fashions?" she offered.

"Yes, ridiculous fashions."

"To make ourselves more appealing to men, and to impress each other, I guess." Her laughter dissolved his tension. "Here, shall I help you?" she offered.

"God yes." He watched in mute fascination as she deftly undid the rest of her buttons and began removing her bodice from her skirt.

He reached for her breasts, cupping them in his hands. Firm and full, they filled his palms. How a pound of flesh could feel so amazing was beyond reason. He rubbed his thumbs across her nipples, deeply gratified as he watched them harden into tight little buds.

"Oh my goodness, James." She arched her back, giving him greater access to her body. Her unbound hair fell across her neck and shoulders like a curtain of lace.

She wanted him, of this he was sure. This time there could be no doubts. He leaned forward, and began kissing her breasts, submerging himself in their sensual softness. A man could get lost in breasts like these.

She reached out and began stripping him of his jacket and waistcoat. Next, she moved onto his shirt, racing to undo the buttons after she had tossed aside his tie.

Having bared his chest, she began running her hands over his skin, her eyes hungry with desire. Pulling him close, she kissed him on his neck and across his shoulders. The touch of her lips warmed him, and aroused him, robbing him further of his diminishing control. He tipped her face up and kissed her again. Passion and sweetness melted into one.

She was no longer the cold fish who had laid unmoving in his bed, nor was she the prim and proper wife who claimed she only wanted friendship. His hand sought bare flesh, but her corset, and yards of fabric from her skirt, bunched between them.

When she reached for his belt and began to undo the buckle, she surprised him. This was not what he expected from his wife, at least not the woman he had married.

As if tuned into his thoughts, her hands paused and she looked up at him with a hint of wonder. This was a damned inconvenient time for her inhibitions to return.

"Do you think it's prudent to continue this here, in the sitting room?" She looked about, as if taking stock of their surroundings, her eyes darting between the two doors that connected to their respective bedrooms.

"Would you rather we move to a bedroom?"

"It seems a tad more appropriate, wouldn't you agree?"

"Your room or mine?"

She put a finger to her lips. "Good question. Which would you prefer?"

"Mine, of course." He liked having the advantage of familiar surroundings.

"Then yours it shall be. Do you mind if I retire to my dressing room to prepare for . . ." It seemed her original shyness had returned.

"Bed?" James supplied.

"Your bed," Rebecca confirmed. "I hope this won't put a damper on your fire while you wait."

"If it does, you'll be expected to fan the flames." His eyes raked over her body and settled to gaze directly into her eyes.

"Oh my, is that a challenge, Mr. Jaffray?" She pulled back with a pretense of being offended.

"I believe it is, Mrs. Jaffray."

"Good." She slipped from his arms and rushed to her room. A moment later her heard her call for her maid.

Would she really follow up on what she had started, or was this her way of wiggling out of something she had no intentions of seeing through to the end. He realized the answer intrigued him more than worried him.

A few minutes later, James lay naked between his sheets, waiting for his wife to come to his room, wondering what to expect. Silly or unreasonable as it seemed, he realized he was anticipating her appearance far more than he had on their wedding night. It was hard to believe they had been married almost five months and yet this was the first time since the week of their marriage that they would be intimate. Of course, that was still dependent on Rebecca—Becca—coming to his room as she promised. What would he do if she didn't show up? What if her seduction had all been a pretense? As retribution for the snubbing he had given her? She wouldn't do that, would she? It made no sense. He wanted to believe in this version of Becca, and trust her as she had asked.

He was still turning over these thoughts in his head when he heard a soft knock, followed by Becca slipping silently through his door. His heart thumped hard in his chest and it took half a second for him to catch his breath. Contrary to any previous impression he might have had, this confirmed his wife was truly beautiful. Standing before him was a vision in white. Becca's frilly, sheer nightgown draped softly over her lush body, showing off a curvaceous silhouette outlined by the single lamp he had left burning. He hoped she wouldn't ask to turn it off, she looked too good to be left in the dark.

Stepping inside his room, she twirled prettily about as if showing off a new gown.

"Do you like it?" she asked with a sly smile.

"I like the woman in it better."

"Good answer." With slow, determined steps she approached the bed. An arm's length away, she stopped. "Mind if I join you?"

"I was hoping you would." He pulled back the sheet for her.

Lifting the hem of her nightgown, she climbed onto the large four-poster bed, but did not slip between the sheets. She glanced over at the lamp.

"Please don't ask me to turn it off. I'd like to see your face."

She nodded happily. "I was hoping you would say that. I'd rather like to see yours too. So, where do we begin, how do we start? I feel as if I hardly know you and yet we're husband and wife."

James sat up with the pillows behind him and drew her into his arms. "We haven't had a good beginning, have we?"

Becca shook her head. "The cards were stacked against us."

"But look at how far we've come." It pleased him greatly to know she had come to him on her own volition.

She curled up next to him and placed her delicate hand upon his chest, her touch heating his skin. "You're so warm, like my own little furnace."

He always ran hot; it was one of the reasons he slept naked. "Do you like that?"

"Oh yes. I always feel so cold." She snuggled closer. "You can keep me warm."

"I would like that." He wondered if this meant she was willing to spend the night with him and not leave after their lovemaking was done.

Her hand slipped lower down his chest and stopped at the sheet draped across his waist. "I get the feeling you're naked under there."

"I'm wondering why you're still dressed."

She pressed her lips together as if repressing a grin. "Only in my nightgown. I thought you liked it."

"I'll like it even more when you're not wearing it."

Again, she gave him that little suppressed grin. "Wishful thinking?"

"I'm fairly confident in my prediction."

"I like that about you, your confidence." She suddenly got a faraway look in her eyes and he wondered what she was thinking.

~~~

"I wonder if this time will be different from the past," Becca asked, thinking back over her past mistakes.

"Different from our first attempts? Of that, I have no doubt. It's already different. This time you've come to me, not only as my wife, but as a willing partner. I can assure you, this will be so much better."

Becca gazed into his eyes. "I think so, too. You're a good man, Mr. Jaffray, and I'm a very lucky woman." Suddenly a dozen questions flooded her mind. Did he know how to swim? Had he climbed trees as a little boy or only social ladders? It seemed he preferred to make love with the lights on, and she wondered if he in fact had ever been in love before. Was there someone else he would rather have married?

Earlier that evening she had decided to become an active participant in this relationship she'd been thrust into and she had every intention of making the best of it. She was no longer Becky Sue Dobson, and she had never really been Rebecca Wheland. She was a whole new woman who called herself Becca and wanted to do right by her husband. She no longer cared about the painting, or the ball, or Jules, or anything else outside of this house. She was with James and she wanted to make the most of her time with him. She wanted to feel loved and appreciated if only for a little while.

She started to unbutton her nightgown but James reached up to stop her.

"Allow me," he said. He sat up straighter to undo her buttons and the sheet covering his lower half slipped away revealing his fully naked, aroused body. Dang, the man looked good.

He continued to unbutton her gown. "It'll be better when you're naked, too." James opened the top of her gown and slid it down her shoulders, revealing her breasts. Becca bent her arms, catching the fabric as it pooled around her waist, but didn't attempt to cover her breasts. James moved his hands to cup them, rubbing his thumb across her nipples before he bent his head to kiss them. She arched her back and moaned, slipping lower onto the bed.

James rolled with her and pulled her against his body. She could feel his arousal fully evident against her thigh. She reached out to touch his shaft; the man was built like a blessed stallion. What a great package. *Yeah for me!*

"Not so fast, my little kitten," he said, gently pulling away her hand. "First I want to make you purr."

She was pretty sure she would do more than purr before the night was through, but she had warned him, she didn't like dangling carrots. If he persisted in taking this slow approach she would have to take matters back into hand.

As her hand drew back across her belly she realized, that although still rather small, and thankfully free of stretch marks, it wasn't quite as flat as it has once been. Would he notice? Hopefully, like most men, he was too distracted by the sight of a naked woman in his bed to get too involved over the particular parts, except of course, the ones that mattered.

With his help, she slithered her nightgown up over her head and he pulled her close beside him, running his hand down her side, sliding over the rounded curve of her hips and over her bottom. When he slipped his hand between her legs, she nearly flinched, but quickly calmed when he whispered sweetly, "Easy now, this won't hurt. Not like last time." After gently stroking her bud, he slipped his finger inside her folds.

"You're quite wet, Mrs. Jaffray."

"And you're quite stiff, Mr. Jaffray. Have you any ideas on what we should do about this?"

"Aren't you the impatient one?"

"If you make me wait much longer, I may change my mind. Remember, weather and women, we're both subject to change.

He chuckled lightheartedly. "I have a feeling this little storm isn't going anywhere until it's all played out."

He was right, of course. She had no intention of walking away until the deed was done and he had strummed every nerve in her body. He dipped his finger deeper inside her and she bucked against him.

"Please, James, don't torture me. It isn't nice."

"Are you sure you're ready?"

"Yes, I'm sure." She was ready to scream, she was *so* ready. Did he want her to beg? She was tempted to reach back and smack his ass to get him moving, but figured that may not look good coming from a nineteenth century woman, so she played nice.

Rolling over her, he settled between her legs and caressed the tip of his shaft against her opening. He teased them both with his slow, smooth rocking, a shallow promise of the pleasure still to come. It was torture. Exquisite torture. She didn't know how much more of this she could take.

"Please, James, don't make me wait."

Sinking deep inside her, he filled her up, turning her sweet torture into ecstasy. Finally! Thank you, Jesus. She gripped his shoulders across that strong, muscled back and wrapped her legs tight around his waist, welcoming and embracing his body. He began to move within her, slowly at first, then gaining momentum until they found a rhythm of thrust and pull, arousing her senses beyond belief. The soul-searing bliss continued to build until she reached her peak of sensual delight as he took her to that place of divine release. Screaming, she called out his name.

Several minutes later, after she had floated back to earth like a weightless feather, and regained her composure, she basked in the glow of their closeness, savoring the lingering aftershocks of pleasure. So great was her pleasure, and so great her release, it was as if none had ever come before. James was the only man who had ever made her feel this good.

"Thank you, James," she murmured as she lay naked cuddled in his arms. She had no idea where her nightgown was, nor did she care. She loved the feel of their naked bodies next to each other.

"Happy?" he asked, sweeping an errant curl from her forehead and tucking the lock behind her ear.

He must have had some clue from all her screaming and moaning. So unlike a proper lady, but he didn't look disappointed. "Quite happy. In fact, I would say you managed to tickle my fancy."

Her comment made him laugh. "That was my intention all along."

"Did you know it takes two to tickle?" she asked, remembering a joke from long ago.

"I don't believe I've ever heard that one before, but yes, I believe it usually works better that way."

"Oh, yes, it's very hard to tickle oneself." She snuggled closer beside him. "Am I allowed to spend the night?"

He rolled over her again and linked their fingers above her head. "I was thinking of tying you down if you tried to leave."

"Oh, my goodness, promises, promises."

He looked at her with an expression of awe. "It's hard to believe you're the same woman I married."

She shrugged off his comment, as if he hadn't just hit the nail on its head. "Maybe I'm not. Maybe I went to Raven's Point and came back a changed woman. Are you disappointed?" Searching his eyes, she awaited his response.

"Disappointed? Are you kidding? I'm thrilled. But I don't think you shall ever be allowed to return to Raven's Point."

"Why not?" she asked, slightly fearful of what he might say.

"I can't risk thinking the old Rebecca might return."

Her heart thrilled with delight. "I don't think you need to worry. As far as I know, the old Rebecca is dead and buried. I left her on Long Island. You'll have to put up with this new version of me going forward."

"That suits me just fine. I much prefer this new Becca. The old one can stay buried as far as I'm concerned, never to be seen again." He bent his head and kissed her again, filling her with passion.

As she wrapped her arms around him, she breathed a sigh of joy and relief. In her own, round-about way, she had just revealed her deepest, darkest secret, risking he would guess the rest, but he had accepted her as she was. It still felt like deception, but at least in some small way, she had warned him.

CHAPTER 11

James couldn't recall a time when he had slept so well, or so little. Something had obviously changed since Rebecca's return from Raven's Point, and he was more than grateful to be the one reaping the benefits. Somehow, Rebecca Wheland, a woman who had once been little more than an angry, grating thorn at his side, had bloomed into a passionate, loving seductress, with a witty sense of humor, and he couldn't be happier. Who would have imagined? Until now, certainly not him.

Apparently, patience has its rewards, and waiting for Rebecca to finally decide she was fully invested in their marriage had paid off in huge dividends. His only fear, if he were allowed to even think such a thing, was that this new Becca would suddenly disappear in a puff of smoke. Thankfully, he had no reason to believe such a thing could happen. For the first time ever, based on their long night of delightfully satisfying sex, he felt reasonably confident they were destined to enjoy a long and happy marriage.

The following morning, James and Becca greeted the day as a united couple, ready to confront the issue of their cook's thievery together. While Mrs. Granger was still gone from the house, they requested the remaining staff to gather in the servants' hall. James had decided he would call each of the staff into the butler's office to question them one by one while Rebecca remained sitting with the rest of them. It was her job to be sure no

179

one discussed what was happening and share supporting alibis. She had wanted desperately to hear what each of the servants had to say, but James felt it was better to let him conduct the interviews, as he had more experience with these types of matters. James began his questioning with Mr. Jenkins, as he was the senior ranking member of the staff.

"Have you ever had cause to question the purchases or expenses of Mrs. Granger?" James asked his butler.

"No sir, I cannot say that I have. As you should know, it's my job to oversee the salaries of my staff, the purchase of all liquors including wine, and the cost of any necessary repairs to the house in general. I do not involve myself with the running of the kitchen. That comes under Mrs. Hewes."

"Has Mrs. Hewes ever mentioned to you any concerns regarding the cost for supplying groceries for the kitchen?"

"No, sir, not that I can recall." The butler's expression remained fixedly neutral. James would hate to play poker with the man.

"Does she normally confide in you?"

"Mrs. Hewes and I have a commendable working relationship, however we both respect each other's authority over our subordinates. I do not question how she manages her staff, nor does she question me."

James nodded in understanding. Every family employing servants developed their own way of distributing the various tasks and it had evolved in the Jaffray house for Mr. Jenkins to be in charge of the groomsman, the footman and the two step-and-fetch-it hall boys who performed the many menial tasks required to successfully run the house. Mrs. Hewes was in charge of the housemaids and kitchen, including Mrs. Granger.

"You've worked for my family for a long time, Mr. Jenkins. If something seemed suspicious, I trust that you would let me know."

"I can assure you, Mr. Jaffray, I would never do anything to upset your trust."

"Thank you, Mr. Jenkins. You can return to the servant's hall and send in Mrs. Hewes. And please assist Mrs. Jaffray with the rest of the staff. They can talk about the weather or what they did at Sunday services, but no one is to discuss anything regarding this investigation. Do I make myself clear?"

"I understand perfectly, sir." Mr. Jenkins gave him a brisk nod of his head and exited the room.

To his butler's credit, he did not question why they were conducting this investigation. Mr. Jenkins either trusted him to tell him when the time was right or figured it was none of his business. The whole staff would know in due time, but Mr. Jenkins would have to wait with the rest of them until he had finished questioning them all.

A moment later, to his surprise, Rebecca's personal maid Katie stepped into the office.

"I'm sure you were expecting Mrs. Hewes, but I asked Mrs. Jaffray if I could go next and she said it was all right. She didn't even ask me why and she was real discreet when she told this to Mr. Jenkins. Your wife is a real smart lady. I think I know something about what's going on and I wanted to tell you as soon as possible."

It was a bit presumptuous of the maid to jump her place in rank, but since Becca had approved he would go along with her decision.

"All right, Katie, what do you think is going on?"

"Well, I might not know exactly, but I can tell you what I do know. When Mrs. Jaffray, your wife, asked to meet with Mrs. Granger and Mrs. Hewes a couple of weeks ago, I heard them talking afterwards. Mrs. Jaffray had wanted to speak to Mrs. Granger about the menus and such. I was in the boot cleaning room when they came back downstairs and they were out in the hallway. They were talking together, and they were close enough for me to hear. Mrs. Granger seemed a might upset and Mrs. Hewes told her she best be afraid or she might find herself out of a job. I didn't know what it meant at the time, but I figured I should remember this in case it was important."

It wasn't enough to convict anyone yet, but James had to admit he was interested. "Did you hear anything else?"

"Yes, sir. I'm sorry to say, I heard Mrs. Granger say a few unkind things about Mrs. Jaffray, your wife I mean, not your mother. Mrs. Hewes reminded Mrs. Granger to be careful since Mrs. Jaffray, your wife, not your mother, was in charge now."

It helped to know that Mrs. Hewes had stuck up for his wife. He had begun to think she was somehow involved in this matter and he was disappointed to think he could lose both a competent cook and a loyal housekeeper. Although, if Mrs. Hewes did know, and had looked the other way, she wasn't as loyal as he believed and he would have to let her go as well.

"Is that everything, Katie? Is that all you know?"

"Oh, no sir. When Mrs. Jaffray, your wife, asked me to tell Mrs. Granger she needed the ledger back in the library and on her desk, she seemed a might upset, Mrs. Granger I mean. She went right in and spoke to with Mrs. Hewes. I didn't hear everything they said, but Mrs. Hewes seemed to think it was only a matter of time before Mrs. Jaffray, your wife, would check the ledger. Mrs. Granger said she wasn't worried because she didn't think you all know what it costs to run a house of this size. That's what she said. Then she asked Mrs. Hewes to cover for her if anything came up."

"Are you sure that's what you heard, Katie? That Mrs. Hewes should cover for her?" James didn't like the way that sounded.

"Yes, sir. Her exact words were; 'you best be sure to cover for me if anything comes up.' Oh yes, and there was one other thing. Mrs. Hewes said 'this is all your doing. I won't have any part of it.' That's all I heard because I had to get back to my duties, taking care of Mrs. Jaffray, but that's why I wanted to come and speak with you before you spoke to Mrs. Hewes. I thought it might help if you knew what I had heard, especially the part about Mrs. Granger asking Mrs. Hewes to cover for her if anything came up. That part I thought was real important."

"Thank you, Katie, you've been very helpful. Please return to the servants' hall and ask Mrs. Jaffray to send in Mrs. Hewes. I trust you'll be discreet about all this. I do not want gossip to spread." This was pretty damning evidence against both his head housekeeper and his cook, but he still wanted to hear what Mrs. Hewes had to say.

"Oh, yes sir, I understand. I don't like gossip myself. It only leads to trouble." She gave a little bob of a curtsy and exited the room.

A moment later, Mrs. Hewes walked in looking morose. "Mr. Jaffray, before you begin asking me any questions, I would like to confess. I knew Mrs. Granger took money from the expenses she submitted for her groceries and I didn't report her. I've got no good excuse except to say I thought she was a darn good cook and I didn't want the house to lose her. It didn't seem like much, she said it was only one or two dollars every now and then, but still, sir, it was my duty to tell you and I didn't. I told her more than once she was taking too much of a risk, but she doesn't always listen to me."

James drew a deep breath. So, Mrs. Hewes was duplicitous after all. This was disappointing to hear. "It was somewhat more than a dollar or two every now and then. From what Mrs. Jaffray has been able to uncover, it seems Mrs. Granger has been taking three to five dollars each and every week, and we don't know how long this has been going on."

Mrs. Hewes gasped and covered her mouth. "Oh, my lord, sir, I can assure you, I had no idea it was that bad."

"Do you know if anyone else was aware of what she was doing?"

"No, sir, I'm fairly sure she was doing this all on her own. She was the only one who kept the ledger and Mrs. Jaffray was the only other one she let look at it, first your mother and then your wife. I only knew about it because one time I saw an extra dollar in the pay envelope she gets each week and I saw her keep it."

"And yet, you said nothing?"

"It weren't much, only a dollar, and I was still new here. She swore she wouldn't do it again, but I suspect she did from time to time. Since before I got here, Mrs. Granger had taken it upon herself to be the one to submit her weekly expenses and pay her suppliers. She said that was the way it was always done around here and there was no need to make any changes."

"Regardless of the size of the thievery, I cannot tolerate stealing in any form. It saddens me, Mrs. Hewes, but I have to let you go as well as Mrs. Granger. She will be informed as soon as she returns." Mrs. Hewes had obviously allowed Mrs. Granger to undermine her position of authority in the house, which was another strike against the housekeeper.

Mrs. Hewes sadly shook her head. The poor woman looked to be on the verge of tears. "I understand, Sir. I just want to say it's always been a pleasure working in this house. I sorely regret I did not do better for you."

"Mrs. Hewes, this seems so unlike you. I have to ask why you let it go on at all?"

Mrs. Hewes looked down at her lap for a moment before speaking. When she looked up, her eyes were misty but her demeanor was strong. "Mrs. Granger is one of twelve siblings. Her family is dirt poor and she said she needed the money in an emergency to help them keep food on their table. In a way sir, it seems rather ironic. She was always concerned about not wasting any food here in this house and wouldn't cook an ounce of meat more than was needed for our meals, nor would she let anyone snitch from the pantry, but she took that money without any remorse. I still can't hardly believe how much she took."

There was something about this matter that still didn't make sense to James and he hoped Mrs. Hewes could shed some light on the matter. "Do you know how she did it?" he asked.

Mrs. Hewes looked confused. "No, sir, not exactly. I'm sorry. I never asked. I suppose I felt the less I knew the better."

Some say ignorance is bliss, but for Mrs. Hewes it was going to be her downfall. "It seems Mrs. Granger added the extra amount in the grand total for each week, but she didn't include it in the amount charged by any of her suppliers. I ask about this because it seems to me it made her stealing easier to find. As soon as Mrs. Jaffray took the time to add up the weekly costs, she found the error."

"I can only guess Mrs. Granger wanted to keep track of what each supplier charged her to be sure none of them tried to cheat her. She was always worried one of them would try to overcharge her, and she never expected your missus to ever check her math."

James shook his head in disgust. "And yet she had no qualms about cheating me. I take it that you never thought to check the accounting for her expenses. It seems as head housekeeper you should have been in charge of that."

"You're right, sir, I should have, but Mrs. Granger had been doing it when I arrived, and sometimes it's easier to not upset the way things are done to keep everyone working together. I can assure you, sir, I will never make that mistake again, although I don't believe I'll ever get a chance. It'll be near impossible for me to get a job without references." Mrs. Hewes wrung her hands together as she spoke.

"It's for Mrs. Jaffray to decide what references she will supply, if any, although I can assure you, Mrs. Granger will not receive a reference from us. You may go now to pack your belongings. I will leave it to you if you wish to say goodbye to the rest of the staff."

"Thank you, sir, but I think it's best if I can make my departure with as little excitement as possible, if you don't mind."

"Understood. I'll leave you to your task while I speak with the rest of the staff."

Mrs. Hewes left the office and James took a minute to collect his thoughts. This was a damn tough spot they were in. They were losing their cook and head housekeeper right before the holidays and he had no idea how hard it would be to replace them. It seemed Becca was going to have some additional burdens to handle, and yet, he had every confidence she was up for the task. A few weeks ago, he doubted he would have felt this way. Now he was grateful to know he had a wife he could trust to manage his house as needed.

~*~

While sitting with the rest of the staff in the servants' hall, Becca began to ask them some questions, but these had very little to do with the investigation James was conducting. Instead, she wanted to know what each servant did, how long they had worked for Mr. Jaffray, and the question she thought most important, what they liked most about their work. Her father had once told her that the best person for a job was the one who wanted it the most, and not always the one with the most experience. He had told her that desire was even more important than a fancy education. He had seen plenty of men with lots of experience who hated their jobs and it had shown in their work, and he had seen a lot of other men who loved the work they were doing and they were always the best employees.

Every one of the staff had their story to tell and she listened with an open mind, making mental notes on changes she wanted to make. When she talked to the young women working in the kitchen with Mrs. Granger, she learned that Molly Brady was an excellent cook's assistant and loved what she was doing, but it seemed Mrs. Granger had held her back by not letting her do more of the cooking. She was only allowed to prep the food.

"Sometimes I want to try new things, such as a new way to prepare mutton, or pork, or a new sauce, but Mrs. Granger said it wasn't my place," Molly told her. "She said it's her job to make each and every meal since she's in charge of the recipes and ingredients and such. It's not that Mrs. Granger isn't a good cook, you understand, but it seems to me that once in a while she should be willing to try something new."

"Do you really think you could be the head cook for a big house like this?" Becca asked. Cutting up vegetables and preparing food was not the same thing as actually cooking the meals.

"Yes, Ma'am, I do, if given the chance. Especially since there's only you and Mr. Jaffray these days, it makes it much easier. I can do all the cooking we need here in the servants' hall, and I'm sure I can prepare proper meals for you and Mr. Jaffray."

"I know it's been that way for a while, but what if I wanted to entertain, say a dozen guests or more? Would you be able to handle that type of service?"

"I'll be honest with you, Mrs. Jaffray. If'en I needed help, I would let you know. Us servants in the big houses, we all know each other, and I've got friends, I can assure you of that." Unlike Mrs. Granger, Molly Brady seemed very likable.

Becca liked what she was hearing, but still needed to know more. "If you were promoted to head cook, who would do your work? Would we need to hire more kitchen staff to keep things running?"

"Well, Ma'am, that's the best part. Me and the other girls think we've more than enough to keep up with the current work load."

Mary O'Brian, the senior housemaid, raised her hand and said, "I have a cousin who is looking to work in a big house. If you're needing more help, this would be perfect for her, begging your pardon, if you don't mind me saying."

"Not at all, Mary. This is all very helpful. As mistress of this house I need to take more of an interest in what it takes to keep this place running. I've neglected my duties for too long. It took me a while to feel settled in, but if I can count on everyone's help," she looked around the table at each of the staff, "I believe we can make this a much better place to work."

Several of the servants exchanged skeptical glances and she wondered what secrets they were keeping. That couldn't be avoided, not completely. She had worked as a teller at a bank in her previous life and she knew there was always some discord in the ranks, no matter how hard management tried to keep everyone happy. She also viewed stealing as one of the most grievous crimes an employee could commit against their employer.

"What about you gentlemen?" Becca asked, turning her attention to Mr. Wallis, Mr. Bates, and the young boys who worked in the stables and below, in the basement, tending to the mechanics of the house. It took a bit more to get the men to open up, but by the time James came back into the room, she had learned a few things. They were happy enough but wondered if they couldn't have a bit more heat in their rooms. Everyone nodded in accord, she noticed, except for Mr. Jenkins, who maintained he was perfectly fine with the current coal supply. Becca made no promises but assured them she would see what could be done. She wanted to talk to James first, but since they would be saving money by eliminating both Mrs. Granger and her stealing, maybe there was some room in the budget for extra fuel. She knew herself how much she hated being cold.

James came to stand at the doorway but didn't enter the room. "Rebecca, may I speak with you for a moment in the butler's office."

Becca left the servants' hall and followed him to the office, anxious to hear what he had learned and bursting to share her news.

"Are you already done with your investigation?" she asked, mildly surprised, since he had only spoken to a few of the servants.

"I think I know all I need to at this point. It turns out Mrs. Hewes knew about Mrs. Granger's thievery, although I'm fairly certain she didn't partake in the stealing. She claimed she didn't know how extensive the amount was; she thought it was only one or two dollars and only once in a while. Regardless of the amount, her silence requires that we dismiss her."

"I'm so sorry to see her go, she seems like such a nice woman, but I totally agree, she cannot stay. It will be hard to find a new head housekeeper, but I have some good news of my own. I talked to the girls who work in the kitchen and the other housemaids. Molly Brady believes she can take over as head cook. Apparently, she's worked with Mrs. Granger for some time now as an assistant cook and has learned how to keep the kitchen running. If you agree, I'd like to promote her to head cook and move the rest of the girls up a notch to fill in as needed."

"Won't we still need to hire more help?" Worry lines appeared between his eyes and Becca wished she could smooth them away.

"Other than a head housekeeper, I don't think so, although, now that I think about it, I wonder if Mary O'Brian or her cousin could fill the position. I'll work closely with them for a while to ensure they know what they're doing, but I think this might work." She rather liked the idea of being able to promote from within.

"That will put an added burden on you. Are you sure you don't mind?"

"Not at all, James. I want to be more involved in running our home. It will make me feel useful."

"Well, if you're sure, I suppose we can give it a try. I will leave it up to you to tell me if it's not working out."

Becca nodded happily. "I will, James. I'll keep you informed."

In all her delight over the improvements she had planned, Becca had nearly forgotten she might not be here in a couple of weeks. If she succeeded in getting the painting Jules wanted, she would be sent back to her own time to live out her life, hopefully better off for having done her penance. And if she failed, she would be sent off on another assignment until she fulfilled her contract. Either way, her life would suck.

But pleasing James and making sure everyone was well taken care of seemed so much more important; she simply couldn't worry about Jules and the painting right now. The WAL ball was still a week away, but that also meant she only had one week to secure an invitation. She desperately hoped Charlene could come through with her connection to Mrs. Beaumont. If not, Becca didn't know what she would do. At this point, she had no other options.

"What about Mrs. Hewes? Where is she now?" Becca asked.

"I've dismissed her. She has gone to her room to pack. She asked that she not be required to face the rest of the servants and I agreed. I didn't know if you were inclined to provide her a reference. I told her I would leave it up to you."

"I would like to speak with her first, if you don't mind."

"Not at all. I think that would be best." Becca was turning to leave when he added, "Thank you again, Becca."

Becca went to him and put her arms around his waist, hugging him tight. "Thank you, James, for believing in me." With a final squeeze, she headed once more for the door but stopped with her hand on the knob. "Do you happen to know where Mrs. Hewes' room is?"

James chuckled lightly. "Up the back stairs, first door on the fourth floor."

Becca nodded appreciatively. "Thanks, I've never been up there." She headed out the door with a satisfied smile, thinking everything was going to be all right. She felt awful for Mrs. Hewes, how the poor woman had allowed herself to be drawn into Mrs. Granger's deceit, and did not look forward to their final meeting. However, she had no such regrets for Mrs. Granger. She could hardly wait for the cook to return so she could give her the boot.

When she poked her head into the housekeeper's room, she noticed that Mrs. Hewes had been crying. Her eyes were ringed in red and she was holding a cotton handkerchief as she sat on her bed. Becca went in and sat beside her.

"How did it happen?" Becca asked. "This seems so unlike you."

"Through my own stupidity and weakness. I was afraid to upset the apple cart and now I'm paying for it. I didn't know everything, but I knew enough about what Mrs. Granger was doing and I should have stopped it, or reported it, but I didn't. She assured me it wasn't anything more than what every other cook does in every big house. Unfortunately, I was more afraid of her than of doing my job as I should. You may have noticed, she can be very intimidating." Mrs. Hewes took a breath as if she had needed to get that off her chest. Confession was good for the soul.

"I understand and I don't blame you, but you must understand why we can't let you stay. I wish there was something I could do, but James has insisted, we can't set a bad example for the rest of the staff. It would undermine our authority."

"No, no, Mrs. Jaffray, you needn't explain. I understand completely. I was starting to worry that Mrs. Granger was becoming too sure of herself to fully consider the risk she was taking. I think she had gotten away with it for so long, she thought she was safe. Instead, she was only making the matter worse."

"I hope the money she stole was worth it for her. She'll not get a reference from us. But you, Mrs. Hewes, I would like to send you off with at least some sort of acknowledgement for the service you have provided."

"Are you certain? It's more than I can ask."

"I understand as well as anyone how someone can intimidate you into doing something you know in your heart is wrong." Much like Mrs. Hewes, Becca had let Ralph intimidate her into staying with him when she knew it was wrong. She went against her better instincts to keep him happy, and the price she paid was losing her unborn baby. The loss of a job seemed minor in comparison. Knowing she shared such a weakness, she was in no place to judge Mrs. Hewes.

~*~

Mrs. Granger was not an easy woman to confront, but Becca was ready for her. She was notified as soon as Mrs. Granger returned and now she was tasked with giving the cook her notice to leave. Mrs. Granger was still wearing her coat and hat when Becca entered the room.

"Mrs. Granger, there's no need for you to unpack. You're being dismissed." Becca wondered if the cook would confess to her thievery or if she would try to deny the evidence in the ledger.

"May I ask why?" Mrs. Granger asked, looking incredulous.

"I discovered your weekly stealing from the grocery money. It's amazing you were able to get away with it for as long as you did, but now you must go."

Mrs. Granger looked at her as if she couldn't believe what she was hearing. "Every cook in the city pads the food expenses. It's not as if you rich folks can't afford a few extra dollars every once in a while. Think of it as helping the poor."

Becca was amazed Mrs. Granger would actually try to defend her actions. "That is not for you to decide. Stealing in any form is a breach of the trust placed upon you. My husband and I will not allow it. Now, if you will kindly gather the rest of your belongings, Mr. Jenkins will stay with you while you pack and see you on your way." She wanted to make it clear she didn't trust the woman. Mrs. Granger might easily try to steal the silver if she wasn't watched.

"How do you think you're going to survive without me here to cook for you?" Mrs. Granger asked with a lift of her chin. Becca had to give her credit, she was a tough old broad.

"Miss Brady has graciously offered to take over your duties until we can get this sorted out." Not that it was any of her business.

"Molly? Why she's only a child." It was obvious Mrs. Granger didn't think highly of her assistant. Becca doubted she thought of anyone but herself, and maybe her brothers and sisters since she had claimed she was taking the money to help support them.

"That is no longer your concern. I'm sure we'll make do. Mr. Jenkins, please stay with Mrs. Granger until she is ready to leave and see her on her way." Becca reiterated her instructions to her butler to be sure everyone knew what was expected.

"What! Are ye worried I'll take something that doesn't belong to me?" Mrs. Granger asked.

"You've already done that. Why would I trust you now?" Becca turned to leave. "Mr. Jenkins, I leave her to you." It was an unpleasant task, but she could no longer stand to be in the woman's presence.

~*~

The moment Mrs. Jaffray had left the room, Mrs. Granger went to her cupboard in the kitchen and pulled out her recipe box. After thumbing through it for a second, she pulled out a card. She went over to where Molly was standing and slapped the card on the table in front of her, pleased when she saw the girl flinch.

"So, you think you can take my place?" Mrs. Granger asked the little upstart. "You think you can plan menus every week and buy the groceries needed? You think my suppliers are going to work with you like they worked with me?"

"If the suppliers are honest, they'll continue to work with us. I'm not worried," Molly said, sounding more confident than she looked.

"I hope you're right, because I won't be here to help you if you fail."

"I won't fail, Mrs. Granger, I've learned what to do, and what *not* to do from you."

"Damned right you did." She pushed the recipe card forward toward the edge of the table. "Here, child. If you think you can take over for me, you best have this. I was planning to serve it for dinner tonight. Now you're going to have to do it."

Molly stared at the card as if she was too scared to pick it up. Mrs. Granger snickered at her fear.

"This is what's on the menu for tonight. You're going to have to make up menus by yourself soon enough, but for tonight, I suggest you stick to what's been planned."

~*~

The meal that evening was excellent, and Becca especially liked the carrot and ginger soup Molly had prepared. Although she didn't recall it being on the menu plan, it had a most interesting taste. If this was what they could expect from Miss Brady going forward, they should have no problems with the transition.

Just before they prepared to retired for the night, James made it abundantly clear he wanted her back in his bed tonight, and every night if possible. "I understand there are times when women prefer to be alone," he

191

said, no doubt referring to her monthly cycle, "but whenever you feel up to it, I ask that you share my bed."

Both surprised and delighted by his candor, Becca smiled sweetly. "I would love to share your bed, it's so big and comfortable," she said, as if that were the only reason. She then leaned closer and whispered, "I also liked sleeping naked next to you."

He reached a hand across her shoulders to hold her close. "Aren't you concerned what the servants will think?" he whispered huskily into her ear.

Becca smiled up at James, feeling wickedly happy. "I have no problems letting our staff know we're husband and wife."

She felt happier than she could ever remember. It didn't matter that she hadn't stood in a church and declared her vows in front of witnesses. As far as she was concerned, she was Mrs. Rebecca Jaffray, devoted wife of James Jaffray, and no court of law in this land would see her as anything else. After finally putting aside their quarrels and disagreements, she and James had become a loving couple. Maybe they weren't yet a couple in love, and maybe her time here was destined to be cut short, but with God as her witness, she planned to make the most of every moment they had together until her time with James was over.

With Katie's assistance, Becca changed into a pretty lace nightgown and combed out her hair. She was humming cheerfully as her mind happily frolicked with thoughts of slipping away to her husband's bedroom when she felt the attack coming on.

Oh no, this can't be happening, not again, not now.

She'd been so careful. How could this have happened? Especially not tonight. Not after they had put their misunderstandings behind them. She was so looking forward to sleeping with James, but if she was right about her symptoms, and she was sure she was, it would be days before she would want anyone to even see her.

The tight churning in her stomach and the nausea that followed was only the beginning. She'd been through this before and knew exactly what to expect, with each exposure being worse than the one before. Rushing into the bathroom, Becca stared into the mirror. Sure enough, her lips were already beginning to swell and turn red with tiny blisters forming along the edges. Soon, her eyes would become red and swollen, and her face would be puffy.

Somehow, she had been exposed to tomatoes. It must have been in something she ate. But what? She thought back over everything she had eaten that day. The only thing she could think of was the carrot and ginger soup, it was the only dish spicy enough to have hidden the forbidden fruit.

Her maid was still standing in the adjoining dressing room putting away her dress when Becca felt the need to vomit. Thankfully, she was close to the toilet, it came on so suddenly. Bent over its rim, she began to retch.

Katie came running into the room. "Mrs. Jaffray, are you all right?"

Becca held her hair away from her face and continued to heave. When the nausea finally passed, she slumped down on the cold tiled floor. "I need a wet wash cloth."

Katie scurried to fetch the cloth for her and Becca used it to wipe her face. With Katie's help, she went to the washbasin and rinsed out her mouth. Sweat beaded down her back. "Now help me to bed and then bring me a bucket or a pot or something I can use if I need to vomit again."

"Mrs. Jaffray, what happened? What should I do?" The maid seemed far more distressed than Becca as she helped her to her bed.

"I must have eaten tomatoes. I'm highly allergic. Please tell Mr. Jaffray I have taken to my bed." She didn't want him to see her this way, not after they had only recently become intimate.

Turning on her side, she heard Katie leave the room. She should have asked her to bring another damp cloth to cool her face. She would ask for it when her maid returned.

A moment later, James was entering the room dressed in a house robe. Drat, she hadn't wanted him to see her this way. Becca turned toward her pillow, letting her long hair cover her face.

"Becca, what happened? Katie told me you were ill," he said as he came to her bedside.

"I must have eaten tomatoes. I'm very allergic," she said through her veil of hair. "I'll be all right, this will pass. It just takes a day or two."

"Tomatoes? When did you eat tomatoes?" James reached out as if to draw back her hair.

"No. Please don't." She raised her hand to stop him, trapping her hair over her face. Their tentative steps toward intimacy were still too fragile for Becca to risk his disappointment if he were to see her red and swollen face. It would be nice to believe it wouldn't matter, but men tended to be visual where women were concerned and her disfigured face was not likely to encourage appreciation.

He drew back his hand in surprise. "Why not?"

"Trust me, it isn't pretty. I think there might have been tomatoes in the carrot soup. It's the only thing I can think of. When you have a chance, can you ask Miss Brady what was in the soup?"

"I'll go ask her now." The anger in his voice worried Becca. He probably felt helpless, and wanted to take action, but there wasn't much anyone could do other than wait for her reaction to pass.

"You needn't disturb her," Becca said. "I just want to be sure I'm right. Right now, the only thing I can do is sleep." The heat from the nausea had passed and she was feeling chilled. She reached out to pull the blankets around her shoulders and felt James's hands assisting her. "Thank you, James. I'm so sorry about this."

"You needn't be sorry, Becca. You didn't know."

"But I was so looking forward to . . . you know . . . sleeping with you." She spoke softly and hoped Katie wasn't in the room or close enough to hear.

"It's all right. I'll stay here with you." He leaned close to whisper in her ear.

She loved the idea of him holding her close, comforting her through the night, but she was too distressed over the way she felt to give in to such desires. "I'm so sorry, but I would rather you didn't. This isn't going to be pretty. For the next few days, I'm going to look and feel like a red, bloated fish."

"I'm sure it can't be that bad?" There was a note of humor in his voice.

"Oh, yes, it can. I won't even be able to kiss you. But don't worry, it will pass. I expect the worse of my nausea is over."

"I hate to leave you like this." He sounded so protective, she wanted to melt.

"Think of it as a favor to me." She drew back her hair enough to let him see her eyes. She could already feel them starting to swell.

"Oh, I see what you mean. I'll leave you alone, then." Leaning closer, he whispered in a seductive husky voice, "Heal well, I'm looking forward to sleeping with you again, soon. We need to make up for lost time."

Becca felt herself smile, though it hurt her lips. Knowing that more great sex with James awaited her was a stimulating motivator to aid in her recovery. "Thank you, James. You just gave me something to look forward to."

~*~

The next morning, Miss Brady came to her room and confirmed there had indeed been tomato paste in the carrot and ginger soup.

"I thought that might be it. But why? Didn't Mrs. Granger tell you I can't eat tomatoes?" Becca asked her new cook.

"No, Ma'am. It was her recipe I used. She told me it was already planned for that evening's meal and that I should stick to the menu."

"And you believed her? The woman was dismissed because of her deceit."

"I'm so sorry Ma'am. Honestly, I didn't know." Miss Brady sounded on the verge of tears.

"Don't worry about it. I'll be all right. Apparently, Mrs. Granger wanted her revenge, even if she wasn't here to see the results. I don't blame you."

"Are you sure you're going to be all right?" The young servant still didn't look convinced.

Becca knew she looked bad and was using a head scarf to hide most of her face. "Yes, I'll be fine in a few more days."

"I wish there was something I could do. I have some ointment us girls use down in the kitchen. It's almost pure lanolin. It helps take the redness and soreness out of our hands after having them in hot water all day," Miss Brady offered, wringing her hands in her apron. "Maybe it can help you too."

"It's worth a try. Please send some up with Katie." At this point she was willing to try anything. In her previous life she had found only one or two creams that helped relieve the pain and burning redness around her lips and eyes, and neither of them were available to her now.

A while later Katie brought the rich, creamy salve for Becca to try. True to Miss Brady's word, it was like heaven in the way it helped to relieve the burning on her lips.

Still, Becca spent all of Saturday and most of Sunday ensconced in her room waiting for her symptoms to clear. It usually only took a day or two for the worst of it to pass. By Saturday evening, the blisters around her lips were healed and the redness, while still noticeable, was starting to fade thanks to Miss Brady's soothing lotion. The puffiness around her eyes was also receding and her eyelids were looking much better. By late Sunday afternoon, she felt recovered enough to make an appearance in the downstairs parlor, but she still wasn't ready to show her face to the world.

Preferring to wait out her symptoms in the privacy of her own home, Becca skipped going to church services. The last thing she needed was for fashionable New York to get a glimpse of her temporary disfiguration. Church and the rest of the world could wait until she was back to her old self.

By Sunday evening, she was back in bed with James, loving the show of appreciation and affection he showered upon her. Maybe her run-in with the tomatoes wasn't all bad after all, not that she wanted to repeat the experience. The amount of attention James had shown her in the wake of her illness more than compensated for a few painful days of red and burning lips. Knowing her lips were still tender, James had found a dozen new and exciting places to kiss her, submitting her to round after round of torturous pleasure until she screamed for release. Becca was starting to believe he rather liked getting her to scream out with pleasure, and together they often shared raucous laughter over their newfound intimacy.

Sticking to her recently established schedule, Becca met with Miss Brady on Monday morning to discuss menus and the process of purchasing groceries from the various suppliers who had previously worked with Mrs. Granger.

"This is a dependable home. Thankfully, Mrs. Granger always paid our suppliers on time, and there's no reason to think they won't continue to do business with you. If you have any problems with any of them, come to me and let me know. I'll find a way to deal with them," Becca assured the young cook.

"I'm sure that won't be necessary, Mrs. Jaffray. I've already met most of the men Mrs. Granger dealt with; they all know me. I expect some of them won't even be surprised to learn she's gone. As you've seen for yourself, Mrs. Granger wasn't always the nicest person."

Becca held back her grin at Miss Brady's comment. "Yes, so I've learned. I'd like us to go over the menus for the coming week and be sure none of your recipes include tomatoes."

Miss Brady leaned forward in earnest. "You've nothing to worry about, Mrs. Jaffray. I swear, I will never allow tomatoes of any form in the kitchen ever again."

"Good idea! It's so disconcerting to know Mrs. Granger intentionally tried to harm me. But she's gone now and I have complete faith in you."

"I won't let you down, Mrs. Jaffray. You can count on me," Miss Brady assured her, sitting up proudly.

"I want to thank you again for suggesting your lotion. It worked wonders for my lips."

"I'm so glad I could help. I felt awful knowing I had caused you such discomfort."

Becca waved away Miss Brady's concerns. "Water under the bridge. Let's keep moving on." Even as she spoke, Becca wondered why she bothered going through these motions. Yes, she still needed to pretend she was Rebecca Wheland, and she still held out hope that she would successfully complete her penance, but it saddened her to think this would all be taken away from her once she completed her assignment for Jules.

Normally at this time of year, Becca would be out enjoying the decorated shops and doing her Christmas shopping, but she had no idea where she would be in a week or two. It was possible she would be gone well before Christmas. The WAL ball was less than a week away and she was no closer to securing an invitation than the day she arrived to take Rebecca Wheland's place. The days were slipping by faster than snow melting in spring.

~*~

Tuesday, December 5, 1893

Becca decided it was time to pay another visit to Charlene. She hated to impose on her sister-in-law, but where else could she go for assistance. Other than Charlene, Becca had done a dismal job of creating new friends.

While sipping tea in Charlene's parlor, Becca admired the fresh holiday accents of red, green, and gold decorating the room. Whoever had provided Charlene's holiday accessories had done a marvelous job. Becca wished she had such talent.

"It seems you're ready for Christmas. Your home is so beautifully decorated," Becca complimented her.

"I can thank Mrs. Herring, my head housekeeper. She has amazing talent when it comes to these things. It's all about hiring the right staff, you know. They take care of everything for me."

"I completely agree. I know firsthand how important it is to have the right people working for you. I've had to let go both my head housekeeper and cook. There was a problem with the cook's ability to do basic math," Becca said, not wanting to disclose more than necessary about her servant's lack of loyalty.

"Oh my goodness, you can't be serious. At this time of the year it's so hard to find good replacements. Is there anything I can do to help?" Charlene looked honestly aggrieved. Becca liked that about Charlene, she really did care about making other people happy.

"That's not necessary. Thankfully we've been able to find replacements from our own staff. If we can make it through the holidays, I'm sure we'll be fine." Becca took another sip of her tea and asked, "Where ever did you get this? It's marvelous."

"It's a special blend my chef gets from his supplier. Can you taste the jasmine?"

"Is that what that is? It's divine. Do you think your chef would be willing to share his supplier with my cook?"

"You know how chefs are, they like to keep their sources secret, but since you have a new cook, maybe I can convince him as a special favor to me."

"That would be so very kind of you, you're such a dear." Becca set down her teacup, anxious to address the reason for her visit. "I was wondering if you've heard from Mrs. Beaumont yet about getting an invitation for James and me to the WAL ball. I hate to be a harpy about this, but it's less than a week away and I was so hoping James and I could attend. We had such a wonderful time at the opera party with you and Steven." Becca hoped she wasn't laying it on too thick, but desperate times called for desperate flattery.

"Oh my, haven't you heard. I don't think Caroline will be back in time. She's not expected back until Thursday."

"But I thought you said . . . I mean, I was rather counting on her to get us that invitation. I was looking forward to being able to bid on the painting the Delafields donated to the auction," Becca said, reminding

Charlene again of her intention to make a large donation to the WAL charity.

"I know, Rebecca, and I feel awful, but there isn't much more I can do." Charlene shrugged, looking sincerely forlorn. "I was hoping to help, really I was, but I can't very well change Caroline's travel plans."

"No, of course not." Becca shook her head, feeling bad that she had put Charlene in such an awkward position. "I didn't mean to impose." It felt as if her chances of fulfilling her assignment were slipping further and further away, leaving an empty feeling in the pit of her stomach. What would Jules do if she failed? She didn't know. But how could she possibly force herself on a society that repeatedly refused to open its doors?

"There's always next year. If you're able to become a member of the Women's Assistance League you'll be assured an invitation," Charlene said, sounding hopeful.

Not wishing to show her disappointment, Becca put on a stoic face. "Yes, of course, next year." Except she didn't expect to be here next year. Or maybe even next month. "What about you? How are you feeling? Any morning sickness?" Becca asked.

"Mostly I'm feeling fine. I've had some morning sickness, but thankfully it hasn't been all bad. It's the funniest thing, but I've been craving pancakes. Can you imagine? I've had to ask Monsieur Lamont to make them in the middle of the day, which he does, but he calls them crêpes."

"I've heard that happens." Becca had craved popcorn when she was pregnant. Hers had been a nearly painless pregnancy with very little nausea, weight gain, or swelling feet. But then again, she had only been pregnant for about five months. She had barely even started to show. Sadly, she could discuss none of this with Charlene. As far as this world was concerned, she had never been pregnant, never been in an abusive relationship, and had not gone through the pain of losing her baby. In this life, none of that had ever happened. "Since you're expecting, I suggest you stop drinking alcohol until after the baby is born. I've heard that what you eat and drink affects the baby and it's best to be safe."

"Really, I've never heard that." The sweet look of perplexity on Charlene's face told Becca she wasn't sure if she should believe her.

Becca wasn't surprised. Doctors in this age were still recommending glasses of wine to keep women subdued and relaxed as they suffered through this difficult condition, as if giving birth wasn't the most natural thing in the world. "I heard it from a doctor from Switzerland, and you know how advanced they are when it comes to a person's health." Becca figured the reference to Switzerland would help lend authority to her claim. "It's only for a few months, certainly a small consideration when it comes to the health and well-being of your child."

"Oh, yes, I totally agree. I shall make a point of avoiding alcohol until after the baby is born. Do you think that includes wine? I do like wine with my dinner."

Becca understood how some habits were hard to break. She had given up coffee for the short time she had known she was pregnant. If only she had given up Ralph instead. "Based on what the Swiss doctor told me, I'm sure it includes wine."

Charlene nodded thoughtfully, as if taking her suggestion under serious consideration. "Does it also include champagne?"

"I'm afraid so," Becca confirmed.

Putting her dismal prospects of going to the ball out of her mind, Becca spent another twenty minutes enjoying her sister-in-law's company, discussing her pregnancy. Dwelling on negative thoughts, or worrying about something that hadn't happened, was only going to make her feel bad. Sure, she was running out of options, but worrying about it every minute of the day wasn't going to do her any good. She was here with Charlene, a charming woman who had shown her nothing but kindness and respect. She owed the woman her full attention and complete support.

~*~

Like some mystical psychic who knew the exact moment she would arrive, Mr. Jenkins was standing at the door, ready to open it while Becca was still climbing the front stairs. As he assisted her with her hat and coat he informed her, "You have a visitor, Mrs. Jaffray. Your brother, Randolph Wheland has come to call and insisted on staying until you returned."

"Randolph!" This was somewhat unexpected. Becca had expected he would send word before showing up on her doorstep.

"Yes, Ma'am, he's in the front parlor."

Rather than being filled with apprehension, a feeling of joy washed over her. She hurried into the parlor and when Randolph stood to greet her, she rushed into his arms as she would a long-lost brother.

"Randolph, dear brother, it's so good to see you. When did you return?" She wrapped her arms around him, freeing a flood of affection flowing through her.

"Whoa, there, little sister. Why the great show of emotion? What have I done to deserve all this? If I didn't know better, I would think you missed me." Randolph asked as they broke their embrace.

"Of course, I missed you. It's been a month or more since I last saw you. Can't a sister be happy to see her brother?" She reached for his hands and drew him back to the sofa to sit. "Come. Tell me all about your travels. How was London? Have you been to see Father?" Interestingly, rather than feeling as if she were greeting a stranger, it felt as if she had known this man her whole life.

"I arrived only this morning, just got off the boat. I stopped off at the house, but then I came here. The last time I saw you, you looked so forlorn, I wanted to see how you're doing." His gaze swept over her from head to toe. "You look changed, Rebecca. For the better from what I can see, as if you're finally happy."

"I am, Randolph, I'm happy. Better than ever, except for my recent illness, but even that is a thing of the past."

"You were sick? What happened?" She loved the show of brotherly concern that washed over his face and it endeared him to her all the more.

"What a story, let me tell you. First, I discovered that our cook was stealing from us by inflating the amount needed to pay for our groceries. Then, when I had to let her go, she told the new cook to prepare a dish with tomatoes even though I had told her I can't eat them. I had a horrible allergic reaction and was in bed for several days, but I'm all better now."

"I don't recall you ever being allergic to tomatoes." Randolph eyed her with a questioning look.

Too late, Becca realized her mistake. She'd been so caught up welcoming a friendly face, she had forgotten she wasn't actually Randolph's sister, the woman he had grown up with. Of course, he would know whether or not Rebecca had ever been allergic to tomatoes. "I only developed the allergy recently, or maybe it simply has gotten worse over the years. I've heard that can happen," she said, trying to mend her mistake. "It seems every time I'm exposed to tomatoes the reaction gets worse. You may not have noticed, but I do my best to avoid them, especially since I've realized they make me ill. But let's not dwell on such a minor matter, it's already come and gone. Tell me about London. Were you successful with your investment?"

"London was a success, Father and Uncle Henry should be happy, but I've discovered I have a greater interest in art and antiques than banking investments."

"Oh my goodness, does Father know?" Becca had a feeling Stanton Wheland wouldn't be too happy to hear this news.

"Not yet, but he'll find out soon enough. I'm sure he'll scream and shout, but in the end, I'll simply nod and disregard what he says. Since I came into my trust fund from Mother, I have the means to do as I please and I want to become an art and antiques dealer. With all the people I know, I should have no problem setting up my business." His eyes left hers and roamed about the room almost as if he were assessing the value of the objects surrounding them. Many of them, Becca knew, were old family heirlooms.

"How can you be so strong? Father intimidates me so." She had only briefly encountered the man and that was more than enough for her.

"Because I stopped caring what he thinks. When he forced me to give up Miss Wilson because he didn't approve, he lost that right. I listened to him, thinking it would make him happy, but I've discovered nothing makes Father happy, at least not for long. The minute I try to please him, he'll find something else to disapprove of. I may as well do whatever pleases me and let him be hanged by his own unhappiness."

"Randolph! Surely you don't mean that." Becca supported him whole-heartedly, but to hear it spoken aloud was more shocking than she had expected.

"Sorry to disappoint you, little sister, but there's no pleasing Father. You should stop trying."

She nodded thoughtfully. "In a way, I suppose I have. James and I are happy, regardless of how Father may have hoped otherwise."

"Bravo for you. It seems we shall be united in our rebellion. It's always good to have the numbers on our side. What made you change your mind? When I left, I worried that you were two steps from leaving James."

That may have been true at one time, but not anymore. "I've changed. Rather like you, I stopped worrying about how to make everyone else happy and decided I need to make *me* happy. I've also found I rather like

James when I'm not trying to fight, or ignore, or avoid him all the time. Did you know it takes an awful lot of energy to hold a grudge?"

Randolph laughed uproariously. "I couldn't agree more. I'll no longer give my energy to supporting Father's resentments."

"I'm happy for you, Randolph. I'm sure you'll be a great success. You have all the right connections." Becca suspected Randolph would be a natural for the job of art dealer. Father may not like his chosen profession, but she could easily see him moving from the art of the deal, which Stanton Wheland so dearly loved, to becoming a dealer of art, which suited Randolph much better.

Considering Randolph's extensive connections, Becca asked, "Since you know everyone in town, do you think you can possibly get me an invitation to the WAL ball?"

Randolph looked perplexed. "Did I hear you correctly? Did you say wall ball?"

Becca chuckled at his confusion. "The Women's Assistance League. They're having a holiday charity ball this Friday and I desperately want to go. Surely you must know someone you can call upon to help. Perhaps one of those pretty little debutantes who anxiously follow you around at parties hoping you'll look their way." Becca had no way of knowing for certain if that were true, but like any other eligible, handsome, and extremely rich young man, she guessed such an assessment would apply to Randolph Wheland.

Randolph laughed at her comment. "I doubt one of my debutantes would have the right access to obtain an invitation, but I'll see what I can do. However, there's a new exhibit opening tomorrow at the Metropolitan Museum I want you to see. I'll make a few enquiries regarding your sought-after invitation only if you agree to attend the opening with me tomorrow. You need to get out more and mingle with society. Then you wouldn't need to come to your brother for these types of favors. You're a Jaffray now, society should be lining up at your door for your attention."

"I would love to see the exhibit with you, of course I agree. Are you able to stay for dinner? I expect James will be home soon. I'm sure he would like to see you."

"I wish I could, but I need to get back to see Father. He's going to want a full report on my business trip and you know I can't keep him waiting."

Becca completely understood. "But you promise to come by tomorrow to take me to your new art exhibit. We can talk more then."

"I'll be here promptly at eleven."

Becca smiled broadly. "I'll be ready."

Randolph stood and offered his hand as Becca also rose from the sofa. Reluctant to see him leave so soon, she saw him to the door and kissed him goodbye. As she watched the door close behind him, she held onto a small glimmer of hope that he would indeed obtain the coveted invitation she needed to attend the ball and successfully bid on the painting as Jules had requested. Being so close to her goal made her wonder even more what was to become of her once she had completed her assignment.

CHAPTER 12

Wednesday, December 6, 1893

It might be cold and snowing outside, but to James, his life had never looked brighter. He had just signed the contract with the New York, Erie, and Western Railroads, making his company, Jaffray Industries, their primary supplier of railcars for the next two years. If all went well, he fully expected the contract to be renewed for another two years after that.

To top it all off, his marriage with Rebecca was beginning to look like a love match. They had been married for nearly five months and suddenly it was as if he was a newlywed on his honeymoon, enjoying passion-filled nights with his loving wife. As his carriage slowly made its way through the snow-covered streets, he felt like a man on top of the world.

With everything going so well, he wanted to do something special for Rebecca, something he knew would make her happy. He should have done this some time ago, but he'd been too bullheaded to concede to her wishes. Feeling generous and lighthearted, he decided to stop on his way home to send a cable to his mother asking her to provide the invitation to the WAL ball Becca wanted to attend.

He had been a fool to fight her. All he had accomplished was wasting precious time he could have spent enjoying her company in his bed. Who would have guessed that somewhere behind her grim, aloof exterior had been a soft-hearted, loving woman willing to fulfill his fantasies and desires? Becca had become a wild woman in bed once she shed her fish-like inhibitions and let down her hair—that gorgeous, sexy, luxurious hair. He loved burying his face in her hair, her breasts, and especially between her legs, which she had willingly allowed. He'd done more than make his little kitten purr, he'd made her scream out in pleasure, and he loved it.

This was not the old Rebecca Wheland he had been forced to marry. This new and improved version went beyond his wildest dreams. For the past few days, they had spent several hours sequestered away in his bedroom repeatedly making love and enjoying the pleasure of each other's bodies. Once she released her inhibitions, and let go of her resentment over their arranged marriage, Rebecca had become a whole new woman. And she had asked him to call her Becca, which he also loved.

A few weeks ago, he hadn't believed such a thing was possible, but as unlikely as it seemed, he was falling in love with his wife. After she returned from her self-imposed retreat, he had repeatedly rebuked her and each time she had remained steadfast in her loyalty and determination to make their marriage better. This new Becca was kinder, sweeter, and certainly more affectionate. How he had gotten so lucky, or what he had done to deserve this, he had no idea, but as a sign of his appreciation, he would cable his mother asking for that coveted invitation. He only hoped his mother had enough time to make it happen.

Feeling confident in his success, James left the telegraph office and stepped into his carriage, anxious to go home to his wife. He all but stopped breathing when he saw the man sitting across from him in his own carriage.

Jules Vanderzeit.

Before he could catch his breath, Jules rapped his cane on the roof and the carriage lurched forward.

"What do you want with me? I told you, I'll no longer work for you," James said after settling into his seat. He would have liked to kick Vanderzeit to the curb, but the carriage was already moving and he'd been raised better than to toss a man out into traffic.

"Is that any way to greet an old friend?" Vanderzeit asked, with his hands resting comfortably on his walking stick as the carriage swayed down the road.

Friend my ass.

Vanderzeit ignored his loathsome sneer and continued speaking. "I've come to make you a proposition I think may interest you."

"I highly doubt it." He was about to rap on the roof to instruct his driver to stop when Jules held out his gloved hand to stop him.

"Hear me out before you decide. I only need a few minutes of your time. Surely you can spare that for an old friend."

"I don't consider you my friend."

"Then for all we've been through together." Jules cast him a meaningful look. James understood. Regardless of what payment he had extracted, the man had once saved his brother's life.

"Speak. And make it fast." He would let the man say his piece, but in the end, his mind was already made up.

Jules relaxed against the seat of the cab. "If you will recall, the last time we met, I offered to give you the money you needed to get you through your rough patch if you agreed to work for me for another six years. Sadly, you refused my offer and went to Wheland for the loan, and in exchange, you were forced to marry his daughter. I understand that wasn't much of a love match. I also understand you just closed a deal that will ensure your wealth and status for many years to come. As such, I'm offering to let you go back to that day when you turned me down, and make a different offer."

"You don't get it. I'm not interested."

"You haven't heard my other offer yet. Hear me out, if for no other reason than for curiosity's sake." Jules leaned slightly forward with a look of earnestness. 'What if I offered to *give* you the money you needed, not a loan, and you only have to complete one assignment for me? There's a painting I want. It's here in New York. It won't even require you to leave this time. You wouldn't have to go to Wheland, you would never have married Rebecca, and five months later, you'll still have secured this lucrative deal with the railroads. Think about it, one little assignment to have everything you need and still be a free man to marry whomever you pleased."

James did his best to maintain a poker face. As far as he was concerned, he held the winning cards. He may not have started his marriage in the best of circumstances, but now he couldn't ask for anything better. Yes, he had been through hell with Rebecca, but since her little get-away, things had gotten better. So much better, he couldn't imagine life without her. Nor did he want to. Vanderzeit could take his offer, shove it in a snow bank, and let it freeze for all he cared.

"So let me get this straight. I'll get the money I need, but I don't have to deal with Wheland, or marry his daughter. And I'll still get the New York, Erie, and Western Railroad contracts. All this in exchange for doing one little assignment for you?" *How important could this one painting be?* He knew better than to ask. If Jules wanted something, he always got it.

Vanderzeit sat back looking extremely pleased. "Correct. I think you've got the gist of it."

James nearly busted out laughing. "Thanks, but no thanks. When I finished my contract with you, I promised myself I would never work for you again. Thankfully, I plan to keep that promise. I'm fine with things just the way they are. You can keep your offer and kindly get out of my carriage." Let him go find some other unsuspecting fool to do his dirty work.

Again, Jules raised his hand to prevent James from stopping the carriage. "Not so fast, one last thing. If it were all taken from you tomorrow, or maybe next week, would you still want things to stay as they are?"

James sat forward in his seat. "You know something, don't you?"

"I always know something. That's hardly the point and not the question."

James became quiet as he mulled over what Jules had said. Wasn't that the way of life? He could never know for certain what would happen next, and yet life was still worth living, as long as he and Becca were together. "After working for you for seven years, I've learned to accept what life has to offer."

"Are you quite sure? One rarely gets a second chance such as this. Take my offer and it will be as if you never married Miss Rebecca Wheland. Refuse it and you can consider yourself stuck with her for life, or as long as you both shall live, so help us God, and all that romantic hooey."

"I'll take the 'so help us God' thank you very much. Now I'm still waiting for you to get out of my carriage."

"No need to get testy. As you wish, my good man. As you wish."

Nearly as one, they rapped on the roof of the carriage, bringing it to a stop. Jules kindly tipped his hat and exited the coach. As James watched the door close behind him, he fervently hoped this would be the last time he ever saw the manipulative man.

~*~

Thursday, December 7, 1893

Becca yawned, stretched, and smiled as she awoke with a feeling of joy and contentment, thinking about how much she loved life and it loved her back. She and James had spent the early hours of the morning making love before he dressed and headed off to his downtown office. The joy of sleeping in his arms and waking each morning in his bed was the stuff that dreams were made of. It was becoming a habit for them to make love each morning and she could think of no better way to start the day. As much as she enjoyed their nightly lovemaking, she enjoyed their morning encounters even more. Waking to find herself lying naked next to her husband in his bed was even more arousing than slipping into his room each night dressed in her fancy lace nightgowns, which James enjoyed removing from her body as soon as he was able.

Each night in his arms, making love with James, filled her heart with joy and left her aching for more. Becca took a few more minutes to enjoy the warmth and sensuous scent lingering in the sheets before she forced herself to leave the comfort of his bed. After slipping on her nightgown that had been tossed at the foot of the bed the night before, she glided back to her room and began to prepare for the day.

Peering out the window, it looked as though they were in for another cold, winter's day, but thankfully the snow had stopped falling and the work crews were busy clearing the streets. She had never liked the cold, snow and ice of New England winters, especially when she had needed to trudge through the snow to get to work. Since there was no place she needed to go today, she decided she would snuggle up next to the fire with a good book.

It was somewhat of a surprise when Mr. Jenkins came to inform her that Randolph Wheland had come to call.

"Randolph, I can't believe you braved the cold and snow to come and visit me," Becca said as she set aside her book and stood to greet her

209

brother. "Mr. Jenkins, please have some hot chocolate prepared, or would you prefer coffee?"

"The hot chocolate sounds good," Randolph replied as he took a moment to warm his hands by the fire.

"Mr. Jenkins, please have Miss Brady prepare some for us."

"As you wish, Mrs. Jaffray." The butler bowed politely and exited the room.

"Let me assure you, after spending weeks in London, I much prefer the snow to constant rain and fog," Randolph said as he took a seat with her on the sofa. "I come bearing good news. I was able to get us an invitation to that ball you want to attend. And of course, you can bring James." He produced two large embossed cards from the pocket of his coat.

Becca cried with delight as she hugged her brother. "Oh my goodness, Randolph, this is good news. How did you do it?"

"It was a simple matter, as I knew it would be. My good friends, Mr. and Mrs. Richard Dorvall, were more than happy to extend us invitations to the ball on their behalf. He owns the Park View Hotel, you know; and is an excellent resource for future art clientele. I can assure you, they wouldn't lift a finger to come to the aid of our father, but they were more than happy to assist me in your quest to attend the ball. They have also offered a place for us at their table for dinner. I' sure you won't mind dinning with them at the ball."

"Randolph, you're too dear, I can't thank you enough. Attending this ball means so much to me."

"Why so? That's something you've yet to explain. You've attended dozens of balls, what makes this one so special?"

Becca hesitated a moment before responding. "I suppose we always want what seems hardest to obtain," she said wistfully. "When I heard about the ball, but hadn't received an invitation, it became somewhat of a quest I needed to complete."

"Really! A quest? How interesting. Tell me more."

"You see, there's an art auction being held at the ball to benefit the WAL charities and I have my eye on one of the paintings donated for the auction."

Randolph looked impressed. "An art auction? Interesting indeed. I'm anxious to see what pieces our Manhattan friends will see fit to part with. I can't believe there will be many masterpieces among them, but one can always hope. It will provide great insight into my intended clientele."

"Always the business man, I see," Becca chided him. "Father should be proud."

"I really don't care whether Father is proud or not. He will not be there either way, and I shall enjoy the evening all the more without him."

"Do you think it's fair we have united against him?" Becca asked, voicing the concerns of her conscience.

"Was it fair he tried to ruin both of our lives with his underhanded control? Not only did he force you to marry Jaffray, he forced me to set aside Miss Wilson." Becca detected a look of hurt in his eyes that went beyond the need to choose his own livelihood.

"You love her that much?" Becca asked.

"Not so much anymore, but at one time, I did, and that's what's important." He waved a hand through the air as if it were no longer a concern. "They say the best revenge is a life well lived, and I for one, intend to seek great revenge against our father by enjoying my life to its fullest. From what I can see, it appears you plan to do the same."

For now, that was true. Still, Becca couldn't help but wonder how much longer her fairy tale life would continue before Jules brought it all to an end.

Mr. Jenkins brought in the hot chocolate she had ordered and set the tray on a nearby table. Randolph accepted a mug from her and took a sip.

"My word, this is delicious. Is this a sample of your new cook?"

Becca nodded cheerfully then took a sip from her mug. "I know, it's good, isn't it? I'm so lucky, we had Miss Brady right here under our noses the whole time."

"I must say, Rebecca, sometimes I think you live under a lucky star." He took another sip of his chocolate and nearly purred with delight.

A lucky star! If only that were true. Although it may not have always felt that way, lately, Becca had to admit, things were looking up.

Randolph stayed for another half hour enjoying his chocolate and sharing bits of gossip he had acquired since his return to New York. Several times, he had her laughing, and Becca rejoiced in the fact that she had such a loving brother to lend her moral support.

She had just settled back in with a book after seeing him off when she heard voices coming from the front hall. Setting aside her book once again, she stepped out into the wide corridor to see what the commotion was all about. Surprisingly, it was James, returning home in the middle of the day. When he saw her at the end of the hall, he came rushing forward.

"I have it, Becca," he said, waving an envelope in his hand. "I have the invitation to that WAL ball you wanted."

"Oh my goodness, James, I thought you said . . ." Up until now he had made it clear he wanted nothing to do with her desire to attend the charity ball.

"It doesn't matter what I said before. I cabled Mother and she arranged for an invitation to be sent to my office." James met her halfway down the hall and pulled her into his arms. "Are you happy, my love?"

"Oh my goodness, James, this is so sweet of you." Though she had already secured an invitation through Randolph, she saw no reason to mention that to James. She'd not do anything to diminish his grand gesture.

"It's the least I could do. I always knew Mother would come through for me, I just needed to stop being so bullheaded and stop fighting you every step of the way. You deserve this, Becca. I want you to be happy."

"I am happy, James. You make me happy." Resting her head against his shoulder, she couldn't deny how important it was to know James had done this for her.

He pulled back and kissed her forehead. "I told Charlene we would sit at her table for dinner and the auction, I hope you don't mind."

"That sounds marvelous. I'd love to spend the evening with your sister." She would have to inform Randolph she wouldn't be joining him and the Dorvalls, but hopefully he wouldn't mind too much. Most likely, he would be happy for her.

"Not the whole evening, mind you," he said, as they started for the upstairs parlor for their usual evening cocktail. "I expect to have a dance or two with my wife."

With my wife. She loved the way those words sounded. "I think you should count on it. Interestingly, I just had a visit from Randolph. He'll also be at the ball. Isn't that wonderful?"

James' expression darkened. "Wheland won't be there, will he?"

"Oh, no. Randolph assured me, no one would ever think to give him an invitation."

His smile returned. "Good. In that case, I look forward to seeing your brother."

"It's going to be grand, James. Such a happy time with family."

As she climbed the stairs with James, it seemed strange to think that only yesterday she had feared she had run out of options, and today she had secured not one, but two invitations from both James and Randolph. All at once, she felt accepted and appreciated by the people who meant the most to her.

CHAPTER 13

Friday, December 8, 1893

Beauty wasn't limited to the way one looked. Beauty was a feeling, and Becca felt beautiful as she stepped into the Fifth Avenue hotel ballroom where the Women's Assistance League charity ball was in full swing. She walked with James, her hand resting possessively on his arm, as they entered the room, its parquet floor polished to a shine under glittering chandeliers. Dotted throughout the room were dozens of cut-glass crystal vases filled with flowers and feathers as part of the holiday decorations. The air was thick with the fragrance of roses, irises, and lilies provided from the finest greenhouse florists in New York. Comfortable, velvet-covered settees ringed the walls of the room where societies' matrons and wallflowers alike could sit and watch the evening's festivities. Music floated through the air provided by a small orchestra half-concealed by lush palms and holiday greenery. Later, at midnight, supper would be served in an adjoining room where the auction would be held.

Lavish gowns, furs, and heavy jewels were on proud display to signify the wealth and standing of the couples in attendance. To think she could be rubbing shoulders with the upper crust of New York society was beyond her wildest dreams. Like those around her, she made a point of appearing unfazed by the opulence surrounding her and restrained from gawking at the outlandish displays of abundance.

The responsibility of keeping society's upper-class safe from the prying eyes of the masses fell to the matrons of Manhattan. They were the gate keepers tasked with organizing the teas, dinner parties, and balls such as this that kept them all connected. For the wives of Manhattan's elite, childbearing was their chore, social life their recreation, and being respected their privilege.

"Are you happy to be here?" James whispered into Becca's ear as they strolled around the room greeting friends and acquaintances. They had already danced together a number of times, and he hadn't left her side all evening for longer than it took to retrieve a glass of wine or greet an old friend.

"I am, perhaps more than I expected," Becca replied in an equally low voice, "but none of this would matter if you weren't here with me. Yes, I wanted to attend this ball, but my greatest reward is having you at my side. I can't help but notice, you've been rather protective of me lately."

He paused with a thoughtful look. "After I saw how you handled Mrs. Granger and what she did to you in return, I suppose I became a little more protective. I'll admit, I realized I took you for granted."

His confession brought a lump to her throat. "But not anymore?"

"No, not anymore. You showed me kindness and respect when I had done little to deserve it."

"I suspect you're being a little too hard on yourself. We've both made mistakes. And we're both trying to mend our ways. I think we each deserve a bit of credit."

"Rightly so, but one of us needed to take the lead or we would have continued down our path of marital self-destruction. For that, Becca, I have you to thank."

Leaning closer still, Becca whispered softly in his ear, "And I have you to thank for showing me how much fun it can be to share your bed. I don't know what I was thinking to stay away for so long. It just goes to show you, we can all learn from our mistakes."

A sinful grin spread across his face. "I believe there may be a few more lessons we've yet to explore. Are you up for the task?"

"With you as my teacher, I'm a willing student." She wondered if her provocative comment was creating the same sort of fantasies for James as it did for her. Stern teacher, naïve student, short skirts and perhaps a riding crop all came to mind. Based on the devilish look in his eyes, she suspected his thoughts ventured down a similar path. Too bad she would be all done-in by the time they returned home. Her lesson would have to wait until she was well-rested. Something told her she was going to need her strength to keep up with her talented teacher.

It was nearly midnight, time to make their way into the large dining room prepared for the guests to sit for supper and the auction. "Have you received your bid number?" James asked as they searched for his sister and their table.

"Yes, they assigned me number sixty-nine. Do you suppose it will be lucky for me?" She batted her eyes coyly as if she had no clue to the number's hidden innuendo.

"Lucky, perhaps. I've always found the number rather interesting."

She peered at her bid card as if perplexed. "It reminds me of something . . ." Pausing long enough to allow him to wonder what she might say next, she turned the card on its side and then upright again. "Oh, yes, I remember now. It's the Chinese symbol for yin and yang. Have you seen it?"

"I believe it means up and down," he said in a teasing manner.

"I think it means dark and light, but close enough." Suddenly feeling overheated, she fanned herself with her bid card, waving it rapidly back and forth.

They joined Charlene and Steven at their table and took their seats, waiting for the auction to begin.

"Do you see anything you like?" Becca asked her brother-in-law as he flipped through the auction catalog.

"Nothing I want to bid on. I'm trying to let things go, not accumulate more. I'll have to remember to donate a few things for next year's auction," Steven said, glancing over at his wife.

Charlene nodded in agreement. "We need to make room for the baby. There are so many things I need, I plan to start shopping right after the holidays."

"My brother Randolph is becoming an art and antiques dealer. If there's anything you want to buy or sell, I'm sure he can help."

"How very thoughtful. I'll let you know." Charlene nodded in appreciation as the first item was being announced, directing their attention to the stage.

Leaning closer to James, Becca explained, "I wanted to let you know, I plan to use the money from my mother's trust fund to bid on a painting. It's something I've had my eye on for a very long time." It occurred to her, if she started bidding without letting him know of her intentions, he might become suspicious on where she expected to get the money. Jules had assured her the money in her account was available for her to use as she wished since it was part of her marriage settlement. She only hoped it would be enough to accomplish her task. As the deadline to her assignment inched closer, her dread over its possible outcome increased. Her future seemed more and more uncertain as the days marched on, and yet she had very little choice other than to continue down the path she was on. However, if she were able to secure the painting Jules wanted, at least she would have something to bargain with.

"Are you sure that's the best use of your money?" James asked, looking less than pleased.

"Randolph assures me that art is a good investment, if I pick a good piece. I'm rather set on buying this one. I hope you don't mind." She hated lying to him, but what else could she do except flat out refuse to do as Jules demanded. Being obligated to the Maestro was becoming a bigger problem than she ever could have imagined.

"I suppose we can trust Randolph's opinion. I'm sure he's earnest about being successful in his newly chosen profession," he said, sounding notably uncertain.

"I'm sure we can trust Randolph. He wouldn't give me bad advice."

James seemed accepting of her plans, but Becca felt a rock in the pit of her stomach.

About three-quarters into the auction, the painting Becca was instructed to buy, the Magic Flute by V.W. Stevenson, came up for bid. Focusing her attention on the action taking place, Becca readied her bid card. From her limited experience, she believed it was best to hang back and not show too much enthusiasm or a competitive bidder might try to quickly out bid her.

The bidding started at five thousand dollars and rapidly began to go up. It seemed there was much more interest in this painting than Becca had anticipated. Eight thousand, ten thousand, whizzed by in an instant. Becca raised her bid card at the call for twenty thousand, but that was quickly upped to twenty-five by another in the crowd. At thirty thousand, Becca made her highest bid, the full amount she had in her account, and still the bids went higher. She dropped her bid card on the table and folded her hands in her lap, feeling defeated. All her work to attend this ball was for naught. She wasn't going to get the painting Jules had requested, and now she had no idea what fate awaited her.

She was barely paying attention when she heard the auctioneer shout, "Sold, for fifty thousand dollars."

Fifty thousand dollars! That was one of the highest bids of the evening and well above what she had been prepared to offer. What was Jules thinking? Did he not know the value of the painting? She looked around, wondering who had made the winning bid, but it was too late. The auctioneer had moved on to the next piece.

She looked over to James and smiled bravely. "Oh well, my loss."

"There will be others," he assured her, covering her hand in comfort.

He had done so much to make the evening magical; she wouldn't let him see her disappointment. The least she could do was set aside her feelings of frustration and enjoy the rest of the party as if nothing was amiss.

Actually, who was she to blame? Jules had known her limits of ready cash. If he had wanted the painting so badly, he should have ensured she had enough funds in her account to make the purchase. She didn't know what would happen to her when Jules found out she had failed, but she couldn't think about that now. Tonight, she was with the man she loved. She wasn't about to let a silly little thing like not knowing her future spoil her night. Tonight, she would drink, dance and be merry, for she truly had no idea what tomorrow would bring.

~*~

It was late in the day when Becca and James finally emerged from their lovemaking cocoon. They hadn't returned home until nearly four in the morning and James had informed Mr. Jenkins they were not to be disturbed for any reason short of the house being on fire.

Since it was Saturday, and James had nowhere he needed to be, they spent the day at home, ensuring the hearths were well fed to keep her warm while they lounged away the day, reading, playing cards, and exchanging coy glances. All in all, Becca couldn't remember a more relaxing or enjoyable day, feeling safe and cozy in the Jaffray mansion while a light snow fell off and on throughout the day turning the streets outside into a winter wonderland.

They talked about going ice-skating in Central Park, but never seemed to rally the energy to leave the house. Becca was feeling especially spent after the morning of lovemaking lessons James had put her through. It also helped to explain her repeated bouts of staring longingly at her husband. Just the thought of him, and what they had done, made her tingle all over. Too bad she had forgotten to ask him if he owned a riding crop.

Occasionally, her mind would wander to thoughts of Jules and what he might do when he found out she had not been able to purchase the painting he wanted. And each time, she vowed to put those thoughts aside. Though she had no doubt a reckoning would soon occur, there was no reason to worry about something that hadn't yet happened. She had done her best to do as the Maestro asked; hopefully that was worth some consideration.

The weekend passed in a blissful, slow moving haze as Becca and James savored their time together comfortably ensconced in their cozy love nest. It took a bit of effort, but on Monday morning, James finally dragged himself from their bed and left for his office.

Becca was sitting at the breakfast table, happily enjoying her second cup of coffee when the butler entered the room.

"This letter just arrived for you, Madam, delivered by personal messenger. The young man who delivered it said it was most important," Mr. Jenkins informed her.

Feeling a mixture of anxiety, fear, and anticipation, Becca reached out and took the letter from his hand. Her full name, *Rebecca Wheland Jaffray*, was written on the front of the envelope in finely curved script; on the back was a red wax seal. She fingered the heavy, cream-colored envelope for a moment before looking up at her butler.

"Thank you, Mr. Jenkins." Hurriedly, she retreated to the sanctuary of her room. Taking a chair near the window, she sat for several minutes staring at the envelope before she turned it over and broke the wax seal.

Becca,
Meet me Tuesday, two o'clock, at the Park View Hotel, room 444.
Bring the painting.
Jules Vanderzeit

219

Tomorrow! She only had until tomorrow. But she didn't have the painting. She didn't even know who had placed the winning bid. It seemed she was doomed to failure, and she had a very strong suspicion the Maestro did not tolerate failure. What on earth was she going to tell him?

CHAPTER 14

Tuesday, December 12, 1893

Not knowing if she would ever see him again, Becca made love to her husband with enough passion to last a lifetime. By the time he returned home from his office, she would be gone to her meeting with Jules, and she had no idea what to expect. When the Maestro sent her on this assignment, he hadn't told her to fall in love with James Jaffray, only that she needed to convince him that she was his wife.

"You keep this up, my dear, and I may never go to my office again," James teased as she reached for him one last time.

"It's nice to know you'll have something to remember me by as you go about your day," Becca told him, trying to sound light-hearted and jovial. If there were any way she could negotiate with Jules to stay with James, she planned to try, but she had a feeling one did not negotiate with the Maestro. She had already struck her bargain with the man, or devil, or whatever he was, and she doubted he would cut her some slack.

"I'm not likely to forget this anytime soon." He leaned over and cupped her face in his large, warm hands. "I believe the last few days have been the best of my life. I never expected I could fall in love with my wife."

221

He loved her. And she loved him. And yet none of that changed what she needed to do. Tears burned at the back of her eyes, but she determinedly blinked them away. She would not let him see her cry.

"I love you, too, James, more than I had ever imagined possible. I wouldn't trade our time together for anything."

"It hasn't always been easy for us, has it. And yet, here we are, five months into our marriage and acting like love-struck newlyweds unable to get enough of each other." He brought his lips to hers and kissed her, fiercely at first then gently roving to her cheek, her earlobe, and down her neck. Hot tingles shot through every fiber of her being.

Breathless, she managed to say, "I don't believe one can ever have enough love. Or laughter, or joy or all the things you've given me. I shall carry this in my heart forever. You, my dear lover, can rest assured you will never be forgotten."

James snorted out an amused laugh. "You needn't be so dramatic. I'm only going to my office. I have a few loose ends to tie up regarding the new contract with the railroads. If at all possible, I'll try to be home early."

"Don't worry about me, I'll be fine." She drew a deep breath, and kissed him again, knowing she had already said more than she should.

Once James had left for the office, Becca attempted to go about her usual morning routine, taking her breakfast in the small family dining room, but it was never long before she once again checked a clock. Time was slipping away and her nerves were beginning to fray. She had an appointment to see Jules Vanderzeit, the Maestro, a man who could orchestrate time. Pretending to be a wealthy socialite was a piece of cake compared to what awaited her at the Park View Hotel.

For the past three weeks, it felt as if Becca had been living a daydream, living in a big beautiful house surrounded by helpful servants and married to a man she had come to love more than she could have believed possible. There were times when she feared it might all be a dream, but for now, it was the only reality she knew.

Thinking back on her life, she realized it was time for her to forgive herself for her past mistakes. Beating herself up over the past and things she had little or no control over wasn't going to change anything. Jules was right, miscarriages happened, some people were downright mean, others died, it was nobody's fault. That didn't make it fair, and it didn't make it right, it was just the way of life. Painfully, and slowly, she had learned how to keep on living.

Now it seemed, no matter how she spun it, she was once again going to be hit with the loss of someone she loved, and hit hard. Why had she allowed herself to become so attached to James? Why had she allowed herself to fall in love? She always knew she'd be leaving this life behind once her assignment was done. Except it wasn't complete. She hadn't gotten the painting as Jules demanded. She had failed in her assignment, and as Jules had warned, if she failed, she would have hell to pay.

Worried that James would return home sooner than she expected, Becca went to her room shortly before noon, telling Katie she planned to rest for a while and asked not to be disturbed. After changing into in her warmest wool dress, overcoat and hat, she quietly made her way down the stairs. Doing her best not to alert any of the servants of her plans, she slipped out the front door and hurried down the front steps. When she reached the sidewalk, she took one last look over her shoulder before she scurried down the street, her feet slipping and sliding on the snow-covered ground. When she reached the street corner, she hailed a hired cab and directed him to the Park View Hotel. The weather had warmed, and what had once been a winter wonderland of white was now only dirty, soot-covered slush.

~*~

James came home early thinking he would surprise Becca, but she wasn't at home and none of the servants knew where she had gone. She had told her maid Katie she was going upstairs to take a nap and that was the last anyone saw of her. Not even Jenkins knew she had left, nor Mr. Bates, their driver. She must have taken a hired hack, which didn't make any sense when she had a perfectly good carriage and driver at her disposal.

A feeling of déjà vu washed over him and James was suddenly struck with a sick feeling that his wife wasn't coming back. She wasn't going to suddenly arrive home, climb the stairs and join him for their usual evening drink. The way she had said goodbye that morning when he left for work sounded as if it was final and he didn't know why. What he needed were some answers, and sitting here alone wasn't going to produce them.

Hoping to find something, anything that could tell him what had happened to her, or why he felt this way, James went to her bedroom.

223

Other than her recent illness, he had never invaded her private rooms, preferring to respect her privacy, but something nagged at him, telling him this was important. He had learned years ago to follow his instincts, and while snooping didn't set well with him, he needed to find some clue to tell him where his wife had gone.

Quiet emptiness surrounded him as he stepped into her bedroom and looked around. Nothing appeared out of order. Her clothes still hung in her closet, her brushes and bottles still sat upon her dresser. Even the scent of her was still in the air, a soft, floral scent he had grown to anticipate every time she was near. He was becoming more and more discouraged when he noticed the half-opened drawer in her bedside table. Stepping closer, he saw that a book had been shoved in the drawer. It looked like a journal.

For a brief second, he resisted picking it up, but something inside him told him this was important. Feeling the heavy thud of expectation beating in his chest, he opened the book and flipped through the pages. It was Becca's handwriting; he recognized it from her accounting worksheets.

He started looking through the last few pages, hoping Becca had left some clue as to where she had gone. He hadn't read very far when a name jumped out at him big as life. *Jules Vanderzeit*. Holy crap, how on earth could Becca know about the Maestro?

James sat on the chair closest to the window and began reading with his heart thumping wildly in his chest. He quickly realized Becca was working for Jules. It was almost too shocking to believe. His own experiences told him how manipulative Jules could be. Her last entry said she had failed to get the painting of the Magic Flute, as Jules had requested, and she was worried to death about what he might do. It confirmed that she had gone to meet him, but it didn't say where she had gone.

He flipped back to the beginning of the journal. What he found there turned his world upside down. The woman he had fallen in love with, the woman he thought he would spend the rest of his life with, was not actually his wife. She was an impostor, sent here by Jules to make amends for a mistake she'd made in another life. From what he read in her journal, she hadn't done anything to cause Rebecca's death; it had merely been a misfortunate accident. But Jules, bastard that he was, had used the incident to make the switch.

224

His heart went out to her. He had made enough mistakes of his own to know better than to judge the errors of others. Becca, once known as Becky Sue Dobson, had taken the place of Rebecca Wheland, and no one was the wiser.

This explained so much, including how she had gone from being nearly lifeless in bed to being a playful, passionate partner. He had questioned how a person could so completely let go of their resentment after only spending one week alone. Now he knew. It was because she wasn't the same person. As he thought about it, he realized she had as much as confessed this to him the night he had first made love to her, but he hadn't taken her seriously. Vividly, he recalled how she had told him that as far as she was concerned, the old Rebecca was dead and buried back on Long Island. At the time, he had thought she was only being dramatic to get her point across. He had never imagined she was actually telling him the truth.

Now that he knew, what should he do? For a brief moment, he wondered if he should go to the authorities, or to Wheland, and expose Becca as an impostor. But who would believe him? And even if they did, what good would that do? Wheland wouldn't care if his daughter was dead or alive as long as she wasn't his burden. Keeping this from Wheland was the best revenge he could ever hope for. It didn't take much to realize he had gotten the better end of this deal. He loved this new Becca and would do anything to keep her by his side. But first, he had to find her.

The journal confirmed she had failed in her assignment, but it didn't say what would happen next, only that she was going to meet with Jules. He needed to find Jules and bargain for Becca. Now that he knew who she was, he wasn't about to let her go. But how? He had no idea how to find Vanderzeit. The Maestro had always been the one to contact him. He had no idea where the man lived, if he even had a home, or where to look.

He looked back at the last entry hoping it would provide a clue.

I've gone to meet Jules and accept my fate. If I don't, I'm sure he will come looking for me, and that can't be good. I can only hope James finds this journal, and it helps to explain what I've done.

This was her message to him, her way of letting him know her true story. It also meant he might never see her again. People who worked for Jules didn't get to call the shots, Jules did. From his own experiences with

Vanderzeit, he had either succeeded in his assignments, or he had paid a price. There had been no exceptions, and no negotiations.

James dropped his head onto his hands in despair. He wanted to howl with rage, he felt so helpless. How did one fight a phantom? How could he, James Jaffray, fight fate? His world seemed out of control.

The journal said she had gone to meet Jules, but it didn't say where she was going. When he had worked for Jules they rarely met at the same place twice. Most often Jules had simply shown up, or sent him a message for where to meet. Becca's journal made no mention of any of that.

His frustration was rising. He was ready to run out into the street and start screaming her name. *Becca, my wife, where are you?*

Except she wasn't his wife, not by law. By law, his wife had died and was buried as Becky Sue Dobson. But in his heart, Becca was his wife, if for no other reason than because he loved her as such. She had become a part of him and now he had no idea how to get her back.

Angry and frustrated to know what he desired most in life was being cruelly stripped away, James lunged to his feet and threw the journal against the wall. As it fell, the pages fanned out and a piece of paper fluttered down to the floor. His heart raced as he bent to pick it up.

Becca,
Meet me Tuesday, two o'clock, at the Park View Hotel, room 444.
Bring the painting.
Jules Vanderzeit

It was time to pay Vanderzeit a visit.

~*~

Becca sat in the lobby of the Park View Hotel, mindlessly flipping through a ladies' fashion magazine that had been left there for the guests, while anxiously watching the clock. At five minutes before two, she set aside the magazine, and began her ascent up the wide sweeping staircase to the fourth floor. It was time to face the music.

Jules opened the door and welcomed her into a large sitting room with a pair of settees flanking a large stone fireplace. "Mrs. Jaffray, right on time. What a pleasure to see you."

With poker face determination, she maintained a polite smile. "I wish I could say the same." She held up her hands. "I've come empty-handed."

"Please, take a seat. It seems we need to talk." Interestingly, Jules seemed neither angry nor surprised.

Looking about, Becca decided to perch in the middle of one of the settees, her hands clasped tightly in her lap.

Jules picked up a large leather case that was sitting on a nearby table, and leisurely undid the buckles. When he pulled out the painting of the Magic Flute, Becca nearly fell off her chair. He already had the painting. How had that happened?

"Lovely, isn't it? A welcomed addition to my collection."

"How the hell did you get it?"

"From the man who outbid you, obviously. I always have a backup plan." His smug expression made her want to hit something, preferably him.

He must have known, even before he sent her the note telling her to bring the painting, that she didn't have it. Her earlier fears were quickly replaced with righteous indignation. "If you already knew I didn't have the painting, why on earth did you tell me to bring it?"

Jules ignored her while he gazed lovingly upon the painting for several more seconds before he replaced it in its case and set it aside. As he moved to take a seat on the settee across from her, the look in his eyes softened from one of grim judgment to something more closely resembling compassion.

Finally, he said, "Has it ever occurred to you, Becca, that you are precisely where you need to be?"

Ridiculous. She was taking the place of a woman who had made a silly mistake, running away from her problems, and had stumbled to her death. If it wasn't for her own accident on that rain-slicked highway, Becca never would have agreed to work for Mr. Vanderzeit. She wasn't where she belonged any more than Rebecca Wheland deserved to be dead. "Don't placate me. What do you want?"

"I know the effort you made, trying to complete my request, has taken its toll. Even though you failed, I'm hoping you've learned something from this experience."

Was that what this was all about? Learning a lesson? If so, she wasn't exactly sure what lesson she had been expected to learn. Keeping her hands tightly clasped, lest she strike out and ring his neck, she shrugged, unsure of what to say.

"Come now, surely you've gained something from this experience."

227

She thought about how Rebecca's resentment had caused her to lose her life and how resentment of a forced marriage had caused James to become hateful toward his wife. "If anything, I've learned that resentment is a mean and ugly thing that can eat you up and the people around you if you let it. Resentment killed Rebecca Wheland and destroyed her marriage. I want nothing more to do with resentment. It takes too much energy to hold a grudge."

"Even against yourself?" Jules asked.

"I don't resent myself," Becca answered, almost without thinking.

"Are you sure? As Becky Sue Dobson, you resented your life. You resented your mother, you resented your brut of a boyfriend, and you most importantly, you resented yourself."

"I couldn't *forgive* myself. If I had left Ralph, he wouldn't have been able to beat me, and I wouldn't have lost the baby. There's a difference," she argued.

Jules shook his head, obviously disappointed by her answer. "Have you not learned? Resentment and forgiveness are two sides of the same coin. Without forgiveness, you only have resentment. The hardest person to forgive is yourself. So, tell me, do you forgive yourself?"

Becca stared long and hard at Jules, taking a moment to consider her answer. "I think it's better to say I no longer blame myself. I can't stop bad things from happening, but hopefully I can learn from them, and move forward." For the longest time, it had felt as if she was either running from her future or rushing to get there. The hardest part for her was learning how to live in the moment and not wish for it to be otherwise, or worry about something that had not yet happened.

"Well now, I would say that's progress, maybe not all that I had hoped for, but significant progress indeed. And while I'd like to commend you for a job well done, I have to ask how much was actually accomplished by you? You obtained the invitation to the charity ball from your brother, Randolph, and by the way, he's also the one who bought the painting. Perhaps I should reward Randolph."

Randolph had bought the painting? This was news to her. He must have known she wanted that particular painting, since she had bid on it at the auction, so why didn't he tell her? Did this mean he was also working for Jules? That would explain why he hadn't said anything. He would have been sworn not to. Not that it mattered; not any more. Done was done.

"I was able to get invitations from both James and Randolph, and James did it because he loves me. *Me*, not Rebecca, and not because I asked him for a favor. I had no idea Randolph was going to bid on that painting," she said, pointing to the case holding the Magic Flute. "I sure as hell wished he would have told me; after all, I am his sister."

"Not in this lifetime."

Jules made her feel as if she was about to lose this battle and she wasn't even sure what she was fighting for. "Does he work for you, too?"

"I never discuss the details of my clients with each other. So, tell me, do you think I should reward you for what someone else has done?" Jules tented his fingers, tapping them together.

"Now you just wait a minute. You never told me *how* I had to get an invitation to the ball, just that I needed to attend, which I did. It's not my fault I was out-bid by Randolph. It could have been anyone. I didn't have enough money. Besides, you've gotten what you wanted. You don't need me anymore."

"My, my, my, it seems you've grown a backbone." Jules seemed to mull this over. "I rarely, if ever, allow my clients to negotiate their settlement, however I will concede you've performed as well as you could, given the circumstances. I wonder how I should *reward* you."

Becca eyed him with caution. "Do I get a say in this?" she asked, hoping he would agree.

"Not so fast," Jules admonished her.

Suddenly there was a pounding on the door. Becca nearly jumped out of her chair.

"Becca, are you in there?" It sounded like James on the other side.

Jules eyed her with mistrust. "What did you tell him?"

"Nothing, Jules, I swear. I never said anything." Fearful of the punitive look on his face, she wondered if keeping a journal and leaving it where James could find it counted.

"Vanderzeit, let me in, I know you're in there," James shouted from the other side of the door.

Jules calmly stood. "I better let him in or he'll have the whole hotel coming to see what the commotion is all about." He strolled to the door and opened it. "Jaffray, what a surprise. Won't you come in?"

229

James barged into the room and rushed to her side. When she stood, he pulled her into his arms. "Becca, are you all right?" He was breathing heavily as if he had run a long distance.

"I'm fine, for now. But how did you find me?"

"Thank God, I found your note from Vanderzeit, or I wouldn't have known what to do," James said, giving Jules a contemptuous sneer.

"Do you know this man?" Becca asked, realizing James seemed awfully familiar with the Maestro.

"I've worked for him before, but not anymore."

"Dang, does everyone work for Jules?"

"Sooner or later, yes," Jules supplied. "Now, where were we? Oh, yes, we were just discussing the final terms of your assignment."

James wrapped his arms protectively around Becca. "Don't take her away. I'll work for you again, for another seven years, or whatever is needed, just don't take her away."

"My goodness, dear man, who said I was going to take her away?"

"But I thought . . . didn't she fail her assignment?" James asked, bewildered.

Jules rolled his eyes. "It would serve you well to remember, these decisions are mine, and mine alone. Since you're here, let's all take a seat and resume our discussion. As I was saying, Mrs. Jaffray, or should I call you Becca?"

"Mrs. Jaffray is fine," Becca said and felt James give her an affectionate squeeze.

"Fine, Mrs. Jaffray. As I was about to say before we were so rudely interrupted, now that your assignment is over, for better or worse, you can go anywhere your little heart desires."

Becca gasped. "Are you serious? I can go anywhere I want?"

The Maestro's brows climbed up his forehead. "Have I ever lied to you?"

She didn't think so, but how would she know. "Thank you, Jules, from the bottom of my heart, thank you. That's the best news I've had in a long time. Perhaps forever." The past was foreign to her, but so was her future. The only real moment she could hang onto was the present, and she knew exactly where she wanted to be. Turning to James, she said, "It's good you're here. I need to ask you something. I'm guessing you know, I'm not really Rebecca Wheland."

He nodded. "Yes, I know. I read your journal. It's how I was able to find you."

She had hoped he would. "Now that you know who I am, or I should say, who I was; do you still want me to stay?"

"Becca, darling, I don't care who you were, or where you came from, but now that you're here, I never want you to leave. Say you'll stay and I'll be happy for the rest of my life."

There was one more matter she needed to confirm. She turned back to Jules. "If I stay, do I still get to be Rebecca Wheland?"

"Of course. It's who you have become, it's who you shall remain, at least for the rest of this lifetime."

Becca sighed, feeling as if a weight had been lifted off her chest and dissolved into nothing. Looking up at her husband, the man who had become the love of her life, she said, "Then, if it's okay with you, I'd like to stay and be your wife."

In answer to her request, he hugged her as if he never intended to let her go. "It would be my honor, Mrs. Jaffray."

Jules rose from his chair and picked up the leather case holding the painting. "It looks as though my job here is done." Putting on his hat, he added, "Until next time."

"If you don't mind, I would prefer to never see you again," James replied.

"My good man, there's always a next time. If not in this life, then the next." With a final bow, he walked boldly to the door and exited the room.

Becca breathed a sigh of relief. "Oh, my God. That wasn't so bad after all." She'd been so afraid for so long, and yet somehow, everything was going to be alright.

James kissed her forehead. "As much as that man irritates me, I'm thankful for one thing. He brought you into my life, and for that I shall be forever grateful."

Becca relaxed in his arms, happier than she could ever remember. "I couldn't agree more. Let's go home, James."

"Perhaps you've noticed, how often it seems we've been here before, and I expect we'll be here again." -- Jules Vanderzeit

The End

231

To find other books of Timeless Romance by Tricia Linden please go to: htpps://tricia-linden.com

The MacNicol Clan Through Time

A Time To Begin – Book 1

A Time To Return – Book 2

A Time To Belong – Book 3

A Time To Forgive – Book 4

Dreaming In Moonlight

Sometimes we wish upon a star.
Sometimes we dream in moonlight.

What he thought was the blessing of a lifetime becomes an unimaginable curse when Lord Gavin Richard Montague, grand duke of Maninberg, agrees to accept immortality from a powerful wizard in exchange for complete control of his kingdom. Now he can never leave.

Besides being a wizard's great granddaughter, Lady Tara Zanders, is an experienced dream weaver who would rather travel the world than submit to seeking a husband. When she finds herself attracted to the charming spellbound duke, her curiosity is aroused and her wanderlust falters. She quickly realizes Lord Gavin is trapped in his kingdom, but she doesn't know why.

There's a battle brewing just outside Lord Gavin's kingdom that threatens Tara's safety. He wants to protect her. She wants to uncover his secrets. Each feels the pull of their passion, but will their well-guarded secrets destroy any hope they may have of finding mutual happiness and truly lasting love?

Until We Meet Again – *a Jules Vanderzeit novel*

Victoria Winters doesn't regret her affair at Woodstock, or that she returned from the past pregnant with a daughter who would never know her father. Her only desires are to be a good mother to her daughter and to live happily ever after. That's not too much to ask.

Unfortunately, she's deeply indebted to the Jules Vanderzeit, a mysterious man known as the Maestro who saved her life in exchange for ten years of service as his time-traveling courier. Victoria has spent the last four years caring for her daughter, but she still has time to pay, and now she's being recalled into service to travel to Manhattan in 1888 to retrieve a lost Stradivarius violin.

Jules has tracked the missing violin to Robert Stevenson, a successful investment banker living the good life in the gilded age of Manhattan. After his wife's untimely death, he seeks to employ a new governess for his young daughter. When Victoria shows up at his front door, it's obvious she's the perfect candidate for the job, even though he suspects there's much more to Miss winters than she's willing to tell.

If Victoria can find the violin within three weeks, she'll earn extra time off her ten-year contract with Jules. If she fails, she risks losing her daughter, and possible her life. Before her assignment is over, she'll be forced to decide what she is willing to lose to have everything she ever wanted.

Until We Meet Again
CHAPTER 1

We may not have chosen the time so much as the time has chosen us.

Present Day

She couldn't be more than a few minutes late for their appointment, and yet the Maestro made a show of checking his pocket watch the moment Victoria Winters stepped into his office. Time—and his precious collection of musical artifacts—were the only things Jules Vanderzeit cared about. People were only useful in their ability to function as couriers to retrieve the latest object of his obsession.

"How nice to see you again, Miss Winters. I was beginning to wonder if you would keep our appointment." The Maestro quickly dispensed with any pretense of pleasant greetings and dove directly into chastising her.

Victoria rolled her eyes with a shake of her head. "Please, Jules, try not to exaggerate. I was only momentarily delayed. I was with my daughter." She took a seat in one of the low, plush-leather chairs across from Jules, as he sat perched behind his oversized cherry wood desk. Regrettably, it created the perturbing effect that he was looking down on her.

"If you truly valued time, Miss Winters, you wouldn't be so prone to wasting yours or mine. Someday you may find that a moment of time is all that separates you from that which you desire most." As if to press his point, unnecessary as it was, he continued, "If you will recall, it only took

234

a momentary distraction for you to switch guitars behind that wretchedly disorganized roadie's back, affording you the perfect opportunity to retrieve one of my most prized possessions."

"Yes, I know . . . the Hendrix guitar I swiped at Woodstock on the morning of August 18th, 1969." She spoke with mocking distain at the often-repeated reminder, though privately she agreed it was one of her finest retrievals. It was far superior to the quick, three-day trip she took to retrieve the guitar Ritchie Blackmore tossed into the crowd at the California Jam at the Ontario motor speedway on the evening of April 6th, 1974. At Woodstock, she'd been allowed to spend two weeks as part of the crew that worked behind the scenes to setup the historic festival. It was almost like a vacation until the rains came and swamped the place in mud. What a god-forsaken mess that was, but she had completed her mission through hell and high water.

"Retrieved, not swiped," Jules corrected her. He liked to believe his couriers "retrieved" his cherished collection of artifacts. They didn't swipe, steal, or rob the rightful owners of those items; they simply retrieved, for his careful safekeeping, items that otherwise would have been lost. "And scoff if you must, but that mission stands as the pinnacle of your success. We both know it's the reason I granted you the hiatus you so urgently requested."

"Silly me, I always thought it was because I was pregnant, and needed time to raise my daughter." For the last four years she'd been back home in California with her daughter, Magdalena, living a semi-normal life, but after being summoned back into service by Jules Vanderzeit, any semblance of a normal life had played its final note . . . at least for the foreseeable future.

"Think what you wish, but motherhood does not release you from your contract. Nor does having an affair while on a mission earn you any bonus points; and with a local boy, no less."

How nice of him to remind her of the error of her ways. It seemed Jules actually enjoyed putting her through all manner of tribulation for perverse, eccentric, and mysterious reasons she would surely never understand.

"If it's all the same to you, I'd rather forego this little trip down memory lane and get right to business. Didn't you call me here to discuss my next mission?" Victoria asked impatiently. The sooner she got on with the mission, the sooner she would be reunited with her daughter. At least that's what Jules had promised. To her, it looked as though he was holding her daughter as collateral to ensure her unfailing loyalty. Since her recall into service, neither of them had been allowed to leave his castle. Of course, he claimed it was for her own good, and to ensure Maggie's safety while she was away, but Victoria had her doubts. As far as she knew, the Maestro had never lied to her; he might deceive her ten ways to Sunday, but he never outright lied to her. Still, if doing whatever was needed to get whatever he wanted could be considered evil, then yes, Jules Vanderzeit—known to his couriers as "The Maestro"—was indeed an evil little man.

"In a bit of rush now, are we?" Jules mocked her, referring to her earlier tardiness.

"Please, Jules, get on with it. Just tell me where I'm going, and what I need to retrieve."

"You're going back to Manhattan in 1888 to retrieve a Stradivarius violin. This particular violin was from Antonio Stradivari's long period, and at the time of its disappearance belonged to a general in the United States army, if you can believe that. Imagine a military general playing a Stradivarius violin. Totally unexpected. It's reported that the general lent it to a fellow musician and the damn fool left it on a train. Such disrespect for such a valuable instrument deserves to be punished, but fortunately, that's not my area of concern. I'll let karma take care of that. My only concern is retrieving the instrument so it can be preserved for all of time."

For all of *his* time maybe, but he certainly wasn't preserving it for humanity. Once Jules obtained an object of his desire, it was never seen again. He collected rare and priceless musical artifacts, but once they were in his possession, they were as good as gone. The Maestro did not share.

"Sounds easy enough. All I have to do is be on the same train and retrieve the violin when it's left behind. Why the intense study period?" For the last several days Jules had packed her brain with information about the manners of the 1880s and the Gilded Age in America.

"Yes, well, one would think, but it's really not that easy. After being left on the train, it was picked up by another man; and that's where it disappears from history. I've already sent three of my best couriers, and each one tells me the same story. A man was sitting next to the absentminded musician and as soon as the violin was left unattended, this man—this thieving poacher—snatched up the case and took off." Jules ran his hands down the front of his impeccable jacket, as if to sooth himself by pressing out non-existing wrinkles before he continued. "Thankfully, I know the identity of the man. Now I need you to go back and establish yourself in his household and retrieve my prize from him."

Interesting. Three failed attempts, and he was still trying. Obviously this violin had become an obsession with the Maestro. It gave her some bargaining power.

She knew better than to ask, but she did it anyway. She liked to push his buttons. "Why not send me back to the moment before the musician gets on the train and let me sit with him? I could even flirt with him. That

236

would give me an opportunity to swipe the violin before your poacher can get his hands on it." She smiled inwardly, knowing how much her question peeved Jules' sense of time management.

"You know very well, perhaps not as well as I do, but very well nonetheless, that events of history cannot be changed. We do not change history, we act within it. It has already been recorded that this musician, if he can even be called such, lost this particular violin on a train. It is not our job to change *his* story, and any interaction with him creates that risk. If you flirt with him, as you so woefully suggest, his report of what happened will certainly change how history records this event. Not acceptable." Jules gave a sad shake of his head, and again she had the feeling he was talking down to her.

"Worth a try," she commented with a shrug.

Jules shook his head condescendingly. "I've already determined how this will proceed and how this will end."

"Really, Jules, don't you think that's a bit presumptuous? You said yourself that you've already had three failed attempts."

"I always know how things will proceed, and yet the effort must be made, the experience must be allowed to play out. How else can we achieve what we want? I want the violin and you want to be with your daughter. For each of us to get what we want, we must work together. Wouldn't you agree?"

"Agreed," she said, although she wasn't truly convinced. With Jules, she often had the feeling he knew something she didn't. And her feelings were usually right.

"Now, as for the man who found the violin . . ." Jules continued.

"You mean your poacher?"

Jules glared at her as if his small piercing grey eyes could bring her into submission. "Regarding the man who found the violin, there is nearly nothing recorded about him, nothing to create a noticeable effect on recorded history. History doesn't know who he is, but I do."

"I see." She tried to look suitably impressed. "I expect you have a plan for how I am going to gain access to his household; something that will cause little or no disturbance to his already unremarkable life."

"Of *course*." Jules rolled his eyes dismissively. She had to admit, she enjoyed making him do that; it was as if she had scored a tiny victory against his staid and overly composed demeanor. "After he has snatched the Stradivarius, his wife will die in the Great White Blizzard in March of 1888, and he will become the sole guardian of their adopted daughter. In June of that year, he will contact the Arthur A. Anderson Agency looking for a governess. It's all here in his file. We will arrange for you to register

237

with the agency at the proper time to take the job as governess to the child."

"Hmmm, very good. Not exactly a servant, but with nearly full access to the man's life. By the way, does our poacher have a name?" She glanced at the manila folder lying on the desk in front of Jules.

"Robert Lucius Stevenson. He's an investment banker. He's done quite well for himself, but in a time of excessive wealth, he's still one of the little people. However, I doubt he sees himself as such."

"You mean he's not an Astor or a Vanderbilt?" she asked mockingly. It was amazing how Jules could judge a man he had never even met.

"Hardly," he said with another roll of his eyes. "History won't even miss him when he's gone."

Victoria had scored one more tiny victory, but his harsh assessment made her wonder; would anyone miss her if she were gone? Probably not. Disappointing as it might be, she'd been estranged from her family for too long to expect prolonged grieving from any of them, and at only four years old her daughter's memories would be short-lived at best.

Jules picked up the folder, but didn't immediately hand it to her. "You'll need to be familiar with his file. And while I'm sure you know, it's my legal and moral duty to remind you that you are contractually prohibited from telling anyone who you really are, where you come from, or why you're there. You will maintain your cover at all times. If you share any classified information, for any reason, you will be recalled immediately and sent directly into seclusion. No more missions, no daughter, and no life. I have agents everywhere, and as you know, Victoria, if you discuss your mission, you fail."

She had heard it all before, several times over. It was just one more thing to regret about her life. Victoria resented being forced to do the Maestro's bidding, but as one of his indentured couriers, as long as he held her contract, she really had very little choice. No matter where she went, or when, the Maestro could track her.

Some people had property and mortgages to pay off, or they risked losing their homes. She had to pay off a contractual obligation of *time*, or risk losing everything she held dear, including her life.

When she'd been struck by a drunk driver and on the verge of dying, agreeing to work for Jules Vanderzeit had seemed like a good idea. Ten years of being a well-paid time traveler with an opportunity to see the world—not to mention that part about being alive—had sounded great. And it was, for a while. But good times don't last forever, and after paying down six years of her ten year contract she wanted out. The four remaining years of her contract felt like an eternity.

Jules pulled a single sheet of paper from the file he was holding and handed it to her. "Read this before you go."

She quickly scanned the paper, front and back. "Is this all you have? I expected more."

"It will have to do. It's important that this mission go as planned. I've already tried to get the violin before it leaves the train. That hasn't worked. I need you in Stevenson's house. I need you to learn his secrets. And please, use finesse. Try not to be a bull in a china shop but rather a fly on the wall. If Stevenson finds out what you are up to, who knows what will happen to the violin."

Leave it to Jules to be dramatic. "How long do I have to accomplish my mission?"

"Three weeks. That should be more than sufficient."

"Why so long? If this man has the violin as you believe . . ."

"I'm quite certain."

"Then why do I need three weeks to find it? How big is his place? Surely I can search the house in less than a week. Why do I have to be away from my daughter for so long?"

"Your daughter will be fine. She will be in my safekeeping. You will need at least that much time to gain Stevenson's trust. He's not a man who gives up his secrets to any pretty little face that comes along. While I have no doubt you'll put your feminine guile to good use as you've so successfully done in the past, Stevenson will not be an easy mark."

It was the second time he had referenced her affair with the stagehand at Woodstock, but she pushed aside the hurt. Yes, she had slept with Robbie Stevers, perhaps foolishly, but the affair had provided her with backstage access and the moment she needed to retrieve the guitar that Jules had so adamantly desired; the one on which Jimmy Hendrix had played his infamous hard-rock version of the Star Spangled Banner.

And while he may have assured her that her daughter would be safe and sound, she knew he wasn't about to let her slide out of her mission or turn in less than successful results. The only thing greater than her desire to pay off her accursed contract, was her desire live out her life with her daughter in the twenty-first century. The moment she paid off her last second of time, she would take Magdalena as far away from the Maestro and his god-awful Grand Central Time Chamber as this little blue planet would allow.

"But I am expected to search the house, right?"

"Of course, search every square inch, leave no stone unturned, but my knowledge of Stevenson tells me he's a cautious man, a planner, and a schemer. He's not one to leave his secrets lying about for all to see."

"How can you be so sure he's the right man?"

239

"Have you ever known me to be wrong?" He glared at her, but there was no eye rolling. No points scored.

She shrugged, "Not that I know of."

He continued to glare. "As I was saying, you have three weeks to complete this assignment. If you can't gain access to the violin by then, you will have failed and will have to return empty handed."

A failed mission meant extra time would be added to her contract; a double whammy. That was unacceptable.

"And if I'm successful, or able to return early? How much time will I earn?"

"Standard pay; two days off your contract for every day out in the field. I'll also give you time off to be with your daughter before your next assignment."

"Come on, Jules, give me a break." She sat forward in her chair, trying to elevate her eye level equal to his. "This is obviously worth more than standard compensation; the chance to retrieve a lost Stradivarius? How often does that happen?"

He eyed her for a long moment before responding. "All right, all things considered, I can agree to a bonus of two weeks; *if* you're successful."

This was amazing. She had never known Jules to negotiate. She quickly did the math; double time plus the bonus would mean two months compensation for three weeks of work. Not a bad deal, but she wanted more.

"Let's think about this . . . You've already sent three couriers and had three failures. It seems to me, if I'm successful, I deserve at least triple time." She knew she was being unreasonable, but figured it was the only way. She had very little to lose and so much more to gain.

Jules gasped. "You must be joking. Triple time is much too generous for less than one month of work."

"Remember, you're taking me away from my daughter. I think the job is easily worth one month for each week away; maybe even two." She put on her best poker face and held his gaze. In for a penny, in for a pound; it was time to play for the jackpot.

"Six months! You dream."

"Really? Do you have someone else who can do the job? You know, I think I might be coming down with a cold." She faked a cough for good measure.

He stared at her for a moment as if considering his options. "Alright, I can give you six months; if you come back with the violin in hand. And if you come back *without* the violin, but can give me substantial information toward its recovery, I will still give you time served."

She nearly jumped out of her chair. This was great news. This was insurance that she wouldn't suffer a penalty for failure. She let the thrill of victory settle in her bones as she sat back and relaxed for the first time since she'd entered his office. "And if I come back early?"

"Victoria, if you're able to retrieve that violin in less than three weeks, I will take a full year off your contract. But if you come back early by even one day without it, all deals are void."

Dang, this was serious. Jules wanted that violin and he wanted it now. She should have held out for more.

~*~

While the Maestro's office back at his castle was clean, neat, and well lit, with a formal wood-and-leather atmosphere that rivaled an old law library, the Grand Central Time Chamber felt musty, ancient, and full of secrets. The dimly lit space was consumed by dark shadows interrupted only by shafts of dust-filtered sunlight cutting soundlessly through the vast circular space. The ever changing rays of light falling from windows lodged high in the arched walls of the time chamber provided hopeful evidence of a world beyond these thick stone walls; one ruled by the logic of day and night. A world where she had once lived and hoped someday to return.

The exact location of the dome holding the time chamber was, of course, a secret known only to the Maestro. It could be anywhere; an overgrown jungle, a wind-swept barren coastal plain, or a frozen mountain top, but one thing she was sure of, it was well protected. Her trips to and from the time chamber were always at night while she was in a drug-induced sleep. It was nearly comical how intensely Jules protected his secrets. She may have traveled for days or only hours to reach this destination, but she had no way of knowing.

Back at his castle, when Jules was giving her last minute instructions regarding her assignment, he had assured her that her daughter was in good hands and would be being well cared for while she was away. It angered her to no end that she hadn't been allowed to meet the couple who would be caring for her daughter, but Jules had insisted that there wasn't time for a formal introduction. She would have to trust him on this or decline the assignment. The possible payoff for this job was too high to take that chance. Only Jules had been at the castle to see her off, but he assured her that Maggie was already settled in with her new guardians.

"Take care, and please, do your best to complete this assignment on time," Jules had instructed her one last time. "Much is riding on this."

"Yes, of course, Jules, I will do everything I can to protect your secrets while I'm out retrieving your precious violin."

241

"Believe it or not, I am concerned for your welfare . . . more than you may think."

The sincerity of his statement surprised her. She didn't know what to say.

Her silence seemed to please him. He smiled. "Well then, I believe you have everything you need. I wish you well until we meet again." With those parting words, he had ushered her into the vehicle that brought her to the Grand Central Time Chamber.

Victoria entered the vast circular chamber dressed from head to toe as a proper governess from 1888. She scanned the room, counting the doors. The number of doors in the chamber was different with each mission; sometimes there were only one or two, sometimes there were more. Once she had counted seven doors; another time there had been twelve. Today, the chamber held three. Three doors leading back through time, but only one door was calibrated to work for her. The others would hold fast against any attempt she might make to test their timely destinations. She knew, because like any good, curious, adventure seeker, she had once tried them all. But that was before, when she was young and daring and brazenly bold in her search for the next grand experience to stir her soul. Now she was a mother, bound by love to do right for her daughter, and every bit as determined as her younger, adventure-seeking self to make the most of this particular opportunity.

If she was lucky, and cunning, and fiercely focused, she could complete her mission early and earn her bonus.

She couldn't help but ruminate that she'd be done by now, free and clear, if she hadn't taken off time to raise her daughter. But it was a useless calculation; meaningless against the priceless years she had spent with her child. Only two months ago she had celebrated Maggie's fourth birthday; now, to think that she'd be away from her for three weeks, was sheer torture.

If only Jules would wait until Maggie was older and in school, this wouldn't be such an issue, but he claimed he had waited long enough to draw on her contract and maintained that she should be more than satisfied with her extended maternity leave. Not everyone was so lucky, he reminded her. And she reminded him that none of his other couriers were single mothers with a daughter who would never know her father because he wasn't from her time.

"And whose fault is that?" he had questioned, pointing out once again the error of her ways.

Ah . . . the perks of time travel.

She wondered if she saw Robbie again if she would even recognize him. Probably not; time-travel had a way of scrambling her memories. She compared it to taking a whirl-wind tour through a foreign country; she might remember the highlights, but it was hard to recall all the details of every place she had seen. Besides, Maggie's father would be an old man by now, if he was even still alive. She laughed, thinking what a shock it would be if he knew he had a four year old daughter.

She questioned the benefit of having all these amazing experiences if she couldn't even remember them; it hardly seemed worth the effort. But that wasn't true. She might not be able to recall every detail of every trip, but the experiences stayed with her nonetheless, adding to the richness of her life. They had brought her to where she was, a proud and happy mother to her beautiful Maggie, and for that she had no regrets. She might not have been able to anticipate the effects of time-travel, but she wouldn't regret the decision to become one of Jules' couriers. It had saved her life.

When Jules had pulled her from the car wreck, he had asked her the strangest question. "What would you be willing to lose, to have everything you've ever wanted?"

She hadn't known how to respond, or even what he meant. Later Jules had explained that his question was a paradox; weighing something we think we want, but would have to lose, against what we really want. She supposed that's what had happened to her. She had agreed to ten years of indentured servitude in exchange for her life. Now it was time to pay down her debits.

She set down the satchel holding her journal and traveling wardrobe, limited as it was, and adjusted her undergarments, again. Nothing she did could compensate for the god-awful, ill-fitting corset. Why couldn't Jules have provided something better; something that actually fit? Whoever had designed this particular garment should be hanged, or at the very least, forced to wear the torturous body-shaping device every day of their godforsaken life, and then be buried in it.

Spandex was so much more practical, as well as comfortable, for containing a woman's figure. And who the hell had determined a woman's figure needed to look like an hourglass anyhow? When she had left for Woodstock, she had worn a long, free flowing, tie-dyed summer dress with cotton panties and no bra. That had truly felt liberating.

Only five years ago she'd been reed thin with long, straight, bleached blonde hair and a golden tan from years of living in Southern California. Now she wore drab grey governess tweeds, her hair had returned to its natural reddish-brown shade, and she was as pale as an English maid due to her prolonged time away from the sun. She had also gained the well-rounded figure of a woman who had given birth. Instead of being a shapeless toothpick, she now sported curves, and best of all, full breasts, which were now being crushed by her confining corset. It was obvious the

243

darn thing was laced too tight. She'd be sure to fix that once she got where she was going.

She needed to pull herself out of the twenty-first century and set her thoughts on 1888. If there was one thing she had learned from her years of traveling through time, it was the value of living in the moment, regardless of where or when she was. It wasn't productive to focus on the vastness of the past, or even on the possibilities of the future. It was best to focus only on the immediacy of the moment before her.

She picked up her satchel and headed for door number three; the one assigned to her. She placed her hand on the door knob and took a deep breath. Within a matter of seconds she would travel through time. She opened the door, stepped into the antechamber, and closed the door tight behind her. On the opposite wall of the small chamber was another door, Victoria took another deep breath as she counted; one-thousand-one, one-thousand-two, one-thousand-three. When she opened the second door again, she was standing on the sidewalk in front of a secondhand bookstore. The large clock tower decorating the bank building across the street read six o'clock. She didn't need to ask anyone to know she was standing in downtown Manhattan on Sunday evening, the tenth of June, 1888. All it took was four small steps and one giant leap of faith.

Tricia Linden, author of timeless romance with a touch of magic.

An International Banker by trade, and a romance writer by desire.

In this lifetime, I've lived in five states, on two islands, and on a farm, and am now living in Northern California. My travels have taken me to Guam, Canada, Mexico, Australia, Hong Kong, England, Scotland, several countries in Europe, and several states in the US. Besides my love of reading and writing romance, I have a great fondness for zydeco dancing, classic rock and best of all, Pink Flamingos. Over the years, I've gathered a rather large collection of the fun pink birds.

I believe in life, love and the pursuit of romance and am living happily ever after with my soul-mate in Northern California. "My life is magical, I am truly blessed."

Website: https://tricia-linden.com/
Facebook: https://www.facebook.com/TriciaLindenAuthor/

Tweeter: @TriciaLinden69
Email: Tricia.Linden@ymail.com